The Nyctalope
and the Tower of Babel

IN THE SAME SERIES

Jean de LA HIRE
The Cross of Blood
translated by
Jessica Sequeira

Emmanuel GORLIER
The Tower of Babel
translated by
Michael Shreve

BLACK COAT PRESS

ISBN 978-1-61227-701-1. Printing. January 2018. Published by Black Coat Press, an imprint of Hollywood Comics.com, LLC, P.O. Box 17270, Encino, CA 91416. All rights reserved. Except for review purposes, no part of this book may be reproduced or transmitted in any form or by any means, electronic or mechanical, including photocopying, recording or by any information storage and retrieval system, without permission in writing from the publisher. The stories and characters depicted in this anthology are entirely fictional. Printed in the United States of America.

TABLE OF CONTENTS

Jean de La Hire

Introduction

La Croix de Sang (translated here by Jessica Sequeira as *The Cross of Blood*) was first serialized in the daily newspaper *Le Matin* in 1941, before being reissued in book form by publisher Simon later that year. It was reprinted in a somewhat edited and abridged version by Hauteville in 1953, bizarrely and meaninglessly retitled *La Croix du Sang*, as No. 16 in their imprint. « Les Grandes Aventures du Nyctalope » [The Nyctalope's Greatest Adventures].

Unlike most of the other Nyctalope novels, *The Cross of Blood* is a fantasy/horror thriller. Its atmosphere is one of subtle terror, and Saint-Clair's foe, Armand Logreux d'Albury, the so-called "Master of the Seven Lights," has powers so deadly that the Nyctalope does not dare to attack him directly—perhaps for the first time in his career—preferring instead to rely on a cunning stratagem.

According to our timeline of the Nyctalope's adventures, *The Cross of Blood* takes place in January 1925. In 1924, Léo mounted an expedition to Tibet (in *L'Amazone du Mont Everest*) during which he had an affair with Queen Mizzeia Khali, which may have cost him his marriage with Laurence Païli (see *The Nyctalope vs Lucifer*). Also, his two previous assistants, Pilou and Corsat, left, and he was forced to recruit two replacements, the Corsican Vitto and Soca, whom he had met during the Great War.

La Tour de Babel (translated here by Michael Shreve as *The Tower of Babel*) was written by Emmanuel Gorlier as a sequel to *The Cross of Blood*, and was originally published in the French edition of *Tales of the Shadowmen*, *Les Compagnons de l'Ombre*, Volumes 15 and 16. It takes place in late 1931, after the battle between Léo and the vampiric princess Alouh Tho (in *Les Mystères de Lyon*). Léo is then

7

married to Sylvie Mac Dhul, with whom he had a son named Pierre—or "Petit Pierre" to separate him from an earlier Pierre whose mother was Xavière de Ciserat (see *The Nyctalope on Mars*).

One character who plays an important part in this novel is Engineer Maur Korridès. Korridès first appeared in *Le Trésor dans l'Abîme* [The Treasure in the Abyss] (1907), *Le Corsaire Sous-Marin* [The Undersea Corsair] (1912-13), then directly against Léo in *Titania* (1929).

Korridès was likely born around 1877 and became a brilliant scientist and engineer in 1900. In 1902, he synthesized *heliose*, a substance not unlike *cavorite* which is attracted by the sun while not being subject to any other attraction. Thanks to this discovery, Korridès built two ships, one to explore the oceans (which could also fly through the air), and the other to travel through interplanetary space. Korridès also invented a revolutionary autonomous diving suit, featuring a motorized articulated exoskeleton capable of operating at great depths. Amongst other inventions of his were a disintegrating ray and a solar-powered helicopter.

Due to overwork and lack of recognition from his peers, Korridès fell into a deep depression and had to be committed to a mental hospital where he stayed until 1907. During that time, his first wife (identity unknown) passed away.

In 1907, he was released thanks to the intervention of an American billionaire seeking to recover a safe from a sunken ocean liner [*The Treasure in the Abyss*]. Korridès provided an underwater vehicle powered by *heliose* and articulated high-pressure suits. The expedition was a success. Unfortunately, *heliose* and gold reacted together, becoming an unstable explosive that caused the death of the billionaire and the destruction of his ship. Korridès then married Marguerite Dormach, who had been part of the doomed expedition.

For the next seven years, the Korridèses, whom everyone believed to have died in the explosion, lived secretly in the United States under the identity of Mr. and Mrs. James Norton.

In 1912, Léo de Malterre, a.k.a. the Black Corsair, having stolen a prototype experimental submarine from the French Navy, declared war on the U.S. and Venezuela, whom he blamed for the death of his family and the disappearance of their fortune [*The Undersea Corsair*]. The Nyctalope briefly intervened in that world-spanning conflict by receiving and forwarding to the French authorities the so-called "scientific testament" of Korridès.

In 1914, Korridès and Marguerite left the Earth to go to Mars aboard a heliose-powered spaceship. The details of their stay on the Red Planet remain unknown. But in 1917, Korridès returned alone, broken, aged and embittered. It is likely that Marguerite died on Mars under brutal circumstances, possibly linked to the destruction of the Martian colony set up by Oxus. This would also explain Korridès' subsequent opposition to the Nyctalope, given the violent role he played in these events.

Between 1917 and 1926, Korridès worked for the Bolsheviks and the evil mastermind Leonid Zattan. After Zattan's death, he married Diana Ivanovna Krosnoview, the Red Princess, and, with her, founded a terrorist group of hashishin, which she ran under the nom-de-guerre Titania [*Titania*].

Korridès and Diana had a son, Hugues Mézarek, who will later return under the alias of Belzébuth. The hashishin attacked the Nyctalope and captured his family. Léo managed to free them and take both villains prisoners. Both die in captivity: Diana is murdered in her cell by a gypsy girl; after learning the news, Korridès committed suicide—or did he?

Now read on!

Jean-Marc & Randy Lofficier

JEAN
DE LA
HIRE

La croix
du Sang

Les Grandes Aventures du "NYCTALOPE"

Editions d'Hauteville

Jean de La Hire: *The Cross of Blood*

PART ONE

CHAPTER I
An Atmosphere of Terror

At 8:30 a.m. on the morning of Tuesday, January 20, checking the day's post at his residence in Paris, Léo Saint-Clair found the following letter:

La Hêtraie[1],
Saint-Christophe-sur-le-Nais (Indre-et-Loire)
19 January 1925
My dear friend,
    Eight years ago, in the unforgettable circumstances of war, we swore to one another immediate and absolute assistance should a grave danger ever threaten one of us or a human being we love. Saint-Clair, by virtue of your oath, come to me—come to us, quickly! I will wait for you.
                    Jacques d'Hermont.
PS. Don't answer. Just come! Come with your men, for there is no doubt that you will need them. You can pay me a "surprise" visit at Beech Grove, to have lunch with me as I have often asked you to do. In case you are invited to hunt wild boars in the Périgord, have your guns and ammunition ready.

---

[1] Beech Grove.

After reading this, the Nyctalope did not hesitate a moment. He picked up the phone and said immediately:

"Vitto? Call Soca. Bring the car and the three Hammerless guns. We leave in half an hour."

At 9:00 a.m., the powerful gray roadster crossed the intersection of the old Porte d'Orléans and raced toward Chartres through Palaiseau, Orsay and Ably. From Paris to Saint-Christophe-sur-le-Nais, the most direct route was 240 kilometers. At 11:45 p.m. exactly, Saint-Clair arrived in front of the town hall of Saint-Christophe. At that moment, a man wearing leggings, a short leather jacket and a kepi with silver braid appeared; he was the county's game warden.

"Monsieur," said Saint-Clair, with a military salute, "would you point the way to Beech Grove?"

The Nyctalope had never visited his brother-in-arms before.

"You can see the castle from here," the game warden replied, stretching out his right arm. "Up there, on the hill, between the two woods."

The three men looked in the direction the game warden had indicated. To the east of the village, down the hill, there was a pretty valley through which a big stream wound its way; it was bordered by elm trees and a railway on the embankment. Beyond it rose a hill, its bare fields on a slope with a big forest on top. Through the gap, one could see a gray building with slate roofs, flanked by two dovetowers.

"To get there," the game warden continued, "go through the village, and, at the next crossroad, take the road that goes over the Nais and the railway. It will take you straight to the castle."

"Thank you, my friend."

Having slid five francs into the hand of the obliging man, Saint-Clair put his car back in motion.

That winter day was luminous and cold, with a strong wind from the northeast. The picturesque village, the valley planted with elms and poplars, and the hill of Beech Grove formed the center of a well-ordered landscape, agreeable to the eye and sweet to the spirit; the country between Tours and Le Mans offered many similarly pretty landscapes for tourists. The Nyctalope had to repeat to himself the pressing terms of the enigmatic letter of appeal he had received to imagine that any drama could take place in such a beautiful countryside, still charming despite the winter.

After a flat stretch, the road started climbing abruptly, becoming like a shallow trench through the fields. Then, quite suddenly, it turned into a beautiful path bordered by two rows of lime trees with branches cut short. Ahead, they spotted a metal gate open between two old walls.

The path went on, flanked by young pines. The roadster skirted a vast stretch of lawn, overhung by a magnificent grove of immense beeches with gray trunks and bare, almost rose-colored branches. The other side of the lawn was bordered by a similar canopy. This grove, stretching out over the high plain and projecting over the bastions of several parts of the castle, circled the main building on three sides.

The front entrance stood between two towers in the southwest and had big front steps, a tall door, eight balcony windows on the ground floor, nine windows on the upper floor and nine skylights in the attic. Certainly, Beech Grove must also have servants' quarters, but none could be seen. Saint-Clair thought they must be hidden behind the castle.

Just then, at the very moment the automobile stopped before the front steps, a smaller door opened within the monumental larger one, and a man appeared. Quickly he began to descend the twelve steps, each of his strides double their usual breadth.

Saint-Clair had jumped to the ground, which was covered thickly with gravel, as Vitto took the wheel and Soca prepared to carry the suitcases.

Now, seeing the man who came toward him, the Nyctalope had trouble recognizing the splendid captain of the Alpine Hunters from the Great War.

In his mind he cried out, stupefied: "Jacques d'Hermont, but a mere ghost of what he once was…" But nothing in his face, his look, his voice, betrayed his thoughts, and he remained distant from this friend, whom he had lost from view after the War, this friend who was now so different from the image he had kept in his mind.

All at once, the "comedy" planned in advance began, as plotted in the postscript in the letter.

"Ah! What a surprise! What a lovely surprise!" the chatelain explained in a shrill voice, taking and shaking the two hands that the Nyctalope held out to him. "My good friend Saint-Clair! At Beech Grove, at last! How is it possible? Why didn't you warn me? The telegraph… the telephone… But it doesn't matter! I am so happy to see you! You will explain everything. But first, let me shake the hands of our companions. They were our soldiers, Saint-Clair, among the very best. You had the power to keep them in your service and they had the pleasure of staying with you. Make yourselves at home, my friends."

After the presentations, he turned back toward the Nyctalope, he added:

"Saint-Clair, you plan to stay for several days, I hope? At last, I have you here, after so many invitations in the past! No? What say you?"

Entering into the game, Saint-Clair laughed energetically, shaking his head. And with a full, deep voice that carried far, he declared:

"I'm going to hunt near Brantôme, in the Périgord, my dear friend! They are waiting for me there to begin hunting wild boars. So I don't think I'll be staying here for more than a few hours…"

"Oh!" exclaimed the chatelain, admirably feigning sorrow and indignation.

Saint-Clair thought: *Why is he playing this comedy so well? Does he know, or believe, that he is being watched? Let us continue this game.*

So, he went on, at once serious and polite:

"But I must say, d'Hermont, that it would be a great sorrow not to accept your very kind offer."

"Yes, indeed!"

This was said with evident sincerity.

"Well then!" said Saint-Clair. "I'll send a telegram. They can hunt the wild boars without me; at least for a few days."

"Ah! Yes!" exclaimed the chatelaine, once again visibly reassured.

"Yes. I don't know this part of the Touraine countryside. It seems very charming. And what sweetness in the air! In fact, a bit of balm for my nervous system is just what I need. The atmosphere, the landscape... and your friendship, my dear d'Hermont! It will be a great opportunity for me to rest a little, and such a contrast to those days and nights I spent with you in the trenches!"

"So you will stay, then?"

"Yes, I will."

"For several days?"

"For a whole week if you like."

"Ah! What pleasure you give me!"

This quick dialogue took place at the foot of the steps. Before taking the first walk with Saint-Clair, Jacques d'Hermont went on to add in a joyful tone:

"Vitto, take the car to the garage; you have to go around the castle. You will find my driver down there; he'll be at your service. Soca, bring the bags."

While climbing the steps, the chatelain continued:

"My dear Saint-Clair, today you will be treated to a late buffet lunch. Normally, we usually have lunch at 12:30 a.m., but my cook Amélie will have the time to prepare a meal worthy of you. I live here with my two daughters and my sister. Her husband—do you remember him? He was killed at Verdun. You will see them before we sit down at the table. They have gone to Saint-Christophe to attend the end-of-year service of a very dear friend."

He sighed for a few seconds, and, with a voice that was very sad, such that his expressive face showed an infinite weariness, he added:

"I lost my wife two months ago. An illness unknown to the doctors, even the greatest ones brought from Paris. They could understand nothing, nothing... And ever since..."

He stopped then to let out a sort of sob, and with a shiver said:

"Excuse me, I still have a great deal of difficulty overcoming my pain... and my fear, yes! my fear... I will tell you everything, my dear friend... After lunch, we will go out, under the pretext of showing you the park... It's remarkable, because my great-grandfather and my grandfather applied themselves with intelligence and happy boldness to enrich the number of trees of the most diverse varieties. Some are so exotic they have never been seen before in this region, although they are perfectly acclimatized. Winter doesn't kill them, for the cold is never very harsh here..."

Saint-Clair didn't say a word. They entered through the front hall of the castle, an immense space lit by two big windows looking onto a patio that prolonged the steps on each side. In the back, a large staircase led to the upper floors. To the right and left, there were tall double clapper doors. A handsome chandelier in wrought iron, garnished with electric light bulbs, hung from the ceiling. Around the edges of the room, there were wood armchairs upholstered with leather cushions. Several radiators spread throughout filled the space with pleasant warmth.

"It's really lovely!" said Saint-Clair in sincere admiration.

"Yes!" said d'Hermont, without false modesty. "This used to be the living-room of the house. There was an enormous fireplace there. I had it replaced by a door that gives direct access to the library, which one can only reach through the front room. But in all other rooms except that one, I left the fireplaces. They still work, and I look after them with care.

On gray, rainy, humid days, a wood fire is pleasant, even if we also have heaters... Let's go to your room now, shall we?"

At that moment, a door opened in the back, to the right of the staircase, and a man appeared in shirtsleeves, a striped vest, black trousers and slippers.

"Firmin!" ordered d'Hermont. "Take some of the bags. We're going to the Red Room."

"Yes, Monsieur le Comte."

And smiling with the evident satisfaction he felt, the chatelain said to Saint-Clair, as they went up the staircase:

"I have three guestrooms. In the one we call the Red Room you will always be attended to, as an honored guest. I know you well enough to be sure it will please you."

What could have made Jacques d'Hermont send that terrified, almost desperate call? Perhaps I will learn the answer from him today? thought the Nyctalope. But he promised himself to do nothing to provoke the confidences of his friend, who seemed resolved not to do so right away. Saint-Clair thought: *It must be one of those secret dramas, which it is important not to force.*

The staircase gave onto a wide landing. D'Hermont walked toward a window overlooking the lawn, the access road and the valley. A few steps before reaching it, he stopped to open a door to his left. Crossing the threshold, he said:

"I will walk in front of you, my dear friend, for the room is dark back there. There is no lighting n the Red Room, except for a fanlight with a hanging curtain, which you can draw back and forth at your convenience."

Saint-Clair said, simply:

"My dear friend, do not forget that, as a Nyctalope, darkness does not exist for me."

"Ah! That's right!" exclaimed d'Hermont. "Excuse me."

The darkness was, in any case, only relative, for the afternoon light of the long hallway penetrated into the room through an open door. Walking side by side with his friend, Saint-Clair heard him whisper in his ear:

"Pardon me, I am prone to lapses. What makes this even more ridiculous is that it is precisely because you are the Nyctalope that I called you to my aid! But everything in its time, I say, everything in its time..."

And in his normal voice, he added:

"This way, my dear friend. Come."

The Red Room was a vast square space, with two windows that also opened onto the front of the castle, the lawn, the entrance road, the valley and the rounded hill on which the houses and the church of Saint-Christophe stood. Everything was furnished in the purest Empire style, with beautiful carpets spread over the waxed floor. There was also a long, deep alcove with the bed, flanked by two tables. A chandelier garnished with electric lights hung in the middle, just over a very beautiful round table. In the fireplace, wood was heaped up on great andirons, ready to be set aflame. The walls were covered with garnet fabric and adorned with portrait paintings in the imperial neoclassical genre. There was also a library, full of books well arranged behind a glass.

"The bathroom is this way, my dear friend."

Moving into the alcove to the left of the entrance door, Jacques d'Hermont pushed open a door on hinges that must have been well-maintained, as it opened without the slightest noise. Saint-Clair saw a room full of light, pierced by a window that also faced the front of the house. It was furnished with a bathtub, a shower, a washbasin, and a marble table of the kind referred to by the expression "modern comfort."

"I admire the way you have modernized your house without damaging what was old and uniquely original about it," said Saint-Clair with sincerity.

"It pleases me that you like it," said the chatelain, satisfied.

Back in his room, he pointed out an open door between the alcove and the entrance, which led to a third room lit by an electric ceiling light. Soca and Vitto had already set down the two bags and hung up Saint-Clair's rifle case.

"Here are the wardrobe and storage closet," said d'Hermont. "Is Soca going to help you settle in, or would you like me to leave you my servant, Firmin, while I take Soca and Vitto to their rooms?"

"Leave me Firmin," said Saint-Clair.

"It is just after noon. The lunch bell will ring when you please."

"Didn't you say that at Beech Grove you have lunch at 12:30 a.m.?"

"Yes, but…"

"My dear host, I won't have Madame your sister and your daughters change the habits of the house because of me. A half-hour will be quite enough for Firmin to empty my bags and for me to freshen up."

"Then I shall leave you, my dear friend."

Followed by Soca and Vitto, the Comte went out. Knowing that his master did not like any doors near him to remain uselessly open, the Corsican took care to close those of the Red Room and dark backroom.

Something struck the Nyctalope right away when d'Hermont introduced him to his two daughters and his sister, Laure Dauzet, a little later in the dining-room. It was the rare quality of the eyes of the youngest of the two d'Hermont girls, who bore the uncommon name of Basilie. Her eyes, a very pale periwinkle blue, appeared immense under her long eyelids with painted eyelashes. At first sight, and even afterward, unless one had the penetrating gaze of the Nyctalope, these eyes gave an impression of angelic candor, an infantile and joyful wonder at all things. They seemed in perfect accord with her round face, haloed by warm blonde curls highlighted in copper and gold, as well as her clear and delicate, yet very healthy, complexion. The girl's lips were bright red, owing nothing to artifice, and her body was at once slender and full, supple and lively. Everything in the young girl was the image of physical and moral health, naïveté and perfect happiness with life. Basilie must have been between eighteen and twenty years-old. But Saint-Clair had the strange thought—was it an intuition?—that those beautiful and splendidly candid eyes were a screen, an impenetrable screen stretched over a secret soul, with an enigmatic life in retreat from the apparent life on the surface. But this was no more than a quick thought, of which he was conscious for only a second or two.

At the same time, Saint-Clair was strongly attracted and intrigued by the entirely different figures of the widowed sister, Madame Dauzet, and the Comte's older daughter, whose first name was Madeleine. Their poor health showed them to be in the same disturbing state as their brother and father, Jacques d'Hermont.

Like him, whom they resembled, their eyes were dark brown and their slim bodies were stiffened by a nervous tension that seemed to need relaxation. Madame Dauzet was in her forties and Madeleine was in her twenty-fourth or twenty-fifth year. They had yellowing, emaciated faces, with feverish circles under their eyelids and folds of bitterness at the corners of their mouths. The expression in their faces was at the same time anxious and yet full of hope and courage.

The identical look of Jacques, Laure and Madeleine, thought the Nyctalope, *explains the call for help in the letter... But then, why doesn't Basilie look like her father, aunt and sister?*

Naturally, he looked again into the eyes of pale periwinkle. But after the introduction was made, the young girl grew distracted, and busied herself with the best arrangement of the beautiful red carnations in a vase on a nearby table. She must have felt the Saint-Clair's look fixed on her face. Without turning and lifting her eyes, she said:

"These carnations are beautiful, aren't they? I received them yesterday from a friend in Nice."

Saint-Clair felt an indefinable awkwardness. Jacques d'Hermont put an end to it by saying in a falsely deliberate tone:

"Shall we go to the table now, my dear friend?"

"With pleasure," said Saint-Clair, smiling. And he offered his arm to Madame Dauzet.

Ample, well-ordered and savory as it was, the meal was nevertheless relatively brief. The master of the house made an effort to animate it with accompanying conversation; Saint-Clair attempted to help. The two war comrades told anecdotes from their fraternity in arms; then, they spoke of the hunt for wild boars, the pretext for Saint-Clair's visit. D'Hermont expanded on the particulars of the hunt in that wild part of the southern region.

"Here, my dear friend," he concluded, "there is nothing to shoot but pheasant, rabbit, and, on rare occasions, hare or partridge..."

The woman and the two girls took part in the conversation, since each of them was a bit of a huntress. For all of the guests, however, it was a relief once the meal was over. Only Basilie had remained at ease and natural, even laughing occasionally, without having to force the brilliance of her gaiety. Nonetheless, in her big blue eyes, the Nyctalope did not see the childishness that she superficially showed.

Is there anything hidden behind her face? he wondered. *Is this young girl anything more than an adolescent happy to live in magnificent health? Does she see that she is the only one well here, in this place touched by the anxiety of mystery? And what is this mystery?*

Saint-Clair declared that he never drank anything after a meal, not liquor or even coffee, without a glass of pure water, and he did not return to the living-room. Madame Dauzet did not insist. Just then, her brother said:

"Ah well! But my dear friend, certainly you will do me the pleasure of taking a walk with me on such a beautiful afternoon, with such bright skies and dry air. Would you like to go right away?"

"Yes, and we can stop by the post office at Saint-Christophe. I must send a postal money order I didn't have the time to send in Paris yesterday. This morning, I left before the offices opened."

Five minutes later, the two friends were outside. They left the castle by the entrance road and continued along the path that descended through the valley toward the village. After they had crossed the bridge over railway tracks and turned a corner, so that they were completely out of sight of the castle, Saint-Clair put his hand on d'Hermont's arm. With the affectionate familiarity that had united the two men so tightly during wartime, he said:

"Jacques, the money order was nothing but a false pretext. Let's stop here and sit on this tree trunk. Talk to me."

To one side of the path, at the edge of the ditch, lay the trunk of an old beech tree knocked down by some storm. Sitting there, elbow to elbow, the two friends looked out over the valley. In the depths below, the narrow and calm Nais wound, blue and silvery between low banks irregularly interspersed with elms and pink-branched poplars. On these natural shores grazed cows, speckled white and red. On the hill opposite, the houses of Saint-Christophe stretched out amidst the gardens until the church bell tower, which pointed into a pale sky where the sun gently shone. All nature was motionless and silent, charmed by the sun's calm serenity. The air was warm, and it almost felt like spring.

Choosing a cigar from a stiff leather case and lighting it with care, Saint-Clair expected Jacques d'Hermont to talk. But, after a few minutes had gone by, he saw that his friend was so tense that he would need to speak first and question him. Gently, he said:

"Jacques, you called me. Your call was pressing. Let's not waste an hour. There is a start to everything. The simplest way is to start, together, at the beginning. So, I'm asking you: how and from what do you suffer, and when did it begin?"

Jacques d'Hermont suddenly seemed freed from a heavy burden. He raised his arms, waved them, lowered them, and, after setting his hands on his knees, spoke with feverish animation:

"That's it, Léo, that's it! The beginning... or rather the first brutal fact, significant in spite of its mystery, was the death of my wife... But wait! This death, sudden because it was unforeseen by us both, and which constitutes what I call the 'brutal fact' because of the terrifying shock it gave my sister, my eldest daughter and myself, this death was preceded for many months by things that no doubt produced this 'beginning' you asked me about. There were symptoms..."

"What symptoms?"

"It started towards the end of August," continued d'Hermont.

Now his voice was firm and his tone energetic, such that his body, with its straight bust and supple gestures, once again took on the bearing of an officer of the Alpine Hunters. The powerfully charismatic influence of Saint-Clair finally had its usual effect: mental lucidity, physical force.

"Yes, it was towards the end of autumn... You know the constant health I am gifted with, from the time we spent together in the war. My wife, Lucile, came from a race of folks similar to mine, and was as solid as I am. I showed you her photograph, do you remember?"

"Yes," said Saint-Clair. "A young Diana, a fine woman, with good features, a calm look, and a grave smile."

"My eldest daughter Madeleine is like her. As for Basilie..."

He hesitated and made an animated gesture as if clearing the air, then said with calm resolution:

"Let's leave Basilie for the moment. I will come back to her, since, by all evidence, she's found and still finds herself outside the infernal and mysterious cycle of illness in which Lucile, Laure, Madeleine and I have been trapped for a month... I continue: it was one of the last days of the season. Summer had been brutal, without a single day of relief from the torrid, heavy weather and thunderstorms that stopped short of bringing rain to the region, always bursting far beyond the Loire valley, on Le Mans and Nogent-le-Rotrou. Here, the whole region suffered from drought, except for Beech Grove and the narrow valley that stretches before us, which, as you can see, is closed off to the north just before the village of

23

Dissay-sous-Courcillon, by the old windmill with its feudal towers, half-hidden behind the oldest and most beautiful poplars in the region."

D'Hermont became quiet, and did not speak for a few moments. Saint-Clair contented himself with nodding as he looked into the distance at the line of tall poplars.

"That was a very unhealthy summer," d'Hermont went on. "Everyone in my house blamed it for the poor state of health we found ourselves in during the first days of September. My wife, my sister, my eldest daughter and myself were all in the same state, sickly without a defined illness, in a state of general weariness that increased from day to day, a lack of sleep and appetite, and a bizarre kind of fever that rose from night to morning, fell abruptly at sunrise to leave us exhausted, and began to rise again at nightfall... The doctor of Saint-Christophe, Doctor Luvier, is my friend. He visited us often. He examined us, observed us, tried to cure us, but in vain. The four of us were not affected to the same degree. More than me, more than my sister Laure, more than my daughter Madeleine, Lucile grew progressively weaker. By the end of September, she was no more than a skeleton. She could be fed only with liquids, which she mostly rejected. By the middle of October, her legs were incapable of carrying her. She was confined to bed definitively..."

Jacques d'Hermont stopped, and, with infinite distress in his feverish eyes, his whole yellowish and emaciated face, he looked at Saint-Clair, who observed him.

"Pernicious anemia?" speculated the Nyctalope.

"No. Luvier didn't think so. Professor Render, visiting from Paris, confirmed his diagnosis, or rather his inability to diagnose. He advised a change of scenery, a change of air and habits, but my wife would not move. So we stayed and now she is dead. I asked for an autopsy to be performed. Her organs were all unharmed, without illness, only diminished in volume and shriveled. 'I don't understand,' Professor Render confessed. And he understood even less, a few weeks later, when my sister, my eldest daughter and myself, after Lucile's death, remained in a stable state—the one in which you see us now. There was one difference between September, October and November: our appetites returned. We began to eat normally again. But we still can't sleep; during the nocturnal fevers that afflict us, we experience only brief periods of rest. We spend our nights plagued by nightmares that wake us with a start, drenched in sweat. Luvier refused to medicate us— what good would that do? All his pharmacopoeia has proved either useless, or had had typical harmful effects."

"What about the change in scenery?" asked Saint-Clair.

"We tried. We all left for Menton. And here I have the strangest and most mysterious fact to report... the most anxiety-inducing, too, because it now seems to me as if the grip of death does not want to let us go, and plays with us as a ferocious tiger does with its powerless prey..."

He stopped again, breathing hard, with desperate panic in his eyes. Saint-Clair took one of his hands, clasped it, and said with irresistible authority:

"Jacques, courage! What is this fact?"

With a voice filled with anxiety, d'Hermont explained:

"The big car that was taking us to Menton had just come out of Tours, when my sister Laure, seated between my two daughters in the back, grabbed my arm. I was in one of the two seats in the front, next to Firmin, who was driving. Laure said to me with violence: 'Jacques, let's go back! Let's return at once to Beech Grove!' Now, my dear friend, after a few minutes, I, too, began to feel a growing repugnance for the journey, which had hardly begun since we were only about fifty kilometers from here. Yes! In my mind, growing minute by minute, was the notion of asking Firmin to take half the day off and bring us back home. This bizarre, unreasonable and crazy desire, motivated by nothing, took hold of me entirely. It produced an irresistible physical need to grab my driver's arm, raise my voice with authority, and say exactly what Laure had just requested. When her cry had struck my brain, it was as if I had uttered it myself. And just as I was opening my mouth, about to give the order to turn back, Madeleine moaned: 'Oh!

Yes, father! Yes! Let's go home!' Only then did I look at the two of them. Laure was tense, shivering, looking like a madwoman; Madeleine's eyes were turned upward and her teeth chattered. I was feeling crazed myself and and confused, as if I was about to faint. So I grabbed Firmin's arm and shouted: 'Turn around! Turn around! Right away! Let's go back quickly to Beech Grove!' Firmin had the good sense and composure to immediately stop the car. His wife, Amélie, our cook, and her niece, Jeannette, our chambermaid, occupied the folding seats in the back. They were frightened, incapable of caring for Laure, who was in the midst of a nervous fit, and Madeleine, about to faint. Furiously, I ordered again: 'Firmin, let's go back, turn around, turn around!'"

Breaking off once more, Jacques d'Hermont gasped, wiped his sweating forehead with one hand, and, in a hoarse voice cut by nervous sobs, finished:

"Firmin obeyed. We returned to Tours, crossed the city, not stopping at any pharmacy or doctor's office. Less than five minutes after the car had turned around, Laure had calmed down, and Madeleine had recovered from her fainting fit. I myself had regained all my lucidity, and felt calm, euphoric even, better than I had felt since the first days of summer! It didn't last, however. At nightfall, fever took us again... Since then, our condition has not ceased to get worse from day to day. Every evening, as soon as the fever returns, it seems as if we're about to die... to be extinguished suddenly, just as Lucile was extinguished at the exact hour of sunrise..."

The Comte had a convulsion, his whole body shook; he took his face in his hands and surrendered to tears and sobs. Formerly so strong mentally and physically, he was now at the end of his resistance. Alone with his friend, Jacques d'Hermont at last allowed himself to cry freely.

Certainly, Léo Saint-Clair was profoundly moved. But he showed it in just the right amount in his words and tone, so that d'Hermont understood that the friend he had called to his aid sympathized with all his heart with his plight, but also kept a cool head. This he was soon again in a state to listen, understand, reflect and speak according to facts and reason.

The Nyctalope expressed the main idea that the confidences of his unfortunate friend had produced in him:

"Jacques," he said, "in my opinion, the most astonishing thing of all, based on your silence on the subject and my own observations, is that your younger daughter, Basilie, was not affected by this mysterious sickness, nor were Firmin, whom I saw looked well, or your niece Jeannette, who served us at the table, or your cook Amélie..."

Complete master of himself once more, his face dry of tears, his eyes clear, Jacques d'Hermont replied firmly:

"Yes! That is something lucky, at least! That mysterious epidemic affects only a limited number of people! It hasn't taken hold of them. Can I confess to you that, like many fathers feel towards their last born, I love Basilie the most? Her aunt and her sister also love her deeply. Our great joy is that she is unharmed. Our greatest fear was that she, so pretty, so beautiful, and so happy to live, with all her magnificent young vitality, might have been taken in turn! We don't hold it against her, of course! It is only human to remain healthy and strong, while we ourselves, on the contrary, pray to God that..."

"Understood!" said Saint-Clair gently. "But Basilie's health... your servants'... who all breathe the same air as you you, your late wife, your sister and your elder daughter... who all eat the same food and share the same daily habits... A question arises, inevitably. You realize it, and rejoice and fear, at the same time, but what did Doctor Luvier say? And Professor Render? For the same evidence must have struck them too, just as it did me the first few minutes after my arrival here."

"Yes, of course!" replied d'Hermont forcefully. "Luvier and Render agreed that the mysterious atavisms, of which we were the victims, did not affect Basilie. It seems that this is normal, that the atavistic process may skip some individuals, sometimes generations even—yes, generations! This must be so, for in the entire history of my family, going back to the Revolution, I have found nothing that compares to this."

His voice dropped as he continued:

"... and I fear we all shall die from it, just like Lucile."

"I'm sorry!" said Saint-Clair, "but your wife didn't share..."

"I know what you're going to say, my dear friend, but your objection is irrelevant. Lucile was, in fact, my first cousin, the only daughter of my father's brother. So we would have shared the same atavisms..."

"I see."

After a gesture to clear the air, Saint-Clair went on with gentleness:

"I must tell you, my dear d'Hermont, that the theory of atavistic transmission by continuous or intermittent effects has never filled me with enthusiasm. It can all too easily be applied explain things that one does not understand. And it does not resolve our problem, which is, right now, how to heal your sister, your eldest daughter and yourself. As you know, I do not like the unknown. Will you allow me to ask you a few questions, which you must answer with absolute sincerity?"

Jacques d'Hermont, very tense but calm, looked at the Nyctalope with an expression of total confidence, and answered firmly:

"Go ahead, question me. And it goes without saying that my answers will be totally truthful."

"Excellent! After the first manifestations of that mysterious sickness, particularly at the time of its most powerful effects... for example, when your wife passed away, or during the scene of the extraordinary return to Beech Tree, a return that seems dictated by some kind of occult power... yes, what was the attitude, what were the reactions, of Basilie and your servants? Firmin, Jeannette, Amélie?"

What appeared to be a genuine and sincere expression of astonishment illuminated the Comte's face. After a moment, not hesitating but reflecting, he replied:

"My goodness! I never asked myself that question. And I don't think that Laure or Madeleine have asked it either... As far as I can remember, Basilie's attitude and reactions... and that of our servants... were what they quite naturally should be... What they are when circumstances produce an accident created by an inexplicable evil... Eagerness to take care of us, compassionate pity, fear even, before the mystery and suffering... Anger and instinctive disregard for the impotence of medicine... Yes, all this was in plain view. Naturally, life for them at home retains its normalcy, and they go on with their day in continued good health."

"Very good," said Saint-Clair. "Another question. What made you call me? More precisely, did you make that call after thinking about it for some time? Or did a sudden event inspire you to do it all at once?"

Once again, the mobile face of Comte d'Hermont expressed a sudden, violent emotion. To Saint-Clair's attentive eyes, he seemed more irritated this time than pained.

"An abrupt event, indeed! Yesterday, I wrote to you. I knew from the newspapers that you had returned to Paris from Corsica. I remembered our friendship and your oath. I did not doubt for a second that you would come without delay. Thank you, my dear friend, for not having disappointed me. As for the event which inspired and decided me, it is one more mystery..."

Jacques d'Hermont concentrated, as if to relate the thing in the clearest way, in the fewest words possible. Then, in a resolute and rapid voice, he began. But his gaze was blurred as if he were hallucinating, as he looked into the calm and steady eyes of the Nyctalope:

"It happened two nights ago—the night of Sunday 18th to Monday 19th—a soft, dark night without moon or stars. This detail has its importance, as darkness is one of the elements of the mystery. I knew that the night was dark because, since the War, I haven't been able to get used to sleeping in a closed room, so my window always remains half-opened at night, even in the deepest cold of winter.

"I could not sleep. Lying on my right side, eyes wide open, sweating and shivering from a rising fever, I saw through the half-opened window the night outside, darker than my room where only the tiny flame of an oil lamp burned in a corner under a pot of tisane. It often happens that my mouth and throat become dry to the point of being painful, and then a sip of the warm infusion..."

He stopped, little haggard, as if the thread of his thoughts had just broken.

"You were not sleeping and you had your eyes open," encouraged the Nyctalope softly. "And then?"

Jacques d'Hermont shrugged, and, once again lucid and clear-minded, he continued:

"Suddenly, I heard a noise—not that noises are unusual in the silence of the night, in a house full of old furniture and antique woodwork like Beech Grove. No, it as an an abnormal noise... I listened to it for a few minutes before I realized what it might be. I can't define it any better than by saying it was a sort of continuous whirring mingled with moaning. This came from the lawn that the window of my bedroom opens onto, as do all the windows in the main rooms and the large hallway on that floor.

"Having more or less determined the nature of the unusual noise and approximately located it, I stood still for a few minutes, listening, hesitating... But as the groans became stronger, even seeming to double in intensity, that is to say becoming different, sometimes together, sometimes alternating, I jumped out of bed. My suddenly galvanized nerves gave vigor back to my body, and after putting on a warm dressing gown over my pajamas, tied with a rope belt, I went to the window and opened it completely...

"I saw nothing. But now, I could situate the whirring and moaning better: the first occurred far away in the valley, and I thought that it was the windmill of the Nais turning. *In the middle of the night!* I thought. *That miller is truly horrible.* As for the moans, evidently human, they were uttered by two persons whom the dovetower in the north hid from my sight..."

Jacques d'Hermont stopped. Telling this story, he had become calmer, his eyes less crazed, as if he felt tranquility or a euphoria of hope in the presence of Saint-Clair, who listened and did not doubt his reason or veracity.

He breathed deeply, and without effort resumed:

"You may have noticed that the lawn in front of the castle is heart-shaped, its tip dividing the entry road in two, the rounded sides containing the two dovetowers. The human beings moaning were on the lawn at its extreme north edge, behind the northern dovetower. Quickly, I put on my leather slippers and left my room. I did not carry any weapon. My old unloaded Parabellum must have been in some drawer of my study. This part of the countryside is far from any main road and perfectly calm; its inhabitants are all from there, and they are the most honest and peaceful in the world..."

Saint-Clair cut in:

"Then why did you tell me to bring my rifle and buckshot?"

"I'm going to tell you! I went downstairs, lighting my way with a small electric flashlight, which I always keep on one of the bedside tables in case the night lamp goes out before dawn. Now, to my great surprise, I found the gate that led to the porch wide open, even though it's almost never open. I thought: *Who's gone out?* But all at once I had the intuition that it was my sister Laure and my daughter Madeleine... But why? Such a thing had never happened before. Or at least I had never had the smallest clue, or slightest suspicion...

"These reflections tormented my spirit as my legs, extraordinarily strong and agile, carried my body. I ran. I followed the curve of the road that goes around the castle, and passed the bulge of the enormous old tower. Then I stopped short, nailed to the ground. I had to cry out, or at least make an effort. For what I saw... Oh! Saint-Clair, believe me! It was not a hallucination! Besides, Laure and Madeleine, when you question them, will tell you the same thing, exactly..."

He paused, panting, a pitiful supplication in his eyes. Saint-Clair clasped his hands and said with penetrating force:

"I believe you, my dear friend, do. What did you see?"

"Ah," exclaimed Jacques d'Hermont. "That is difficult to express, to define... The idea I have is that of an aurora borealis... I hope you understand. Yes, a kind of aurora borealis, but right there, before me, on the lawn, not in the sky... An aurora borealis in nimbus... Wrapped around two completely still human forms, standing side by side on a broad pedestal that had once supported a statue, but that had been empty since a lightning bolt had shattered it into a hundred pieces... Yes, on that pedestal, inside a great nimbus of light, stood two pale human forms... and it was from there that the moans came from... Oh! I can still hear them! They were moans of pain mixed with ecstasy, suffering mingling with voluptuousness! But I did not remain still and nailed to the ground for long, for I was aware that a force was attracting me toward the luminous nimbus, toward the two moaning forms which—I was now certain—were those of Laure and Madeleine...

"I remember very well how I ran... But, when I was no more than two or three steps away from the stone pedestal, the nimbus was extinguished. It disappeared. It vanished. Despite the sudden, opaque night, I could still make out the two human forms. From them a double cry broke out and I saw them grasping one another, hugging, staggering, collapsing... I advanced. I opened my arms. I received them heavily on my chest and fell beneath them. But then, with as much skill as was in my power, I disengaged from them. I got down on my knees and, with my still-lit electric lamp, which I'd kept mechanically in my clenched hand, I illuminated the faces of Laure and Madeleine. They looked as if they were dead, their faces more emaciated than ever, their eyes closed. But their lips were frozen in a smile... a smile of unspeakable happiness!"

He went silent, and closed his eyes.

Looking at this man, whom he had known as one of the most balanced officers in the French army, Saint-Clair did not have the slightest doubt: Jacques d'Hermont was not mad. He had not dreamed the events of that night; what he had just told him was the living truth, which he had heard with his ears and seen with his eyes.

Given the exhaustion of one and the meditative observance of the other, the two men's silence lasted for several minutes.

At last, Saint-Clair said:

"Did they remain passed out for a long time?"

"A little above an hour," replied d'Hermont.

"But you took them to the castle right away?"

"Yes! One after the other, of course. Each one to her bed. They had gone out from their rooms, from the house, without putting on any clothes over their night dresses. They were frozen. I was strong, agile, lucid, although in a state of intense fever. I did not call either Amélie or Jeannette. I took care of my sister and daughter alone. Fortunately, the heater was working at its full. I quickly filled two hot water bottles and prepared a grog, using powerful English salts. Once revived, Laure and Madeleine passed instantly from their fainting state into normal sleep.

"In the morning, when they were awake, I called them to my room and told them what had happened, I questioned them and they remembered everything—yes, everything! It was summed up first by each one separately, then by the two of them together: they had woken up with the irresistible desire to go out, and had jumped out of bed. They had met each other in the hallway, and from there, taking each other by the hand, they had gone running onto the lawn toward the pedestal, above which they could see a beautiful halo of light twinkling and palpitating!

"Then they were seized with an exultation at once painful and pleasurable which had kept them there. This sort of conscious ecstasy had stopped abruptly once the inexplicable light had gone. They had felt themselves bathed in ecstasy, having the sensation of being penetrated and impregnated. The abrupt cessation of such a state had given them a kind of brutal trauma, which had thrown them into unconsciousness. There it is, my dear friend."

D'Hermont gave a heavy sigh. Saint-Clair murmured, as if to himself:

"This is one of the strangest things I have even heard in my life—which has been so full of strange things."

In another tone, he said:

"What happened afterward, Jacques?"

"That's when I thought of you and wrote to you. Oddly, after this extraordinary nocturnal episode, my sister, my elder daughter and myself felt less exhausted, and were given a return of vitality and hope, which undoubtedly contributed to the letter I sent you. Saint-Clair, you are our only recourse! What we face is beyond the natural order of things, and I know that you see clearly not only through tangible darkness, but also through... How can I put it...?"

"The occult?" suggested Saint-Clear.

"Yes," exclaimed Jacques d'Hermont, illuminated. "For it is from within the occult that the phenomena from which we suffer, from which my wife has died, from which we ourselves are in danger of dying, originates! Yes, in danger of dying, and soon! Because..."

He stopped, panting again.

"Because?" asked Saint-Clair, calmly.

"There is something else..."

"What is it?"

"I found out just this morning, after such an extraordinary night, that, for the first time in months, Laure, Madeleine and I have slept normally! It was just because of this beneficent, restful sleep that Laure and Madeleine were able to accompany Basilie to the church of Saint-Christophe, to attend the yearly service of a friend..."

"Is there anything else?" asked Saint-Clair.

"Yes. This morning, Laure and Madeleine told me a secret. They betrayed an oath that my wife Lucile had demanded of them when she was bedridden. They thought this oath no longer held, and that I should know everything."

"Well?"

"A few nights before the bed rest from which she would go to her tomb, Lucile had a night of painful and voluptuous ecstasy on the pedestal, trapped in the same luminous nimbus!. After that, she enjoyed a few days of the same vital renewal that Laure and Madeleine presently enjoy. And then, the relapse was brutal, complete, definitive... My dear Saint-Clair, if I hadn't written to you yesterday, after that inexplicable night, I would surely have written to you this morning after that revelation. Do you understand what this means? If your intervention is ineffective, in a few days, my sister and my elder daughter will take to bed the same way that my wife did, and soon after... death!"

"Enough moping!" said the Nyctalope, almost violently. "Courage and calm, Captain d'Hermont! Do not fall again into despair. Listen to me, look at me! I do not know if I will be able to discover the cause of the abominable attack, but I am going to do everything in my power to find out the truth and to battle on behalf of you and your family—and win! Have you told me everything? Do I need to know anything else?"

"Thank you! Thank you!" answered d'Hermont, seized by enthusiasm.

"Do I know everything that Laure and Madeleine know told you

"Yes! I am sure of it."

"I must insist! Did they hide anything from you?"

"No! They swore they told me everything, and know nothing else... Besides, you will speak to them and..."

"Today! Let's go, Jacques, let's move!"

Saint-Clair was already standing. His friend rose. They walked with a quick step, elbow to elbow, on their way down into the valley. Thinking, Saint-Clair contemplated the landscape, infinitely pleasant and sweet on that serene afternoon with so little winter in it. Suddenly, he said:

"Jacques, do you have any errand to run in the village or around there?"

Surprised, the chatelain hesitated, but then he said:

"No, not exactly. But I could go and talk to one of my farmers, who told me yesterday that some repairs were necessary in his stables. Why?"

"Because I would like to talk right away to Doctor Luvier, your physician and friend. And I would like to do so alone. Perhaps he will say some things to me alone that he would not tell you, even if they are only vague thoughts, hypotheses..."

"Yes, indeed..."

"Will I find him at home?" asked Saint-Clair.

"Today? Let's see, what is day are we?"

"Tuesday."

"Ah, yes! Precisely on Tuesday afternoons, Luvier stays home to give consultations."

"Good. Point me toward his house. Can you walk a little faster?"

"Of course."

"Let's go there with our military march!"

At the bottom of the valley, the road took a curve, crossed the Nais over a little metal bridge and entered between the houses of the village. Turning several times, it climbed up to the church, then traveled left toward the square partly bordered by lindens. There stood the most beautiful and opulent houses of Saint-Christophe, with a large garage for cars at the entrance; there was also the habitation, nobly bourgeois, of the local physician.

"Here!" said Jacques d'Hermont, pointing to the house with a gesture. "As for me, I'll take that road..."

He pointed to a road that wound upward, and continued:

"We should return together to Beech Grove. Where should we meet?"

"It's a lovely day," replied Saint-Clair, smiling. "The sun is still hitting the front of the hotel. This terrace is fine. It's important that people see us together. I'm a friend who's come to spend a few days with you. But let's give me a false name: Dubois, Dupont or Durand, anything you like. I have the intuition that it's better to leave everyone ignorant of the presence of the Nyctalope in your house. Without vanity, but with caution, I can say that I, too, am well known in the world not to attract attention and suspicions of which even I remain ignorant. In this respect, have you thought of giving an order at Beech Grove to say nothing about me to the outside world?"

"My goodness, no!"

"Ah! Please do so this evening. Let's hope that my incognito has not already been betrayed."

Jacques d'Hermont took the arm of his friend and said in an anxious, passionate tone:

"Do you have an idea? An intuition?"

"No. To tell the truth, none whatsoever!" said Saint-Clair, shaking his head a little. "But I sense that all precautions are necessary, and we must give no one outside Beech Grove the least suspicion that I'm here to investigate this mystery."

"I understand. How about you being Charles Dumont, one of my brothers-in-arms from 1917?"

"Understood. I'll be Charles Dumont, starting now."

"Perfect!"

The two friends parted. From the threshold of the café-hotel, a man and a woman saw the Comte d'Hermont enter the Rue Haute, which five hundred meters farther turned into a dust road and filed along the plateau between the crops. They also saw the unknown gentleman go straight to the house of Doctor Luvier, push open the gate, climb the front steps, ring the doorbell and disappear behind the door, which had opened and then immediately closed.

In a very bourgeois drawing room, with a piano and a library, richly furnished and in good taste, Léo Saint- waited in the company of a young peasant woman nursing a child and a petty bourgeois in his Sunday best. To the rustic valet who had let him in him, he had said:

"Please announce Monsieur Charles Dumont, passing through for a consultation."

Well settled in an armchair, arms crossed and eyes vague, he waited, meditating on everything he had learned so far. It was so extraordinary that, despite his will, he suffered a little from the atmosphere of anxiety that seemed to surround Jacques d'Hermont.

The wait did not seem long. In fact, it lasted only a quarter of an hour. The peasant woman went in first, then the petty bourgeois. Finally, the voice of the doctor said:

"Monsieur Dumont?"

"Ah! Yes!" said Saint-Clair, half distracted. "Pardon me."

He entered the consulting room and introduced himself under his real name, all the while observing the doctor. He was: a young man, stocky and of small size, his face at once powerful and fine-featured, his brown eyes clear and lively, his look decisive and with a sympathetic aspect.

"The Nyctalope! Of course, I've heard of you!" exclaimed Doctor Luvier with spontaneous joy. "My friend d'Hermont has often spoken about you! And your exploits all around the world! How you defeated that madman Lucifer! If you had taken the time to look at my bookshelves, you would have seen your two volumes on the exploration of Occult Tibet."

Smiling, the Nyctalope nodded. Then the doctor said:

"But why are you here, in Saint-Christophe, in the guise of Charles Dumont?"

"I will explain," said Saint-Clair. "But have your consultations ended?"

"Yes. Your predecessor was the last of my patients today."

"Is it possible for you to close your doors for at least an hour? I must talk to you about some very serious things…"

"Oh!" said Doctor Luvier, who stopped smiling. "I think I can guess after all. The mystery of Beech Grove."

"Yes."

"Very well. Please take a seat. I will give the order that if someone asks for me, my valet will say I have gone out."

He disappeared and was gone for two minutes. Then he returned and closed the door again, with care. After turning the lock, he said seriously but with the sort of spirit the Nyctalope appreciated:

"There we are. I am at your service for as many hours as you please."

"I'm grateful."

The conversation lasted for over an hour.

When, after enjoying an aperitif with Jacques d'Hermont and Doctor Luvier on the still sunny terrace of the café-hotel, Saint-Clair once again found himself alone in the company of his friend on the return path to Beech Grove, he said simply:

"Nothing, my dear Jacques. Doctor Luvier knows no more than you do, and he gave up after weeks without making even the slightest hypothesis about the mystery of the Beech Grove. He waited... He himself said to me: 'I waited as if I were in an atmosphere of anxiety.'"

"I thought so," said d'Hermont.

For several minutes, they continued to walk in silence. Suddenly, Saint-Clair stopped short, grabbed the arms of his friend and cried out:

"My goodness! We have forgotten to clarify something important. It totally slipped out of my mind."

"What clarification?" asked d'Hermont, surprised.

"The reason why you asked me to bring my rifle! Hunting wild boars was only a pretext, I imagine."

"Yes, of course. What you say is true: it slipped my mind, too. How odd..."

"Tell me quickly."

"Well! Here it is... You know that often our senses of smell, hearing, sight and touch, register impressions and sensations in which our spirit does not participate. These later return at some point, as if from the depths of our being..."

"Yes," said Saint-Clair.

Very animated, d'Hermont went on:

"Yesterday morning, after I received the confidences of Laure and Madeleine, and before I wrote to you, I went for a walk in the park to be alone and to reflect on my idea to as you for help. Instinctively, I walked toward and around the pedestal, all my senses giving rise again in my thoughts to the episodes of that incomprehensible scene I had witnessed two nights earlier. Then, suddenly I remembered, yes, for the first time I remembered, or rather I became aware, that, as I was running toward the pedestal, just before the nimbus was extinguished, I had seen against beech trees, beyond the lawn, a shadow—a shadow cast by the luminous halo against the light gray trunks of the trees. My eyes had perceived an all-black human form for only a second! That human form had then leaped, running away no doubt, into the total darkness of Beech Grove!"

"Well! Well!" said Saint-Clair.

"As soon as that image resurfaced from the depths of my mind into the light of day, I ran to the place where I had seen that shadow. I inspected it well in the sun. At the foot of a tree, in the bare and humid soil, I found the footprints of shoes... And here, my dear friend, is the essential thing! In this same place, I found an object, which I immediately picked up and examined. Here it is!"

D'Hermont buried his right hand deep in the pocket of his jacket and withdrew it. Between his thumb and forefinger was a small shiny object of nickel and copper, which he presented to the Nyctalope. It was the ball-cartridge of a pistol.

With his usual composure, Saint-Clair pronounced:

"Browning 9mm HP 35."

"Yes!" exclaimed Jacques d'Hermont. "I, too, recognized it at once. Note: a cartridge intact, not shot. Now look here, Saint-Clair. My German Parabellum is not of this caliber. No one at Beech Grove, or in the immediate dependencies, possesses a Browning 9mm. So I thought to myself: During the phenomenon of the luminous nimbus, a man stood there who observed the two women. He must have been protecting himself against a possible risk of attack, for he was carrying a gun. No doubt he was absorbed entirely by the task that had brought him there, because while loading the Browning, he had to do it twice instead of once, mechanically passing the cartridge of the magazine over the barrel, in a dry movement of the cylinder head. The first cartridge was ejected, and fell to the ground. This is why in my letter to you, I wrote: *Have your guns and ammunition ready*! That's all!"

"That, my dear friend, is tremendous news!" exclaimed Saint-Clair. "These footprints and this cartridge are not supernatural elements, but very tangible evidence! They constitute the first knot of the thread of Ariadne that will lead us to the solution to our problem, the explanation of the enigma at the bottom of this mystery."

Saying this, the Nyctalope took up his march again. D'Hermont followed his example. And without saying a word, the two friends returned to Beech Grove.

CHAPTER II
"She Gave Her Soul To The Devil"

The sun was setting. The cold became intense. At the top of the steps, before entering, Saint-Clair said to d'Hermont in a low voice:

"My dear friend, the sky is clear and the breeze is beginning to blow from the north: the night will be frozen and it will not rain. That means that tomorrow morning, the footprints at the edge of the park will be visible. Let's go in. I will stay in my room until dinner. I want to speak with Vitto and Soca. No staying awake after the meal: I will say that I got up very early this morning and that I simply need to sleep. Tomorrow, I will find a way to talk, out of your presence, with your sister and elder daughter."

The two men crossed the threshold.

On the order of his master, Firmin went to inform Soca and Vitto that Monsieur Saint-Clair had summoned them to his room.

Five minutes later, in the Red Room, the Nyctalope had his two Corsicans helpers sitting before him.

Born in Sartène and friends from childhood, Soca and Vitto had served together in Champagne and Verdun under Saint-Clair's orders. After the war, they had returned to Corsica, but when their former commander had needed them, they had answered his call. They were his companions and, in whatever way he might need then, his soldiers. Vigorous and agile, intelligent and devoted, without restrictions or limits, they both loved and admired the Nyctalope, just as much as they were appreciated and loved by him. They were fit for all kinds of trades and for the most varied kinds of work. And they were so used to the Nyctalope that they understood him at the slightest word.

This time, they were not given a brief order to carry out. Saint-Clair applied himself to bringing them up to date on all he had learned during the day, down to the slightest detail. He showed them the Browning 9mm bullet, which he had kept, before putting it back into one of the pockets of his jacket.

At the end of the conversation, he confided in them:

"Sometimes it is necessary to lie. I lied to Jacques d'Hermont when I told him that Doctor Luvier had not kept secret any of his hypotheses. In truth, there is one hypothesis that he definitely kept quiet, and will keep to himself until some new fact convinces him to say it publicly. Here it is. The doctor told me in his own words:

" 'There is a possibility that some criminal poisoning has taken effect, through methods of which I have not the slightest suspicion. We still have witch doctors in our countryside, magicians who openly identify as bonesetters and secretly serve as spell-casters, that is to say: poisoners. Our modern science still does not know all the *virtues*, if I may call them that, of certain plants and their amalgams of vegetable juices. Through word of mouth, from the Middle Ages, secret formulas have been transmitted to our days. The d'Hermonts might be victims of a subtle, slowly staged poisoning that attacks the very centers of their vitality in a way that I cannot discover. This has been done in the distant past. Why shouldn't it happen again?'

"Then I said:

" 'It's possible, indeed. But why has only Mademoiselle Basilie, out of the whole d'Hermont family, been spared?'

" 'Ah!' exclaimed the doctor. 'That's just what I ask myself.'

"So I continued:

" 'Whom would gain from such a crime?'

" 'I asked myself that question too,' the doctor replied.

"After a moment of meditative silence, which I did not disturb, Doctor Luvier took my hand and pressed it, very moved. Then he said:

" 'Monsieur Saint-Clair, I want to be frank with you. I have had, I have always had, strange thoughts, and maybe they are awful in their injustice. But I cannot defend myself. Listen! You asked me: *Who would gain from such a crime?* The answer is: *Every single member of the d'Hermont family!'*

" 'Ah?' I said, very intrigued.

" 'Yes!' the doctor went on. 'You mentioned that all are affected except Basilie, and so Basilie becomes our prime suspect. I myself made this observation. At the examination, she showed no symptoms. But to begin with, Basilie is a child, an innocent and happy teenager, deliciously full of joy of life, clear as water from a pure spring, and clean of spirit. She would be unable to conceive of such a crime—the slightest ugly action from her seems to me absolutely impossible. What's more, the fact that only she is well does not seem to constitute an absolute proof against her. The poisoner could very well have absorbed the substance voluntarily, precisely to divert suspicion and appear to be a victim... The guilty party would only have to dose the poison carefully in order to be ill, but not to die. After the murder, he or she would heal and...' "

Saint-Clair broke off. Silent as always when their master spoke to them in this way, Soca and Vitto listened with extreme attention, without interrupting. Both of them kept the remarks or questions that occasionally came to their minds for the end. After a moment of silence, the Nyctalope continued:

"I confess that I was astounded. I could not, and still do not, see why my friend Jacques d'Hermont, his sister or his daughter would strike with such diabolical perversity, with such demoniacal obstinacy, trying to spread death in their own family. I know very well that the immense estate of Beech Grove belongs to the Comte, as the head of the family, but I also know that his sister and daughters freely enjoy his wealth. Why would one of the members of the family desire to become the sole owner of the estate? Besides, I know the character of Jacques d'Hermont well... As for his sister, his elder daughter, his younger daughter, such a monstrosity would be beyond belief... No! I said all this to Doctor Luvier. But he replied:

" 'I think and reason exactly as you do; nonetheless the hypothesis of criminal poisoning seems to me the only one, in the end, that fits with the facts. Who is doing the poisoning? By what means? Why? Alas! Faced with this frightful mystery at Beech Grove, I am not Sherlock Holmes. I am happy to watch and wait. But I must admit that all my observations so far have come to nothing, nothing.'

"So, I asked:

" 'How do you explain the scene of the illuminated nimbus in the night? The painful and voluptuous ecstasy of the two women on the pedestal? The clear view that d'Hermont had of all this, with his conscious senses?'

" 'I did not know about that,' replied Luvier, 'for you were the first to tell me about the phenomenon. I am astounded, and I don't understand it. Maybe it was a hallucination, transferred from Laure and Madeleine to Jacques? Note that this is supposed to have have happened in the middle of the night, when the paroxysm of that strange fever possesses these unfortunates.' "

Saint-Clair paused again, then resumed, nodding his head:

"At the time, I did not know the triple fact of the human shadow, the footprints and the Browning cartridge. I could only repeat, with the doctor: 'Collective and communicative hallucination, due to a state of intense fever.' But now, I do not believe it was a hallucination. I am convinced that the mysterious luminous nimbus, the ecstasy of Laure and Madeleine, and Jacques' state of conscious lucidity were real, just as real as the human shadow he saw, the footprints, and the cartridge."

With a gesture of both hands, he concluded:

"There, my friends, now you know everything."

Although neither of the two Corsicans was very talkative, Vitto was the more taciturn. Unless he was induced to speak from an irresistible impulse, he usually left it to Soca to respond. As usual, the latter took his time before saying:

"Monsieur, we think that, in addition to obeying your orders, we should listen and watch, speak only with extreme prudence, and ask questions with a subtle appearance of naïveté or indifference. That is, we should work to give you the most information possible."

"Yes," said Saint-Clair. "Just that, to start. You will live with the staff of the castle, and will be able to see the persons who come from the outside for one of the thousand tasks of life in the countryside. You will keep your eyes and ears on constant alert. As for specific orders, I do not have any to give you at the moment. I know nothing more about this mystery than what I have told you, and you now know as much as I do. As for Doctor Luvier's hypothesis, let us not dismiss it altogether—let's keep it in mind. After all, everything is possible in this world, where the forces of evil have unfathomable powers. But let's not also pay too much attention to it, for hypotheses of this kind are tyrannical and can cast a veil over knowledge. Understood, both of you?"

Vitto joined his voice with that of Soca in replying:

"Yes, Monsieur."

Saint-Clair having risen, the two Corsicans followed him and went out.

The Nyctalope put on his pajamas, prepared a bath, enjoyed it for ten minutes, then strolled about his room until dinner time. He took a long time dressing, and glanced through the Sunday papers he'd brought with him from Paris.

In the dining-room, brightly lit by chandelier and torches, the chatelain of Beech Grove and his guests not only dined in fine style—for Amélie was a first-rate cook—but with what even almost approached joy! Vivacious Jeannette, who was serving, was at once excited and bewildered. This relative euphoria seemed to be due not only to the presence of the famous and lively Léo Saint-Clair, but also to the obvious and extraordinary fact that Jacques d'Hermont, his sister Laure and their older daughter Madeleine, had suffered hardly at all from the stubborn fever which usually started at sunset, worsened around midnight, then remain stationary and disappear abruptly at dawn, leaving its victims in a desperate state of mental anxiety and physical depression.

Now, on the evening of the first day of Saint-Clair's presence at Beech Grove, it was evident that the victims, except for their thinness and yellow complexions, were far less sick than on any other previous evenings, and ate with pleasure and a strong appetite.

As for Basilie d'Hermont, she looked even freer and happier than usual, contributing the most amusing, spiritually childish and malicious sallies into the conversation. Saint-Clair observed her closely, and saw in the deep clearness of the young girl's pale periwinkle eyes nothing but honest wonder and the innocent, joyous egotism of living.

Jacques d'Hermont, his sister and his daughters were very sincere in begging him to stay up late—Laure would play the piano, Madeleine would sing, because she felt "so much better," and Basilie would recite some fables of La Fontaine, which, her father said, she did "with a naturalness and a naive drollery that verged on genius," but Saint-Clair held fast in his decision to retire almost immediately after dinner, and at ten o'clock, he shut himself up in the Red Room.

According to his habit, he had eaten hardly anything, and only out of courtesy—for at home, in a hotel or at a house familiar enough for him to enjoy some freedom, the Nyctalope rarely dined at night. He had practically suppressed the evening meal from his life. A fruit, an infusion, a bowl of milk, often with a simple glass of Vichy or Vittel water, was his normal supper. As an exception, he consented to sit at table when he was a guest at a house, or in company where worldly convenience made him consider his duty to not stand out and act like everyone else. Even then, skillful and discreet, he ate very little without it being noticed.

Once again in his pajamas, Saint-Clair settled himself in an armchair in front of the fireplace with a blazing fire, and began to smoke a pipe while reading the monthly review of *Les Œuvres Libres*. This evening hour of reading and smoking was for him the most pleasant hour of the day, and its solitude, abstraction, relaxation and forgetfulness of everything helped him transition between the activities of day and the rest of the night.

He didn't even mentally review the events of the day. No! The day was over. Now it was time to rest, to sleep. Tomorrow would be another day! His mind would be fresh, and he would resume his activities at the peak of his powers. Night was made for man to sleep, just like almost all of nature's creatures. Saint-Clair slept like a log during the nights, usually without exception.

This night—the night of Tuesday 20 to Wednesday 21 January 1925—was no exception. After closing his eyes a little after midnight, Saint-Clair reopened them after the normal duration of sleep, somewhere around 6 a.m.

He opened his eyes, stretched, rubbed down, washed, and changed out of his pajamas, breathing in the fresh air from the window he'd left half-open during the night.

It was 6:45 a.m. when Saint-Clair rang the bell. Two minutes later, Firmin entered the Red Room.

"Good morning, Monsieur. Has Monsieur slept well?"

"Yes, very well, thank you. Good morning, Firmin."

"Does Monsieur want me to light the fire?"

"Yes, and close the window. When will breakfast be served?"

"Monsieur le Comte has given orders. A breakfast spread will be served at exactly 7:30 a.m. Does Monsieur want it here?"

"Yes, please."

"Very well, Monsieur."

From the moment he woke, until breakfast, while washing, dressing, and eating, Saint-Clair did nothing but review again and again the circumstances of the drama at Beech Grove. Lucid and lively as his well-rested mind was, however, nothing emerged to throw light on the mysterious drama.

After a hearty breakfast, Saint-Clair murmured:

"First of all, the footprints. Classic and banal as they are, they often give valuable clues. Then, a private interrogation of Laure Dauzet and Madeleine d'Hermont. Finally, a detailed visit of the castle, the servants' quarters, the gardens and the park. That will be the program for the day. This afternoon, I will send Soca with a letter for the Prefect of Tours, to request a list of all the citizens of Saint-Christophe who may have registered the possession of a Browning 9mm. It is an expensive weapon, and therefore not very common. Unless that 'human shadow' comes from farther away, which is unlikely, I hope this list will allow me to narrow my list of suspects…"

He then asked himself:

"I wonder if the condition of our three victims will be as euphoric today as it was yesterday?"

The answer to this question was given to him at 8 a.m. when, descending to the ground floor, he heard talking in the dining-room. He entered and said:

"Good morning, Madame, Mesdemoiselles, my dear d'Hermont… Please, I beg of you, do not disturb yourselves!"

Chocolate, coffee, milk, toasts, butter and jam were on the table. The chatelain, his sister and his daughters were tucking into the first meal of the day. Jacques, Laure and Madeleine were visibly well. In front of Saint-Clair, who sat in an armchair between the table and a French window, they continued to eat with an appetite. Basilie reminded him of a fresh, beautiful, perfumed flower, still almost a bud, whose magnificent blossoming one could not imagine without a certain pleasant disturbance.

Through the large window with drawn curtains, one could see that this day, while colder than the previous one, would still be sunny.

"Would you like to go hunting?" d'Hermont asked Saint-Clair.

The latter gave the answer expected by his friend:

"My goodness, no! I feel lazy. If you permit, my dear fellow, I will amuse myself by strolling through the park that must still be magnificent despite the winter, with corners of truly Lamartinian romanticism.[2] Am I mistaken?"

"Not at all, Monsieur Saint-Clair," said Basilie, laughing heartily. "But my father never told us that the Nyctalope had a romantic soul."

"Bah! It depends on the day, Mademoiselle. Everything is within us. It's simply a question of not systematically rejecting any impulses."

"Well! As for me," the young girl replied, "I don't believe there's anything romantic about me. I'm more the sporty type. Papa even reproaches me for being a frightful materialist. You're going to despise me: I hardly ever read a book. I love horses, cars and bicycles; in winter, canoeing, and in summer, swimming in the lake to the north of the park. It's beautiful, you'll see. I admit that its banks may strike you as romantic, but I limit myself to finding them picturesque. Above all, they're an excellent hunting ground, full of game. Our clever Bottot has created a little place there, next to the water, for breeding pheasants.

"This Bottot is no doubt your gamekeeper?"

"Yes, of course." And, with a naive vanity, she added: "The head gamekeeper, in fact, for he has three subordinates."

"Yes," explained d'Hermont. "Our park is bordered by some large woods and natural meadows that form a vast hunting ground. To the west, the estate is bordered by the national road from Tours to Le Mans. Prowlers and poachers would have good game if I employed only one gamekeeper. Four at least are indispensable. They live in pavilions in the woods. I will show you all this, my dear friend."

And in another tone, paternally tender, he added:

"The weather's so very fine, Basilie. Will you go out riding this morning?"

---

[2] After Alphonse de Lamartine (1790-1869), French writer, poet and politician.

"Yes," replied the young girl, surprised. "Ah! It's true, I was seated when you came in, and didn't get up. You didn't see that I'm already in my riding breeches and boots."

"Very well! Will you give me the pleasure of going to the Fosses-Blanches? The farmer there bought two horses the day before yesterday, at the fair of Château-du-Loir. I'd like you to examine them and give me your impression."

"No, not my impression, my reasoned opinion," corrected Basilie in a tone at once so pert and so assured that it was almost comical, to the extent that Saint-Clair himself could not help but laugh, as did the Comte, Laure and Madeleine. They were all decidedly well that morning, at least as much as they could be after months of the progressive weakening of all their vital organs—a weakening during which their weight, yellow complexion and hollow eyes revealed the seriousness of their ailment and made a disturbing in contrast with Basilie's dazzling health.

Saint-Clair observed everything and everyone. He said to himself:

"Can my presence alone be responsible for this reprieve? In that case, the influence of the mental on the physical is even prompter and more effective than even the illustrious Cabanis affirmed, explained, and demonstrated.[3] Patience! We shall see."

After breakfast was over, they all got up. Laure and Madeleine occupied themselves, as they did every morning, with the progress of domestic life, which involved talking to

---

[3] Pierre Jean Georges Cabanis (1757-1808), French physiologist and materialist philosopher. His principal work, *Rapports du physique et du moral de l'homme* [On the relations between the physical and moral aspects of man] (1802), is a sketch of physiological psychology. Psychology is directly linked on to biology, for sensibility, the fundamental fact, is the highest grade of life and the lowest of intelligence. All the intellectual processes are evolved from sensibility, and sensibility itself is a property of the nervous system.

the cook, the chambermaid and the servants. Basilie went out to the stable, passing through the pantry to pick up Firmin, her groom.

D'Hermont said to Saint-Clair:

"If you want, my dear friend, I will take a little walk with you. But in half an hour, I will leave you, because I have some accounting to do. I plan to come back and shut myself away in my office until noon. When you return, Laure and Madeleine will keep you company until lunch."

"Thank you. I'll take Vitto and Soca; I enjoy their company."

"Understood!" said d'Hermont. "I remember what they were to you, and you to them, during the War."

While they spoke, the two men had passed into the grand entrance hall, which Laure, Madeleine and Basilie never entered.

Saint-Clair put on a large coat with a fur collar, which Vitto had hung the day before on the coat stand. Jacques d'Hermont threw a pelerine over his shoulders. Summoned by a bell that they had specially arranged, Vitto and Soca appeared from the office, also wearing large jackets similar to that of their master, except with collars of padded cloth. Completing their look with boots, peccary gloves and a Basque beret, the Nyctalope and his two Corsicans followed the Comte, who himself wore an old gray felt hat, wool gloves and tightly laced-up shoes.

They exited through the door of the great portico. D'Hermont showed his admiring friend the beautiful spectacle of the valley still wrapped in gauzy mist, as well as the houses in the amphitheater valley of Saint-Christophe, illuminated by the rising sun. Here and there, the glass shimmered and sparkled.

Saint-Clair had packed a short pipe and now lit it. Then they set off toward the north side of the lawn, where the low squat pedestal stood without a statue. As they circled the large dovetower, they heard a clear voice cry out with joy:

"Hey! Hop! Diane!"

A fine bay mare trotting along came to a halt. It was mounted by Basilie, head bare, gold hair flying in the wind. She wore a kind of fitted blue jacket, trimmed with fur at the collar and sleeves and molded about her firm bust.

Passing ten steps in front of them, the modern Amazon took them in with a keen glance and made a gesture of salute. They had no time to reply, for at that very moment, making a quarter-turn, the impatient mare carried its light and lively load down a forest path.

Saint-Clair said softly:

"Jacques, let's wait a while."

While they waited, they looked closely at the outside of the castle.

"I don't want anyone to see us while we examine the imprints of the shoes," explained the Nyctalope.

For no apparent reason, Comte d'Hermont was suddenly very moved, and did not look to suppress the emotion, also revealed in the expressions of his face and voice:

"At this hour, no one has any business on this side of the castle," he stated.

Glancing in the direction of the woods, Saint-Clair made sure that Basilie had taken the turn about two hundred meters into the forest path. Then he said:

"Well! Come on."

They only had to walk fifty steps.

Beyond the bulge of the lawn with its pedestal and the circular path with its thick layer of gravel, the green front area in front of the first row of trees was a bare space of three to five meters in width. In it there alternated random patches of grass or moss and patches of soil, frozen from the cold. This space was not very trafficked, as the humans in the castle and outbuildings had the habit of entering the park only by one of the many paths that stretched around the lawn and buildings.

At a rapid clip, Jacques d'Hermont led his three companions to the foot of an enormous and immense beech tree. Its great trunk was divided, almost at the level of the earth, into three diverging segments that projected their branches nearly horizontally ten or fifteen meters around them.

Just one step in front of the tree with light gray bark, Jacques d'Hermont stopped. Leaning forward, he held out his right arm, pointed his index and spoke in a slightly hoarse voice.

"Saint-Clair, there they are... There are the footprints... Right there, just between those two parallel footprints, is where I picked up the intact cartridge."

"Good," said the Nyctalope softly. "Would you move slightly, my dear friend? That's enough... Vitto, take the measurements. Soca, write them down; please also note all the details you see. It's necessary to have take impressions, and we need an exact and complete description... You know how to do these things. Hurry up!"

Then, to d'Hermont, he asked:

"Did you see the human shadow running away?"

"Yes," replied the Comte.

"Where did it go?"

"Ah—that, I'm not sure. At first, I could see the shadow, then it melted into the night."

"When you first saw the human shadow, you said it seemed to peel away from the light gray of this trunk, which received some light from that enigmatic nimbus. When the shadow saw you heading with such energy towards the pedestal, it fled. One leap is enough for anyone to pass from here into the nearest path. Most likely the man went that way to avoid giving away his trail. If he had plunged into the woods, he would have made the dead branches creak on the ground and rustled the living branches in the thickets. So he must have gone the other way... Well then! Vitto, Soca, where are you?"

Soca did not hesitate:

"Indeed, Monsieur, it's very clear. The footsteps came, trampled about a bit, stayed for a while in absolute immobility, and suddenly left."

"Where did they go?"

"Down this path, Monsieur, where the impressions that interest us are lost among the many other footprints of men and animals... Unfortunately this is a forest path that crosses the park, which no doubt everyone uses."

Jacques d'Hermont had been listening attentively. He smiled at this last statement, before saying cordially:

"No, Soca, not everyone. Only the people of the castle and the gatekeepers. It's true, this is enough to blur traces as banal as those of a shoe... For if I've seen right, they are some kind of shoe, aren't they?"

"Yes, Monsieur le Comte," replied the Corsican after looking at Saint-Clair, who gave him a brief smile of encouragement. "The shoes that made those impressions are not very remarkable, at least as far as their soles go. All the same, Vitto has noticed a peculiar detail—nothing escapes him."

"Ah!" said d'Hermont in a lively tone, advancing a step toward Soca. "This detail, what is it?"

Saint-Clair intervened.

"Vitto, you discovered the thing. Answer."

The taciturn Corsican was kneeling on the ground. He had finished observing, measuring, dictating to Soca. He stood up with a smooth movement. After having also sought the approval anticipated from the Nyctalope, he faced the chatelain and replied:

"Monsieur le Comte, the shoes that left their impressions here are ordinary country shoes, the kind with nails, not too thick. In short, they are strong lace-up shoes with thick soles, carefully hobnailed. The left shoe, however, has a peculiar detail about it—one might describe it as a fissure, or a crack, produced in the middle of the sole by exposure to a strong source of heat. I imagine a man who has returned from a walk in cold weather, warming up before the fire; he brings his left foot too close to the fire, and leaves it there too long. The leather of the sole dries up abruptly; it shrivels, cracks, splits. And this crack gives the footprints a very neat, very significant form in the dirt, impossible to mistake. I will add that the footprints came from old shoes that have worn for a long time;

many of the nails are missing, and those that remain are flattened. What's more, the man who usually wears these shoes has legs that are rather far apart, with the tips of his feet turned out. He must be heavy; large or small, he is no weakling. There it is, that's all, Monsieur le Comte."

"That's quite a lot!" said Jacques d'Hermont, impressed.

"And it's as definitive as it is beyond doubt," said Saint-Clair. "Vitto speaks rarely and briefly. What he has just told you, my dear Jacques, is a very long speech for him. He has said nothing useless, and everything he said was important. As for the footprints and soles of the shoes, we would learn nothing more now, even if we had the shoes under our eyes, unless you can identify them as belonging to a man of your acquaintance. They are certainly the shoes of a man of quite large size..."

"Forty-two wide," Soca said calmly.

"I will think about this," said d'Hermont, puzzled. "Yes, I will think... We'll talk some more about it later, Saint-Clair."

But the Nyctalope went on, calmly:

"In the meantime, Vitto and Soca will continue to work on the footprints. That is to say, they will try to find and separate out from the path the steps of the man whose left shoe had a split sole. Perhaps this investigation will lead them in a direction that is, or could be, significant. During the day, they will also arrange to see all the existing shoes, worn or not, in the castle and its outbuildings... Isn't that right, my friends?"

"Yes, Monsieur," the two Corsicans said together, with a peaceful assurance that d'Hermont admired, despite the fact that he already knew that these two men were unparalleled servants and incomparable bloodhounds.

"Good!" said Saint-Clair. "On you go, then. Now, my dear d'Hermont, I believe you have work to do in your office. Meanwhile, I would like to speak to your sister and eldest daughter. Where can I find Madame Dauzet and Mademoiselle Madeleine?"

"Come with me, dear friend. My sister and daughter are expecting you. I warned them that you wished to speak with them."

"Very good."

No doubt Madame Dauzet and Madeleine had rushed that morning to attend to their usual occupations, for d'Hermont and Saint-Clair found them waiting in the little drawing-room, visibly moved.

D'Hermont said only:

"I leave you to it."

And he disappeared through the door that gave direct access to the living-room library.

There was no preamble. Immediately taking a seat before the two women who had, at his gesture, arranged themselves side-by-side on a couch, Saint-Clair spoke in a contained but penetrating voice:

"I address myself to you both. Your brother, Madame, your father, Mademoiselle, has told me all he knows. But do you know anything beyond what he does? Is there something you have hidden? If I am to have a chance of clarifying the tragic and painful mystery enveloping Beech Grove in who knows what mortal evil, you must tell me everything you know, with no restrictions, down to the vaguest and most secret of your thoughts."

The aunt and niece resembled one another closely. The two of them shared more than the "family air" one notices between blood relatives. They had the same eyes and dark hair, the same tanned complexion, now sallow from the mysterious illness, the same cut of the face which hardly varied from the difference in age, the same body shape, normally solid and full, but reduced to skeletal thinness because of physical illness and moral anguish.

After the Nyctalope's sober but energetic plea, there was a brief moment of silence. The aunt and niece took one another by the hand, and clutched each another convulsively. With a look at once trusting and anxious, they stared at their grave and calm questioner.

At last, turning her head slightly toward her aunt, Madeleine sighed:

"You say it!"

"I shall," said Laure Dauzet, with a breath.

And in a low voice, a little hoarse, for her throat was contracted, she said:

"As far as the facts go, we told Jacques everything. But as far as our thoughts..."

She stopped, trembling.

The Nyctalope knew the power that he had to communicate his will to others through the fluid from his hands. He leaned toward Laure and Madeleine, and though he did not touch their clutched hands, he took hold of their other hands that the woman and the girl had left at rest at the edge of the couch, one to the right, the other to the left. Their fingers were frozen. He touched them, held them, caressed them, and kept them in his warm palms, electrified by his intense vital fluid. With a dominating familiarity, he commanded:

"Laure, speak!"

At the same time he looked into Madame Dauzet's eyes. They opened wide, and soon appeared as if fascinated. The patient abandoned herself to the Nyctalope's hypnotic grip. Suddenly softening, becoming less stiff and strained in all of her body, she started speaking in a low, slow voice:

"Our thoughts... I do not know which one of us first became aware of *it*. It was two weeks ago, barely two weeks, that Madeleine and I first communicated with one another during the night, obeying a simultaneous impulse. Our rooms are next to each another. After the death of my sister Lucile, we were afraid at night, and began to leave open the door between our rooms. Just as in my brother's room, in each of our rooms a nightlight gives a weak light..."

She paused and sighed, seeming to hesitate. But the Nyctalope increased the pressure of his hand. Laure went on:

"One night, we slept less well than most nights. I had just heard the great grandfather clock on the landing sound three... All at once, we got up and started walking towards each other, meeting on the very threshold between our two rooms. Quickly I said:

" 'Madeleine, I have to talk to you.'

"She replied:

" 'And I to you, Laure.'

" 'Come here!' I said.

"And embracing Madeleine, I brought her to my bed, where we sat hugging one another. Shuddering, we spoke the same words at the same time. I was conscious, as was Madeleine, that we were saying the same words, expressing the same thoughts, learning nothing from each other since we were thinking the same way. But we had to say what we did so that our souls would be liberated..."

She stopped then, but Saint-Clair did not let her rest. He insisted:

"And what was that?"

With a great shudder, her face expressing a frightful horror, Laure whispered:

"Basilie!"

"My God!" moaned Madeleine, clenching her hand within the hand of Saint-Clair.

Coldly, the Nyctalope asked:

"So, what about Basilie?"

Then, with a quick and gasping speech, as if the unfortunate woman were anxious to "liberate herself" from a thought that filled her with fear, shame and remorse, Laure spoke once again:

"She is so different from us! In the essence and aspect of her whole being, she resembles neither my brother, nor my sister-in-law who bore her, or me, her aunt, or Madeleine, her sister, or either of our grandparents from the south of France. She, Basilie, looks like she's from one of the Nordic countries where most girls have her deep blue eyes, fine blonde hair, flushed cheeks, innocent look... Innocent maybe, but only on the surface..."

Laure then fell silent, her mouth shut tight, as if she had made a sudden decision not to speak anymore.

But Saint-Clair applied more pressure to her hand:

"A thought is no more than a name, an ensemble of statements of fact. Her name, Basilie. A fact: the lack of resemblance of your youngest niece with the entire d'Hermont family. A name, a fact. So be it! But your thought, and Madeleine's, did not limit themselves to this name and this fact. So what is it? Speak, Laure!"

She obeyed, but with her head lowered, and in a voice so low that Saint-Clair could barely hear her:

"Our thought came from jealousy, it seems. This is what gives us shame and remorse. But we cannot drive it away; the jealousy destroys us. We are afraid to hate Basilie, because out of all the d'Hermonts, she, alone, is free of the evil that tortures and kills us... From jealousy to hate! My God, it is horrible! From hatred to suspicion..."

She sobbed, her whole body convulsive. Madeleine, also agitated with violent shivers, leaned her whole weight against her.

"What suspicion?" asked Saint-Clair intensely.

"Oh! No! No!" moaned Laure, twisting.

She would have fallen backward on the sofa with Madeleine, if the hands of the Nyctalope had not kept the two convulsed bodies seated upright.

"Yes! Speak!" he ordered.

With an evident effort of her whole being, Laure continued:

"*To make us die, she gave her soul to the devil!*"

And with this extraordinary utterance, which astonished Saint-Clair, for he had never imagined a conclusion of this kind, Laure was seized by a nervous tremor, so sudden and violent that the Nyctalope, neglecting a half-fainting Madeleine, turned his attention completely to attending her.

He had anticipated, if not exactly this, but at least some kind of physical trouble due to the exasperation of her nervous system. In his pocket was a tiny bottle of subtle and powerful English salts.

Saint-Clair nursed Laure, who soon calmed down, relaxed and had a healthy cry, while of her own accord Madeleine slowly regained consciousness.

During several minutes of progressive return to calm, not a word was exchanged. Saint-Clair alternately caressed the hands of Laure and Madeleine, at first glazed and stiffened, then more and more lukewarm and supple. He looked at them with infinite gentleness. In this way, they returned almost to how they were before the start of their dramatic confessions. When he judged their spirits had become lucid again and their bodies were calm, the Nyctalope spoke again:

"Laure, I beg you to keep your composure, with all the strength you have. You too, Madeleine. Can I count on you two?"

He smiled at them.

They replied with a pale smile and a distinct "yes."

Saint-Clair went on:

"The thought you expressed in saying: '*To make us die, she gave her soul to the devil!*'... We must carefully examine such a thought, consider things cautiously, for this resides on a very different plane than the one I discussed with Doctor Luvier, or when I examined the footprints and pistol cartridge in the presence of your brother. Yes, this is on an entirely different plane! Laure, Madeleine, I beg you to answer me with complete sincerity. First, do you believe in God?"

"Yes!" the aunt and niece said together.

"Are you practicing Catholics?"

"Yes."

"And pious too?"

"Yes."

Laure added:

"Even very pious, in the judgment of the world, for we rarely pass a week without taking communion."

"Good!" said Saint-Clair. "But am I right in remembering Jacques, without being anti-clerical or an atheist, as being..."

"My brother is indifferent, that's all," Laure cut him off gently. "All the same, out of affection and tenderness for us, he accompanies us to Mass on Sunday. And of course, he would never make the slightest derogatory remark about our faith and practices of piety..."

Then, Saint-Clair asked, clearly:

"What about Basilie?"

Neither the young woman nor Madeleine were surprised by the question. They had been expecting it. Madeleine whispered, shrugging her shoulders:

"Oh! Basilie, her faith, her piety..."

Laure answered coldly:

"I am convinced that the soul of Basilie is closed to God. My niece accompanies us to Sunday Mass and holiday celebrations, but for eighteen months, she has not taken communion. She did not even go to the Easter Mass last year. She has not confessed, even once. Jacques, her father, has never questioned her about this failure to fulfill her fundamental religious duties. Madeleine and I have kept the same reserve. We believe that each person is responsible only before God and their own conscience. Thus, as far as religion is concerned, a way of life has been established at Beech Grove whereby each acts according to his or her own will, without attempting to influence the conduct of others, and without allowing oneself any commentary in attitude or words. We feel, Madeleine and I, that this is the will of our brother and father. Jacques, the last Comte d'Hermont, is now the head of the family, a sort of function of dignity and authority with respect to keeping old traditions alive. The will of our brother is thus respected. We do not judge her—even in the most secret depths of our souls."

"That is good!" said Saint-Clair.

And he stood up.

With the same movement, the two women rose, astonished. The Nyctalope noted their surprise.

"Yes," he replied. "That is enough. You have told me enough for today. I have to think, now. But I also need the two of you to reflect well, before our next conversation. I do not want your reflections to remain silent. Tell them to me sincerely, examine them together and analyze them, if I dare use that word, a little pedantic in the circumstances. Do you understand me? Then you will tell me everything you have discussed amongst yourselves."

"We agree," said Madeleine.

"Agreed," echoed Laure, who added: "But what should we think about, in particular?"

Saint-Clair looked into the two faces with his extraordinary gaze and said slowly:

"About this: *To make us die, she gave her soul to the devil.*"

He took one hand of Laure's and one hand of Madeleine's, raised them, bowed, and touched one, then the other with a kiss. Letting them go suddenly, he turned and walked out.

But before he reached the door, he stopped, turned again towards the two women who had remained motionless, and, in the same deep, slow voice, said:

"During our next conversation, I will also ask you to tell me how you explain the phenomenon of the luminous nimbus and your kind of ecstatic prayer on the lawn pedestal."

He saw them blanch with new emotion. Without adding a word, he left the room.

CHAPTER III
The Cracked Sole

Léo Saint-Clair had resolved the problem of the existence of God for himself in a definitive way, one that filled his soul with stoic serenity. As far as religions went, he was informed. He had conversed with the Pope in Rome and with the living Buddha in Lhasa; he had devoted himself to studying at the Islamic universities of Morocco and at the most venerable temples of China; as friends he could count on the Superior General of the Jesuits, a great Dominican orator, a venerable pastor from Heidelberg and the president of the Geneva consistory. In consequence, he thought that if a young girl "gives her soul to the devil," this young girl is either an ungodly mystic, or the devil in question is represented by a man of flesh-and-bone, visible, tangible and very alive.

He said to himself:

"In the eventuality, doubtful if not improbable, that Basilie d'Hermont plays an occult role in the mysterious drama of Beech Grove, is she possessed by the madness of demonic mysticism? Or is she instead the instrument, conscious or not, of a man seeking to do deliberate harm? The footprints of the size forty-three shoes and cartridge of the Browning caliber 9mm make me lean toward the second hypothesis..."

From the little drawing room where he had left Laure and Madeleine, Saint-Clair headed to the library.

"Well?" asked Jacques d'Hermont, who had been anxiously expecting him.

Saint-Clair replied calmly:

"Your sister and eldest daughter, my dear friend, have entrusted their secret thoughts to me. But its nature is such that I do not think I ought to reveal it to you. I need to think and come to a decision. I will tell you later, in my own time. I beg you not to question me, and above all, not to let Laure and

Madeleine suspect I have alluded to their strange thought before you."

Without hesitation, Jacques d'Hermont gave his promise.

"I appreciate it," said Saint-Clair. "Now I would like to visit the whole castle, including the rooms of your sister, your daughters and yourself. Will you allow me?"

"Certainly! Would you like me to accompany you?"

"No, it's better for me to do this alone."

"As you please," said the chatelain obediently. "We are in the habit of never closing the doors here. You will be able to enter wherever you like."

"Thank you. One more thing: have you had your servants for a long time?"

"Yes, all of them," replied d'Hermont. "Firmin and his wife Amélie came here twenty years ago, just after their marriage. The maid Jeannette, their niece, was born on one of my farms, the closest one to the castle. The gardener, Francis, and his wife, Charlotte, in charge of the farmyard, have been at Beech Grove for thirty years. Finally, our head gamekeeper, Bottot, is the son of his predecessor, who was hired and trained by my father. I can tell you that I know all these people as well as I know myself. They have not only our confidence, but also our affection."

"Very good!" concluded Saint-Clair, visibly satisfied. "This afternoon, I will first talk to Firmin. I have been watching him: he seems a man of good sense, with a typical peasant calm, based on concrete realities."

"Exactly!" approved the Comte.

"Well! Until tomorrow then, my friend. I am going to make a complete tout of your home. No, don't bother describing the rooms to me. I already have a sense of the inner layout of the castle. I will make my tour without hesitation."

D'Hermont nodded in agreement, and Saint-Clair left the library.

Of course, the Nyctalope did not try to open doors that were closed or did not have a key in the lock. But he did not hesitate to make forays wherever his hands could access something without breaking in.

He spent only a short time in Jacques' room; but spent a long time, though still and thinking for long minutes, in the rooms of Laure Dauzet, Madeleine and Basilie d'Hermont. All the rooms of the castle and outbuildings were made up by the young servant, Jeannette, whom he found occupied in the laundry with a bit of mending. With kindness, he questioned the young woman about herself, her parents and the Gasse family, the brother and sister-in-law of Firmin who worked as farmers at La Migeonne. This was a medium-sized farm with buildings located not far away, at the edge of the park, about a kilometer away from the castle.

From Jeannette, Saint-Clair learned a fact that he lodged in his memory. For six months, in the farmyard, barn and stable of La Migeonne, the cattle had become ill and died in number singularly higher than in all the other farms of the area. What is more, the farmer, Hector Gasse, and his wife Anna, Jeanette's parents, had been in poor health for six months, although before, they had been "strong as oaks."

Saint-Clair gently risked a question:

"Do their discomforts resemble those suffered by your master, his sister and his elder daughter?"

"I do not know," replied Jeannette innocently. "They are weak in the legs above all, and sometimes in the evening, they suffer from dizzy spells with a bit of fever."

"Has Doctor Luvier seen them?" asked Saint-Clair.

"Yes, Monsieur."

"And what did he say?"

"He said that it is a fever from the damp. La Migeonne is on the edge of the biggest pond in the entire estate, and last summer, it drained only halfway. The bottom took a long time to dry up in the sun. It seems that this created a bad air, miasmas."

"That's possible," said Saint-Clair.

But Jeannette went on, with a smile of contentment and hope:

"Monsieur le Comte had all the rushes and herbs in the pond removed. Now the water has filled up the basin again, and the overflow goes to the Nais by a small, clean stream. The doctor said that my father and mother will be fully recovered by the spring."

"That is also probable," concluded the Nyctalope.

Saint-Clair left this reasonable and robust country girl, ruddy and in perfect health, to her work, and exited the laundry room to continue his visit. Already, however, he had promised himself to make a visit that afternoon to the farm of Hector and Anna Gasse.

At 11 a.m., he had finished his first general foray, and began his return to the library. Passing through the grand entrance hall, he saw two figures through the ground-floor window, open to the sun for the daily airing-out. These were his two Corsican aides, making their way through the park toward the castle.

He went through the big gate to meet them. On seeing their master Vitto and Soca stopped, and Saint-Clair realized that they wished to speak to him at a distance far enough from the castle so that no one would overhear them. He took a step toward them, and stopped. Soca said immediately:

"Monsieur, we have found more footprints of the shoe with the cracked sole. They are faint, but sufficient for us to follow their track. They led us straight to a farm at the edge of a large pond. In the yard, before the front porch, the trail is lost in a muddy ground trampled by the men and women of the farm. A servant was turning over the manure in this yard, and looked at us. We pretended that we were only taking a walk, and wanted to admire the yard, which is indeed remarkable for its antiquity. Then we turned back."

"Very good!" concluded Saint-Clair.

He then added:

"We need to find out if, at this farm, which is called La Migeonne, there is a man with a shoe size forty-three, who owns old studded shoes, with a cracked left sole. But we will not do this today—at least not you, Soca, because this afternoon, you will go to the Prefecture at Tours. There you will deliver this letter from me to the Prefect, requesting a list of citizens in the area who have declared ownership of a 9mm Browning. Vitto, you will stay with me. Maybe we will go together to La Migeonne. Soca, hand me your notebook."

"Here, Monsieur."

"Is everything written down here about the footprints?"

"Yes, Monsieur."

"Good. You are free until after lunch. I will see you at 2 p.m. sharp. Now, I am going to rejoin Comte d'Hermont."

Two minutes later, Saint-Clair went into the library. There he found Basilie, buttoned-up in her uniform and with a whip in hand, reporting to her father her conversation with the farmer at the Fosses-Blanches.

With a small gesture, he signified that he would wait for their conversation to finish. For a few minutes, he could watch the young girl at his leisure.

When he entered, she flashed him a brief and charming smile. Basilie, very animated, was evidently very concerned by the little affair of the Fosses-Blanches, perhaps chiefly because it was a question of horses. She continued her explanations, or rather, her well-informed criticism of the choice of horses the farmer had made at market. She concluded by saying:

"The best, Papa, would be for you to go see the horses for yourself. You will certainly agree with me. It is necessary to resell them at another market and purchase others with greater vigor. I insist: these ones are too fine for the work destined for them on the hard soil of the Fosses-Blanches."

Saint-Clair admired—it astonished him a little—that a young girl like Basilie took so much to heart a question connected with the mere exploitation of a farm. He had assumed she was of the old stock of country gentlewomen and rural chatelaines, solidly attached to the land. Soon, however, his astonishment disappeared. What's more, it seemed impossible that there could be anything abnormally criminal, to say nothing of "selling her soul to the devil", in this modern-day amazon who appeared so well-informed, so practical, so balanced, so endowed with good physical and moral health, with blue eyes and beautiful red lips uttering words that, in spite of their reason, were those of a child passionate about toys, in her case, horses.

"The soul of this adolescent is both naively practical and youthfully fiery," he said to himself. "I do not imagine her as 'giving her soul to the devil" to secure from infernal powers the death of her mother, father, sister and aunt, against whom she shows no visible interest and no hatred with suspicious motives. On the contrary, she seems united to them with blood and family ties of a natural tenderness that nothing in this life would seem able to threaten... Then what are the grounds for the atrocious thoughts of Laure and Madeleine? That is what they will not tell me. It's true that I did interrupt the logical chain of their confessions, but I will lead them back to the right place."

Meanwhile, Jacques d'Hermont said to his daughter:

"It's decided then, my darling. I'll go this very afternoon to the Fosses-Blanches."

"Very good, Papa! Now, I'm going to take a bath. I need it. I was so full of energy during the argument with that stubborn Boussin! And then I took Diane on such a gallop..."

Light and cheerful, she went out with a rebellious shake of her head and a new smile for Saint-Clair as she walked by.

The two men waited a moment after the door closed behind Basilie. Then d'Hermont asked with sudden uneasiness:

"So, my dear friend, how was your visit of the castle?"

Saint-Clair let himself sink into an armchair, and looking distractedly at the shelves of the library lined up before him, he said:

"My word, everything was fine!"

After another brief silence, he added:

"But yes, there was something. In the laundry room, I found Jeannette, and chatted with her for a bit. Without the slightest ulterior motive from me, the slightest mental restriction, she told me certain things. Come, you must have noticed that all things living at the farm of La Migeonne, men, women and animals, are in a poorer state of health than that of the inhabitants and livestock of your other farms?"

The chatelain frowned and answered energetically:

"It's true! Yes, it's true."

And after a kind of hesitation:

"But I admit that not once did it occur to me to make a connection between..."

He broke off, shivering and very moved.

"Between Beech Grove and La Migeonne, from the point of view of the mystery?" said Saint-Clair calmly.

"Yes! It is true that the losses of cattle at La Migeonne increased last year, and that the farm is now in a much less flourishing state than my other farms. The veterinarian attributes this to the extreme avarice of the farmer, Hector Gasse, and his wife, Anna. Their avarice is legendary in region; it is spoken about at all the fairs and market. As for the state of health of Hector and Anna, Doctor Luvier attributes it in part to the miasmas given off by the water of the big pond last summer, which evaporated in extraordinary proportions, breathing out years of accumulated stores. On the other hand, this same avarice that plagues the Gasses makes them feed themselves as poorly as they do their cattle. This is why my valet Firmin, Hector's brother, demanded that his niece Jeanette be hired here as a maid. Her father and mother agreed enthusiastically: for them, it was one less mouth to feed, and profit without risk, for their daughter gives them half of her wages every month."

As he gave these explanations, Jacques d'Hermont had little by little recovered his ease and calm. In the end, amused no doubt by the memory of country anecdotes linked to the avarice of the Gasses, he smiled.

"So that's how it is," said Saint-Clair. "All that is plausible, but there is something else."

"What?" asked d'Hermont, once again anxious.

"Perhaps it is unrelated to the Gasses, their avarice, their ill health or the deficiencies of their cattle, but it is worth noting nevertheless... I'm beginning to realize that, to solve the mystery of Beech Grove, nothing must be neglected... Everything that is part of the existence of the beings and things at the castle, on the farms, and in the village of Saint-Christophe, and all the bourgeois and chatelain residences of the surrounding countryside, must be taken into account... Please excuse the vagaries of my reflections, which must still be sorted out... I said there was something else worth noting. Here it is."

He took a breath and continued:

"On a path in the park, Vitto and Soca were able to find more footprints with a cracked sole. They led straight to a kind of mud pit that stretches out in front of the old porch of the farmyard of La Migeonne. They led there; then, unfortunately they disappear. The footprints are not found again anywhere else in the area, in other directions than that of the entrance to the farm... So the question arises: Did the man who wore these shoes go into the farm? Given the late hour of his walk, this would seem to suggest that he is one of the people who usually lives at La Migeonne. Or did he lose his cracked shoe at some point while crossing the muddy area, intentionally or not, continuing across without it so that he left no footprint in the solid mud? We find ourselves faced with an alternative of two propositions. It is important to choose one."

Saint-Clair fell silent.

"Indeed, yes, indeed!" whispered d'Hermont, nodding. "Yet another bizarre detail to add to the thousand that make up this mystery."

But the Nyctalope said calmly:

"By means of one or several of these details, or others that will be added to the list, we will eventually reach the end of the thread of Ariadne, leading to the solution of the mystery. But we are not yet there. We must not waste another minute. This afternoon, Soca is going to the prefecture at Tours. You know why. I will go with Vitto to La Migeonne. May I ask you to drive us there? The pretext is simple and perfectly credible: you are showing me around your magnificent estate, and very naturally, you are starting with La Migeonne, the farm closest to the castle."

"Excellent!" said d'Hermont. "We will go La Migeonne after lunch."

He said no more. Tired, slumped down and sinking softly into the back of his chair, he seemed overwhelmed. His yellow face and fixed eyes expressed a gloomy despair, as if he were resigned.

Looking at his old comrade with infinite pity, as well as an intense curiosity, the Nyctalope said to himself:

"Did he hope that I would come with a magic wand of pure and brilliant light to dispel the murky darkness, thickened by months of this diabolical mystery? I use 'diabolical' in the human sense of immorality, cunning and human perversity, rather than its religious meaning. Come now, I must bring the man to his senses!"

And seizing one of Comte d'Hermont's hands with authority, he pressed it against him, and said with persuasive force:

"My dear Jacques, I beg you not to succumb to these dark thoughts which..."

But d'Hermont did not let him finish. He sat up, flashed Saint-Clair a resolute look and exclaimed:

"Oh! Léo! How right you are! They are unworthy of you... Of me! You know, these overwhelming events have turned me into a wreck! Everything has been so terrible! Yes... So horrible... To die would be nothing. You have seen me brave death a hundred times, in harsh circumstances... But to feel that I am becoming an old man, increasingly moribund... To see those I care for threatened by death, my eldest daughter, formerly so happy with life, my sister, who had at last accepted her widowhood with some stoic serenity and tender devotion to her two nieces... Seeing this, after having seen weaken and die the woman whom I loved with the gentlest part of myself and all the strength of my being... Ah, Saint-Clair!"

He stood up and clasped a hand to his forehead.

"But you're right! You said it. I must be strong, and go with you bravely wherever this thread takes us."

The Nyctalope answered, smiling:

"Didn't you feel better yesterday, all of you? Your sister and eldest daughter fell asleep at the normal time last night. And today, you all look physically better off than yesterday."

"Ah, Léo, that is due to your presence!"

"Perhaps. The influence of my morale on yours, and thus on your bodies, is not to be underestimated. It is a phenomenon that I have seen before. But it would not have lasted if you, Laure and Madeleine, had not energetically bandied together with all your thoughts, all your muscles and nerves, for this battle for life, at once lucid and obstinate, that has become our struggle. Isn't that so, Jacques?"

The Comte agreed, with a smile that remained a little wan:

"Yes, Léo, that must be it. At least, I hope so. I wish it to be so. If we give way to despair, my daughter, my sister and I, whip us! Set us straight. You are the master here. Be an attentive and stern teacher."

"I will," concluded Saint-Clair gravely.

Without another word, he separated from his friend, left the library and went back to his room to freshen up before lunch.

This meal was less sinister than the one the day before. The weather was fine, dry and clear, and the enormous dining-room, where nothing of bad taste shocked the eye, gleamed under the sun. On the damask cloth of the table, the glass, porcelain and silver sparkled. Comely, fresh and smart, like a maid in a cloak-and-dagger novel, Jeannette attended smartly to the service. The dishes Laure Dauzet had ordered, chosen with care and grouped into a simple but thoughtful menu, tasted delicious, and the wines were of the first order.

Although, as we have noted, he was not in the habit of dining in the evening, Saint-Clair, with his solid constitution, greatly enjoyed the midday meal. For him, it was necessary for the satisfaction of his appetite, and he took a great and delicate pleasure in doing honor to the dishes and bottles.

In good spirits now, he recounted picturesque episodes from his adventures. Jacques, Laure and Madeleine did little more than listen to him. With her lively and curious spirit, however, Basilie was eager to question the Nyctalope and made spontaneous sallies. When giving his replies, Saint-Clair mixed unruffled admiration with gentle, mutinous, joyously youthful irony. Basilie, in turn, told anecdotes of her meetings with the peasant farmers, and Saint-Clair quickly discerned that she had a natural faculty for acute observation, always just and often profound. In the expression of some of the young girl's thoughts, he also found the practical and even calculating sense that had been revealed to him in the library, during the account she had made to her father about her conversation with the farmer at the Fosses-Blanches.

"Strange girl!" he thought. "With her natural attitude of observing, laughing and making fun of every point in the compass rose, it seems that she will never lose her north. She joins the solid qualities of d'Hermont with a clairvoyant and ironic intelligence, and a lively sort of spirit that I have never noticed in Jacques, and of which Laure and Madeleine seem to me completely destitute. Yes, what a strange girl! But isn't she just a child, impulsive and barely aware of the vitality she carries within her? Her youth, health, loveliness, beauty, the assurance of wealth? When one possesses all of this, one can be with sincerity and simplicity all that she is—all that she appears to be—without anything left remaining to be discovered."

So the Nyctalope reasoned to himself, all the while remaining the main animator of life around this sunny table, so pleasant and seemingly untouched by any atmosphere of pain, unhappiness or mystery.

In the little drawing-room, where Jeannette served coffee and where the Comte arranged the liqueurs, cigar cases and cigarette boxes on a table, all remained the same as in the dining-room. But when the cups and little glasses had been emptied and the ashtrays were full, Basilie spoke. Turning suddenly toward her aunt and sister, seated beside each other on the same sofa, she said:

"Auntie, Mad, will you come with me in ten minutes?"

"Where?" asked Laure, who extraordinarily and for the first time in half a year, was blissfully smiling.

Madeleine asked with nonchalance:

"Will it be far?"

"A bit," replied Basilie, "but we'll take the big cabriolet. We also have to stop at the pharmacy and pick up some absorbent cotton and medicines."

"Does Mother Ploch have rheumatism?" asked Laure.

"You guessed it, Auntie. It was Boussin, the farmer at the Fosses-Blanches, who told me. Big mama Ploch's gout comes once a year regularly, Doctor Luvier told me. Let's go, the three of us, to the farm at the Priory where, despite her pains, Mama Ploch will make us some of her incomparable eggnog. And let's take our rifles; we can shoot starlings. Nowhere in the country are their flights at dusk, their crisscrosses, columns and circle arcs, as rich in the number of birds as above the wood thicket of the Priory. Monsieur Saint-Clair, do you like starlings, grilled and skewered between slabs of bacon? They are exquisite. Papa enjoys them, Auntie appreciates them, Mad licks her fingers, and I can't get enough of them myself!"

Speaking once again to her aunt and sister, Basilie concluded:

"So, are you coming?"

"We're coming, aren't we, Madeleine?" replied Madame Dauzet.

"Yes we are."

A minute later, the three of them had left the room.

Saint-Clair then said:

"My dear Jacques, I think I've noticed something. Correct me if I am wrong…"

"What is it, my dear Léo?"

"It is that, to my knowledge, no matter to whom she is speaking, never has Basilie alluded to the sickly and deadly drama of Beech Tree. Never, not in speech, or even in her look. She does not inquire about your health, or that of her aunt and sister. In the morning, when she sees you for the first time at the beginning of the day, does she ask you how you slept? Today, to you, Laure and Madeleine, she said only, 'How are you?'"

"My God!" said Jacques d'Hermont, surprised. "I never thought of that. But it's true... Never has Basilie... Oh! What a strange thing that is!"

"Not at all!" replied Saint-Clair energetically, worried about giving his friend a new subject of alarm and perplexity. "It's not odd at all. On the contrary, it can be easily explained. It is even very intelligent and wise on the part of Basilie. As a natural optimist, she deliberately refuses to appear gloomy, and would rather spread as much joy as possible around her. Instead of aggravating things with vain lamentations, a constant display of the anxieties and doubts, that to you three might seem normal but would have no beneficial effect, she has continued to live with youth, joy and vivacity, and treats you exactly as if your health were as hearty as her own. Come, Jacques, does any of that prevent her from being helpful when a crisis presents itself, as she was for example when you returned from your unsuccessful attempt to leave for the Riviera?"

"It's true! It's true, my friend!" exclaimed d'Hermont, reassured. "I understand. But then, why did you ask me if..."

"To know if Basilie ever left her stoic attitude that I just commented upon."

Changing his tone, the Nyctalope said:

"But it's time to leave, at least if, during our trip to La Migeonne, we want to enjoy the last sunny hours of this beautiful day."

"Right! Let's go!" said d'Hermont.

The Nyctalope knew that Soca had already left for Tours in his fast roadster. He thus only had to call Vitto.

76

"Let's take the rifles," said the Comte in the hallway. "There are a lot of water birds at the edge of La Migeonne. We can bring back some of those birds for Amélie, who will make us excellent salamis. Do you have your own rifle, Saint-Clair? Or do you want one of mine?"

"One of yours will be fine. The lightest."

At the far end of the entrance, to the left of the staircase, was a small room furnished with a rack of arms, various pieces of hunting equipment, and cupboards with numbered drawers. In the drawers, cartridges with lead bullets of distinct calibers, buckshot and pellets were methodically filed. Saint-Clair took a gun from the hands of his host. Vitto arrived, and took another one for himself. Each of the three men put one or two handfuls of bullets in their pockets. Then they covered themselves in overcoats, put on hats and caps in preparation for the fierce cold of the undergrowth, pierced by the whistling winds of the valley, and went out.

On their way out, the Comte let out two dogs specially trained to chase the water hen.

In adventures like the one in which he was engaged, the Nyctalope preferred, as a general rule, not to expect anything, or to put forward any hypothesis beforehand. Instead, he would study the country, the land, the human beings, the animals and the objects he saw. He would look, listen, watch and properly classify all things in his brain, reflecting on everything and forgetting nothing. This way, he would have many chances to make a first hypothesis, one automatically born in his mind from all the elements that were capable of being plausible, or at least worthy of a thorough examination. The process tended to reduce errors. With this approach, Saint-Clair was also least exposed to wastes of time, red herrings and false trails.

With this in mind, he went to the farm at La Migeonne, where he would view all the inhabitants as both victims and suspects, without viewing any subject with either preconceived notions or positive ideas.

While walking, he said to Vitto and Jacques d'Hermont:

"I would like you to know that I am not going to La Migeonne either to accuse or play doctor. I will do nothing but look, listen, observe and perhaps speak. D'Hermont, you will be my guide. Vitto, if you discover that a little isolation is useful, you can say you want to see a water hen, and then go where you want. That way, you can follow the trail of the cracked sole."

"Understood, my dear friend," replied the Comte.

"Very good, Monsieur," said Vitto.

The buildings of La Migeonne were very picturesque.

"An old hunting lodge, with a stable, a kennel and a room for the guards," said Jacques d'Hermont, when after leaving the north side of the park they had the farm in full view beside the water. "All of it has been transformed into a proper residence for a farming family, and internally expanded with the construction of a barn, a stable and a pigsty. But the enclosure of the walls remained untouched. Frankly, it's a bit run down now. I only carry out repairs when strictly necessary to maintain the walls, porch and dovetower, such as you see them. I confine myself to this not from greed, believe me, but in order to not destroy the character of the whole edifice. The buildings look good against the landscape, with this magnificent spread of water in front, and that double curtain of poplars in the back."

"I understand," said Saint-Clair. "It is very beautiful like this. And I imagine that farmer Gasse is not too concerned about the enclosing wall, porch or dovetower."

"Him! So long as I do not raise the rent or skimp on repairs at the places he inhabits and uses, the walls, porch and dovetower could crumble! You see, my dear Saint-Clair, I know the men of this land, the peasants. It is possible that sometimes they feel the beauties of nature, but I do not think they are aware of them very often, and I know they never speak of them. The weather is always 'fine' or 'poor' not according to its beauty, but to whether the lands, sowing, grains, potatoes and beets, need snow, rain, moisture, sun, or dry air. And this is quite natural."

"Indeed," said Saint-Clair.

Vitto, who possessed four chestnut-trees and two hundred vine stocks in Corsica, approved of these remarks and others of a similarly rural nature, adding exclamations or monosyllables of agreement. In such a way, the three men occupied the time it took to walk around the vast body of water, following a broad dirt road along its northwest bank.

On the outskirts of La Migeonne, the barking of dogs welcomed them. The beasts, two handsome but slightly scrawny "red-paws," quickly recognized the supreme master in Jacques d'Hermont, and there followed nothing but yelps of pleasure with groveling, jumps and running in circles. The hunting dogs kept their distance with dignity, rendering the leash held by the Comte unnecessary.

Thus they arrived at the small esplanade that stretched muddily between the edge of the pond and the carriage porch of the farmyard. It was there that Soca and Vitto had lost track of the footprint of the cracked sole.

"La Migeonne has two entrances," said Jacques d'Hermont. "This is the lesser used, for the dirt road that leads to it comes only from the park and the castle. The other, more frequented, leads to various farmlands, and, via a detour, to the departmental road that runs through Saint-Christophe."

The three men crossed the porch and entered the courtyard.

"At night, are the doors to this gate closed?" asked Saint-Clair.

"Yes, and with good reason. Not because of tramps and thieves, who are unknown here, but because of the four-legged marauders, the foxes, who come to sack the whole farmyard despite the dogs."

"I see," said Saint-Clair.

He stopped, and his two companions did likewise.

By all evidence the Gasses, husband and wife, were of the race of peasants that was clean and tended to its affairs. Nothing useful or useable was out of order in the farmyard. Nothing was there that could not be used wisely. The manure pit, deep and marked off well by a rectangle of cement blocks, did not allow any trace of its precious matter to spread around it. The ground, entirely paved, was kept neat except for a semi-circular radius a few yards from the porch, where the horses, cows, pigs, sheep, goats and other animals came to drink at the pond, bringing with them the mud of the outer path.

A very gentle slope in the bank of the water, and a slight convexity in the side of the farm, did not allow for the slope necessary that would create a flow of water to bathe the feet of the horses and cows. Saint-Clair saw and remarked on this, for in an investigation like the one he was conducting, he never neglected to explain all that offered itself to his eyes.

But that was it for the afternoon. Their inquiries did not lead to any revelations. A quarter of an hour of difficult conversation with Hector Gasse and his wife, Anna, in the common room of the farm; another quarter of an hour to visit everything, to meet a young valet and a big, red-faced woman busy in the pigsty, then a handyman with red hair and a ruptured right eye; finally, a few minutes at the gate, to survey the naked fields that, beyond a double row of poplars ,rose toward the sky and defined the line of the horizon; all of this produced nothing.

Even the certainty that Hector and Anna Gasse were not in good health; that the little "handyman" was "quite weak;" that the red-headed, one-eyed valet, after a few weeks there, was becoming weaker and feebler by the day; that even the big reddish girl complained of sometimes having legs like cotton; and that all the animals, from the bull to the smallest hen, were lacking in good health, prosperity, in a word, life...

Except that Jeanette the maid had already told them all this in substance. The Nyctalope had not learned anything new.

Neither had Vitto. As it was pleasant out, under the pretense of looking at the water hens and rabbits, he had wandered for half an hour or so around the farm, but had found no traces on any path, trail or area of bare earth, of the character-istic imprint of the cracked sole.

While they were returning toward the castle, skirting the area of water on the northeast side to gain access to the hunt-ing ground and fire at water hens and pheasants, the Comte unhooked the two spaniels still on their leash. Saint-Clair said to d'Hermont, and Vitto understood:

"Unless we find some new information, I'm inclined to agree with the doctor and the veterinarian; the general state of health at La Migeonne is deficient because of malaria and malnutrition."

"I've always thought so," said d'Hermont. "Against ma-laria, I did what was necessary to make sure that, in summer, the body of water kept a part of the overflow from the rains of February and March, and I opened a special credit to Luvier so that he could freely administer quinine to Gasse and his wife, the valets, the girl and the handyman. A similar credit went to the veterinarian for care of the animals, which the Gasses by stupid avarice would leave to die rather than spend ten sous more to the veterinarian. As for undernourishment, I can do no more than scold them. But Hector only replies by laughing si-lently: 'Go on then! We eat too much! That's why the cows have swollen up, the women have indigestion, and even the men look tubby like I do!' There's nothing to do, my dear Saint-Clair. These peasants are stubborn. Hector and Anna Gasse are—as they often say throughout the country—'stubborn as an ass, which is worth a hundred peasants'."

"Well then!" said Saint-Clair, laughing. "I have recorded everything we saw and heard at La Migeonne in my mental file. But nothing explains why the cracked print of one of the shoes the 'human shadow' was wearing the night of the lumi-nous nimbus followed a path discovered by Vitto and Soca, which ended just in front of its the yard, and became lost in the mud..."

"Monsieur..." said Vitto.

"Yes?"

"Next Sunday, it seems, there is a gathering at the hamlet of the Priory. If it does not rain, between one and four p.m., all the people from La Migeonne will be there. If Monsieur le Comte permits it, I can visit the farm discreetly, to take a better look at all the shoes there. As for those worn by the Gasses and their servants, I will prepare a small stretch of land on the path from the other exit, where they will clearly leave their footprints."

Saint-Clair gave a satisfied smile. But Jacques d'Hermont added gravely:

"My dear Vitto, all things are permitted to Monsieur Saint-Clair and his assistants."

Then, in another tone, he objected:

"But Hector and Anna are bound to lock and double-lock everything."

"Oh! Double or single turn of the key, it's all the same!" said Vitto smiling.

Saint-Clair explained:

"My dear Jacques, did I forget to tell you that Vitto and Soca are expert technicians in the art of pre-burglary?"

The Comte replied, amused:

"What you call 'pre-burglary' is no doubt the mechanical and artistic work of opening closed doors, closed cabinets and secret drawers?"

"Exactly, my dear friend."

"Ah! Very good."

And for the first time in months, Jacques d'Hermont burst into real laughter.

CHAPTER IV
The Nyctalope's Second and Third Nights

If during that day, the atmosphere of anxiety at Beech Grove had dissipated considerably, it was evident that it had reappeared and, once again, had begun to condense around Jacques, Laure and Madeleine.

From the start of dinner, Saint-Clair noticed that his friend, the young woman and the young girl, were rapidly losing their appearance of good health. At the fall of night, the usual fever had returned and seized them.

Despite the efforts of the Nyctalope, helped by Basilie—consciously or not? he couldn't decide—the conversation could not be sustained, and the meal took on a gloomy silence. What's more, Saint-Clair himself felt that his whole body was entering an abnormal state of mortal anxiety and physical unease.

Irritated for a moment by this impression, this ill-defined sensation, he reacted with his entire will to observe himself effectively. Without taking the trouble, which seemed to him useless, of giving any pretext whatsoever, just after the dessert, he declared that he was retiring to his room, and, after a few dull words of courtesy, he left the dining-room.

He had seen Soca return from Tours and had received from him the names of those living in the area, who had registered at the town hall their ownership of an automatic pistol of 9mm caliber. Before dinner, he had not had time to examine the document, or to speak of it alone with Jacques d'Hermont. This was therefore put off until the next day.

Before he crossed the threshold of the dining-room to enter the hall and go upstairs, the Nyctalope suddenly remembered that he had wanted to speak with Firmin Gasse, the valet for the castle and the brother of Hector, the farmer of La Migeonne.

Before Saint-Clair lay down to rest, in order to chat a bit more, he called Firmin, pretending he needed his services to change the "uncomfortable" arrangement of the furniture in the Red Room.

But he got nothing from him. Not because Firmin wished to conceal the slightest of his thoughts, but because this man, so intelligent and naturally observant, knew nothing, thought nothing, imagined nothing, that the Comte himself had not already observed. Nothing in what he said was of any use to the Nyctalope.

The room was now pleasantly warm: two radiators gave out central heating, along with a wood fire burning inside a large chimney, according to the Nyctalope's preference.

In the bathroom, Saint-Clair undressed, stretched for ten minutes doing Swedish gymnastics, dressed again in light pajamas and went to sit in a comfortable Voltaire armchair in front of the crackling fire.

On a little table he drew toward him, he had arranged his pipes, big tobacco pouch and metal box lined with matches that formed part of his travel necessities. He carefully stuffed the largest pipe and lit it. Then he began to smoke, meditating.

These meditations were at first fed entirely by the facts of the afternoon and the previous day, but soon they evolved in such a way that Saint-Clair began to meditate on himself— observing his behavior, analyzing his own moral and physical condition, forbidding himself any surprise, for he did not feel at peace with himself as he usually did.

According to his custom, when battling something in his spirit, he started by formulating his thought verbally. This produced a sort of inner monologue, his lips moving but not making a sound that could have been overheard by attentive ears, even two steps away.

"Let's see! What do I have here?"

The forefinger and thumb of his right hand grasped his left wrist. He looked at the dial of the beautiful Empire clock gently ticking on the mantelpiece, and waited a minute.

"My pulse is quicker than usual. Around my eyes, I feel the first touch of a fever. I also feel something like light strokes on my back. Now, I am sure that this is not a cold. For twenty years, thanks to the a healthy lifestyle and some of the practices I learned in Tibet, I have immunized myself against the common cold. This extraordinary state must therefore be caused by an extraordinary factor. And this state is distinctly progressive. I felt the first attack in the library. Later, as Jacques, his sister and his daughters talked about their afternoon, I waited for it to pass in the dining-room. The start of my abnormal state almost coincided with the astronomical hour of sunset. At the same moment, I noticed that Jacques, Laure and Madeleine shuddered almost simultaneously, suddenly losing their serenity of mind and the visible physical wellbeing, which for some extraordinary reason, they had enjoyed throughout the day. What does this mean? Is the same mysterious affliction striking me as well?"

Saint-Clair let go of his left wrist and, with his right hand, took up his pipe again, which rested on the table and had not been extinguished. As he moved his lips with the words that expressed his thought, he brought the pipe to his mouth, took one or two puffs, and pushed it away, eyes staring without seeing into the dancing flames of the hearth.

Except for the slight crackling of flames and an occasional scattering of sparks and embers, the silence in the room was absolute. No sound came from outside. If some nocturnal animal or dead branch falling from a tree had resounded in the park near the castle, it did not reach the enclosed room with its windows shuttered and heavy curtains drawn.

In this silence and solitude, Léo Saint-Clair was alone with himself, his body under fine silk and his lucid mind functioning perfectly, despite the rising fever.

A rising fever—this was undeniable. He had the idea of making a graded elevation. His suitcase always contained a small, carefully composed, travel pharmacy. A thermometer was tucked away in a metal case. Saint-Clair rose, went to grab the thermometer and, without interrupting his smoking, placed the glass tube under his left arm. With his arm pressed to his side, he waited calmly and even with a sort of ironic amusement, for this analysis of his own state.

Patiently, he let five minutes pass.

Then he removed the thermometer, looked at it and whispered:

"Thirty-seven point nine.[4] In the evening, my normal temperature is thirty-seven point two. Unquestionably the fever has risen. At midnight, my temperature will exceed thirty-eight point five.[5] Bizarre! All the more bizarre since, sitting here calmly, I feel in my legs and my thighs a soft and already painful heaviness, and I am suffering clearly in my liver, too—I who have never suffered from liver problems before! It therefore seems without question that I have entered personally and effectively into the drama of Beech Grove. This is interesting, but I do not know if I have any cause for worry yet."

Laying the thermometer on the table, he continued to smoke, observe and analyze himself, without neglecting to maintain the fire with a basket of dry logs within reach of his hands.

His pipe finished, he let himself fall asleep and dream, without fully losing consciousness. From time to time, he opened his eyes and looked at the clock.

A little after 1 a.m., he put the thermometer under his arm again. It now said his fever was at thirty-nine point two.[6] He was sweating. For an hour, he tried to sweat it out. Then he stood, staggering on his weakened legs, leaning on the furniture and walls, and went to the bathroom. There, using all his energy, he managed to remove his clothes, dry himself with a towel and put on clean pajamas. He also took a large dose of quinine and went to bed. Soon he fell into a deep sleep.

It was relatively brief, for when Saint-Clair woke with a start, the clock only read 6 a.m.

---

[4] 100.2 F.

[5] 101.3 F.

[6] 102.6 F

The Nyctalope's head felt heavy. But he did not have to make a mental effort: his brain was sharp and his ideas were clear. He stood without difficulty, and felt his body. His liver was painful, his muscles soft. He perceived that his mouth tasted bitter, but he did not dwell on it. He relit the fire, as the coals were still alive under the ashes. Then he drank from a powerful cordial in his pharmaceutical kit. He forced himself to perform a meticulous toilette, after a thorough shave. Finally, dressed from head to foot, and wearing his tall lace-up boots, he took note that his body temperature was now only 36.4.[7] It was 7.00 a.m.

He rang the bell. Three minutes later Firmin entered the room.

"Good morning, Monsieur. Did you sleep well?"

After these ritual words, the intelligent servant, accustomed to a familiarity at once respectful and free, did not hesitate to say with an expression of astonishment:

"Monsieur looks tired. The face of Monsieur..."

Then Saint-Clair said gently:

"It's true Firmin, I slept very badly, with a heavy bout of fever. But I beg you to say nothing to anyone, do you understand? Not even to your wife or Jeannette."

"Yes, Monsieur. Monsieur can trust me: I know how to be discreet."

"I trust you, Firmin. And the proof is that I will give my permission to Vitto and Soca to speak to you as we do amongst ourselves of what we call the Mystery of Beech Grove—a mystery that began with the evil that led to Madame d'Hermont's death, and has continued inflicting unspeakable pain on Monsieur d'Hermont, Madame Dauzet and Mademoiselle Madeleine—the same evil of which I myself last night felt the first attacks. I am at Beech Grove to solve this mystery and put an end to this evil. Let it affect me—I will only have better information to find the truth. So, Firmin, calm and discretion. I'm counting on you."

---

[7] 97.4.

"Yes, Monsieur!" said the man, moved.

"Good. Before breakfast, we have time to talk. Go tell Vitto and Soca that I want to see them right away. And come back with them."

A few minutes later, Firmin returned, bringing the Nyctalope's two assistants. Saint-Clair made the three men sit, then sat down himself. In minute detail, he told them what had happened to him, hour by hour, through the night. He concluded, speaking directly to Vitto and Soca:

"I see that it was not the same for you two. You have slept normally, and did not feel anything out of the ordinary, am I right?"

Their replies of "No, Monsieur" merged into one.

"Like Firmin," continued Saint-Clair, "and like the other inhabitants of the castle. This evil appears to affect only the masters, except for Mademoiselle Basilie. This is remarkably strange. Firmin, have you seen Monsieur d'Hermont this morning?"

"Yes, Monsieur. Just before you rang."

"How was he?"

"Ill. That is to say, like every morning, except yesterday. And to me, he even seemed even weaker, even more overwhelmed. The crisis of the night must have been stronger than usual."

"I see. The mysterious evil made only a superficial truce yesterday, due no doubt to the mental blow it received because of my arrival. That's why it's important to hide from our hosts that I was attacked last night. Besides, I now feel almost back to normal. After a substantial breakfast, I will be quite well. Listen to me, Vitto, Soca! Today I will have to make even more significant progress in our investigation than yesterday. Whether this mysterious evil comes from a human entity hostile to the d'Hermonts, or from a natural cause with its source in who knows what elements of nature, we must learn soon, very soon, which of these two hypotheses is correct, to arrive straight at the principle of that evil. Now as far as mental clues go, we have none. But with respect to material clues, we have one: the footprint of the shoe with the cracked sole."

"But, Monsieur," exclaimed Soca, "we also have the cartridge of the 9mm caliber gun!"

"Yes, but does this cartridge constitute a second clue? Let us examine the list of names you have brought me from Tours. Give me the paper, over there on the dresser."

The examination was made quickly. Only fourteen citizens of the department of Indre-et-Loire had officially declared themselves the owners of an automatic pistol of 9mm caliber. Eleven lived in Tours, one in Chinon, one in Membrolle and only one in Saint-Christophe-sur-le-Nais.

"Ah!" said the Nyctalope, visibly content. "Here we may have found the owner of our pistol... A Monsieur Armand Logreux... The odd thing is that, out of all the names on this list, his is the only one for which the official declaration was filed not by the owner of the gun, but by the gunsmith. For in the margin of the name 'Armand Logreux,' I read this handwritten note: 'The possession of a 9mm Browning was declared not by its owner but after a police cross-checking of the records of the gunsmiths of Tours and a statement of arms sales.'"

Saint-Clair paused. Then he said, in an imperious tone:

"Firmin! Soca et Vitto will bring you up to date on all the facts in a minute—at least those which you do not already know, such as the discovery of the cartridge we are discussing. But you must tell me right away what you know out this Armand Logreux. You must know something, since he lives in Saint-Christophe."

Firmin Gasse replied with calm, but also a sort of astonished perplexity, evident especially in the expression of his light brown eyes:

"Monsieur, the domain of Beech Grove extends into three communes, of which one, Dissay-sous-Courcillon, is in the department of the Sarthe. Saint-Christophe remains our village, however, for the Town Hall, Post Office and daily suppliers. I know everyone there. Monsieur Logreux does not live in Saint-Christophe. He lives... Well, from here, you can see the old mill that a Logreux, a hundred years ago, transformed into a castle-like dwelling. He even gave it a pretentious name: The Manor. A few years later, this was expanded to *The Manor of the Cross of Blood*!"

"What a strange name!" said Saint-Clair.

While speaking, Firmin had walked toward a window. He turned around and said:

"Monsieur, may I open it? From here, you can all the way to Monsieur Logreux's manor, and the rest."

"What do you mean, 'and the rest'?" asked Saint-Clair, moving toward the window with Soca and Vitto.

"Monsieur Logreux is also the owner of a very important estate used mostly for livestock farming, which on one side borders the property of Monsieur d'Hermont for more than six kilometers."

Firmin opened the window wide, and standing to one side stretched out an arm:

"As Monsieur can see, at the end of the valley in front of this magnificent curtain of poplars, there is a ramshackle ensemble of buildings, towers and pepper-pot roofs. This is the so-called Manor of the Cross of Blood."

Saint-Clair remembered that, two days before, while going to the village with Jacques d'Hermont, he had admired, but from a different viewpoint, those poplars so numerous and so tall, seen over the roofs and towers of the village. He said nothing, but repeated:

"What a strange name!"

With simplicity, but not without the complaisance of a man proud of being well informed, Firmin explained:

"Before a Logreux transformed it, the building was called the 'Mill of the Nais.' Then it became the 'Manor.' But a few years later, there was a drama, which has become a bit of a local legend. One morning, in a large area that borders the Manor to the west, a large pool of coagulated blood was found. A bloody trail led to the dam of the Nais. There, a corpse was found, that of an unknown man. The gendarmes and the police never solved this mystery, about which, moreover, there was no complaint filed. A judicial investigation was ordered by the Public Prosecutor of Tours. But it was not possible to establish the identity of the dead man, whose throat had been slit, and who had been thrown into the water. Not the slightest clue about his murderer, or murderers, could be discovered. The case was finally closed. The Logreux had the bloodied earth dug out and remove. Then they covered it with a large slab of granite, and erected a wrought iron cross on it."

"I see," said Saint-Clair. "The Cross of Blood. And this name was added later to that of the Manor by the locals."

"Yes, Monsieur."

"Close the window again, Firmin. But the present Monsieur Logreux, what kind of man is he?"

"Oh! Monsieur, I know very little. One almost never sees him on the roads leading to the d'Hermont estate, for there have never been any relations between Beech Grove and the Cross of Blood. He appears only rarely at Saint-Christophe, and all his correspondence is addressed to Poste restante at Dissay-sous-Courcillon, where a servant goes to pick it up every day. To replenish stock of any kind, the Cross of Blood goes to Dissay, or the Château-du-Loir, or even Le Mans. In Saint-Christophe, the Logreux have never been loved, because they've always kept themselves apart from the village and its inhabitants. Only the notary communicates with them, but he is a man who speaks little. Perhaps Monsieur le Comte knows more than I do?"

"It's possible, Firmin, even likely," said Saint-Clair in the same calm tone with which he had said "I see" a few minutes before. "I will ask him. But you, Firmin, not a word to anyone about this. Starting now, I ask you to keep the same silence regarding your conversations with Vitto and Soca, or me, as you do regarding the mystery of Beech Grove."

"Monsieur can rest assured."

"I will, Firmin. Another thing: this morning I will have breakfast in the dining-room. Yesterday, I observed that Monsieur d'Hermont and his daughters have the habit of taking it together. I will do the same. Will you come to let me know when it is served? The same as yesterday, please."

"Yes, Monsieur. But does Monsieur see any objection in my informing Monsieur le Comte?"

"No, on the contrary, since I was going to instruct you to tell him. But why do you ask?"

"Because in that case, Monsieur le Comte will doubtless want me to take up another habit of the castle at breakfast hour. The bell rings, a light sound that is repeated. The ringing was cancelled yesterday and was to be cancelled again this morning, so long as Monsieur is here, in order to avoid waking Monsieur, if Monsieur..."

"Right, I understand. You may ring the bell as usual, Firmin."

"Yes, Monsieur."

Saint-Clair smiled at this meticulous servant. Then, speaking to his two assistants, he said:

"I will see you after breakfast, when I have chatted with Monsieur d'Hermont."

And the Nyctalope remained alone, having slipped into one of his pockets the list brought by Soca from the prefecture of Tours. He waited, seated on an armchair and meditating, to hear the bell announcing that breakfast was served.

As soon as he heard it, he left his room.

Just as the day before, in the dining-room he found assembled Jacques d'Hermont, Laure Dauzet, Madeleine and Basilie d'Hermont. But unlike the day before, no one was seated: they were all waiting for their guest. There was an even more moving difference. Neither Jacques, nor Laure, nor Madeleine were, as had been the case the previous day, visibly well. On the contrary, the chatelain, his sister and his older daughter had visibly suffered as much, and perhaps even more, during the night. It was no less obvious that this strange evil continued to spare Basilie, who, like the day before, inspired the Nyctalope with the thought: "fresh, beautiful, perfumed flower, still almost a bud, whose magnificent blossoming one could not imagine without a certain pleasant disturbance."

Jacques, Laure and Madeleine had suffered too much not to be withdrawn into themselves, and they did not discern on the face of their guest the slight sign of the same physical fatigue. But Basilie, precisely because of her normal and habitual serenity, of which she thought nothing, noticed these signs. After the usual greetings had been spoken, everyone sat for breakfast, and Jacques, Laure and Madeleine, all too aware of their relapse, thought only about hiding the suffering and shame that made them so different from what they had been the day before. Basilie, however, fixed the pure gaze of her fathomless blue eyes on the Nyctalope, and with a gravity at once timid and attentive, asked:

"Have you had a bad night?"

Saint-Clair was not expecting this. He had not even imagined that the question would be asked of him by Jacques, so sure was he of his preparations, of the influence of his will upon the physical features of his face. He thought he had erased all traces of the "bad night" he had experienced. It was astonishing that the question came from the lips of the young girl, who had never previously shown herself to be such a good observer. But Saint-Clair had experienced many surprises of this order, and had never let himself shown to be surprised. So he replied immediately, in the most normal tone:

"I? No, not at all."

This was the unthinking, mechanical, immediate response of a man feeling well, who affirms this truth.

But he let some time pass, as he took a seat beside Madame Dauzet. Then, with just the right expression of slight astonishment, in an amicably cheerful tone, he asked:

"But what, Mademoiselle, makes you think I had a bad night?"

With a seriousness at once timid and attentive, without lowering her eyes or turning them away, Basilie replied:

"Your face is pale and a bit contracted. Your eyes, or rather the area underneath, looks swollen and circled."

"My goodness!" exclaimed Saint-Clair, with admirably feigned enthusiasm. "How observant you are! It's true that while washing my face, I noticed this too. But it's such a small thing! It's likely fatigue from a first day spent being very active in the countryside. With us Parisians, as you know, the open air gets the better of us after three consecutive months in the city. Also, this morning, I rose early and turned myself completely to a very difficult work of ethnography, a chapter of the narrative of my last trip to India. Congratulations, Mademoiselle, on your discernment."

Basilie blushed, and with a sort of sadness that Saint-Clair noted for the first time in the look and voice of the young girl, she murmured:

"It's nothing, Monsieur. I have become so used to watching faces here."

Now she did lower her eyes, as she began to pour coffee into the bowls, starting with her father's.

During this brief, unexpected dialogue, the Nyctalope was able to observe Jacques, Laure and Madeleine. All three had listened to the exchange, and had now their eyes fixed on the face of their guest. None of them showed any unease beyond that which tortured them personally. None seemed to want to speak. But Saint-Clair knew well that the alteration in his face was scarcely perceptible, and in his heart, he continued to be astonished that Basilie had shown such perspicacity—as well as, hidden beneath her timid exterior, such a brutal frankness. He wanted to know if Jacques, Laure and Madeleine, now informed, saw what Basilie did. In a playful tone, he added:

"Jacques, and you, Madame, and you Mademoiselle Madeleine, looking at my face, do you think it so far gone?"

"Oh!" cried Basilie with an abrupt laugh. "I didn't say that!"

With an effort, as if speaking were physically painful, Jacques d'Hermont said:

94

"Yes, your face bears traces of fatigue. You rose very early, and did not sleep enough after a day in the open air and two or three hours of work."

"That's it," said Laure.

"Yes," whispered Madeleine.

A minute later, Jeannette and Firmin had arrived, carrying eggs and ham for Saint-Clair, hot chocolate for Basilie, buttered slices of toast for everyone.

They spoke no more of the face of Saint-Clair. In fact, they did not speak at all. Jacques, Laure and Madeleine ate without appetite, with effort. They showed a bleak sadness that they did not try to hide, let alone conquer and dispel. Basilie, now obviously embarrassed, hurried to devour the toasted and buttered bread, which she dipped into her hot chocolate. Saint-Clair, determined to remain natural and eat as if he still had his usual appetite, did nothing to break the general silence.

All the same, he thought that, when the meal was over, he would not leave them without expressing a few ideas.

It was Thursday, January 22. The day had begun with overcast skies, humidity, fog and a dreary cold that sank into the body, softened it, and made it shiver with discomfort. The Nyctalope waited for the Comte or Basilie to speak again. During this wait, he noticed that the young girl was once again dressed in her riding costume despite the unattractive weather. This surprised him a bit. He thought: "With her, riding borders on fanaticism. To be carried through this fog at a trot or gallop on a horse... Few Amazons would find pleasure in it. What is this young girl hiding? Is she even hiding something?"

It was Basilie who again broke the silence. She stood up and said:

"That's it! I'm done!"

She walked around the table and went to kiss her father's foreheads, then her aunt's and sister's, quickly, like a rite that had become routine.

"I have an appointment with the gamekeepers at the Cross of Oaks. And it's on your behalf, Monsieur le Nyctalope!"

"Ah?" asked Saint-Clair, once again surprised, without concealing it.

"Yes!" said the young girl, with a somewhat exaggerated disinterest. "But you don't know the reason. At least, not yet. At noon, when I return, I will reveal my secret."

She laughed, swirled around in a pretty gesture of good-bye, and left quickly.

Jacques d'Hermont rose, immediately followed by Saint-Clair. Before their bowls still half-filled with milky coffee, Laure and Madeleine remained motionless, prostrate, their lost gazes fixed straight ahead, their minds absent.

Then the Nyctalope said, with energy:

"Jacques, I must speak with you. I would like it to be in the presence of your sister and daughter."

"Let's go to the library?" suggested the Comte, softly.

"Wherever you like."

And leaning over the table toward the two women, Saint-Clair said in a low and penetrating voice:

"Laure, Madeleine, I beg you, listen to me! Two new elements have appeared for consideration. First, the same mysterious evil came to me last night, and intensely! Second, it is possible that the pistol from the bullet cartridge found in the wake to the mysterious shadow belongs to a Monsieur Armand Logreux."

"Oh! Oh!" exclaimed the Conte, suddenly sitting upright, his eyes bright.

At the first words of Saint-Clair, Laure and Madeleine had stood up. When the name of the owner of the Cross of Blood was spoken, they experienced a similar galvanizing effect.

"Good!" said Saint-Clair. "I see that you know something about this Armand Logreux. Let us move to the library."

Two minutes later, all four were sitting in the comfortable leather armchairs arranged by Saint-Clair himself in a semi-circle around the fire. During the ritual morning aeration, carried out by Firmin, the outside humidity had entered this vast room. But the windows were closed, the radiators blasted heat, and the flames of a wood fire burned, crackling up the big chimney and beginning to dry and warm up the atmosphere. They felt well there. Saint-Clair sighed with ease. The day was not very lively, and in other circumstances, Jacques d'Hermont, who did not like the half-obscurity, would have lit the electric bulbs of the chandelier, adding bright artificial light to the wan light of the sun veiled by the enormous thicknesses of wet fog. Now, however, the mysterious conjectures of the hour were better adapted to a dim clarity. The Comte sat down without touching the light switch.

Immediately, Saint-Clair spoke in a calm and low voice:

"First I will say a few words. Yes, Basilie has glimpsed the truth: I had a very bad night."

In detail, he described his successive states from evening to morning. With a terror that they did not conceal, and which turned their faces into tragic masks, Jacques, Laure and Madeleine recognized in this psycho-psychological account all the signs of their own state.

"And not from the beginning!" said the Comte with excitement, when the Nyctalope had finished. "No! For you, my dear Léo, the first attack of the evil manifested itself with an intensity that we only knew and suffered after many weeks of progression."

"Indeed!" said Saint-Clair. "But let's speak no more of me. A second experience is necessary. Perhaps I will be subjected to it tonight. I dare say, I hope for and desire it, for I no longer doubt the existence of this mysterious evil, and I'm all the more determined to get to its root... Now, let's speak of Armand Logreux. Listen carefully. I will be brief and precise."

He remained silent for a moment. Then, he spoke passionately as Jacques and the two women anxiously listened:

"In our region, the police know only of one 9mm Browning. It belongs to Armand Logreux. It is not through his declaration that its existence came to light, but thanks to the well-kept accounts of the gunsmith in Tours who sold him that gun. There is, therefore, a high probability that the cartridge, found at the foot of that beech tree from which the 'human shadow vanished after the 'luminous nimbus' phenomenon, fell from the pistol belonging to Monsieur Logreux."

"Well, well!" said Jacques d'Hermont.

"I said this to Firmin, in my room before breakfast, in the presence of Vitto and Soca. He opened a window and showed me, quite visible in front of the big poplars, even through the morning fog, the Manor of the Cross of Blood. He told me the name of the family that, for a length of time that he did not specify, has owned that manor and its surrounding estate. But Firmin did not say anything else, for he did not know anything more. I think that you three know something, so I will listen to you. Jacques, please speak first."

The sight of Comte d'Hermont, his sister Laure and his older daughter Madeleine, confirmed for the Nyctalope that he would be told all he needed to know about Armand Logreux; but this look of fierce and passionate anticipation, against an obvious background of enormous astonishment, made him also think that, until the last quarter of an hour, the victims of the mystery of Beech Grove had never dreamed for a single minute that the owner of the Manor of the Cross of Blood could have had any connection with this enigma. For Jacques d'Hermont, Laure Dauzet and Madeleine, the intrusion of Armand Logreux into their life was as staggering and inexplicable as it was unexpected.

Saint-Clair had attempted to speak in a calm, easy tone that would put his friends at ease. Now it was Jacques d'Hermont's turn to speak:

"My dear Léo, it is with pleasure that I add what I know to what you have already learned from Firmin, which is correct. At the time of the drama that ended with the raising of a cross on the piece of earth tainted with the blood of an unknown man, the owner of the Manor was Stanislas Logreux. He was a strange man, both a Republican and a very pious practicing Catholic. He was a widower, without children. He remarried very late and built his fortune from scratch. My father knew him, and it is from him that I have learned those details: the first Logreux appeared in Touraine, in Tours to be exact, in 1791, and, with a fistful of *assignats*,[8] bought up a great many of the properties previously held by the Priory of Saint-Christophe, which, for centuries, under the *Ancien Régime*, had shared with my ancestors all the land between Tours and Château-du-Loir. During the Restoration, the Logreux revealed that their true name was Logreux d'Albury, a Scottish branch which had helped Louis XVIII with his fortune, when this prince was only the Comte de Provence, an émigré.[9]

"Despite this, or because of the authenticity of the name and the reality of the services rendered to Louis XVIII, the Comtes d'Hermont, legitimists and jealous of their prerogatives in the region, never associated with the Logreux, from whom they kept rigorously apart. My father continued as his father had, and like I have, to avoid any sort of relationship with the master of the Cross of Blood, even that which one might call "good neighborliness." Our properties border one another for several kilometers. When an incident occurs as a

_____

[8] *Assignats* were paper money issued by the National Assembly in France from 1789 to 1796, during the French Revolution. Backed by the value of properties formerly held by the Catholic Church, they became immediately a source of political controversy. While their proponents argued that land was a more stable source of value than gold or silver, the opponents saw them as based on an illegitimate seizure of property.

[9] Louis XVIII (1755-1824) was a monarch of the House of Bourbon who ruled as King of France from 1814 to 1824, except for a period in 1815 known as the Hundred Days. He spent twenty-three years in exile, from 1791 to 1814, during the French Revolution and the First French Empire, and again in 1815, during the period of the Hundred Days, upon the return of Napoleon I from Elba. Until his accession to the throne of France, he held the title of Count of Provence as brother of King Louis XVI.

result of this, our respective notaries deal with it without either I or the current Logreux, named Armand, entering into a relationship, even by mail.

"Besides, Armand Logreux d'Albury is never seen; all the ordinary life of the manor and the property of the Cross of Blood is directed toward the north and east—Dissay-sous-Courcillon, Château-du-Loir and Le Mans—while the whole existence of Beech Grove is focused toward the south and the east—Saint-Christophe, Saint-Paterne, Château-la-Vallière, Tours, etc. Our parks and hunting grounds luckily do not touch: vast fields of cultivation separate them. We live, the d'Hermonts and the Logreux, in mutual ignorance, except, if necessary, through our notaries. There has never been any conflict. Our honest and skillful lawyers have always amicably resolved the minor disputes and other matters that spring up between people who own two vast, adjacent agricultural properties. That, my dear Léo, is all I know. But, it must be admitted, that the fact that the 9mm cartridge..."

"One moment, my dear Jacques, one moment," said Saint-Clair, raising his right hand with authority. "Let us examine the new facts together. But I read in the eyes of your sister and daughter that they know more than you do about Monsieur Logreux, and I see that they are trembling from both the impatience to speak and the temptation to remain silent..."

He turned toward Laure and Madeleine, seated elbow-to-elbow on his other side, and continued:

"Isn't that so? That you are impatient to speak, I understand. But that you are tempted to remain silent... Why is that? Are you afraid, Laure and Madeleine, that Jacques will hear you?"

Then, in a low voice filled with an ill-contained passion, her black eyes fixed on Saint-Clair, Laure Dauzet said:

"The day of frankness and truth has come. I will answer you. Brother, father of Madeleine, there is no harm in your hearing this truth, but as you are also the father of Basilie..."

These last word, her niece's name, was spoken with great violence in a low but hoarse voice.

"My God!" moaned Madeleine, hiding her face in her clenched hands.

Jacques d'Hermont turned abruptly toward his sister, with a look of astonishment.

Extremely intrigued by the grave threat of everything that Laure might reveal, and well aware of the importance of this revelation, Saint-Clair did nothing to stop the outburst or lessen its brutality. On the contrary, hoping to precipitate it, he said firmly:

"All of it, Laure! Speak the whole truth!"

With a sharp gesture, Madeleine uncovered her face in tears, stretched out her arms toward her aunt and pleaded in a fiery voice:

"Yes, tell the truth! Perhaps it will help you to destroy the frightful suspicion that you and I have of the man mentioned here."

Jacques, after a violent shudder, commanded:

"Laure, speak! I beg you to speak to the father of Basilie, to reveal everything... everything!"

Stiff, her face pale, her eyes fixed but clear, with a lucid reason and firm will, Laure said slowly:

"Basilie has been in contact with Armand Logreux."

Saint-Clair had been expecting this, and it did not come as a surprise. But he wondered why Laure and Madeleine had not revealed this to him during their conversation the day before. Out loud, he asked them as much. Without hesitation, Laure replied:

"I did not think of it."

"Nor did I!" said Madeleine.

"We didn't think of it," explained Laure spontaneously, "because the fact dates from several months ago, and to our knowledge, the contact has not been renewed. In reality, we forgot to tell you because it had no connection in our minds with the mysterious evil of Beech Grove... Even when, in our darkest hours, Madeleine and I could not help but envy and hate, and even vaguely suspect, Basilie, when comparing her life to ours, we did not establish any connection between these nightmarish events and the fact that Basilie and Armand Logreux were one day seen together by Madeleine and I, riding side-by-side, chatting and laughing... No, no connection, no link... As for Basilie, when questioned and warned by me, she promised not to permit Monsieur Logreux to approach her again. Then Madeleine and I thought no more of it... There... Now you know as much as we do..."

"No!" spat Jacques d'Hermont, with such violence that Saint-Clair took his hand, clasped it and said in a quiet voice:

"Jacques, be calm. Let me question Laure and Madeleine, who, as you can see, are sincere and well-intentioned. Everything must be made clear between you three, in front of me. And everything will be. First, I will give your sister and your daughter a few minutes to calm down. Let me tell you in full the conversation I had with them yesterday morning."

The Comte, composing himself, said in a simple tone:

"My dear friend, you told me nothing of this conversation yesterday, except that Laure and Madeleine had confided to you their secret thoughts. You added that you needed to reflect, and that you would speak of it in your own time..."

"Yes!" said Saint-Clair, letting go of his friend's hand. "And it is clear that the hour has come. Here is what Laure and Madeleine revealed to me. Do not expect concrete facts. Their revelation consists entirely of the expression of a thought, a secret thought that Laure and Madeleine had at the same minute and that they communicated as one; a thought they came to believe from two observations: the first, that the mysterious evil of Beech Grove in no way affected Basilie; the second, that Basilie has liberated herself completely from all duties of faith and religious exercise. This thought that was, and perhaps still is, in their mind can be formulated in these words: *To make us die, Basilie gave her soul to the Devil.*"

"Oh!" exclaimed Jacques, taken aback once again.

"Jacques, my friend," said Saint-Clair softly, "do not lose yourself in your surprise. Keep your mind lucid. Everything has just begun. We must go toward the truth with a sure step and brains that work well. Keep your calm, your cool. Do you understand?"

"I understand you, my dear friend, and I obey. As for you, Laure and Madeleine, do not be afraid, for I will take care not to judge your actions, your thoughts, your acts, your way of being toward Basilie. Yes, I will take care not to judge, until the moment when the truth becomes obvious, irrefutable..."

The Comte had spoken in his ordinary voice, his body composed but not rigid, his face now expressing nothing but gravity, attention and kindness.

"Very good!" said the Nyctalope.

And, in this atmosphere less burdened by surprises and potential storms, he went on with calm, as if pursuing a conversation that was merely of academic interest and devoid of any mysterious, dramatic atmosphere:

"Laure, I beg of you, remind me the exact date, the circumstances..."

"Oh! It was more than a year ago!" replied the young woman, without hesitation. "It was in October '23, on a very beautiful day in autumn, at around 10 a.m. I had the idea of climbing to the very top of the south tower with my grandfather's old telescope, to amuse myself by looking into the distance at the farmers working in the fields, or the cars on the road from Le Mans and Tours. It was a childish whim, one of many I had at the time. Basilie had left on horseback, as she did almost every day. I called Madeleine and, laughing, invited her to take part in my whim, and I offered her first use of the telescope. She accepted..."

With this, Laure fell silent and looked at her niece. Madeleine, blushing a bit at first, then suddenly becoming very pale, continued in a feverishly animated voice:

"Yes. And all at once, I saw Basilie on her half-blood chestnut. To my great shock, she was not alone. At the pace of her horse, Basilie was advancing boot-to-boot with another rider. They were facing me, on the road from Dissay-sous-Courcillon to Saint-Christophe, on the section that stretches on beside the hillside for a long way. I cried out:

" 'Oh! Auntie, I see Basilie! She has a companion. Who is it? I don't know him!'

"I remember very well that Aunt replied, laughing:

" 'So, does your sister have a secret flirtation? In the countryside! Who might it be?'"

Turning toward her aunt, Madeleine fell silent in her turn. At once, Madame Dauzet went on, with an excited expression:

"I took the telescope. Now, a few days before in Saint-Christophe, while I was chatting with Doctor Luvier in the square, a man had passed us by and greeted us politely... A man of forty to fifty years, who nicely filled his well-cut suit. I asked the doctor:

" 'Who is that?'

" 'That's right,' he said, 'you don't know him. He's recently returned from a long journey to China and Tibet. That is Monsieur Armand Logreux d'Albury, the chatelain of the Cross of Blood.'

"I said no more, except for a sound of surprise... and antipathy. For I knew that the Logreux had always been estranged from the d'Hermonts, and that no relationship had existed between our families.

"Five minutes later, I had forgotten this gentleman. Nor did I think of him once during the days that followed this chance encounter. But through the clear round of the telescope, I suddenly recognized the riding companion of my niece Basilie: it was Armand Logreux!

"I was all the more astonished to see him laughing, speaking animatedly and making gestures, and seeing that Basilie replied in the same tone, with the same free, amused ease. I forgot to tell Madeleine, who asked me:

" 'Do you see them?'

" 'What is she doing with that man?' I asked myself, while continuing to observe Basilie and Monsieur Logreux. Suddenly, where the road sloped down toward the Nais, the two riders disappeared behind an unbroken curtain of trees.

"I adjusted the telescope. Very disturbed, as well as perplexed, I said to Madeleine:

" 'I will ask Basilie. No doubt she was joined by that rider, who came up with who knows what excuse to speak with her. She must not have known who he is. I will tell her. This will not continue. But we must not tell your father, who will be irritated.'"

Once again, Laure fell silent. The silence continued, this time, for a long while. Madeleine kept her head lowered. Neither Jacques d'Hermont nor Saint-Clair, said a word. At last, looking straight at her brother, Laure Dauzet went on, with a calm will in her tone of voice and the pronunciation of her words:

"When Basilie returned, I questioned her. She answered without any trouble. It was as I had supposed. As she was returning at a light trot from Dissay, a rider had joined her at a gallop. Surprised, she had mechanically stopped her horse to let the stranger pass—a surprise as she had never met a rider in the country. The latter halted his beast and saluted, saying:

" 'Mademoiselle, isn't this yours?'

"He presented her with a square of blue silk. It had slipped from the pocket of Basilie's jacket without her noticing. She took what belonged to her and thanked him. All at once the rider said:

" 'Aren't you Mademoiselle Basilie d'Hermont?'

"He nudged his horse to start walking. Amused and curious about this man, whom she told me she immediately found 'remarkable' both for his appearance and for his beautiful horse, Basilie kept her half-blood walking at the same pace.

"The gentleman began to speak with wit and good humor, pleasantly apologizing for not introducing himself 'precisely to pique the curiosity of a young Amazon,' in his own words. There followed an animated conversation, in which a very amused Basilie held her own with the somewhat mocking vivacity you can imagine.

"When she reached the branching in the path that led to Beech Grove, she burst into laughter and said: 'Goodbye, mysterious stranger!' Then she gave her horse a half-turn and set it off at a gallop. Turning back round, she could see the rider laughing too, saluting from afar with his cap. This is what Basilie told me."

Another brief silence followed. Then, with calm, Laure continued:

"I told Basilie that this 'mysterious stranger,' who had committed the impropriety of not introducing himself from the start, was Monsieur Armand Logreux, from the property of the Cross of Blood. Still very much at her ease, my niece then said:

" 'Ah! The hereditary enemy? I won't let him speak to me and will avoid meeting him in the future, then. But it's a pity. He's so interesting. He's just come back from China, Tibet. Oh well, all the worse!...'

"She left my room, where I had begged her to follow me at first. On the threshold, she turned and said:

" 'Auntie, have you spoken to father about this?'

" 'No,' I replied. 'I think it is better to remain quiet. Madeleine won't say anything either.'

" 'Yes, that may be better,' said Basilie with her spoiled child's face. 'Well! We'll have a little secret, the three of us. Bah! Let's forget about it!'

"She shrugged and gave a small laugh. Then she went out. That's all, that's really all."

But the Nyctalope, calm, said:

"No, dear Madame, I think that is not all. One more question, if I may?"

"Yes," said Laure, now weary and resigned.

"Thank you. Since then, do you think that Basilie has seen Monsieur Logreux d'Albury again?"

"I don't know. I really don't know. The strangest thing is that neither Madeleine nor I have ever had the courage to question her on the subject, though we have often been tempted to do so. My niece has never made the slightest allusion to the incident."

"And the telescope?" insisted Saint-Clair. "Have you ever used it again?"

"No! Never! That, too, Madeleine and I have often been tempted to do. But I do not know what pride, what reserve... what apprehensions and fears... have always prevented us."

"Well then!" said Saint-Clair. "I have finished now. Thank you. Excuse me if I ask you to leave Jacques and I alone."

"There is no need to ask permission, my dear friend," said Laure, emphasizing the last three words slightly.

She rose, immediately followed by Madeleine, who saluted her father with a tender look and smile.

And the aunt and niece, having taken one another by the hand, left the library together with a slow, heavy, harassed step.

Saint-Clair did not leave Jacques d'Hermont to the thoughts that had, as their sole and inevitable focus, the meeting, perhaps more cautiously repeated, of Basilie with Armand Logreux d'Albury. For the Nyctalope had still not got to the essence of the facts that he had come to learn. Immediately after the double doors had closed after Laure and Madeleine, Saint-Clair spoke:

"My dear friend, let us get to the point. Leave your daughter Basilie to one side. We will come back to her when I have acquired some indispensable additional information. There is something more serious, in my view, in need of a urgent examination. Will you listen to me?"

"Yes," said d'Hermont. "Yes, of course!"

His attentive eyes expressed the most fervent confidence in his friend.

"Good! So let us see what we have. There is a distinct possibility that the 9mm caliber cartridge leads us to the pistol owned by Armand Logreux, and therefore to the man himself. There is also a possibility, but without any probability at present, that the print of the shoe with the cracked sole may also lead to the Cross of Blood. I hope that if I work closely with Vitto and Soca, I will soon have some exact and clear solutions. But now I have in my mind a third fact... Do you not see it?"

"My goodness, no!" confessed the Comte.

"It is the fact that Armand Logreux d'Albury has lived in China and, above all, Tibet. You did not tell me that. Were you aware of it?"

"No. Doctor Luvier revealed it to my sister by chance. He must not have told me, as he avoids speaking to me about anyone at the Cross of Blood. I have never given him a reason to do so. I did not know and remain unaware of almost everything about this Monsieur Logreux, his life, his surroundings, even his presence or absence, about which I never inquire. I think of him no more than once a year perhaps! But why do you ask?"

"Tibet, my dear friend," Saint-Clair pronounced gravely, shaking his head. "I have been there. You have read the two volumes I wrote about my journeys and experiences in that far-off land. Remember! In some monasteries, totally unknown to Europeans, and even to the vast majority of Asians, the most vertiginous secrets of life and death are passed down through the centuries, by word of mouth. I know some of them, but I would never make use of them, first because I have never had the will to learn the details for my use, and second as a logical consequence of the fact that I lack the technical science and the necessary practice... But another man, passing through Tibet, visiting some of the same places I did, may have been curious in ways that I was not, and perhaps learn things that I did not, undertake experiments that did not tempt me... Someone like Armand Logreux d'Albury, for example..."

Saint-Clair went silent, his lively eyes fixed on the dilated ones of Jacques d'Hermont. With sudden new emotion, blood returned to the Comte's face, and his emaciated, livid face became filled with color for an instant. He stammered:

"Oh! My friend! So you think...?"

"Now, now!" the Nyctalope interrupted him, raising his right hand. "I don't think anything. I imagine, I suppose... And now, I've added another project to those I was planning to undertake with Soca and Vitto, about the cartridge and cracked sole... Tomorrow night, a third project I plan to carry out may enlighten me so much that the sole and the cartridge, without losing their importance entirely, may become entirely secondary..."

"Tomorrow night!" murmured Jacques d'Hermont, trembling all at once with hope and curiosity.

"Yes. But I will say nothing more at this time!" said Saint-Clair forcefully, as he rose.

In a softer tone, with a smile on his lips, he added:

"Excuse me, my dear friend, if I tell you nothing else. It is precisely because it is possible that we may transition abruptly from the material plane, in which we have operated until now, to the spiritual plane, which is pulsing with fearsome mysteries. Not only is the slightest word about it dangerous and imprudent, but thought itself must be kept from irradiating into the outside world by too great an intensity, too great a clarity. I will thus be quiet, until I can speak without imprudence or danger. Even I will have to carry out certain special rites to protect hermetically my own thoughts..."

Jacques d'Hermont, trembling, had risen. Saint-Clair took him by the hand, held it between his own and in a penetrating voice said:

"My dear friend, have confidence! And avoid reflecting or making conjectures about what I have just told you."

Almost playful, he then added:

"Let's see! Do you feel physically able to go out, walk, go talk to your farmers, or even hunt a bit while chatting with your brave Bottot? And with Basilie?"

Subjugated, but also reanimated by the influence of the Nyctalope's powerful will, the Comte replied somewhat cheerfully:

"But of course! Well, I think so."

"Well then! Go! Join Basilie and Bottot at the Cross of Oaks. At noon, we will meet again in the dining-room. It's probable that I will be busy all morning with Soca and Vitto.

But I will pretend to run an errand to Tours, and will leave by car from Beech Grove. At dinner, we will meet once again, of course. Do not think, Jacques, do not think! Get moving, occupy yourself actively and chat with whomever you can in the countryside, about anything that might feel like an ordinary conversation. Right away!"

Separating from his friend, Saint-Clair exited the library. He went up to his room, called Firmin, and begged him to alert Vitto and Soca that he was waiting.

With his two assistants, but out of the presence of Firmin, he had a conversation in a low voice.

When all was agreed upon, he dismissed them. Then he remained alone in the red room, which Jeannette had made up while he was downstairs.

He wanted to think, but as he had said to Jacques d'Hermont, he wanted it to be in such conditions that his thoughts would be hermetically sealed and confined to his own mind, and none of it produced emanations that another man might be able to receive and capture.

For this, certain rites had to be observed. He observed and accomplished them.

To be precise, this is what he did: first, he closed the windows, the shutters of plain crossed wood, and drew the curtains in such a way that the light of day would trickle as little as possible into the room. Then he closed the doors that led to the antechamber and bathroom. On the hearthstone, the wood fire from the morning was no more than ashes. Saint-Clair checked that no embers were hidden there; for more precaution, he then scattered the ash over the whole of the hearth, and carefully slotted the polished wood panel into the large inner frame of the chimney. Finally, having placed an armchair in the middle of the vast and now dark room, he sat in it, clasped his forehead with both hands, closed his eyes, and little by little, entered into the ascetic state in which a man becomes both blind and deaf, and hardly takes a breath.

Later, there was a surprise: Laure Dauzet and Madeleine did not appear for lunch. Without emotion, for it was not the first time this had happened, Jeannette announced that "Madame and Mademoiselle Madeleine" were feeling tired, had decided to remain in their dressing gowns and take their lunch in the small bedroom of their shared apartment.

Jacques d'Hermont contented himself by saying, in a very low voice:

"Too bad."

Saint-Clair, now in a good shape and seeming not to suffer from any traces of his nocturnal fever and morning depression, spoke a few words, expressing his regrets and wishes.

As for Basilie, very animated by her walk in the woods in the company of Bottot, the head gamekeeper, she declared casually:

"I'll give them a little hello. I won't be five minutes, Papa. Excuse me, dear Monsieur."

The Comte and the Nyctalope waited, in front of the sunny window, for the return of the girl. They exchanged no more than a few words.

"Courage, my dear friend, courage and hope!" said Saint-Clair.

"I have both, my dear Léo," murmured the chatelain. "But I feel physically exhausted."

"This afternoon, you will rest. After the meal, I will give you an elixir to drink that I used myself this morning, with benefit. It is both tonic and calming. And tonight, I will give you a dose of a soporific, whose secret formula I have brought back with me from Tibet. You will sleep soundly. You must. For perhaps tomorrow..."

He fell silent.

"Tomorrow?" asked the Comte, rather keenly.

"I can't speak to you about it until tomorrow."

His tone was affectionate, but firm.

"So be it," conceded Jacques d'Hermont.

All was silent until Basilie's return.

111

The young girl spoke only these words about the state of her aunt and sister:

"Nothing special."

The three of them took their places at equilateral points of the table, which, for this meal, had only three place settings.

Then, to create an atmosphere without heaviness or embarrassment, Saint-Clair said:

"Mademoiselle, you told me this morning that you were going to prepare a surprise for me with Monsieur Bottot. I am impatient to know what it is."

Basilie's beautiful blue eyes sparkled with pleasure, and with joy she declared:

"I will not put your patience to the test. Tomorrow, Bottot and his men are going to set up a fox hunt!"

"Ah!" said Saint-Clair. "I'm delighted! I hope we shall have good weather."

"It's likely," the young girl assured him. "The barometer is steady. The moon is nearly full. The wind blowing from the northeast is light and steady."

As she spoke, she served herself from the selection of foods set out by Jeannette, and began to eat with her lovely appetite, still sharp from the morning march through the woods.

Saint-Clair was hungry too. Energetically resolved to fight against weakness in every way possible, Jacques d'Hermont forced himself to eat. Since even in the slightest appetizers, the professional qualities of Amélie the cook affirmed themselves to be of first rank, the excellence of the dishes made it easier for him to take in food, despite his lack of appetite. Thus the first quarter of an hour was passed in almost complete silence. Only brief words were spoken about trivial details of table and service.

A Trout au gratin in provençal style followed the appetizers. This was one of Amélie's triumphs. Exquisitely presented, in well-ordered forms and rich, warm colors, the dish was at once mellow and firm, tasty and flavorful, without an excess of spices. If anyone spoke now at all, it was only to praise the incomparable qualities of the cook.

Before the roasted pheasants, which the Comte began to cut with obvious pleasure and subtle art, the conversation resumed. This was done by Basilie with her usual spontaneity, both timely and innocent, for it was she who spoke first, casually addressing Saint-Clair:

"Dear Monsieur saint-Clair, for you who have traveled the world on a thousand adventures, the fox hunt will be but a modest entertainment. I imagine you have chased the elephant, shot the tiger at close range, applied force against the antelope and stabbed the panther right in the heart? All the same, for a real hunter, the fox is not without interest. But perhaps you have already had the experience...?"

"Of hunting fox?" asked Saint-Clair, smiling. "Yes, my dear girl. Although it's true that, as a hunter, I've tackled the big beasts you mentioned, not without some irony, I am also able to appreciate the difficulties and seductions offered by a simple fox hunt. But a question comes to mind. You know the hunted fox does not hesitate to leave its usual area and lead its pursuers all over the countryside. If the prey passes through land that does not belong to you, do you follow it? In this region, you have an agreement between owners on the subject, I believe, isn't that right?"

"An agreement? No. But a tolerance that is tacit, yes. The configuration of the hunting grounds of Beech Grove lead the fox along the long edge of a bushy area when chased, so that it enters into the thickly wooded part of the neighboring estate, the Cross of Blood. It is precisely there that we will wait for him, so that we can flush him out and hunt him down. The gamekeepers of the Cross of Blood have never opposed our incursion. We maintain the same tacit reserve and courtesy toward them, when their foxes take refuge at the edges of Beech Grove. I heard Bottot once say once that it had always been so between the two properties, but only for foxes. For any other game, 'no way!' as Bottot put it: trespassing is rigorously forbidden! The codes of small and fragmented parts of the French countryside, Monsieur le Nyctalope, are far from the freedom of the virgin forests, savannahs, steppes and pampas of the world!"

And she laughed with joy.

When she laughed, Basilie was a feast for the eyes. Her eyes sparkled, her pink cheeks were marked by a dimple, her beautiful white throat was exposed, and her fine pearly teeth sparkled between her delicate red lips. When she pronounced the name of the Cross of Blood, her father looked at her with extreme attention, and interrupted the cutting of his second pheasant. But neither the look of the Comte, nor the softer but more profound look of the Nyctalope, appeared to trouble the serenity of the young girl.

"Indeed, nothing at all in common," said Saint-Clair with an amused smile.

Her father returned his entire attention to the light, skilful, quick work of his hands, armed with a knife and fork.

It was like this throughout the meal. D'Hermont hardly entered into the intermittent conversation, while the Nyctalope attempted to make Basilie speak, by bringing her with subtle insidiousness back to the subject of the Cross of Blood. In a throwaway tone, with just a hint of a question, as if by accident, he even pronounced the name of Armand Logreux d'Albury. But Basilie neither frowned, nor blushed, nor grew pale. In the simplest and most natural tone, which seemed to be sincere and true, she replied without saying anything more:

"I do not know him."

At that moment, Jacques d'Hermont looked at his daughter. He asked himself: "Is she lying?" Or had Laure and Madeleine both dream it all up? Even if Basilie was lying, it was a lie agreed on long ago with Madeleine and Laure...

Confused, perplexed, even overwhelmed by this new subject of anxiety, he lowered his eyes. But Saint-Clair did not let up. He made a movement of his head which addressed the father as much as the daughter, and asked a question in a tone of surprise:

"By chance, I learned the name of your neighbor and also the total absence of interaction between your property and his. Does he never come to talk to you?"

"Never!" replied d'Hermont, gravely.

As for Basilie, Saint-Clair had the clear impression that she was purposely evasive, addressing him in a tone of false ingenuity, an imperfect mask. With a falsely confidential air, the girl murmured:

"Monsieur, at Beech Grove everything that has to do with the Cross of Blood is taboo: one does not speak of it!"

And deliberately, she broke the thread of the conversation by saying in her normal voice:

"Papa, eat your pheasant quickly! What a delicious smell! I still have the hunger of a wolf!"

From then on, until the end of the meal, nothing more was spoken except indifferent banalities.

Rising first, the Comte said to his daughter:

"What are you doing this afternoon?"

She replied without hesitation:

"I am going to keep Auntie and Mad company. If they want, I will read to them out loud a wonderful novella by Guy de Maupassant that I read yesterday. It talks about peasants, marriage and inheritance; it's quite a thrill... Then I will receive Bottot, who will give me a report on his preparations. In sum, I do not think I will go out at all. Do you have any requests of me, Papa?"

"No."

"And you, Monsieur, Saint-Clair, may I be useful to you in any way?"

"No, my dear girl. I don't see how. Thank you. Besides, I'm planning to go to Tours, to see an old friend, a curator at the local Museum..."

"Then let me say good-bye now."

She gave Saint-Clair a little bow, at once sweet and mocking, and offered her left cheek to his paternal lips. Then, her step light, balanced and harmonious, she went out.

Ten minutes later, alone in his car, Léo Saint-Clair drove away from Beech Grove. He had not seen Soca and Vitto again, but they had already received his instructions for their afternoon's work.

In fact, the Nyctalope did not go straight to Tours. First, he stopped at Saint-Christophe, where, in the secrecy of his medical office, he had a long conversation with Doctor Luvier.

At 3:30 p.m., he arrived in Tours, not to see any curator, but to call from a telephone booth at the local post office his secretary, Marcel Dubost, based in an outbuilding of the mansion on Rue Hallé where he presently lived. He was back at Beech Grove at 4:45 p.m., that is to say about half an hour after sunset. From there, he went straight to the room of Jacques d'Hermont, who had been waiting for him.

"How do you feel?" asked Saint-Clair.

"Bad. Worse than yesterday at the same time. Tonight, the fever will be dreadful—if you do not succeed in helping me sleep..." replied the Comte with dejection.

"Not quite! It was to calm you, this morning, that I promised you a strong soporific. You will not sleep until at least midnight—but neither will I. We will stay up together, but not here."

"What?" asked the other, astonished.

"I mean, not in your room, nor in mine. Listen to me, Jacques. You know my theory that Armand Logreux's long stay in Tibet is crucial to solving this mystery. Do not question me. It is important that the mental in you has no influence on the physical during the entirety of this experience. I cannot explain anything in advance. Afterward, everything will be made clearer, or at least, I hope so. All I ask of you is to follow me. Will you do this?"

"Obviously, yes!" said Jacques d'Hermont with fervor.

"Good. Call Firmin right away. First, tell him that you will have only a glass of warm milk for dinner, which should be served in your room. Second, have him go and ask Madame Dauzet and Madeleine to come here immediately, for you must speak to them. That's all for the moment."

Without replying, d'Hermont held out his arm and pressed an electric bell that emerged out from the tapestry, next to the fireplace where the great dry wood fire, all embers, was dying slowly. Saint-Clair sat in one of the armchairs.

Two minutes later, the valet appeared.

"Monsieur le Comte has rung?"

"Yes, Firmin. I will not dine downstairs. In half an hour, bring me a glass of warm milk and some biscuits."

"Yes, Monsieur le Comte."

"Also, go tell my sister and older daughter that I would like to see them in my room right away."

"Yes, Monsieur le Comte."

Shortly afterward, Laure and Madeleine came in. They were both wrapped in warm wool dressing gowns, gray for the Laure, dark red for Madeleine.

When, after a few words about the state of health in which the three patients found themselves, they had sat down in two other armchairs before the fire, between the Count and the Nyctalope, Jacques looked questioningly into the eyes of his friend.

"I will speak first," said Saint-Clair.

Turning toward the two women, who had the same attentive and confiding look, he went on in a calm tone:

"This evening, I am going to take some steps that I very much hope will provide the solution to the mysterious problem of Beech Grove. Jacques and I will have roles to play, and you two as well. Do not ask for any explanations now. You must do exactly as I tell you. Understood?"

"Yes!" replied the aunt and her niece, together.

"First, you will make an effort to go downstairs and have dinner with Basilie. Then you will ask her to follow you back to your apartment and keep you company, reading and chatting without any music, until she can no longer resist sleep. Understand that you have to keep her with you as long as possible. Can you do this?"

"Oh, yes!" said Laure. "Although we have never asked her to do that before."

"If it seems necessary to insist," Saint-Clair went on, "then you must insist. And without letting her realize that you are observing her, you will do so. Perhaps she will remain as she always is. Perhaps, on the contrary, she will suffer first from the constraints she may be obliged to impose on herself in order to comply with your request, or from a more or less progressively rapid discomfort, a sudden outbreak of fever, a violent desire, hardly fought or not fought at all, to leave you and return to her own room... If this happens, you will give back her liberty only when she visibly cannot take anymore. Have you understood me?"

Once again it was Madame Dauzet who answered:

"Your instructions, yes, but not your purpose."

"You will understand it later. Use all your energy not to be overwhelmed by the usual evil. Hold on until Basilie leaves. Afterward you can abandon yourselves to the fever and the depression without further struggle. Tomorrow morning, you will wait for Jacques to come and see you. That's all. No! One more thing. Neither your brother nor I are going down to dinner. You will tell Basilie that I am not hungry and that I would like to keep Jacques company. Do I have to add more details? Do I need to be more precise?"

"No," said Laure, clearly.

"What about you, Madeleine?"

The young girl did not hesitate any more than her aunt:

"No. I have understood what we must do," she said. "It is very simple. But how long will we have the strength to hold out ourselves?"

"I do not know," confessed Saint-Clair, smiling. "But I repeat: draw for as long as you can on the energy of which your nervous natures are capable. You will be astonished, both of you, to see what high point this energy can reach, especially in a single and expected case of voluntary tension."

He fell silent. It was clear he had no more orders to give. And they knew in advance that he would not explain anything.

Laure looked at her brother. During the conversation, Jacques d'Hermont had not said a word or made the slightest gesture. Slumped in the low chair, elbows on his knees and chin on his folded hands, he had listened, looking in turn at the eyes of his friend, of his sister, and of his daughter. Looking at Laure, he understood that he himself had to conclude. So he straightened up, rose with a slow and painful movement, and with a firm voice said to the two women rising at the same time as Saint-Clair:

"I join our friend in imploring you to be strong, clever and attentive. Laure, Madeleine, I will see you tomorrow."

He opened his arms. Together, his sister and daughter came to him with lightheartedness. He drew them into an embrace, kissed them on the cheeks and, drawing back a little, detached from them. For Saint-Clair, the women had a smile and a look at once submissive and grateful.

When they had gone away and the door was closed, Saint-Clair said simply:

"Jacques, let's wait for Firmin. I do not think it is useful to speak."

"As you like," said d'Hermont, docilely.

They sat down. The Comte took out a log from the basket of wood at the outer corner of the fireplace and laid it on the pile of red embers. Soon a flame leaped up, and danced broadly and capriciously, colorful, luminous and, at times, playful—a sight before which a man with an active interior life could spent hours thinking and dreaming. The vast room was gently illuminated by this moving flame and by the electric bulb of a bedside lamp veiled by a green shade. No sound could be heard from the night outside. In this half-light, this silence, the two friends did not speak a word until discreet blows were struck on a door.

"Come in!" said the Comte.

Firmin appeared, a tray of biscuits balanced on his left hand. He placed it on the thickly-marbled pedestal table in the middle of the room.

"Will Monsieur le Comte need anything more?"

"No, Firmin."

"When shall I bring the hot milk?"

"In ten minutes. I am going to bed early."

"Very well, Monsieur le Comte."

Turning toward Saint-Clair, the intelligent valet hesitated, but he immediately overcame this and asked:

"What about you, Monsieur?"

"In fact, Firmin," said Saint-Clair, affecting a tone and aspect of great weariness, "I do not feel the slightest appetite, no matter how succulent the dinner prepared by Amélie. Madame Dauzet will excuse me along with Mesdemoiselles Madeleine and Basilie. I am not going down. And the notion of a glass of warm milk makes me wish to imitate you, Jacques..."

He fell silent. Firmin asked:

"Would Monsieur like for me to bring him a glass of warm milk, as well?"

"Yes, Firmin, definitely yes. But without biscuits."

"As Monsieur wishes."

Firmin went out.

Quite naturally, the Comte thought of waiting for Saint-Clair's milk to be brought, so the two of them might take this light evening meal together. As the fire was no more than embers, to occupy himself during his friend's silence, Jacques d'Hermont began to put more wood in the fireplace. But he was interrupted by a gesture and a touch from Saint-Clair, who gently said:

"My dear Jacques, if you expect the room to be heated and brightened by a fire burning slowly during the second part of the night until morning, you must arrange the logs differently. But if you want beautiful flames at once, I warn you, we will be leaving this room in under a quarter of an hour, that is to say as soon as you have eaten a biscuit and drunk your milk, and I mine. Besides, you are trembling and sweating from fever. I advise you not to eat and just drink your milk in small sips. I will do the same, for I too... Hey! There it is!..."

For a moment, he shivered, and with a clacking of teeth he stopped speaking.

"The fever!" moaned d'Hermont, who at the Nyctalope's first words had abandoned the fire. "I feel so miserable... And you, too.."

"It is beginning again... a little more brutally than yesterday... But I expected it... Jacques, we will soon leave here... I will..."

The Nyctalope had to stop, so strongly did his teeth suddenly begin to chatter. He let himself be overtaken by this attack for a moment. Then, reacting, he continued in a tight voice between clenched jaws:

"I would like... We will retire to a room located as far as possible from your room and mine, a room situated on the axis northwest-southeast of the castle. Think... If there are central heating and comfortable armchairs, all the better. We will suffer less physically. Do you know this room? My dear Jacques, we will have to go there and stay secretly, without anyone knowing it, not even Firmin. During my visit to the castle, I saw a painter's studio, currently unoccupied..."

"Yes, yes," whispered d'Hermont, whom the fever had left exhausted and annihilated, whereas it had made Saint-Clair nervous and agitated. "Yes, there are two rooms... a painter's studio and a room to the northeast... well heated by many radiators... There are also two chimneys all filled with wood ready to be lit. I had them set up for a painter with whom I have close relations, a Belgian whose character and paintings I like... The four still lifes in the dining room are by him. You admired them yesterday... I..."

"Yes!" cut in Saint-Clair, between two violent shudders.

At that moment Firmin reappeared with the two glasses of milk.

While placing the second tray on the table, he looked at his master, then his guest, and did not refrain from saying to Saint-Clair:

"Monsieur has a fever, like Monsieur le Comte did yesterday..."

The Nyctalope replied:

"Like Monsieur le Comte, no! But like yesterday, yes. Firmin, you will tell Madame Dauzet, Mademoiselle Madeleine and Mademoiselle Basilie straight away that your master is in bed, and that as I am giving him some exotic medication gathered during my travels, they should not come to say goodnight. As far as they're concerned, of course, I don't have a fever at all, is that well understood?"

"Yes, Monsieur."

And in another tone:

"Monsieur le Comte has no more orders to give?"

"No, no, go!" sighed Jacques d'Hermont, between two gulps of milk.

Firmin bowed and stammered:

"I wish, er, a good night to Monsieur le Comte... to Monsieur..."

Then he turned on his heel and left.

Immediately they both began to drink the very hot milk, with little sips. When they had emptied and set their glasses back down, the Nyctalope stood up and quickly said with a kind of violence:

"Now, let's go! Let's go fast, for the love of God!"

Jacques d'Hermont felt too weak to walk without support.

"Léo," he said, "give me your arm."

"Here. Are you sure we will not meet anyone in the corridors?" asked Saint-Clair.

"No one. My sister and Madeleine are in their apartment. Basilie must be in her room. Besides, we are going straight into a corridor where all the rooms are uninhabited."

With one hand, Saint-Clair set the grate in front of the fire. On the way out, he switched off the bedside lamp. He removed the inside key from the door and closed it from the outside, with a double turn of the key. Then he slipped the key into one of his pockets.

A minute later, the two friends had entered a dark vestibule. But as we know, there is no such thing as darkness for the Nyctalope.

D'Hermont said:

"Léo, is this the door I see in front of you?"

"Yes."

"Let's not turn on the light. Let me guide you."

With care, Saint-Clair closed the door of the corridor again. With his left hand, the Comte crossed the vestibule, crossed another threshold and closed another door. Only then did he switch on an electric light. A large ceiling lamp lit up, shedding generous light.

The studio was large, comfortably furnished and in good taste, illuminated during the day by a high canopy at present hidden by an immense curtain of bisected canvas. A monumental chimney showed a pyramid of logs in the fireplace. On a small adjoining table was a box of matches and a cigarette box.

"That's good!" said Saint-Clair, smiling.

The Comte sat down heavily in an armchair. The Nyctalope set fire to the paper and the twigs placed under the logs. Immediately the flame rose, sparkling, to give joy to the eyes of the two men seated near one another. Saint-Clair drew up an armchair and settled into it.

"There! Now we wait," he said, with visible satisfaction.

He didn't try to suppress the shivering and chattering that gripped him again. It lasted several minutes, under the anxious glances of Jacques d'Hermont, prostrated by immense fatigue but strained to the full by curiosity and expectation, hope and fear.

The Comte stammered, his voice low and hoarse:

"Wait... wait for what... my dear friend?"

Rubbing his sweaty palms on his handkerchief, Saint-Clair calmly replied:

"What will happen soon, if my hypotheses are well-founded. I did not give you any quinine, nor have I taken any myself. It is important this evening not to fight the evil with artificial means. There's something else I'm waiting for, which is the rapid diminution and cessation of the fever that afflicts and overwhelms you, and that overexcites my nerves, overwhelming me too as well. Patience! Speak, if you wish to do so, but let us speak of something other than the mystery of Beech Grove. Come, tell me how you met this Belgian painter. The canvas I see on this easel, if I am not mistake, represents a view of Saint-Christophe. It reveals a talent even better than the still-lifes in your dining-room. His name, his career, his character, his manners. Tell me! Tell me! You would not believe how much it interests me right now."

Was Léo Saint-Clair sincere? Did he only want to give his friend an easy and abundant subject of distraction? Revive him by engaging him in bringing the past to life? Dupe or not of this subterfuge, if subterfuge it was, Jacques d'Hermont began to speak, at first slowly and painfully, in a low and halting voice that searched for words, then with greater ease, and eventually with obvious pleasure.

As if he were, in fact, deeply interested in his friend's account, Saint-Clair cut in to ask questions, clarify details, dates... He even interposed digressions on painting in general, discussing the modern Belgian-Flemish school. He set forth ideas that d'Hermont, very "classical" in his tastes, fought with an ardor that was friendly, but intense, and a great lucidity of thought and lively ease of speech...

Then, all at once, a silvery sound rang out gently. One, two, three... The two men went silent. Twelve chimes rang out. With the uninterrupted tick-tock of its clock, an old pendulum in a high painted case had just sounded midnight.

With the twelfth sound of pure silver, Saint-Clair rose with a supple leap and stood up straight. Then he laughed, without a sound, his whole face illuminated. Arms stretched toward his friend, hands open, he spoke clearly:

"Jacques, get up! Oh! I know you are still very tired, depressed and weak. But it's only physical, and it's incomparably less effective now than on every night for the past few months. Get up!"

"Ah!" exclaimed the Comte at length, rising.

His tense face and his eyes, now very sharp, expressed infinite astonishment as well as joy. For he did not content himself with standing up, but began to walk. From one end of the studio to the other, for a length of nine or ten meters, he came and went, his step alert. He breathed deeply. He laughed with triumph. Then, finally coming to a rest before a smiling Saint-Clair, who had not moved, he cried out:

"By what miracle...?"

The Nyctalope, a hand on his friend's shoulder, replied:

"Don't get me wrong, Jacques. You are not healed, at least not completely. The mysterious evil has, if not destroyed, but at least diminished the healthy power of various vital organs of your body. Tonight, what's taking place is not a cure, but a transition between mortal evil and regenerative convalescence... In my body, which was only touched for twenty-four hours, in an extremely brutal attack, the evil hasn't had time yet to put in roots, so I am healed altogether. Anyway, that's not the point. The main thing, at the present hour, is the confirmation of my conjectures. My diagnosis was correct, Jacques! And now..."

He stopped, lowered his head and meditated. The Comte, stupefied, did not think to interrupt this thinking with a single word. Finally, raising his head, Saint-Clair fixed his grave and hard eyes on those of his friend, and said in a slow and firm tone:

"So long as the enemy is not informed and does not risk all in an offensive that might kill us, Jacques, I am sure that I can save us, save Laure and Madeleine, unmask the monster, take his power away, and lastly, divine the depths of Basilie's sphinx-like soul... if, at least, Basilie is not the pure and innocent girl she appears to be."

"My God, Léo! My God!" moaned d'Hermont. "What are you talking about?. When will you explain to me...?"

But with cold resolution, Saint-Clair said:

"Not yet, not yet! I have only one thread of the plot, which is demoniacally complicated. Patience, Jacques! Patience and trust! How do you feel now? What is your physical, mental and moral state?. Come, let's sit down again. Do not speak right away. Examine yourself, question yourself, analyze yourself. It's necessary that I have of you, that you have of yourself at this important hour, a knowledge that is perfect in breadth and depth. It is necessary, Jacques, absolutely necessary!"

Jacques d'Hermont spoke to himself at first, slowly and with pauses, in a low voice. Then the two friends questioned one another, to arrive after an hour at these conclusions: since midnight, the action of the mysterious evil had been nullified on Jacques d'Hermont, and his happily restored morale had reacted with immediate, obvious effect; likewise, the same evil no longer had any effect on the Nyctalope.

"But how had this happened? And why?" asked Jacques, with a curiosity as cheerful as it was ardent.

"I hope I can tell you soon," said the Nyctalope cheerfully. "Now let us get some real rest. Me, I will sleep in this armchair. You, go to the next room. You're in your pajamas already: slide under the covers and sleep. I always wake at the hour I have determined in advance. Today, this will be seven. We therefore have five hours of sleep before us. Let us not lose a minute. Not a word more, Jacques. Go! Go!"

The Comte obeyed.

Five minutes later, in the total darkness of the room and the half-darkness of the studio, where the embers were glowing, the two friends were overtaken by sleep.

This continued without interruption until Saint-Clair, suddenly opened his eyes, and heard the silvery ringing of the old pendulum sounding 7 a..m.

He got up, shook out his limbs and went right away to wake up Jacques. Very awake and conscious now, he said:

"How do you feel?"

The Comte slipped out of bed, stood up to make some gymnastic movements and laughed:

"Very well, indeed! Oh! Not like before the mystery began! But much better than any morning since then."

"Perfect. But careful, Jacques. No one... do you understand me? No one should see you today, nor even suspect you are convalescing. Also, you shouldn't let anyone know that you and I spent the night outside our respective bedrooms. You will lock this room and the workshop with a key, in such a way that no one can enter. We will come back tomorrow night."

"Saint-Clair!" cried d'Hermont, his eyes shining, "I think I am beginning to understand!"

"Stop! Say nothing! Not even to me!" commanded the Nyctalope. "And do what I ask. In short: you and I will pretend to be worse off this morning than we were yesterday. It's a matter of playing the comedy well. It is of capital importance. Agreed?"

"Agreed."

"Then let's go. Go back to your room, lie down and pretend you're ill. I will go to mine and do the same. No arranging oneself this morning: the slightest ablution could give us a healthy air, which we should not have. As for the continuation of the comedy—which, of course, risks becoming a tragedy, will not hide this from you!—wait for my further instructions. I will give them to you either verbally or in writing, at the appropriate time. Come, enough talk. Let's leave now! Ah! One more thing! If today you see any change whatsoever in the state and attitude of Basilie, or Vitto and Soca, think what you like, but no matter the circumstance, you must act and speak according to our plan. You and I are more ill than we were yesterday. Even if you begin to feel better, speak and act as if nothing new had happened to us between yesterday and today. That's it! This time, I have finished. Let's go!"

It was exactly 7:20 a.m. when Saint-Clair, without being seen in the corridors, returned to the red room.

There he found Vitto and Soca, who had shut themselves away the night before on his orders, at the very moment the sun had set. The two Corsicans were sitting in armchairs almost facing one another, before the burning fire.

"So?" asked Saint-Clair, as soon as he entered.

Soca replied:

"Ah, Monsieur, what you predicted happened, just as you said. At midnight, Vitto had a fever of 39°5 and I had one of

39°8. We shivered, chattered our teeth and sweated. Now we're exhausted."

"That's perfect!" exclaimed the Nyctalope, with the liveliest and most evident satisfaction.

But immediately he added:

"I'm sorry, of course, but it had to be tested. Now, off you go. Back to your room. Take the dose of quinine I have prescribed. Do you have the tablets in your pockets?"

"Yes, Monsieur," the two Corsicans replied together, standing with a bit of effort.

"Wash, shave, get dressed and eat well, even if you're not hungry. Go take a walk in the woods. It's a nice day. I have my reasons to be sure that the fox hunt will be called off. And don't forget the slightest item in the instructions I gave you yesterday."

He accompanied them to the vestibule, then returned to his room, where he dressed fully, but did not shave or shower. Opening the window, he let the fresh air and sun freely enter the room for a few minutes, then rang for Firmin.

CHAPTER V
Defensive Tactic

After the customary "Good Morning, Monsieur," Firmin said, sounding content:

"I see that Monsieur is very well today, though he has not shaved."

"Yes, Firmin, all is very well. But keep that wise remark to yourself. I must seem to be worse off than yesterday."

"Very well, Monsieur! Will Monsieur take breakfast downstairs all the same?"

"Yes. But first, sit down, my friend..."

"Oh! Monsieur!" exclaimed the valet, confused by the armchair that Saint-Clair pointed out to him.

"Sit down. We need to speak for a few minutes; it's important."

"Yes, Monsieur."

Firmin sat next to Saint-Clair, who was already seated in his armchair. The Nyctalope went directly into the heart of the matter:

"My friend, you should know that it is not just me to whom good health has returned this morning. It has also come back to your master. Oh! The Comte is not healed yet, but tonight, for the first time since the attack of the illness, the evil spell did not afflict him and did not worsen his state. As the influence of the moral on the physical exercised itself fully, his condition quickly improved, to such a point that your master cried out there had been a miracle. Do you understand?"

"Oh! Monsieur," replied the valet, without false modesty. "I am not completely ignorant. I read a great deal. I borrow books from the library, and not just novels. I have read the astonishing chronicle of the Monsieur's journeys to Tibet."

"Very good. I will not delay in explanations then. Anyhow, do not ask questions. I have not even explained anything to your master. To you, as to him, I request no more at the moment than for you to listen and follow my instructions. Understood?"

"Certainly, Monsieur!" said the man, with force.

"Good! Now, take this key. It belongs to the studio and room that your master had set up for that Belgian painter, Van der Lass. The Comte and I spent the night there.. In the future, and until further notice, your master, Madame Dauzet and Mademoiselle Madeleine will only pass through their respective rooms after dinner. They will make it look as if they were sleeping in their room, but in reality, they will go to the Van der Lass apartment and spend the night there. There is already a bed and a large couch. You will make up another bed and couch. Madame Dauzet and Mademoiselle Madeleine will sleep in the room, and the Comte and I in the studio. All three will not return to their own rooms until after sunrise, a little before the usual time at which Mademoiselle Basilie rises. In fact, does she rise at a regular hour? And what does she do then?"

By his physiognomy, Firmin Gasse expressed his determination not to be surprised by anything, to understand without asking for explanations, and obey even if he did not comprehend. He answered with ease and simplicity.

"Well, Monsieur, Mademoiselle Basilie follows her alarm clock, which rings at 7 a.m.—6 a.m. after March 15th. She dresses alone and never calls for help. She stays in her pajamas if she plans to remain in the castle, and dresses for walking or horseback if she intends to go out. Then she comes down to the dining-room, where Jeannette serves breakfast. Usually Monsieur le Comte is there, too, and frequently Madame Dauzet and Mademoiselle Madeleine as well. If her aunt, sister or father have not come down for breakfast, Mademoiselle Basilie goes up after the meal to check on them..."

"Good," Saint-Clair interrupted. "Another thing, Firmin..."

"I'm listening, Monsieur."

"Your niece Jeannette... Are you sure of her intelligence and discretion? Listen to me! Absolute discretion with regard to everyone is necessary, even vis-à-vis Mademoiselle Basilie—in fact, her above all!. Your service would be easier, and there would be fewer risks of surprises, if Jeannette, under your orders, collaborated with you in the delicate and complicated day-to-day actions I consider essential to save Comte d'Hermont, his sister and his daughter, from death!"

Firmin maintained his sharp and naturally frank gaze on the Nyctalope. It was in a grave, firm tone that he replied:

"Monsieur, I am sure of Jeannette, absolutely. But you must also bring my wife into the secret. Otherwise, Mademoiselle Basilie will perceive something unusual at one time or another, for if I understand correctly, everything must be done without her having the slightest idea that things have changed."

"Yes."

"Well, then! Monsieur can trust me. With the help of Amélie and Jeannette, I will be in a position to carry out your instructions without anyone suspecting. I will answer for my wife as well as for my niece. But Monsieur will excuse me if I appear troubled, for Monsieur surely understands my emotion..."

"Firmin," said Saint-Clair with kindness, "from now on, when you and I are alone, or in the presence of Vitto and Soca, do not address me in the third person. Direct formulas are more natural and rapid."

The frank face of Firmin expressed a lively contentment, and in a very moved tone the man said:

"Thank you, Monsieur. May I ask you a question?"

"Let's hear it."

"Mademoiselle Basilie... She is not to be told anything... Is it because...?"

He hesitated. Saint-Clair cut in clearly:

"Firmin, I was expecting this question, and I understand your emotion very well. All I can tell you at this time is this: Basilie must be kept in ignorance of our defensive, and eventually offensive, steps taken against the evil that is attacking Beech Grove, at least as long as I myself do not know why she

131

has been preserved, at least until now, from that same evil that killed her mother and now threatens her father, aunt and sister."

With these words, which Saint-Clair pronounced slowly, in a low and grave voice, Firmin turned pale. All at once he exclaimed, in a voice that was quieter but heavy with emotion:

"Oh! Monsieur! You have said just what I was thinking when I asked you that question. But, in the words you have spoken, there is something which overwhelms me. You said 'preserved until now.' Does that mean…?"

Saint-Clair replied gently:

"Yes, if my hypothesis is right, last night, Mademoiselle Basilie must have fallen ill, along with her aunt and sister whom she kept company. Following my plan, which Madame Dauzet and Mademoiselle Madeleine cleverly executed, Mademoiselle Basilie must have felt the first violent attack of the mysterious evil."

"Oh!"

Saint-Clair added, with authority:

"I have not gone astray, Firmin. I shall soon know with precision in what state Basilie was last night and this morning… For the moment, let her be and wait for my further instructions."

"Very well, Monsieur. I will."

And Firmin showed, in his attitude, that he was a man capable of exercising an energetic authority over his emotions.

"Let me recapitulate and summarize," Saint-Clair went on. "Tonight, the Comte, his sister and his older daughter, will sleep in the studio apartment. Everything will be prepared by you, your wife and your niece, so that Basilie has not the slightest idea of this change. I will also give detailed instructions to Jacques, Madame Dauzet and Mademoiselle Madeleine to that effect. You, Firmin, will organize the switch in the most discreet and secure way."

"Yes, Monsieur."

"Now, pay attention, my friend! If my hypothesis is correct, your master, his sister and his older daughter, will progress toward health by the hour, attaining a state of convalescence that will be increasingly favorable. But the three of them must hide their progressive well being from Basilie, even if it is painful! They must pretend that the evil still has a hold on them, and is overwhelming and weakening them more and more. You, Firmin, Amélie, and Jeannette, must act as if it were really so. Do you understand?"

"Perfectly, Monsieur! But how long will this last?"

"Oh!" said Saint-Clair, smiling, "not long! For the affectation of illness might, if it goes on too long, impair the correct progress of the cure. Keep calm! Soca, Vitto and I will act our part too, so the need for comedy won't last more than a few days, a week maximum..."

Saint-Clair paused, and said in a less serious tone:

"Firmin, we have reached the point where I must speak to you about Vitto, Soca and myself. I will be brief. First, I want you to know that the three of us are going to disappear."

"Oh!" exclaimed Firmin. "Disappear?"

"Yes, we'll be leaving Beech Grove, to continue our journey toward the Dordogne."

"Ah! Truly?" Firmin said in a tone of incredulity.

Saint-Clair smiled.

"Bravo!" he said. "I see that you are intelligent. Our departure will be real only for Basilie... and maybe a few others. But as far as the Comte, his sister and older daughter, you, Amélie and Jeannette, we will not be far from here. We will even be very close. When the time comes, you will learn everything, Firmin. For now, I will say no more."

He stood up; Firmin stood as well, saying:

"Very well, Monsieur. Do you have any orders to give me for now?"

"Oh! Just this: at 8 a.m., serve my breakfast. I will come down. Unless I'm mistaken, I will be alone this morning, in the dining room."

"Ah?"

"Yes, Firmin. For I expect Mademoiselle Basilie to be ill. She will ring Jeannette, if she has not already done so. Go, my friend, go, and carry out the service as usual. You will not bring your wife and niece into our secret until the afternoon, when you can be alone with the two of them, far from any curious ear. Ah! A detail! Do not forget that I was taken ill this morning too. But as the evil's grasp on me is recent, I am still in control."

"Very well, Monsieur."

"Let us seal the pact, my friend. Your hand."

"Here, Monsieur!"

And the pact was sealed by a frank, cordial, solid clasp of hands from man to man.

Saint-Clair entered the dining-room at 8 a.m. sharp. Ten minutes later, Jeannette appeared, bringing eggs and ham. The young maid did not have her normal expression of smiling and good humor, however, and her "Good morning, Monsieur" lacked any joy.

"Good morning, Jeannette," said the Nyctalope. "What's the matter? You seem upset."

Jeannette put down the plate, folded her hands and said quickly, with sharp breaths:

"Oh! Monsieur! Now Mademoiselle Basilie is ill too!"

Saint-Clair felt a deep satisfaction, but he did not let it show. On the contrary, he feigned a very sad surprise:

"Mademoiselle Basilie, ill! But how?"

"I don't know. Madame Laure is with her. I was called to serve her tea with lemon in her room."

"Has the Comte been told?"

"I don't know, Monsieur."

"But your uncle..."

"I'm going to tell him right now that Mademoiselle Basilie..."

At that moment, a door opened and Firmin entered. He went straight to Saint-Clair. Right away, he said:

"Monsieur, I have just informed Monsieur le Comte that Mademoiselle Basilie is not well. Last night, in Madame Laure's music-room, Mademoiselle Basilie was suddenly taken ill with a violent attack of the fever. She suffered more and more until midnight. Now she is extremely dejected. Monsieur le Comte himself and Mademoiselle Madeleine are even worse than usual. Madame Laure too, but she has so much courage! She is at Mademoiselle Basilie's bedside. Monsieur le Comte asks Monsieur to go see him—but not before Monsieur has had his breakfast."

"Very well. I will go to your master in a quarter of an hour," replied Saint-Clair, pretending for Jeannette's sake to feel a deep anxiety.

Then he sat down. But before he started to eat, he said:

"Firmin, call Doctor Luvier. Tell him to come at once, if he can. In the case of Mademoiselle Basilie, suddenly taken ill, perhaps there is something to be done to stop this sickness from the start, one with which we are starting to have some experience. And you, Jeannette, serve me quickly."

Twenty minutes later, having unhurriedly satisfied his robust morning appetite, Saint-Clair went to see his friend.

They were alone in the room, and could speak freely. They did so, however, only in low voices, Saint-Clair sitting on the edge of the bed where d'Hermont was lying. The Comte said at once:

"Your predictions, Léo..."

"...Have been confirmed, yes. Basilie had her first bout of fever, of an extreme violence, Firmin told me. This very violence justifies and strengthens my confidence in my hypothesis. I have had Doctor Luvier called. Yesterday, he gave me some good advice. He will take care of Basilie, and also Laure and Madeleine, who were attacked last night with the same violence. We have agreed to keep the medicines at their current levels, to avoid risking an aggravation of their condition. There is one more thing, Jacques..."

"What is it?" asked the Comte, at once anxious, curious and trusting.

"Doctor Luvier suggested that Basilie should stay in her room and that an experienced nurse be summoned from Tours. But I am letting you know that this nurse will, in fact, come from Paris. She already left this morning, since yesterday I sent a long telegram to my secretary from Tours. Now several things must happen..."

"What things?" asked the Comte.

"Someone will call me on the telephone. After this call, I will say that I have to leave Beech Grove with Vitto and Soca. Basilie will believe that I have gone to the Dordogne, and that my stay there will last a few weeks. But you, Firmin, his wife and his niece, know that I won't be very far away. Listen, my friend..."

Leaning in closer, as if he were afraid that the walls had ears, Saint-Clair spoke for a long time. Not once did Jacques d'Hermont interrupt him. And listening with eagerness to the Nyctalope, the Comte's face took on expressions at first of astonishment, then of anxiousness, and at last of admiration, but mixed with terror... A terror that, when Saint-Clair fell silent, made the Comte say in an anguished voice:

"But then Basilie..."

"No, Jacques! No! Do not judge. Do not blame. And, above all, do not suffer from the atrocious pain to come... Such an abomination seems impossible to me. I believe Basilie to be innocent—I truly do. And her innocence will show itself when I have exposed the criminal source of the mystery. For to admit that Basilie is guilty, would be to despair of everything, and no longer admit that a pure gaze reflects a pure soul..."

Saint-Clair went quiet again. He said nothing because he could not say everything he thought. It was, in any event, very much hypothetical. But he was able to give his face an expression of such sincerity, that Jacques d'Hermont breathed a sigh of relief. Saint-Clair went on:

"Do you need me to clarify anything in what I have just told you?"

"No, I understand. Everything here will go according to your plan."

"Perfect. Now, there's no need to continue to pretend to be ill all the time. Your real state has to be hidden only from

136

Basilie. Only when you go see her must you take the precaution of seeming to be in bad health. As for Doctor Luvier, since yesterday, he has known my plans. Everything is on the right track now. Both our improvement last night and Basilie's illness have begun to justify my hypothesis. I called Luvier about half an hour ago, and told him that what I had dared to predict came to pass. He will act accordingly. That is all. I will see you soon, since I will come back with him after he's seen Basilie.

"Very well, my dear friend. I will wait for you."

Jacques d'Hermont accompanied the Nyctalope back to the door with a long steady gaze, and an indefinable expression.

Downstairs, Saint-Clair did not have to wait for long. Just as he was coming into the vestibule, Firmin was opening the front door to Doctor Luvier.

"Good morning, Doctor," said Saint-Clair.

"Good morning, Monsieur Saint-Clair."

They shook hands. The doctor was both worried and curious. Firmin disappeared.

"So?" asked Luvier. "Are you and d'Hermont well? And has the evil come to Basilie? Is everything as you foresaw, expected, hoped?"

"Exactly!" said Saint-Clair.

"I confess that it terrifies me."

"With good reason. But dominate this terror, my dear doctor. For your role here is going to be important... and perhaps very difficult."

"My God! I've been thinking about everything you said since your visit. I didn't sleep at all last night. But do not worry, I will act in a way that is worthy of your confidence, and I hope not to disappoint you. Before I see Basilie, do you have anything more to tell me?"

"Nothing—if you remember everything I told you."

"Ah! Even if I lived a hundred years, I would never forget a single one of your words. Let's go then?"

"Yes."

What was happening then, Saint-Clair had predicted the day before in front of Doctor Luvier. The arrangements had been made in advance, and they did not exchange another word.

Upstairs, in front of the door of Basilie's room, they separated. Led by Jeannette, who was waiting for him, the doctor entered the antechamber and passed into the room. Meanwhile Saint-Clair continued down the corridor and opened another door with caution. Thirty seconds later, he found himself in Basilie's bathroom. He was separated from the bedroom of the young girl by only two curtains that, while very thick and completely drawn, did not prevent him from listening. If he slipped a finger between them and the doorframe, he could even see into the room.

Jeannette had not entered the room but instead discreetly closed the door behind her, as she had been instructed. Doctor Luvier was greeted by Laure Dauzet.

"Oh! My dear Madame!" said the doctor, impulsively but containing himself. He stopped, hands raised, eyes both pitying and disapproving.

Laure gave a hopeless smile and murmured:

"Yes, my face says it all! I tell you that I am at the end of my wits, and should be in bed, instead of playing the nurse. But then, who would watch over Basilie? Madeleine has less resistance than I, Jeannette is incapable of certain things, and Amélie has her work that gives her so much to do. That leaves only me..."

All that Doctor Luvier was going to say and do had been agreed in advance with the Nyctalope. The circumstances fit very well into the plan drawn up the day before between them and there was nothing in it that clashed with Luvier's professional duties. He replied, in a low yet emphatic voice:

"My dear Madame, you must not undo through your excess of devotion the actions of a man now on the way to save you all!"

"Oh!" whispered Laure, taken by surprise. "What do you mean?"

"Monsieur Saint-Clair will tell you himself, soon enough, I hope. And you will obey him, for I believe that his way is the right one. But I would never have dared think the impossible could exist at this level! Come, excuse me, I am rambling. Is Basilie asleep?"

"No, but she is very weak. She does not react."

"Let me see her."

Passing before Madame Dauzet, Doctor Luvier walked toward the alcove.

The room was vast, like most of the bedrooms in the castle. And like most of them, it had two parts: one that could serve as a salon, study for intimate work, studio, a music room or simply room in which the alcove was only the extension; the other, the alcove itself, with ample space for the big bed, two bedside tables, a narrow wardrobe, and one or two seats. There the alcove was separated from the room by a double curtain of white muslin, now half raised by two parallel braces.

The double room was open to the outside by only a single window, but one that was wide and tall, a French window that gave onto a balcony. Oriented to the southeast, at this hour it fully received the first rays of the clear sun and was gilded by the pure, cold, transparent light of a beautiful dry winter morning. These rays, crossing the room almost horizontally, brushed the curtains of the alcove, so that it was both brightly and gently illuminated.

In the narrow girl's bed she had used for many years, and which she laughingly said she wanted to keep until marriage, Basilie was not lying but sitting, her back and head resting on two large propped-up cushions.

Extremely pale, even a little emaciated, with bluish rings under her closed eyes, she slowly lifted her eyelids at the muffled sound of steps on the carpet. She fixed a blank look on the doctor, walking in front of Madame Dauzet. This look was so different from all the living looks Doctor Luvier had previously seen in the young girl, that even warned as he was, he became upset for a few seconds. Mechanically, out of the instinct to keep his normal expression, he began to speak with the familiarity that was long established between himself and the daughters of Comte d'Hermont.

"Well then, Basilie! Is it from vanity that you are ill? To make yourself interesting? Let's see here…"

Over the nightdress put on a few minutes earlier, the young girl was wearing a pajama jacket in white silk buttoned under the chin, with sleeves reaching to the wrists. The doctor gently took hold of the left wrist and counted the pulsations, following with his eyes the hop of the second hand of the face of a little clock on the bedside table.

Basilie did not react in any way. In response to the words of the doctor, the "excellent Luvier" whom she admired, there was no answer. She was insensitive up to the wrist. Her sluggish gaze itself could not focus, her head did not give the slightest hint of movement, her long blonde eyelashes drooped and her face showed no expression but fatigue.

A minute went by.

"Good, good!" said the doctor, drawing away his light fingers from the wrist. "A normal depression after an abrupt and violent bout of fever. The cause of the fever itself? Hmm… Perhaps a bit too much walking in the woods yesterday, alongside the pond? And probably a slight blast of cold when passing from the sun of a clearing to the icy shadow of the thick undergrowth... Basilie, can you hear me?"

The pale lips of the young girl barely opened, and a "yes" came out like breath.

"Good! Above all, do not worry! It's nothing. The right diet, a little quinine, silence, a half-day rest... A hot water bottle at your feet, replaced often... There, I will leave you now, my little one..."

All these words of such perfect professional banality were pronounced in a restrained but sure tone, confident and even warm.

Luvier turned his back to the bed, and preceded by Madame Dauzet, left the room without hurry.

From his vantage point between the curtains, Saint-Clair avidly watched Basilie, and saw that her face did not change position, expression or appearance; that her hands remained motionless on the sheet; and that, above all, her closed eyes did not open even once...

Patient and attentive, he remained in observation five long minutes.

Madame Dauzet returned after accompanying the doctor back to the corridor, and sat down in an armchair at the foot of the bed. Resolved to hold out until the arrival of the nurse from Tours promised by Luvier, she pulled a rosary from the pocket of her dressing gown, and began to move through it with a barely perceptible movement of her lips.

As for the young girl, half lying against the cushions, she seemed to be asleep; her breathing was so light that her small, round, firm breasts, visible under the thin linen, were without a single movement.

"I like it better this way," said the Nyctalope to himself, letting the drapes fall. "Depression and complete lifelessness. Everything will be easy and remain secret."

Leaving Basilie's apartment, he went straight to the room of Jacques d'Hermont. Doctor Luvier, who had just spent a few minutes with Madeleine, came in immediately afterward.

The three men did not waste time on useless words. From everything Saint-Clair had told him the day before, Luvier knew the situation, which was just as the Nyctalope had predicted as a result of the evening arrangements. Basilie was in the apartment of Laure and Madeleine, and Jacques and Léo were in the studio of the Belgian painter. The consequences were a new virulence in the illness of Laure and Madeleine, a violent appearance of the same evil in Basilie, bouts of fever and depression in Vitto and Soca, and lastly, an obvious improvement in the state of the Comte and the full recovery of the Nyctalope.

"It's all clear!" concluded Luvier, after having delivered his sober and rapid medical summary.

"We must confine ourselves to defensive tactics," said Saint-Clair.

"For how long?" asked d'Hermont.

"Until I have obtained the results I hope for from the offensive tactic which I shall begin tomorrow morning—a tactic which only you two, for the moment, know in its essential plan. I will not reveal anything to Laure and Madeleine, who in the unconsciousness of a bout of fever or subsequent state of depression, might talk and be overheard by Basilie. Nor will I reveal my plans to Firmin, or his wife Amélie, or their niece Jeannette. These three servants will be informed only that I am leaving Beech Grove with Soca and Vitto, to better continue my work. They will strictly obey you, my dear Jacques, with respect to my defensive arrangements."

"What about Laure and Madeleine?" asked the Comte, anxious.

"For now, they will sleep in the room adjacent to the studio, while you, Jacques, will remain near them in the studio itself. Thanks to the care of Firmin and Jeannette, your usual rooms will be made as if you had used them every evening. We must mistrust—not Basilie, you must understand!—but a Basilie that is deceived or enchanted. Yes, that's what I said: deceived or enchanted. Unless... But no! No! I refuse to believe such an abomination!"

And as d'Hermont made a sharp gesture and opened his mouth, Saint-Clair continued firmly:

"Do not ask me any more today. Soon I hope to enlighten and relieve both your mind and your heart."

In another tone, he went on:

"This morning, a nurse will arrive, supposedly from Tours, called by doctor Luvier, but in reality from Paris and summoned by me. She will be in charge of watching over and caring for Basilie in her room, as well as accompanying her and distracting her outside—that is, if you, Doctor, think it is good for the patient to go out a little. For now, she remains in a sickly state after the violent fever of last night, but this state will not get worse, for she will no longer stay at night in the apartment of her aunt and her sister."

Saint-Clair became quiet. Head lowered, he meditated. Neither the Comte nor the doctor disturbed this meditation. At last, raising his head, the Nyctalope concluded:

"I believe I have told you everything. What time is it?"

Before he had consulted his wristwatch, Luvier answered:

"Twelve after nine."

"Good! In fifteen minutes, I will receive a telephone call from Paris. Firmin will fetch me, and I will return to tell you I have been called urgently to the Dordogne. I will say the same thing to Madeleine in her room, and to Laure in Basilie's room, where Basilie is certain to overhear. You, Doctor, at Saint-Christophe, and at the farms where you visit your patients today, you will create occasions to repeat that the guest of Monsieur d'Hermont and his two servants have left Beech Grove to continue their voyage to the Dordogne. It is necessary that everyone know this. After what I have told you yesterday, and you as well, my dear Jacques, you understand the very important reason for this lie, and the need for it to be spread as widely as possible. There! Now that is really all."

At that very moment, a knock was heard on the door.

"Come in!" said the Comte.

Firmin appeared:

"Monsieur Saint-Clair is wanted on the telephone."

"Thank you. I'm going."

Ten minutes later, all the inhabitants of the castle including Basilie, whom Saint-Clair found with her eyes open, and with whom he exchanged a few words of circumstance, had learned that the Nyctalope, along with Vitto and Soca, would take to the road again at 3 p.m., after lunch.

At 11 a.m., in a hired car from Tours that had left Paris in the morning, a young nurse named Anna Large arrived at Beech Grove. Firmin received her at the foot of the great steps, and she was immediately led to the library where Comte d'Hermont and Léo Saint-Clair were waiting. They spoke for a good quarter of an hour.

Anna Large, registered nurse, then spent a few minutes in the room that had been prepared for her. Bareheaded, dressed in a white smock and slippers, she was introduced first to Madeleine, then to Laure Dauzet, then to Basilie, by the Comte.

Anna was a brunette with an attractive face and simple, easy features. She had a fine, light, supple build and was about thirty years-old. Her special trait was her voice: a light contralto that was music to the ears. She spread immediate sympathy, and, after a brief conversation, Basilie smiled and looked at her with cordial vivacity.

"It's all right!" said Saint-Clair, satisfied, when a few minutes later, Laure reported to him the first contact between the nurse and Basilie.

And he added:

"You know, I was sure of it. With her great energy, which she's careful not to show when it's not necessary, Nurse Large is charm itself. All her male patients adore her, and her female patients can't help but love her."

Laure, who knew that, from the next night, she and Madeleine would begin the same "convalescence" that her brother and father had enjoyed the night before, smiled widely. Taking the hand of Saint-Clair with a lively gesture, she quickly kissed it and said:

"You are a magician!"

"So I am! Working only for the forces of good!" said the Nyctalope, with a laugh.

At lunchtime, only Basilie was absent. She remained in her room, in the company of her nurse.

The meal, though without sadness, lacked a certain spark of joy, despite the new wellbeing felt by Jacques d'Hermont, and the marvelous hope that now animated Laure and Madeleine, still exhausted by the nocturnal evil. As for Saint-Clair, serious and meditative, he spoke little.

This was because he was conscious of the possible precariousness of his "defensive tactics," as well as undecided as to the efficacy of the "offensive tactics" he was going to put in motion in a few hours.

His reasoning and intuition were on alert, and he made many varied observations of the castle and its surroundings, from human beings to material things. Based on these, he started to believe that he possessed most of the facts that could help him solve the "Mystery of Beech Grove." But what would happen to all the beings and things he observed when he would take direct action against the source of the evil?

"If I have not been mistaken during the last twenty-four hours," said the Nyctalope to himself, "direct action will be both difficult and dangerous, and even more so for Jacques, Laure and Madeleine than for myself."

At 3 p.m. on Friday, January 23rd, his bags in the trunk of the car, accompanied by Vitto and Soca, Léo Saint-Clair left Beech Grove.

PART TWO

CHAPTER I
The Sunday Gathering

A seven-kilometer country road led directly from Saint-Christophe-sur-le-Nais, in the *département* of Indre-et-Loire, to Dissay-sous-Courcillon, in the Sarthe. Narrow and winding, it was little frequented, as cars usually took a short-cut three kilometers to the west of Saint-Christophe, since the national road from Tours to Le Mans crossed Dissay.

At its halfway point, the country road accentuated the picturesque quality of the landscape by rising alongside the hillside, where it overlooked for about five hundred meters, facing East, the pretty valley of the Nais. There was a rounded depression where the railway tracks were hidden behind rows of trees and bushes, and the little river winded with a hundred little twists and turns between elms and poplars. Then, at last the water spread out into a lake and gardens, watered by the Nais. To the north were two magnificent columns of poplars, the oldest and most beautiful in the whole region, and before them rose the buildings of the Cross of Blood.

Bordering the hills, a path ran alongside the gardens of the Cross of Blood. Tall thickets of trees rose up here and there from the slopes, knocked down by the saws and axes of woodcutters. On precisely the east-west line, where the manor of the Logreux d'Albury was located, the hill was hollowed by the roadside into a sort of half-moon of about twenty meters in diameter.

This small esplanade between path and wood was the preferred spot for vagabonds, Roma gypsies and small-time caravans of journeymen of various origins. A very old tolerance maintained by the current municipal council of Saint-Christophe authorized them to stay there, for free and in peace, for at most a week.

This place had a very pleasant view, from which one could look at the most beautiful part of the valley of the Nais, stretching from north to south, with the Cross of Blood in the background. In the foreground, there were wooded hills, and far to the right, on a very tall rise, the pepper-pot towers and white façade of Beech Grove.

On Sunday, January 25th, at around 10 a.m., the half-moon esplanade was occupied in a few minutes of rapid and skillful installation by two caravans. These were led by two very handsome Catalan mules, animals that were well cared for and never ran out of good feed. The caravans, without being luxurious, new, or even recently repainted, were in very good condition and kept clean.

As for their occupants, any passer-by who might have stopped there a moment out of curiosity could have admired them as pure samples of the Romani race, whose modern kingdom, with its headquarters at Seville, extends to Granada, Toledo, Saragossa, Barcelona, Perpignan, Beziers, Arles and the Saintes-Maries-de-la-Mer, with extensions to Lyon, Paris and Lille. Having arrived in Dissay in two wagons, this little tribe of Romani gypsies was on its way back to the south of France, Catalonia and Spain.

Four men and three women—one very old, one dark-skinned and one very young—as well as two children of seven to nine years-old—a girl and a boy—made up the tribe. The four men were about the same age, ranging from forty to forty-five years-old. One of them, whose name was Andrès, was the husband of the dark-skinned woman, named Joachina, who was herself the daughter of the older woman, Luisa, and the mother of the little boy and little girl. The three other males, Pedro, Juan and Anton, were single and not related to the Andrès family. The three of them occupied the first caravan, half the size of the second. This belonged to the grandmother, who lived there with her daughter, son-in-law and grandchildren, as well as with the young woman, for whom a kind of independent compartment with private door had been set aside, opening onto the left side of the car between the wheels.

A simple passer-by, somewhat observant, would have understood all this in two minutes. At least, he would have, if he understood the language of the Romani, who, while attending to the ordinary labors of setting up camp, did not deprive themselves of speaking and chatting while helping one another. During that time, the little boy and little girl amused themselves by running and chasing each another along the road.

This language was the pure Catalan idiom of the province of Barcelona, which is also spoken in a less accentuated and very French manner in the area of the Pyrénées-Orientales, the administrative district of the old French Roussillon region.

If the passer-by had also been somewhat familiar with the Corsican language, which resembles it very much, he would have noticed that Juan and Anton mingled with their Spanish-French Catalan many words that belonged to the homeland of Napoléon.

The men were dressed quite comfortably in solid shoes and shirts, without collars, waistcoats, trousers or jackets of whatever kind, used but in good condition. The two women wore *caraco*-style jackets [10] and traditional skirts, in violent colors faded by wear and time. The two little children were half-naked, in spite of the sharp cold of that dry winter morning, a cold they did not feel when playing in the sun.

But the most remarkable personality of this nomadic group was the young woman, or rather young girl, named

---

[10] A style of woman's jacket that was fashionable from the mid-18th to early 19th centuries. Caracos were thigh-length and opened in front, with tight three-quarter or long sleeves. Like gowns of the period, the back of the caraco could be fitted to the waist or could hang in pleats from the shoulder in the style of a sack back. Caracos were generally made of printed linen or cotton.

Nieve, which in Spanish means "Snow." By some kind of anomaly, Nieve was fair-haired, a pale blonde with the silvery reflections of the Nordics. One could guess that, under the tan of her life in the open air, her skin was white, as it appeared furtively when the movements of her body between the edges of the bright red scarf she had over her shoulders, revealed her back or the start of her breasts.

Nieve was a coquette: her beautiful hair, long and well-combed, was twisted into a high and heavy bun like Minerva's, and held in place by silver pins and brilliant combs studded with rhinestones. Under the blanket, her white, immaculate bodice was made of satin, and her skirt, red like the scarf, was short and pleated, cut from a section of pure wool. Although her legs were bare, her feet were covered in socks also made of red wool and Greek laced-up leather shoes with a thick sole and flat heel. Nieve's face was extremely beautiful, with lips in the arc of Cupid and big slightly-slanted green eyes, but aloof due to the straight line formed by her forehead and nose. Her medium-sized body was at once slender and full, supple and muscular, but with the broad shoulders and narrow hips of an Egyptian statue. This accentuated the strangeness of her whole being.

A singular detail: when speaking to her, only Pedro addressed her with the familiar "*tú*." All the other members of the tribe, including the old woman Luisa and two children, spoke to her in a very respectful ceremonial Spanish, in the third person and often repeating "*usted*," which means "you," with a very clear shade of reverential consideration.

While, with the exception of the girl and boy, everyone was working on the set-up of the camp, the outside fireplace for the kitchen and the preparations of the meal itself, young Nieve gathered various objects into a large, light basket with a handle, a small and very fine work of wicker and matting, a delicate art that was ingenious and miraculously free of vulgarity.

When the basket was full, she hung it from the crook of her left arm. Then, approaching Pedro, who was caressing one of the two mules, she said:

"Capo!"

The word "*capo*" means "chief."

The man interrupted his work, turned around, smiled at the young girl and said with gravity:

"You are more beautiful than ever, Nieve!"

"Thank you, Capo!" sighed Nieve, blushing a little under her tan.

"You have forgotten nothing of what I prescribed you?"

"Oh! Nothing, I am sure!"

Pedro, still smiling, nodded.

"Me too, I am sure!" he said.

And with a gesture, he brushed the tips of his fingers over the smooth, straight forehead of the young girl:

"Go then, Nieve. But today, even if the circumstances change, do not be delayed. Do you have your watch? Yes? Well then! Come back by noon, for after the meal, we have much to do. Go!"

Nieve smiled and bent her knee a little, in a sketch of reverence. Then she set off down the road with a balanced, quick step.

The whole tribe, immobilized for a moment and turning in the same direction, watched Nieve move away, until she disappeared down a side road hidden by a tall hedge of wood-thicket bare in winter.

The country road was on a gentle slope. Fifty yards after it branched off, it passed under a sort of monumental doorway, dilapidated and without doors, from which ruined walls forked away to the left and right. Still rather high in places, they were the neglected remains of an enclosure that, in the sixteenth century, must have been a sight to see.

Beyond this were the fields of the gardens of the Cross of Blood. Lawns and groves, flowerbeds bare at the moment, but that, in the spring, would be lined with flowers, for even now, in full winter, everything showed the constant care of industrious gardeners. The groves were composed of many trees of different species, and the pines, fir trees and cypresses of other families were colored in deep shades of green.

Still walking with her harmonious and rapid pace, Nieve soon arrived at a large space all covered with pink gravel. Beyond this stood the castle itself, whose flanking towers and main building did not completely conceal the tops of the buildings, no doubt standing behind an inner courtyard.

Without hesitation, Nieve stepped onto the gravel, which she crossed with her light steps. She went straight to a stone double staircase, which between the two branches of her horseshoe halfway, circled a basin, in the middle of which sprang a stone nymph from a dripping pedestal, a dolphin of cast iron in her arms, with an open mouth that projected clean water gleaming in the sun.

The two staircases led to a terrace that stretched from one side of the façade to the other, between the huge walls of the two square towers. A large central door stood between four mullioned windows and nine windows on the second, and the building was topped by slate roofs with round skylights and tall chimneys.

Nieve thought: *It is grand and very sad. Although the valley is large, this feels like being in a hole. I wouldn't like to live here.*

Since crossing the threshold of the front yard, she had been looking for a human being, but in vain. If the windows had not had their shutters open, one might have thought that the main body of the castle contained no one to see the unusual arrival.

At the foot of the right branch of the staircase, Nieve hesitated a brief moment. Then, with ease, she moved up the steps. Arriving at the terrace, she crossed it so as not to stop before the door, a single leaf of solid wood, on which old fittings and big headed-nails, very shiny and without the slightest trace of rust, were arranged in a Moorish design.

No doorbell, no knocker. But on the middle of the door, a siren of wrought iron sounded its tail into a round hammer.

Nieve lifted the siren and let it fall. The blow sounded loudly and echoed in a vestibule that must have been of great dimensions, for the sound was hollow and went on for a long time. Silence followed for a few seconds, and then the door began to open slowly without the slightest sound: the hinges were oiled well.

The man who appeared in the broad, high frame of the door did not show any surprise at the sight of the visitor. And Nieve, whom Pedro had prepared for all manner of strange things, remained as impassive as the servant. He was evidently more than a domestic servant, this old man with a thin yellow face and shaven head, a black robe closed over his hips by a cord, and bare arms and feet.

For a good half-minute, the old man and the young girl observed one another. At last, Nieve spoke in a soft but fearless voice, in French with a light Spanish accent:

"I read hands and know the language of the tarots. I deliver the possessed, comfort the depressed, and soothe the worried. I also sell small works which my hands have crafted to the rhythm of my dreams."

With a brief pause and a penetrating look into the attentive eyes of the man, Nieve added with a sort of natural pride:

"All that I sell is worthy only of the masters. That is why I do not go where only servants are lodged. Are there masters here, and will they receive me?"

The old man was not surprised. Without turning his eyes away, he replied in a French oddly distorted by an indefinable accent:

"I saw you coming. There is only one master here, and he does not receive visitors. But he will receive you, if I describe to him your face and body, and repeat to him your words not of this country."

With just as much ease, Nieve replied:

"You don't belong to this country either. That is why I spoke to you in my true language. If you had been only a servant, before you I would have been no more than a merchant of pretty and useless things. Go to the master of this house, describe me, and repeat to him my words. I will wait."

"Sit here, please," said the old man.

He pointed out four oak armchairs covered in leather, around a large low table of black marble. They were in the middle of the immense hallway of the castle, and refracted the rays of sun that entered through a window with little squares.

Without a word, Nieve went to sit in an armchair and placed her basket on the table.

The man followed. He leaned toward her and asked:

"What is your name?"

"Nieve," the young woman replied simply, and immediately added: "And yours?"

"Hambad Sin."

"I am a Romani from Spain, from a family with roots in ancient Egypt," she said.

In the same tone, he said:

"I am a Tibetan from Lhasa."

For the first time, Nieve smiled, and with a sort of caressing sweetness, she said:

"Hambad Sin, Grandfather, I thank you."

And he, also smiling, said:

"Nieve, young one, you are welcome."

He placed his two hands flat on his chest and bowed. Then he turned and disappeared through a dark door, which he opened and shut without noise.

For several minutes, Nieve remained there, motionless, impassive, her gaze lost in the sun that was sieved and divided by the small window into little squares.

A few minutes passed. Nieve was less absorbed than she seemed. With a subtle movement, she raised the frills of her left sleeve just slightly enough to reveal a tiny wristwatch. The young woman counted the minutes that she waited, for she was to make a detailed account of her visit to the Cross of Blood to her chief Pedro.

When Hambad Sin reappeared, without noise, another movement made the white satin fall over the watch. The sharp face of Nieve lost none of its impassiveness when she heard the old man say:

"The Master has gone out—I didn't realize. Often he leaves his apartment by a door to which he alone has the key, and which lets him see the sunrise from the most heavily wooded area of the park. I saw that he has saddled his horse. It's likely that he won't return until just before noon, and that immediately afterward, he will dress for his meal. If time doesn't matter to you today, Nieve, I advise you to wait. But if it does, return before sunset. On Sunday afternoon, the master never goes out. You'll be announced. I promise you that he will receive you, and that he'll buy whatever you bring. Perhaps he will even give you his hand to read, and consult you in the science of the tarots. In any case, he will be generous, for he'll feel, just as I do, that his soul has the same essence as yours, beautiful Roma of Egypt..."

All these words were spoken slowly, with an infinite gentleness and an almost paternal tone. The tiny, very black eyes of Hambad Sin seemed to rejoice. At the last words, he put his long dry hand on one of the girl's shoulders and gave her a sort of furtive caress.

After a brief silence, Nieve replied:

"I will not wait. The family of the tribe I travel with is celebrating a ritual meal, with a sacred feast. I must not be late."

She stood up, delicately looping the basket onto the handle of her left wrist.

Smiling, she went on:

"I'll come back when the sun is halfway down. Tell your master I came because from the place where we camp, I saw the weathervane on top of one of the towers, and recognized the figure of the Pentacle. Do you understand me, Hambad Sin?"

"I understand you, Nieve!" said the old man gravely. "When the master returned to live here, in this house on the land of his ancestors, he built the Pentacle of Solomon in the disguise of a weathervane, so that if the gods brought some initiated soul to the land, the castle could be a temple of brief or prolonged rest. In all these years, this is the first time that the Pentacle has been seen by the eyes of a spirit capable of understanding. My old age blesses you, Nieve."

"My youth thanks you, Hambad Sin."

With the handle of the basket on the crook of her left arm, the young Romani walked toward the great door. The old man began to follow her. When she had crossed the threshold, he bowed at her passage, deeply, with both hands raised high.

Nieve took the direction back from the castle to the crossroads. A hundred yards further on, white smoke rose between the two wagons into the calm and luminous air.

The previous day, after having rejoined the main national road of Tours to Le Mans, the Nyctalope's automobile had driven not in the direction of the Dordogne, but toward a much nearer goal: the big market town of La Chartre-sur-le-Loir, only about twenty kilometers to the northeast of Beech Grove.

By one of those coincidences that fill the life of men of action and abound when people live in close contact, for five days, the great market town of La Chartre was hosting the Romani caravan of Andrès del Borjo, an authentic "king" of the only tribe of Spanish Romani, whose origins went back by an undisputed tradition, surer than any written document, to the Romani of Egypt, those priests and priestesses of Isis the Mysterious, Occult and Learned. Saint-Clair was a longtime friend of Andrès del Borjo, whom he had met in Morocco in 1921, and still kept up a frequent correspondence with this strange man.

On his way from Paris to the Touraine to answer Comte d'Hermont's enigmatic call for help, Saint-Clair had learned that in a week's time, Andrès' caravan would set up camp in a municipal field of La Chartre, one of the southerly communes of the *département* of Sarthe, not far from Saint-Christophe. The Nyctalope thus had planned to pay a visit to the Romani master and his tribe during his stay at Beech Grove.

Only a month before, he had lunched with Andrès del Borjo at his "royal" table, in the midst of the wagons and tents of the tribe, while it camped at Fontenay-Saint-Père, near Mantes in the Seine-et-Oise. He had not then foreseen that he would come to visit the tribe again in the Touraine so soon after. He was especially interested in *Nieve-la-Dorée*, "Golden Nieve," because of her hair, or the "Sybil," as the Romani called the young girl.

While at Beech Grove, thinking about what could be the real cause of the evil that plagued the d'Hermont family, except for Basilie, Saint-Clair had naturally thought of turning to Andrès for help, and in particular, Nieve.

When he left Beech Grove, he drove directly to Le Chartre, and talked for a long time with Andrès and Nieve. Then, two wagons were detached from the caravan, which had six others that would remain at Le Chartre until further orders. Saint-Clair transformed himself into "Pedro," while Vitto became "Juan" and Soca "Antonio." Not shaving, modifying the cut of his hair, applying a make-up so skillful that even in the sun it was not discernible, dressing as a Romani, speaking the Catalan language, which was his native language (as Saint-Clair had been born in Banyuls in the Roussillon) and which his two Corsicans assistants knew well enough, was all that was needed to make the transformation believable. Even Doctor Luvier would have been unable to identify, in sight and voice, the Nyctalope and his two companions.

When Nieve, returning from the Cross of Blood, appeared on the road, Lilla and Pépito, the two children, saw her first and ran toward her. She welcomed them at the same time with an affectionate smile and a gesture pushing them away from her skirt, for they had dirty hands after playing with the earth, the grass, the trees and a hundred other things.

Old Luisa and her daughter Joachina were working on the final preparations for breakfast, and had set up a coffee table in the sun, on which a beautiful linen tablecloth was stretched.

Andrès del Borjo was chatting with Pedro, a.k.a. the Nyctalope. They had just sat down on the slope on the side of the road, a few steps from the first trailer. As for Juan-Vitto and Antonio-Soca, they were playing to see who could best turn a golden plate of terracotta on a stiff index finger.

Unburdened of the children called by their mother, who wanted to clean them, wash their hands and serve them their meal before everyone else sat down to table, Nieve stopped in front of her "king" and "Pedro." They questioned her with their eyes. She replied in Catalan:

"I did not see him. He had gone out, and will not return until about noon. I didn't want to wait for him. But I have to go back in two hours.

With precision she described all she had seen, drew the portrait of Hambad Sin, and repeated the words the Tibetan had said to her.

"Well!" said Saint-Clair. "Everything remains as according to plan then, Nieve. You will do this afternoon what you could not do this morning."

He turned toward Andrès and said:

"We must be patient. The issue has multiple angles, and is very complicated. It has to do not just with the life of my friends at Beech Grove and the destiny of a young girl whom I still believe is innocent, but also with our own lives. For if my hypothesis is correct, the man we seek will not pull back for any reason, except his own death. In order to achieve our objective, we must succeed in encircling him from all sides, materially and mentally, before he can even conceive the slightest suspicion of any action directed against him. Is this your opinion, Andrès?"

The "king" of the Romani, a forty-year-old with a intelligent, serious face of simple features, did not hesitate to reply:

"That is my view, friend Léo. You may act and command as you please, as I told you. You will be obeyed and followed. We have plenty of time."

The two men smiled at Nieve, and Saint-Clair made a small gesture dismissing her. The young girl replied to the smile with a happy flash of her eyes, and went to put her basket in the second caravan. Then she went to Luisa and Joachina and began to help them set the table.

A quarter of an hour later, the meal began. It consisted of a very plentiful bowl of Valencia-style rice and a salad of oranges. There were also coffee, cigars, cigarettes and pipes, as a serious conference took place amongst the four men. The women remained silent. At 2 p.m., Saint-Clair stood up. Addressing himself to Vitto and Soca in the manner that was by now his practice, that is to say in the Catalan language, and calling them by their Romani names, he said:

"Juan, Antonio, prepare to accompany me to La Migeonne."

And to Nieves, he said:

"Sibyl, in half an hour you will return alone to the Cross of Blood."

That Sunday afternoon was the day of the gathering in the hamlet of the Priory, located two kilometers west of Saint-Christophe. Each person in the small Romani caravan had his or her role to play. The old woman Luisa kept watch over the caravans, mules and children. Andrès and his wife Joachina went to the gathering, allegedly to sell wickerwork, but in reality to take a good look around, for at this gathering, all the peasants of Saint-Christophe and its neighboring villages would congregate to exchange gossip, joyful talk, and plan future fairs and markets. Eyes and ears like those of Andrès and Joachina, duly informed and instructed by Saint-Clair, could see and hear things that might be useful.

Nieve had her own specific mission. No less precise was that of the Nyctalope and his two assistants, who wished to put an end to the riddle of the shoe with the cracked sole, and in addition make a thorough investigation of the buildings of La Migeonne, left empty for a few hours by Hector Gasse, his wife Anna, and their three servants.

Yes, left empty—and open, for, in that region of Touraine, the honesty of inhabitants was truly total. In this land, in human memory, there had not been a break-in, a theft, or even any notable pilfering. On festive days, whether it was for a fair or a simple gathering, the villagers, tradesmen, artisans and peasants took the day off, closed the ground floor doors and windows, shut up the barns and stables, and went to the provincial place of rejoicing. No one was left even to steal a rabbit. As for vagabonds, tramps and hobos, they were not seen outside the immediate vicinity of the great national road from Tours to Le Mans. If someone went astray on a road near the entrance of a farm, the guard dogs were usually sufficient to keep him at a distance, all the more so if the vagabond knew that the barking would wake up a farmer or valet in the house. Saint-Clair knew all this already, through Jacques d'Hermont. The operation at La Migeonne would thus be very easy.

The previous night, after they had returned by bicycle from Le Chartre-sur-le-Loir, Soca and Vitto had sprinkled large quantities of sand in two places on the dirt road taken by the inhabitants of the farm to go at the hamlet of the Priory. The shoes of the Gasse family and their servants would leave imprints there.

Everything had been planned well. Saint-Clair and his two assistants hoped to find the shoe with the cracked sole, or at least its trace, to determine if the individual wearing it on the night of the luminous phenomenon was one of the five people living at La Migeonne.

Before their departure, Vitto slipped several pieces of raw meat wrapped in paper into a large pocket of his simple jacket. Soca went armed with a bag of nightingales. Neither they nor Saint-Clair carried any weapon. But each of the three men kept on him their identity papers in case they ran into some kind of trouble with the local gendarmes.

To arrive at La Migeonne, the three men skirted the gardens of the Cross of Blood, crossed the Nais in a jump, climbed the slope of the railroad track and followed a path that meandered through the thickest section of the great wood that occupied the borders of the property of Beech Grove on each side. They did not travel directly through the woods and fields. As an added precaution, Comte d'Hermont had given formal

159

leave to all his gamekeepers to go with their wives and children to the gathering at the Priory.

The weather would probably remain fine all day long, for wind was still blowing from the east and the air was crisp. Chances were that the peasants would linger at the gathering until after sunset, as the evening light would last long enough to light their way back from Saint-Christophe to the scattered hamlets and farms.

Without difficulty, and without having been spotted, Saint-Clair, Vitto and Soca reached the immediate vicinity of La Migeonne. After making absolutely sure the surroundings were deserted, all three crossed the threshold of the open porch together. On the pavement of the front courtyard, two dogs were sprawled in the sun. They rushed forward, barking. But Saint-Clair called them by their names, and calmed them with a voice that soothed them into absolute stillness. Vitto threw them the pieces of raw meat he had brought. Attracting them with further chunks of meat and whispering flattering comments, he led them toward a kind of dark recess on the side of the pigsty and adroitly shut them away. The dogs quickly occupied themselves in gnawing on their meat, and satisfied as they were, did not start to bark again.

Then Vitto went to post himself to watch for any possible arrival at the opposite gate, on the side facing the dirt road. The latter had two doors that could be locked from the inside, but there was a wide gap between them, through which the watchman could easily keep an eye on the road running straight across the fields toward the point that the hill began to slope toward the valley of the Nais.

Meanwhile, Saint-Clair and Soca walked rapidly to the small building that contained the living quarters of the farm. There was just one door and three windows, of which two were closed. The lock on the door did not long resist one of Soca's tools; its bolt gave way, and the two men entered.

Saint-Clair knew the lay-out of the farm from having come there with Jacques d'Hermont: kitchen, dining-room, living-room, etc. Quickly but carefully, he made a search that turned up nothing. There was only one piece of furniture shut with a key: a solid old country cupboard, containing some silver cutlery and table linen. Nothing suspicious, nothing even a little significant.

The next room was obviously the bedroom of Hector and Anna Gasse, the farmer couple.

"Curious!" said Saint-Clair, amused. "Everything here is cozy and perfectly maintained. The terrible greed of the Gasses does not prevent them from maintaining a certain personal ease, a private luxury, in secret. Attention, Soca! Everything must be displaced somewhere. The smallest corner must be examined, even the frame of the bed, as well as under the mattress and cabinet. But then we must put everything back in its place, and it must look as if we have not touched it."

"Naturally, Monsieur!"

In this room full of furniture, with its glossy hardwood floor covered with a large rug, window trimmed with thick white tulle and red curtains with a double layer of pink sateen, the investigation went on for much longer than in the living-room. Everything was meticulously searched without result.

They ended with the cabinet, a most remarkable piece of furniture. This item, supposedly from the First Empire, did not look antique at all. It had four drawers stacked above one other, all locked, and a table made of thick black marble. At first Soca lifted and removed the marble, fixed by its weight alone. He set it on the floor and leaned it against the wall. Under the marble was another slab, made of a single plaque of very thick wood screwed, studded and strongly glued to the four massive columns that ended with a ball foot. When the marble was removed, however, one could not see the inside of the upper drawer, as one usually does with this kind of furniture.

Standing in front of the cabinet, the Corsican cautiously opened the four drawers, which he pulled fully open without removing them completely. Each time he felt a clear resistance, a sharp jerk.

"Fixed brackets are holding them back," he said, "but I can touch and see the bottom without difficulty."

While Soca was engaged in the work of successively opening and closing drawers, Saint-Clair stood two steps to the side: a movement and halt that were not calculated, or even conscious. He did not think there was a secret hiding place in a piece of furniture. He had always thought that the hiding place, if it did exist, would be in a well-concealed hole in the wall, in a sordid and little-frequented place in the house.

But his eye was naturally observant, and with his mind sharpened, he was quick to see, notice, compare, deduce, and conclude. In front of the piece of furniture, or standing at a slight angle, Saint-Clair would probably only have seen what Soca saw, and not remarked on anything, compared anything, or deduced anything else. He would have concluded that they only had to empty the drawers methodically, and put everything back that they contained.

When the first one was opened, Saint-Clair thought: "Obviously the shoe with the cracked sole cannot be inside, any more than in the furniture we have already seen. But I am not only looking for that shoe. With a criminal of the rare nature I suspect, if there is an accomplice at La Migeonne, I must look for clues of a very different kind!"

By chance, he found himself two meters to one side of the cabinet, so that daylight passed between the drawn curtains and cast it into full light. Then he clearly saw the full width of the drawers pulled out of the furniture.

He heard Soca say mechanically:

"I can touch and see the bottom without difficulty."

And the mind of Saint-Clair thought logically:

"So, this bottom I can see from here does not extend fully inside the cabinet."

Saint-Clair's eyes saw, and his mind noticed, that the width now visible from the drawers, front to back, measured barely more than two-thirds of the extension of the cabinet. And his mind deduced:

"So the drawers, when pushed in, do not reach to the back of the cabinet!"

He exclaimed sharply:

"Soca!"

"What is it, Monsieur?" asked the Corsican, looking at his master.

"I'll explain. But do not move, for luck has positioned me well to see precisely what all our efforts might have caused us to miss!"

"What?" exclaimed Soca.

"Yes. There's something abnormal about this cabinet."

"What must I do?"

"Find the fixed brackets, remove them with as little damage as possible, and take out the drawers completely, placing them on the carpet. Be calm, but quick, because one false move could break something, and we have neither the time nor the means to repair it."

"Understood, Monsieur."

Quickly, but with method, the Corsican emptied the upper drawer, and carefully set all the contents on the carpet. There was only linen, rough but good quality, sewn by peasants. With his eyes and fingers, Soca studied the bottom of the drawer, and the walls and inner walls of the cabinet.

"I have it, Monsieur. There is one bracket on each side. The wood at the bottom of the drawer juts in, and the brackets have been applied under the table. Now the whole system is coming apart: the three drawers, top to bottom, are held together. The brackets of the table keep the first drawer in place, the brackets of the first keep the second in place, and so on. It's not bad. I do not need to completely pull out the drawers of the cabinet to empty and inspect them. But I do not see the reason for such joy on your face..."

"You will see, you will see soon," said Saint-Clair. "Continue and do not speak at all!"

"Yes, Monsieur."

And without speaking, at least until his master questioned him, the Corsican continued to work.

Unscrewing the eight brackets was for him a quick job.

At the end of it, Saint-Clair said:

"The ease of the extraction of brackets proves they were not placed with the intention of permanence, and even that someone took them out and screwed them back in before you did so yourself, Soca. No doubt this happened a long time ago, for the countryside is damp, and even in this closed room, moisture penetrates. Not touched for months, the screws would be rusty. But they are perfectly sharp and shining, and their heads bear scratches from the blade of a screwdriver. The fingers that handled them were obviously less skillful and light than yours, Soca."

Saint-Clair went silent, obviously delighted. But he still had not asked a question, so the Corsican did not say a word.

The last drawer was pulled out and set on the carpet, and the cabinet revealed its empty belly.

Then Saint-Clair said:

"Soca! You may speak now."

"What should I do, Monsieur?"

"Measure the length of the drawers and the cabinet table by eye. And at last you will see!"

Two glances were enough for the Corsican.

"Ah! Monsieur! I see now! The drawers, pushed in, do not reach to the back... they are too short! Or rather, they go to the back, but there is a double back! Top to bottom, the wall of the cabinet is double. And between the two walls there is a space..."

"Yes! Soca, yes! A space that constitutes a very clever hiding place, and therefore must not be empty. Find the mechanism to open it."

"Yes, Monsieur."

The Corsican pressed his knees against the inside of the cabinet. Then he stuck his head, arms and torso inside.

"Can you see?" asked Saint-Clair.

"Yes, Monsieur, I see very well."

The Nyctalope was calm. Secret as the system of opening and closing the double back was, clever as the cabinet-maker might have made it, Soca would find it. And quickly.

So quickly that Saint-Clair was going to point out that two minutes had already passed, when Soca said with joy:

"Monsieur, I've figured out the trick. But do I have to open it myself?"

"Yes! The honor is yours!"

"Well then! Here it is, Monsieur. It is open. I see packages tied with string."

At the bottom of the cabinet there was a light creaking, and the slap of a wood tablet, which fell and touched another dry piece of wood. Soca began to leave the cabinet. But Saint-Clair said:

"No! No! Don't come out. Empty the cache. Give me everything. And take the things methodically, top to bottom and left to right. For, I insist, everything must be replaced exactly."

"Understood, Monsieur!"

One after the other, in under a minute, Saint-Clair received nine packages that he set in order on top of the cabinet.

These packages were different from one another in their wrapping, dimensions and weight. But they all had a cubic, rectangular form, one that rendered their wrapping more or less well-adjusted and uniform. These packages were small, for even the most voluminous was no more than thirty centimeters in width, twenty in breadth and fifteen in height. The envelopes were made of fine linen or solid gray paper, and they were tied with red string, without superfluous knots.

Saint-Clair said cheerfully:

"The Gasses are not at all miserly in this room. Instead of wrapping and tying these packages with just anything, they have used cloth of excellent quality, brand new paper and string from a fancy ball of thread, all bought for this purpose, for we saw nothing else like it in the house."

"The ball of thread, paper and fine linen are in a corner of the hiding place, Monsieur," said Soca, even more cheerful than his master. "Do you want them?"

"Hand them over, hand them over, Soca! Empty it completely!"

"There is nothing else, Monsieur."

And Soca, backing out, finally left the cabinet.

"To the packets then," said Saint-Clair. "I will undo them, and you will wrap them up again."

"Yes, Monsieur."

The most voluminous packet was opened first.

"Oh! Oh!" exclaimed the Nyctalope. "This is unexpected."

He held it in his hands and leafed through a bundle of shares of the Indian Oil Company. To find these Anglo-Indian assets in the possession of a very ordinary peasant born, living and likely to die in the countryside of the French department of the Indre-et-Loire was indeed very unexpected!

"It is unbelievable," added Saint-Clair.

He gave a small dry laugh. Then he went on:

"The most recent coupons have been detached recently."

For a minute at most, he remained unmoving and meditative. Pushing the bundle toward Soca, he at last said:

"Tie up this packet. To the next one."

The second contained ten pinned notes of a hundred francs. Ten thousand francs! The Gasses were not poor!

The third contained only letters and family portraits.

The fourth contained five pinned notes of a thousand francs.

"Fifty thousand francs!" whistled Saint-Clair. "The Gasses are decidedly rich. And this does not come from the profits of the exploitation of this farm, intensive as it may be. In ten years, the Gasses have accumulated a fortune, monetary or immediately negotiable, of more than a million, at the value of the Indian Oil shares this week. What do you make of it, Soca?"

Tying up the third packet with care, the Corsican replied gravely:

"I think that so much money here reeks of crime..."

"Or complicity with crime!" corrected Saint-Clair. "Only complicity, Soca. For the crime itself is of a type that neither Hector Gasse nor his wife have the means to commit. They have only a very vague, superstitious and vulgar idea, based on the practices of peasant witchcraft and a use more or less skilful of poisonous plants. But I am hoping that, through the accomplices, we will arrive at the master-criminal. The essential thing for us, you see, Soca, is that he should not suspect that we are on his trail. For if he should come to do so, we may be dead long before we reach him!"

Such words, spoken by the Nyctalope! And in such a simple and grave tone, from which the slightest bit of irony and bravado was excluded! Courageous as he was, Soca could not help but go a bit pale.

Saint-Clair opened the fifth package, harder under its wrapping than the preceding ones. It was a cardboard box that had previously contained fifty cards and envelopes for correspondence, but was now filled with one dozen rolls of coins, like those produced by banks. Each roll had fifty gold *louis*, worth twenty francs, stamped with different effigies.

"No need to undo the other rolls. There are ten thousand gold francs in this box. My guess is that this is the genuine old peasant fortune of the Gasses, accumulated little by little over two or three generations of patient, laborious and secretive avarice. The Gasses were patriotic enough to get themselves wounded or killed during the war, but too cautious, suspicious and calculating to let go of their gold unless it was absolutely obligatory or prodigiously fruitful. There are many peasants like these in our beloved France, Soca. And in a sense, it's not a bad thing, for sooner or later, the country benefits from these clandestine savings."

There were only three packages left: they contained paid invoices, receipts of money orders, notes on craftsmen and suppliers, all the accounting of La Migeonne for ten years, except that of the year immediately preceding, the papers of which had no doubt been classified and packed away to take their place in the "safe" of the old solid trunk.

That was all.

With a quick glance, Saint-Clair had read the essential of these papers: not a line, not a word, not a name that gave any clue as to the mystery of Beech Grove.

"Good!" he concluded. "Let us pass over the bundles of banknotes as we have passed over the rolls of gold. These were won from other peasants, from the honest sweat of their foreheads and the work of their laborious hands. But the shares of Indian Oil still need an explanation... Soca, quick, put everything back in its hiding place. I am going to pass you the packets one by one, in the reverse order that you gave them to me."

Ten minutes later, everything in the room was back in its normal state, and Saint-Clair and Soca left the room to continue their investigations.

Examined thoroughly, the house offered no other clues.

As Vitto continued to keep watch, Saint-Clair and Soca inspected all the farm buildings, even the most squalid. Above the stable for the cows, a vast loft contained two beds, dirtily kept. A wardrobe without doors showed a mixture of linen with male and female clothes.

"The farm girl and farm boy both sleep here," remarked Soca ironically. "This promiscuity is good business for the Gasses: as neither nor the boy nor the girl go to seek their pleasure outside, they do not lose time hanging about with gentlemen and ladies, and there is no risk of debauchery for the profit of another farm."

"Exactly!" said Saint-Clair.

They came to the last dwelling. It was in the courtyard adjoining the pigsty, a kind of bricked-up hole where Vitto had locked up the dogs. Immediately friendly when they were let out, the dogs did not bark. Soca stayed inside while outside, Saint-Clair stroked the two four-legged guards, so easily neutralized.

Then suddenly the Corsican reappeared, holding in each outstretched hand a large muddy shoe. He laughed:

"Monsieur! Here is the cracked sole!"

And he presented the left shoe, showing the sole. The crack was partly filled with dried mud, but it was perfectly clear.

Saint-Clear looked at it with a serious eye.

"There's no doubt. This is the shoe that was on the left foot of the mysterious man, on the fateful night. The evidence is obvious. Whether he left La Migeonne or came from elsewhere, before his walk to Beech Grove, the man came here and took the shoes from this nook. On the way back, he put them back. Well done! Soca, show me the exact place that you found them."

And following the Corsican, he went in.

A kind of shed leaned against the wall of the pigpen. Built of well-fitted stones, barely bricked in here and there, it was a little over two meters in height, from the floor covered in rubbish to the roof made of corrugated iron. Its width and its length were no greater. In the back, on the ground, there was a trough full of stagnant water. There was no other opening but a narrow, low door made of poorly fitted and unpolished wood, closed with a rusty iron latch. In one corner, near the door, was an old tin-plated basin with holes. Objects could be seen in it: a thick piece of rope, wood pegs, a small iron rake, a big ladle with a twisted handle.

"There, Monsieur," said Soca. "The shoes were in this basin. They must have been thrown this way from the entrance, sent flying."

"Very good. This shed must be used to lock up a pig when it has to be separated from the others. That's all. I've seen all I need. Give me the cracked shoe."

Saint-Clair took the object, and looking closely at the sole, convinced himself definitively that the shape and depth of the crack corresponded exactly to the traces so carefully examined during the first investigations between Beech Grove and La Migeonne.

Then he said:

"Leaving here after he was chased, the man must have walked not on the muddy space that separates the porch from the edge of the body of water, but on the stony ridge that runs along the wall of the farm in the direction of the park. When he set out, the crack was empty, or it lost its old dry mud during the walk on the stony ridge. That is why it left its trace in relief on the sandy soil, where you and Vitto identified it in several places. The wet sand took the form of the crack, but the rest stuck to the ground; this is why the print and protrusion are reproduced so clearly. But, on his return, the man crossed the muddy esplanade, and the crack was filled with the mud that we now see. Very good. We now know what I wanted to know, and more, for even if I hoped to find the shoe, I never suspected I would have more than half-million shares of Indian Oil before my eyes."

He laughed, and threw the shoe into the basin.

"Should I throw the other one too?" asked Soca.

"Yes, naturally!"

"There we are, Monsieur."

"Let's go out, shut the door again," called Vitto.

And the three men returned to the Romani camp, Saint-Clair meditating while Soca, happy to speak freely, told an attentive Vitto the details of the search.

Meanwhile Nieve-the-Sibyl had gone, at the appointed hour to the Cross of Blood, wearing a hooded mantle that draped over her shoulders and reached to her knees.

She was once again received at the top of the steps, on the threshold of the patio, by the old and smiling Hambad Sin.

"The Master is here," he said at once.

The young girl replied with a friendly glance and a brief nod.

"I spoke to him about you," the Tibetan went on. "I showed him your picture and told him you would return today."

The man gestured toward the inside staircase and added:

"He is waiting for you."

Then, with a smile of accentuated benevolence:

"Follow me, Nieve. Give me your mantle. But keep your basket. The Master likes works that are made by skillful hands, according to the meanderings of thought as it progresses in a subtle mind. Such are your works, Nieve. The Master will look at them with pleasure, and no doubt buy from you those that please him most."

Once again, Nieve answered with only a look and a tiny bow. When Hambad Sin began to walk, she followed him.

The staircase led up to a vast landing from which stretched a long corridor, at the end of which were two tall windows with small tiles tinted in translucent red. The sunlight, entering the window on the right, gave the corridor from one end to the other a clear color of blood.

Just opposite the entrance of the staircase was a huge double-door with a prominent stone frame and Arabic engravings. It cast dark-red shadows in the form of writing on the white walls, turned pink by light.

Hambad Sin knocked three times with his fist on the left door. Head leaning forward, he listened. Nieve did not hear anything. But the Tibetan must have received the expected answer, for he quickly put his hand on the door handle and took a step back. At the same time, through the play of an automatic mechanism, a second padded door opened into a room that seemed at once vast and full of sunshine, in Nieve's attentive eyes.

At the gesture of her guide, the young girl moved forward, crossed the threshold and took a few steps into the room.

Before her, in the bright light that entered through a single large bay window, was a man wearing polished shoes (this is what she saw first, for she walked with her eyes lowered) and dressed in black silk pajamas over a white silk shirt with collar. From this collar emerged a magnificent neck that held up the most original head ever to meet the eyes of the young Romani.

A straight forehead, broad and high, crowned by naturally glistening waves of thick black hair; an aquiline nose of noble line; cheeks of matte whiteness, somewhat emaciated, with prominent cheekbones; a powerful jaw, closely shaven, around beautifully drawn lips at once ironic and sensual, disturbing and seductive, eloquent and silent, showing love and cruelty, experienced wisdom, discernment, prudence. But above all, it was the eyes that were extraordinary: between the long eyelids with their tight, slightly clamped lashes, they were wide open, with a color that was indefinable and seemed infinitely changeable, a dark blue with gold spikes that made one think of an eastern night and its stars.

Nieve, who kept her cool, was moved to an admiring surprise. She saw that at this moment the man's eyes expressed nothing but curiosity, but the sort of curiosity that deliberately envelops, caresses, penetrates.

She thought, lucid: *If the Nyctalope hadn't warned me, I would have been caught off my guard! I must appear to be subdued.*

The matrons of her tribe and life had already taught her to be a good actress. She turned pale, she blushed, she pretended to be disconcerted. She fixed her eyes on the man, as if fascinated by him, and stammered, trembling:

"Monsieur, I came to this castle because I saw on your roof, disguised as a weathervane, the image of Solomon's pentacle..."

She hesitated. The man completed the expression of the crystal-clear thought of his visitor. In a voice at once masculine and velvety, he said:

"For you are a daughter of Egypt, initiated by the Romani, isn't that true?"

She sighed:

"Yes. I am Nieve-the-Sybil, your humble servant."

And gently, she bent her knees in reverence and prostration before the acknowledged Master. But he put out his hands—his long and fine hands, which though delicate looked to be of great strength—and grasping the young girl by the shoulders, he drew her to him, saying with grave simplicity:

"I am Armand Logreux d'Albury—in this country. But in another land, where history is shrouded in the night of thousands of centuries, and which some day will rule all others, as befits its status as the center and light of the entire terrestrial world, I am known as the Master of the Seven Lights."

For an indeterminate length of time, all was immobility, silence, the sparkling dark eyes of the man fixed on the light green eyes of the girl, that, at that moment, were dilated in the apparent fascination endured, but endured without revolt, almost religiously.

Then, the hands having let go of their grip, Armand Logreux said in a courteous and cheerful tone:

"Nieve, set down your beautiful basket here. Sit down. Show me your work. I will choose some of them to keep as a souvenir of your passage in my solitude. Then you will take off your clothes and I will gaze upon your form, so that your beauty remains alive in my thoughts. Maybe then I will speak to you about the Seven Lights..."

Without reacting, except with immediate obedience, as if judging all the words spoken by the Master normal, Nieve placed the basket on a low table and sat on a large leather ottoman beside it, while Armand Logreux took his place on another ottoman, bending his legs in Turkish style while facing the young Roma girl.

Nieve would not have seemed natural if she hadn't shown the most ordinary curiosity. Seated, she looked around her with a sort of bold timidity.

Permeated and enlivened by the light of the sun, the high, long, broad room was at once library, study, smoking room and oriental bedroom. Books, paintings, statues, couches, cushions, drapes, carpets, antique furniture, coffee tables, armchairs and leather ottomans: everything was luxurious, comfortable and in good taste. Nothing barbarian, nothing ultra-modern, nothing mysterious or even bizarre. A room dedicated to the existence of a rich intellectual with a taste for the things of the East, who liked to surround himself with them, without excess.

If Armand Logreux d'Albury had not introduced himself as the "Master of the Seven Lights," the setting where he received the young Roma would not have been enough to suggest that he was one of the great scholars of the Occult. Even the weathervane shaped in the form of Solomon's Pentacle might only have been the fantasy of a chatelain that made an amusing find at some antique dealer's.

In the ornate chimney hearth, dry wood flamed and crackled. But more pedestrian heaters were also present.

Nieve understood at once that the real "home" of the Master of the Seven Lights was not this room, which in a sense remained banal. She knew she would have to go far in the confidence of Armand Logreux to accomplish the mission given to her by the Nyctalope. But she also remembered what the Master had just said: "You will take off your clothes and I will gaze upon your form." And so she waited.

After looking around, Nieve lowered her eyes toward the basket she had placed on the carpet in front of the man. It contained objects with very fine weaving in different colors of delicate taste and infinite variety, embroidered in designs inspired by geometry or simplest flowers and wild plants. There were glove boxes, tobacco pots, bowls of flower petals allowed to fade until their perfume had faded, and placemats fine and supple as silk, to slide beneath vases or glasses...

With her pretty hands with their almond nails, gilded delicately by henna, the young girl took up one after the other of these humble marvels, presenting them with skill to the gaze, soon amused, of Armand Logreux. Soon he had less attention for the mobile display than for the face, eyes and lips of the Romani girl. Above all her lips!

The lips of this young girl could be the symbolic image of voluptuousness. They were not just a static image; rather, they lived, sometimes grave, sometimes smiling, occasionally lightly ironic, revealing at moments fine clenched teeth of an imperceptibly pearly whiteness. Whatever their expression, they were made of such flesh, colored with such blood, alive with such sap, that they seemed to be modeled and animated precisely for kissing: for the kind of kiss that gives and takes, that breathes and penetrates, that all at once excites, overwhelms, exalts, exhausts...

And Armand Logreux d'Albury, Master of the Seven Lights, who had traveled around the world and known the kisses of hundreds of women, thought: *I have never seen lips like these. And her body, what a divine beauty her body must be!*

The chatelain of the Cross of Blood had been chaste for months, since the day he had met Basilie d'Hermont for the first time. He had returned that morning to spend the night outside Château-du-Loir, in a villa where a kind of "governess" kept two young women for him alone, discreetly. In the countryside, they passed for the nieces of this respectable lady, who referred to herself, according to the purest tradition, as the "widow of a superior officer."

After having met Basilie for the first time, Logreux had not returned to the villa. He even gave definitive leave to the lady and her "nieces," and now a couple of old servants kept up the little pleasure cottage, bought under a borrowed name shortly after his return from the Orient, empty but in good condition.

The voluntary chastity of this ardent man proceeded from a mysticism to which the ascetic men of India and Tibet sacrificed most of the pleasures of the flesh, if not all. To reach the goal he had been aiming for, since his meeting with Basilie, however, Logreux did not need to live as a monk. He did not refuse himself any of the other physical pleasures enjoyed by a rich man. A gourmet and connoisseur of fine wines, he ate with a rational sobriety that was at once a delicate sensuality. He did not deprive himself from smoking a cigar, a pipe or a cigarette, according to his mood. And he looked after the hygiene of his body with vigorous exercises that conserved his health and the supple qualities of youth.

Today, in just a few minutes, a profound revolution had taken place in this man, who had calculated his appetites as strictly as his fortune.

Nieve had entered his existence in a perfectly unexpected way, just as Basilie had. The man said to himself:

She will not leave again. For the pleasure of my days and nights, I will unite Nieve to Basilie, until they begin to grow old as I remain young. They are good only to raise the children I shall have with them. Then I will enter into the third stage of my life.

Such were the strange thoughts of Armand Logreux d'Albury, as he let drop from his hands the objects that Nieve handed him, and pushed the basket aside. In a calm and serious voice, he said:

"You will leave all this here, Nieve. And in exchange, you will give the chief of the tribe a sum of money that will enrich it for many generations. As for you, I will soon tell you my desire, but first, you must stand and remove all your clothes."

Before, when the Master had said: "You will take off your clothes and I will gaze upon your form, so that your beauty remains alive in my thoughts,." the young Romani girl had not expressed any astonishment. Nor did she show any now, when she heard the words that, this time, were not the expression of any desire for future satisfaction, but an order that required immediate agreement or refusal.

She did not stand. In a voice equally calm and serious, she said:

"My body is not of the type that one displays casually, without veils, in a profane place. A Master of the Seven Lights must have a secret sanctum, if he is not wandering on the paths of this world. Take me there and you will see me naked."

Was he expecting this reply? Or did it take him by surprise? Neither his eyes nor his face let any of his inner thoughts appear. Yet, he hesitated. Brief and contained as this hesitation was, Nieve discerned it. Her green eyes grew languid and her lips opened in such a way that, in it, Logreux saw a promise that increased his intimate trouble.

Hiding his agitation well, for nothing in this man showed itself openly, he replied:

"That is fair, Nieve. I would like you to know the sacred rites. We will observe them. Come!"

He held out his left hand. She gave him her right, which he clasped. Together, with one supple movement, they stood up. Guiding her at her own pace, they crossed the room. In the corridor lit by electric light, the Master raised successive flaps and opened a series of doors. Then, all at once, he stopped, as did Nieve at his side.

They were now in a room much longer than it was wide, gently illuminated by two electric ceiling lights and several torches with porcelain screens. At the left end, a tall hanging drapery concealed a door. At the right end, a bay window had replaced the entire wall. It was made of a single pane of glass that reflected every object in the room, but Nieve saw that it was not a mirror, because a curtain of corrugated iron masked it from the exterior. This metallic curtain could be raised and lowered by an electric mechanism fixed at arm's height on the large frame of glass. The glass itself was mobile, as one could see from the metal handles that glistened at the bottom of its crystalline mass.

The walls, of a slightly greenish white, were bare. There were no paintings, no bookshelves, no tapestries, only the door in the back, on the left. The floor was bare too, made of wood tinted like the walls, and absolutely clean. Three glass cases were stacked with various instruments, intended for what Nieve had not the slightest idea. There were seats, stools of wood tinted in pale green. In the corner, between the door and the largest of the windows, there was also an immense low couch on which many cushions had been tossed randomly. Stretching along the length of the floor was a magnificent black panther skin. The velvet and silk coverings of the couch and cushions were black as well.

At the bedside, a sort of marble chest held up drinking glasses and many large glass vessels, containing liquids of various colors. Above and along the length of the couch, the wall was covered by a broad band of purple silk on which, in gold and silver, there were embroidered images of the twelve constellations of the zodiac.

Finally—and this was the only thing that surprised the young girl—in the middle of the room, a massive wood pedestal held up a strange machine. All at once, Nieve could only look in its direction, and she wondered what it could be used for.

At first, she thought she had never seen anything like it. Then, as she contemplated the machine, she remembered a vision from her childhood. The caravan of her tribe had passed by the harbor of Villefranche, on the road that borders the sea. Great nautical festivals were prepared there in honor of the navy squadron that anchored in the harbor. On a large pontoon near the shore, sailors were setting up a sort of apparatus that Nieve later found out was a powerful projector, used to throw long, wide jets of moving light into space.

In this sanctum, belonging to M. Armand Logreux d'Albury, Master of the Seven Lights, the young girl recognized the projector of the harbor of Villefranche. It was the same sort of machine, standing on its enormous pedestal, directed toward the immense bay window, surrounded on all sides by mechanical devices, electric cables and wires.

The machine looked so monstrous, so forbidding, and so sinister that Nieve quickly turned her gaze away from it, after having first examined it with such interest.

She looked toward the sofa, where, to her surprise she saw the smiling Master sitting on the edge of the bed, amongst the cushions.

"Nieve," she heard, "I am waiting for you to show yourself to me in all your beauty."

A short silence. Then the same voice continued:

"Come. Approach. Stand naked on this panther skin, which will be soft under your feet."

She obeyed, and moved forward.

Before she reached the silky black skin, she removed her shoes and stockings. Her feet trampled the furry hide of the beast. But her flesh was not moved, for her mind remained in control.

With slow, almost ritual gestures, she began to undress.

It took a long time. In the Romani fashion, the young girl wore several skirts and layered petticoats. One by one, she unlaced them, and they fell softly around her legs. Before the last petticoat, she unfastened her bodice, letting it slide off with a supple movement of her shoulders. Soon, she had on only a very fine linen shirt, tied with a cord over her breasts. She undid the cord, and the shirt slid down to her knees. Then, raising her legs one after the over, she took a step forward. There she stopped, standing straight, arms folded and fingers on her shoulders, in an attitude as sculptural as it was simple. Her wide eyes, fixed on the face of the man, seemed empty of all thought.

The beauty of Nieve was perfect. The beauty of the young girl would, in its womanly form, take on a little more roundness in certain places, thought Logreux, but it would remain for a long time as it was now, if it did not deform in an ill-attended and ill-treated maternity. A slim and firm beauty, it would not be destroyed by the weight gains and relaxations of her many years to come.

For several minutes, the Master contemplated Nieve in admiring silence. He had sat down on the edge of the couch, his back almost straight, leaning against the piled-up cushions. Hands clenched his knees, his tension betrayed his excitement. But he made no other sign. His face with its serious eyes remained impassive.

Suddenly he said, in a slightly hoarse voice:

"Nieve, you are the most beautiful of all girls, and there will be no woman more beautiful than you..."

A silence. Nieve seemed not to have heard.

The male voice continued:

"Nieve, turn around and walk away. Then come back."

The statue grew animated. She uncrossed her arms, and her natural movements were like waves. She walked a dozen steps, turned, came back, and was still again, standing in front of her clothes on the panther skin, her arms hanging on her sides.

In a dull voice, the man commanded:

"Approach again."

A flash shone in the green eyes of the living goddess. And her lips opened slightly to utter:

"No."

The man frowned, contracted his jaws, tightened his lips and tightened his fingers even more on his knees.

"No!" repeated Nieve, after a brief silence. "If I were within your reach, you would touch me. I can only allow a man to touch me during the twelve days before the Purification. Do you not know the Law of Virgins who do not yet want to be mothers?"

"I know it," said the man with visible effort.

"Then you will obey it, as I do."

Then, in a voice surprisingly supplicating and firm at the same time, he said:

"Nieve, at this moment, I do not command, I beg. But remember that this is the first time in my life, and it will be the last. I beg, do you hear?"

"I am listening," said the girl, still impassive.

"Stay here for an hour. Live in this room as if you were alone, dreamily idle. Would you like to try some exquisite liquors? Here they are. Would you like to smoke? Here are Egyptian cigarettes, with tobacco that has been lightly dipped in opium. I will get up and move away from your body. I swear to you that I will not approach close enough to touch you, even once. Sit or lie down as you please. Just live and forget that I am here."

He stood up. From the bedside cabinet he drew out boxes of cigarettes, an electric lamp that he plugged in and several small fine towels that he placed on the table near the vessels and glasses.

He said:

"Are you hungry? I can have Hambad Sin bring fruit and jam, sweets..."

"No. I will neither drink nor eat. I will only smoke. I see there is a radio there: that is something I know about. Today is Sunday and the time is right. Let me listen to music... pure music, without a human voice... a big orchestra... or wild jazz..."

"Yes," he said. "Yes!"

Then Nieve stretched out halfway amidst the cushions, which she had arranged around her. The cigarettes and small electric lamp were within reach of her left hand. Immediately, she began to smoke. She was happy. She hoped she would soon have reason to be even more so. The temperature of the strange room remained constantly warm. Nieve was naked. And for the first time in her life, she knew the pride of dominating one of the most powerful of men by the virtue of her beauty and the calm force of her secret will alone.

Meanwhile, Logreux had turned various dials of the apparatus without hesitating. A large invisible orchestra billowed forth in a complex magnificence of sound waves.

"Beethoven," he said.

But the young girl's taste for music did not extend to musical erudition. Depending on the state of her soul, or the whim of her temper, a Caribbean song could delight her as much as the most sublime concerto. The Beethoven symphony that the radio was now broadcasting was a storm of fierce violence, with oases of sweetness and charm, caresses and dreamy repose. This suited Nieve perfectly for a few minutes.

When this charm was over and the voice of the speaker was heard, the girl said:

"Enough! Now, I would like some jazz—or songs from the islands... or a popular Spanish tune."

A fanatic of music, making intelligent use of the invention of radio, Armand Logreux d'Albury subscribed regularly to various publications that listed the programs for multiple radio channels.

Amused, for he was conscious he was obeying this girl as a pinnacle of beauty, and trembling with a powerful emotion that mocked his apparent smiling docility, the Master of the Seven Lights selected a pamphlet, flipped through it and after a few moments of research, said:

"Here!"

He changed the music to a well-known dance tune, with the voice of Raquel Meller and the clicking of castanets. [11]

Then Nieve slipped her feet onto the panther skin and stood up. Taking two steps forward to reach the smooth floor, she danced. Clapping her fingers, she followed the rhythm of the music with the whole of her wonderfully soft, light body. Her face was serious, her eyes were unfathomably deep and her slightly smiling red lips revealed the bright whiteness of her teeth.

Logreux gazed at her with admiration and desire. He had leaned against the door at the back, and before him, three paces distant, the disturbing Sibyl swayed, leaned, straightened up, turned, jumped, twirled lightly on her toes and raised her legs in a harmonious motion, that showed her splendid beauty in a thousand angles and a thousand fleeting attitudes.

When the music ceased, Nieves froze, straight, on her stretched legs, hands on her shoulders, breasts projecting their hard brown nipples, as if with voluptuousness.

Then, suddenly, the man came away from the door, moved forward and held out a hand. But a flashing glance and a brief word stopped him.

"No!"

And with a sigh:

"No!" Nieve repeated. "The rite is sacred. You will not touch me today."

Sure of her power, she lowered her arms and walked back to the couch. Her left shoulder, in passing, brushed against the trembling fingers of the man.

---

[11] Raquel Meller (1888-1962), a Spanish singer and actress. She was an international star in the 1920s and 1930s, appearing in several films and touring Europe and the Americas. A vaudeville performer, she sang the original versions of well known songs such as *La Violetera* and *El Relicario*.

She sat down, took a cigarette, lit it and smoked a little, dreamy.

Then Nieve glanced calmly around the room, until her gaze stopped at the mysterious machine that rose in the center. She laughed, the pretty pearly laugh of a young girl, as her eyes sparkled with curiosity.

"Look at this!" she said. "What is it?"

In this way she broke the charm.

Standing with a hand on his forehead, all at once Logreux jerked and stood up straight. In his normal voice, he answered:

"There are mysteries of which the Master speaks with an initiate only when the latter has given himself to him entirely, body and soul. You are not there yet, Nieve."

"It's true, I am not there yet," she said gravely.

Calmly. she stretched out and tossed aside the cigarette, which landed on the floor. Then she closed her eyes and made as if she wanted to sleep.

He took a stool and sat in front of her. Her posture suggested total abandonment, but he knew that to touch her was not a possibility.

Sinking into her gaze, her perfume, he revered his voluptuous beauty.

CHAPTER II
Conclusion

The first to return to the gypsy camp that Sunday were the Nyctalope and his two companions, Vitto and Soca.

Evening fell with a spreading plume of clouds. Andrès del Borjo finished tending to his mules, as Joachina and Luisa, assisted by Lilla and Pépito who brought them twigs of dry wood, prepared the evening meal. As soon as he saw "Capo Pedro," and his two assistants, Andrès hurried toward them.

"So?" he asked, looking at the Nyctalope.

"We have discovered something new," replied Saint-Clair. "But it isn't the time to talk about it yet. Has Nieve returned?"

"No," replied the chief of the tribe.

Hearing this, Saint-Clair's face showed a fleeting expression of simultaneous impatience and anxiety. He knew the sort of danger into which he had sent the beautiful and seductive young girl. Without speaking further, he walked toward the caravan that he occupied with Soca and Vitto, and dismissing his two men with a gesture, shut himself away.

Neither Vitto, nor Soca, nor Andrès, needed precise orders to understand that the main thing now was to wait for Nieve's return and report her arrival at once to the Nyctalope. So all three, silent as they usually were, walked back and forth over the two hundred meters of the path, with a quick step to battle the harsh cold of the late winter day.

They did nothing but wait for the one they sometimes called the "Sibyl." In regard to the mystery the Beech Grove, and consequently the Cross of Blood, they knew they did not have all the facts. Until then, they had been directed by Saint-Clair. Now, at the expression of his face when Andrès had answered "no," they realized that a grave possibility was present. This possibility was that Nieve would not return.

184

Minutes passed, minutes that seemed interminable. They came closer and closer to the branch of the road leading to the Cross of Blood. Tempted to take it, they consulted each other with their eyes, but the orders of the Nyctalope, given once and for all when they had arrived in the region, were clear: make no movement that could give away their presence to any visible or invisible observer. Except for Nieve with her basket of goods, no other member of the tribe would approach the castle with medieval towers at the bottom of the valley.

So the three men stopped short, the moment their steps were about to take the forbidden path. They couldn't help but remain there for a few minutes, in the course of which their impatience and anxiety increased. As all three were men of a rude and violent character, anger threatened to add itself to their anxiety.

A few more minutes passed. The cold of the evening, which grew darker and darker, reaching their relatively unprotected bodies, and they shuddered at almost at the same time. As they were taciturn beings, they kept silent. Consulting one another yet again with a glance, they made a half-turn on the spot and set off down the road. When they arrived back at the encampment, they heard Joachina cry out in a voice that echoed their own feelings:

"Where is Nieve?"

Andrès shrugged, and, without replying, he turned again with the same movement as Vitto and Soca. Once again, the three men went as far as the crossroad leading to the Cross of the Blood. Suddenly, together, they uttered a cry, which their habitual prudence had stifled. Bright against the shadow of the hollow road, a form moved forward in which they could clearly recognize the girl that they hoped to see again. They did not commit the indiscreet awkwardness of waiting for her. Quickly, with the same precipitate steps, they returned to the encampment. Knocking at the door of the Nyctalope caravan, Andrès said in a joyful tone:

"Capo! She is coming! Here she is!"

The door opened immediately. Skipping the wooden staircase, Saint-Clair jumped straight to the ground. Nieve had just emerged from the path leading to the Cross of the Blood. She advanced rapidly and lightly, swinging her basket at the end of her left arm. The four men immediately saw that it was empty. Andrès del Borjo said gaily:

"She has sold everything."

"Except herself," said Saint-Clair.

Separating from the three men, who remained discreetly on the spot, he went to meet the girl.

When they were face to face, almost touching, Nieve dropped the basket on the floor and offered both of her hands. Saint Clair took them, pressed them slightly, united them to one another, held them tightly, and stared into the eyes of the young girl.

"Will we be victorious?" he whispered.

"Yes!" she replied, with a somber ardor.

Saint-Clair seemed to hesitate. Nieve felt the hands of the Nyctalope contract over hers and perceived the slight alteration in his voice, when he asked:

"Without giving anything of yours?"

Nieves did not reply immediately. With a supple movement, she clasped the Nyctalope's fingers. Fixing on him an expression full of triumph and humility, she answered:

"Without giving anything of mine."

Why did the Nyctalope not dominate himself as he usually did? And why were there traces in the features of his face that expressed feelings the intuitive Nieve recognized as joy tinged with a kind of pride? This lasted only briefly, however. A flash, the duration of a glance. Then the male face expressed only an affectionate satisfaction, as from his mouth words flowed with natural ease. He did not try to disguise their banality:

"Very well, my dear. I'm proud of you. Come on, first you are going to have a nice dinner, then you will come in and tell me everything down to the last detail. All that you have seen, heard, said and done. I hope you won't omit anything and forget nothing."

Then, after a small burst of silvery laughter, she replied:

"Be patient! If I could be vain before you, I would say: you will be satisfied with me."

He made no reply. They walked side by side, with a quick step. He kept the girl's right hand in his left hand, and as they walked, they swung their hands to the united rhythm of their steps.

Saint-Clair never dined. At Beech Grove, he had sat down at the table of Comte d'Hermont, first out of affectionate courtesy toward his former companion in arms, then not to lose the opportunity of observing d'Hermont himself, his sister, his eldest daughter, and perhaps, most importantly, Basilie. At the encampment of Andrès del Borjo, he did not have the same motives for complying with a presence at the table, the ordinary rites of which he found tedious. So while the Bohemian family, as well as Soca and Vitto, took the evening meal in the dining room of the caravan, the Nyctalope remained in the other caravan, waiting for Nieve, smoking a pipe and meditating.

His wait did not last long. Hardly a quarter of an hour had passed when three knocks were heard at the door.

"Come in!" he said.

The door opened and was closed by Nieve, who remained motionless.

"Well?" said Saint Clair. "Already? This is not a reproach; quite the contrary."

The girl smiled, while answering:

"I was not hungry. I also drank and ate very good things at the the Cross of Blood. Monsieur Logreux took good care of me."

One of Nieve's feet touched a sort of large leather-covered ottoman next to the canvas chair in which the Nyctalope was seated. She dropped softly onto it, and, crossing her hands on one of Saint-Clair knees, she raised her head. She gave him a look brighter than the flames of the five candles on the small table. Then the Nyctalope, caressing the half-naked shoulder of the girl with one hand, said:

"Tell me everything."

In a voice that was sometimes quick, sometimes slow, expressing herself in the Catalan language which she spoke without apparent effort, along with perfect French, Castilian and Arabic, Nieve made a minute report of all she had heard, said and done during the two hours of the afternoon she had spent at the Cross of Blood. During the course of this narrative, she kept her eyes fixed on the Nyctalope's face, but Saint-Clair did not look at hers, keeping an absolute immobility. He smoked with small, slow, spaced-out puffs. His eyelids seemed closed. Nieve looked in vain for the expression of a thought or feeling on his impassive face; yet, she recognized to some extent the reactions provoked by the details of her story, in the slight tremors and brief contractions of his hand on her naked shoulder.

Not once was Nieve interrupted. Even after she was done, Saint-Clair remained silent. At last, she said with a shade of nervous irritation:

"I have finished!"

Then the Nyctalope, putting his pipe on the table, turned his head a little, looked at the girl with an expression of gravity and said:

"I have been listening. But I have no thoughts for now. Or at least, I will not tell you today the reflections I have made. Maybe tomorrow."

Their eyes mingled. On the man's lap, the girl's crossed hands were contracted and burning. The silence lasted a few minutes, before finally Nieve could not take it anymore:

"But when I return to the Cross of Blood, what shall I do?"

The fingers of Saint-Clair grasped her quivering shoulder abruptly, and in an almost brutal tone, he said:

"Will you return? I do not yet know. Perhaps it may indeed prove indispensable…"

All tense, and in a voice that vibrated with passion, she replied:

"You know I may be killed there?"

"What of it?" said Saint-Clair, raising his eyebrows. "You know what is at stake."

Then Nieve, dropping her head onto his knees, gave a brief sob and whispered:

"If I must, then let me kill myself before I..."

Saint-Clair made no reply, but stroked her head softly.

During the hour that passed, the man and the young girl scarcely moved. They did not look at each other, and did not say a word. With her eyes closed, Nieve seemed to be asleep. With his eyes wide open, the Nyctalope reflected. Even when he took his hand off the girl's shoulder to lift her up a little, he did not speak. His movement made Nieve understand at once, and she got up herself.

For a moment they stood face to face, their hands united.

"I shall have to go back?" asked the girl in a breath.

"Yes," said Saint-Clair, sadly. "But first, go back to our caravan and sleep. Tomorrow may be a terrible day for you—and for me. Tonight, I must leave. But I want to be sure you sleep well. I know that your will commands your body and brain; so you must obey me in that respect."

Nieve said:

"Do not worry about my rest, but do not forget what I have begged of you."

"How could I forget?" said Saint-Clair, with sudden violence.

Then, pushing the shoulders of the young girl, he said:

"Out you go!"

She obeyed. As she went out of the door, she heard him order:

"Send me Vitto and Soca right away."

Half an hour later, after a brief conversation with Andrès del Borjo, Saint-Clair and his two assistants took the great road in the icy darkness, which by a detour below Saint-Christophe led them to the park of Beech Grove. They did not make this journey side-by-side or close to one other, but spaced out at about fifty meters apart, Saint-Clair in the middle, Soca and Vitto serving as front and rear guard scouts.

Nothing was reported that might seem suspect. At this nocturnal hour and in this season, no encounter was likely. The three men, now together, crossed the park where its width was the smallest, and reached a small door in the castle, which led directly through a private corridor and staircase to the apartment-studio where, for the past two nights, Comte d'Hermont, his sister Laure Dauzet, and his eldest daughter Madeleine, had slept.

The Nyctalope had a key to that door. He left Vitto and Soca, who had well-defined jobs outside, to enter the corridor and go down the stairs.

He was the Nyctalope. There was no darkness for his eyes. No electric lamp could betray him. There was no need to touch switches to turn on lights. Without anything to reveal his presence, not even the slightest noise, for he had put rope slippers over thick woolen socks, Saint-Clair reached the little landing with the main door of the studio apartment, where according to his arrangement, Jacques d'Hermont, Laure and Madeleine were to sleep.

Anxious to make no noise, the Nyctalope opened the door with a *passe-partout* his friend had given him. But on the threshold, he stopped short, suddenly prey to the most acute anxiety. The studio's bedside lamp was lit, and, on the divan, illuminated by this lamp, Jacques d'Hermont was seated against a pile of cushions. His eyes were dilated; he was burning with fever; his body trembled and his teeth chattered.

Saint-Clair quickly controlled the emotions that came over him. He understood at once, and his decision therefore took only a moment. He closed the door, walked toward the divan and took the sick man's hands.

"Jacques! Jacques! Did it start again? Here!"

At first, d'Hermont was unable to answer. More than by a feverish attack of terrible violence, he was possessed by an infinite terror. Nevertheless, the Nyctalope's clasp of hands,

190

his gaze and voice, at once imperious and full of affection, soon calmed the unfortunate man enough so that he could stammer:

"Léo! My friend! Yes, it began again today, as soon as Laure, Madeleine and I entered this studio. Go and see them; I heard them moaning a little while ago. In the beginning, we wanted to get out of here, to go to another part of the castle, to rooms long abandoned, but we could not... We could not! You see, although the door is open, we were nailed to the spot. They are still in their beds, no doubt, and I am here. Are they dead, my God? Are they dead?"

Saint-Clair let go of his shoulders, on which his fingers had been clenched. He got up and ran into the adjacent room. Between columns and a sort of draping canopy was the huge bed that had had belonged to the Belgian painter, and on which now, both in bathrobes, Laure Dauzet and Madeleine d'Hermont were stretched out side by side. A bedside lamp was lit, screened by a shade of pale green silk, and in its light the two faces seemed inanimate.

It was very rare for Saint-Clair to swear, but now all his tumultuous feelings expressed themselves in a curse of anger. He leaned over the two bloodless faces, with their closed eyelids and tight lips. Although pale, a very slight shudder rippled through the temples, the cheeks, the lips and the drops of sweat at the roots of the hair.

"They are still alive," thought Saint-Clair. "But in what condition! And for how long? I did not foresee this... I did not bring anything."

He remained there, perplexed, anxious and furious, for a few seconds that weighed on him as much as hours. Finally, an idea came to his mind, a reaction took place in his being and he acted immediately. He had a great deal of energy, and the exhausted bodies of the young woman and girl did not weigh much. He clasped them both to him, one in each arm, and carried them away.

"Ah!" he cried, so excited that he expressed his thoughts out loud. "No matter if Basilie is innocent or guilty, conscious or bewitched, only beside her alone is salvation to be found! I may have been mistaken about many things; but I am sure, absolutely certain, that salvation lies near Basilie."

He left the apartment, crossing the studio. He did not wonder what Jacques might think of his double burden. He had only one desire, one goal. Rushing into the darkness of the staircase and corridors, which fortunately for him were as bright as in daylight, he reached the door of the apartment of Basilie d'Hermont.

If his instructions had been observed, Nurse Large would be awake in the little drawing-room next to Basilie's room. No more precautions! Saint-Clair kicked his foot violently against the door, and called:

"Nurse Large, Nurse Large!"

The next moment, the door was open. With a look, the intelligent Anna understood at once that this was one of the most dramatic acts in her existence. Saint-Clair said:

"Quick! Help me put these two women on the bed with Basilie, next to her, on her right and left. I want all three of them in the same space of a few square meters. We'll put Jacques d'Hermont there too. Quick, quick!"

Accustomed to caring for inanimate bodies, ones that, even in a waking state, could not move, the nurse made the skilful and strong movements that were necessary.

In under a minute, Laure and Madeleine were stretched out beside Basilie, who had suddenly awakened and was gaping with astonishment.

Saint-Clair said:

"Take care of them. Doses of ether, if necessary. Revive them. Let them move, talk, but not get out of bed. In two minutes, d'Hermont will be here."

He ran out. Two minutes later, he had Jacques d'Hermont sitting in an armchair, leaning against Basilie's bed.

Then, with no more attention for the three patients and Basilie, Saint-Clair questioned the nurse, who had just given them two quick doses of ether.

"What happened since I left?"

Calm, Anna Large replied:

"Nothing, really."

There was a silence during which the Nyctalope reflected, his head lowered, his hands thrust into the pockets of his overcoat. Finally, raising his head, he said:

"I see. So the bout of fever that seized Jacques, Laure and Madeleine up there was the first one since I left?"

"Yes," replied the nurse. "And I did not know of it. When I said goodnight to Monsieur d'Hermont, Madame Dauzet and Mademoiselle Madeleine about three hours ago, they were all quiet and smiling."

"What about Basilie?" said Saint-Clair, as if forgetting that the girl was there, looking at him and listening.

"Mademoiselle Basilie is also getting better," the nurse replied after an imperceptible smile. "However, she is not yet completely cured of the fever that seized her the day before your departure."

Saint-Clair, turning to Basilie, said quickly:

"Yes, the same fever that seized her when she went to spend the night in the apartment of her aunt and sister."

He stepped forward, took his his trembling hands from his pockets and stretched them toward the young girl, who had just sat up against the pillow and was buttoning her pajamas over her throat.

The gesture of the Nyctalope pleaded and threatened at the same time, as he asked in a harsh voice:

"Basilie, what do you know? What do you really know? How could you have lived for months, so joyfully alive, as you witnessed the martyrdom and slow death of your father, aunt and sister? And that of your mother, who was killed? Basilie, I beg of you, answer me, or do I have to make you do so? No, don't close your eyes! Look at me!"

The eyelids with their long eyelashes drooped. Then they rose again, and once again, he saw her eyes, so clear, so blue and so deep that one always wondered whether there was a thought behind them, or if they contained nothing but a happy basic instinct to live. But at that moment, those eyes, while losing nothing of their innocence, expressed an infinite anguish, while her trembling lips murmured something that Saint-Clair and Anna Large could barely make out:

"I don't understand, my God! Why do you look at me like that? Why do you say such words to me?"

Suddenly, clutching her hands to her face, Basilie began to cry.

This had the immediate effect of calming the Nyctalope. For he saw that Basilie was not crying like a guilty woman or a terrified girl, but like a desperate little child, who really did not understand. She did not understand the death of her mother, the illness of her father, aunt and sister, her own immunity until today, her recent bout of fever, the anger of the Nyctalope. He said to himself:

"Is it possible that her understanding should become conscious only at this moment? How is it that she did not understand or seemed not to understand in the past? My God! When I told her to look at me, she hid her face in her hands. Parents know that, even among little girls, especially among them, there are some great actresses..."

He had moved a few steps from the bed. On his right, Nurse Large also watched Basilie. For several minutes there was no other sound in the room but that of her convulsive sobs and groans. Laure and Madeleine remained motionless, although thanks to the dose of ether, they were visibly revived. As for Jacques d'Hermont, stiff in the armchair, hands clenched under his arms, he looked from Saint-Clair to Basilie with eyes so extraordinarily dilated that he seemed crazy.

Suddenly, Saint-Clair seized Nurse Large's arm, and drew her to the farthest corner of the room. In a low voice, but with extreme vigor, he spoke to her:

"Anna, listen to me. I must speak. I must express my thoughts in words to make them clearer before my judgment. I have told you everything, so you understand what is going on here. According to my theory, based on verifiable ideas, only those living from sunset to sunrise in the library, the Comte's study and the apartment occupied by Madame Dauzet and Madeleine, became ill. The soundness of my theory has been demonstrated by the fact that Basilie was attacked the day she spent hours in the apartment of Laure and Madeleine. Also, the Comte, Laure and Madeleine did not have an attack of fever on the nights when they moved in to the studio apartment. Finally, although I was attacked the third night of my stay here, I was unharmed on the fourth night because I stayed in that same studio. Soca and Vitto were attacked because I put them in my room. Conclusion: Well! Come on, Anna, say it yourself!"

Nurse Large responded at once:

"This is obvious: whatever place the evil comes from, by whatever process it is created, the man or woman who directs it knows the movements of the people who are here. In your case, he knew forty-eight hours after your arrival the room you occupied. As for the Comte, his sister and his eldest daughter, the criminal was not warned until forty-eight hours after their nocturnal relocation to the studio apartment. And he or she was also not warned when Basilie remained, according to your arrangements, in the rooms where the same evil took place."

"So," said Saint-Clair, seizing the nurse's wrists and pressing them, "Basilie is not guilty!"

Nurse Large had a moment of hesitation. Finally, in a dubious tone, she said:

"Directly guilty? No, no doubt. But as an indicator..."

"Come," said Saint-Clair, impatiently, "use your reason better. She cannot have been an indicator for three days, since you have been watching her and she has not left her room. How are we to explain that Jacques, Laure and Madeleine were attacked in the studio tonight?"

A silence.

Nurse Large said softly:

"Let's say she is innocent. Then why is she alone immune? And who is the snitch, if we assume that the criminal is not at Beech Grove?"

"There," said Saint-Clair, obviously satisfied, "that is a well-framed question. I am now absolutely certain that the criminal is not at Beech Grove. But I also believe that the snitch is someone here, for it would be impossible otherwise to know of the changes that were made in the sleeping arrangements if one does not live in the castle. Another related but important question is: when and how does the snitch communicate with the Cross of Blood?"

At this name, Nurse Large started.

"The Cross of Blood?" she said.

"Yes. I sent a friend there, and she spent the afternoon with Armand Logreux d'Albury. First, in a small room, then in his sanctum, where she noticed something unusual—an instrument that looked abnormal and sinister, but which is quite meaningful to me. She has given me only a brief description of it, for she herself did not understand it, but I recognized it..."

Another silence. Finally, he said:

"First, it is necessary to know how Armand Logreux d'Albury was made aware of the movements of people at Beech Grove. It is child's play to figure it out knowing that the shoes with the cracked sole were hidden in a corner of La Migeonne. Then, everything becomes immediately clear, even the more astonishing events, such as that incomprehensible scene of ecstasy and pain on the lawn, with the luminous nimbus..."

"Excellent!" said Anna Large.

"My God, all of this is exciting," exclaimed the Nyctalope, with intense pleasure. "But first, we must reassure this poor weeping child, who is herself dreadfully part of the mystery! What role did she play without knowing what the consequences would be? Or does she really know nothing and understand nothing? Let's see, Anna, what was Basilie's attitude during those last few days when you had her under your immediate care?"

The nurse replied with precision:

"By your instructions, and with the help of Doctor Luvier, after her extraordinary attack of fever, Basilie was kept in a state of physical and mental weakness, which, without endangering her health, made her my prisoner in this apartment. She spoke very little, and only about the small necessities that presented themselves. I tried not to share confidences, as this would have been premature of me, but I did watch her reaction to some pointed comments I made. But I saw in her only a kind of childish incomprehension. And yet, Monsieur, the truth is that, in spite of everything, I cannot help but feel a certain uneasiness around her."

As she went silent, Saint-Clair insisted:

"Why?"

"Because of her eyes. I found them sometimes fixed on my face, on my own eyes. Oh! It was only a flash. But once, using mirrors, I was able to look at them for a good minute."

"Yes? What did you find?"

"They are too clear, too deep, too unfathomable. Ah! They are not childish, I assure you. And I said to myself: Is it possible that there is nothing behind this void, this frightening, inhuman void?"

She was silent again. Saint-Clair frowned. He meditated for a couple of minutes, and then shrugged his shoulders:

"Bah! We will see! The essential thing is that, unless I am wrong, I shall soon have before me, in my eyes, and between those two hands"—he waved his hands clenched like talons, almost touching the pale face of the nurse—"yes, I will have the criminal. Woe to him if, at that moment, Nieve is not alive and intact! Come, I will try to calm Basilie."

With a quick step he walked to the bed. The girl was no longer sobbing. She was thrown back on the cushions, offering her whole admirable neck, her head inclined a little to one side. Her arm and hands rested softly on the sheets. Tears slowly fell from her half-closed eyelids and shone brightly on her cheeks. The Nyctalope bent down, took the two long pale hands, carried them one after the other to his lips and kissed them gently.

Then he said in the caressing, enveloping, penetrating voice he used when he wanted to speak in a certain way to a woman:

"Basilie, my girl, do not be afraid. All this will end. And it will end well. Your father, your aunt, your sister will recover. You yourself will no longer feel the fever from which you are still suffering. I can see that you do not understand me, and for this very reason, I am beginning to make sense of things. Basilie, come my dear, open your eyes, look at me, look at me with confidence, with friendship..."

Without her pretty head moving, her eyes opened and fixed on the Nyctalope a dreadful look he could not bear.

In her eyes, Saint-Clair had now perceived the truth. The supreme decision, the definitive thought, sprang into into his mind, and he did not hesitate a moment.

"Basilie," he said, "be happy! You will be saved today. All of you, especially you, who would have run a danger worse than death!"

Turning around, he walked back through the castle with quick steps to rejoin Vitto and Soca outside.

"Go straight to La Migeonne," he commanded them. "You know what you must do."

They set off immediately through the park, lighting their way through the night with a small electric lamp.

As for Saint-Clair, he set off at a run, for a quarter of an hour through the country.

Once at the encampment, he immediately woke Andrès del Borgo and Nieve.

"You," he said to the girl, "dress quickly and be ready to follow me. We are going to the Cross of Blood. You, Andrès, keep watch here in case I send little Pépito, whom we will take with us, back to you with more instructions. Quick, help him get dressed!"

The whole camp was in a state of excitement. Saint-Clair went to his caravan, opened a small suitcase in a wardrobe, and took out a box, the lid of which opened with a spring.

From this case he chose a ring with an agate stone set in gold. Under the light of an electric torch, he examined it and several times operated the mechanism it contained.

Satisfied, he opened a drawer and was about to grab a high-caliber Browning, when, withdrawing his hand, he growled:

"No! No weapons! What Nieve has will be enough, I hope. If I am mistaken, then as usual my salvation will come from my brain and bare hands."

He was still wearing the overcoat he had brought from Beech Grove, and that he had left unbuttoned. He now buttoned it back up, and with the ring clenched in his left fist, he left the caravan. Nieve and Pépito were ready and waiting, the girl and the child protected from the cold by long hooded capes.

"Let's go," he said.

Clouds filled the whole sky, and the night was dark. For the Nyctalope, it did not matter. But Nieve and Pépito could only keep up with his pace by holding his hands.

It took only a few minutes to reach the steps of the Cross of Blood. No dog barked or showed itself. The master of the house did not believe he needed any dogs to protect himself.

During the journey, the Nyctalope had spoken to Nieve, who listened attentively, but did not say a word.

At the top of the steps, after handling the door knocker several times, Nieve waited a good five minutes. Finally the heavy gate opened, and, after a few words exchanged between her and Hambad Sin, the gate closed behind Nieve.

"If all goes well," thought the Nyctalope, "I will only have to wait ten minutes."

All did go well, for according to the luminous dial of his wrist-watch, he counted only seven minutes before the portal was reopened.

"Come, Pépito."

Nieve welcomed them into the hallway.

"All is well," she said with a splendid smile. "He has not touched me, even with his fingertips."

Exultant, Saint-Clair allowed himself to be guided by the girl who walked before him. He neglected Hambad Sin, who seemed to be sleeping in an armchair on the landing.

They found Armand Logreux d'Albury stretched out on the black couch of the sanctum, where the projector of evil rays was pointed over the great open bay in the direction of Beech Grove.

The Nyctalope looked at Logreux and murmured:

"His mind will be able to live a few more years, but his body is now paralyzed forever. Hambad Sin will look after him. You only pricked him once, Nieve?"

"Yes."

"And Logreux, five times?"

"Yes."

"All is well then."

He went straight to the projector, studied the machine, then quickly began to dismantle it.

"I was right!" he said, nodding his head. "Just as some radiologists are victims of X-rays, so were the occupants of Beech Grove, except for Basilie, victims of these undiscovered rays. For for centuries, the priests of the Aggartha in Tibet have used a complex set of crystals and mirrors to protect their sacred city from western explorers. This defense has always been victorious, as no expedition has yet reached the true summit of Mount Everest."

Leaving aside this machine, which he planned to turn over to Government, so it would be stored in a safe place, the Nyctalope turned towards the divan. At this very moment, Armand Logreux d'Albury opened his eyes; but only his gaze could speak, as all the muscles of his body, including the vocal cords, had been paralyzed by the poison contained in the agate ring, which had slipped out five drops when Nieve had applied her ringed finger to the man's virile neck as he had grasped her in a violent embrace.

Saint-Clair spoke, for although Logreux was silent, he was not deaf:

"You coveted Basilie and the estate of the d'Hermonts. And you realized that you could only have her, and it, by creating a void of death around her. You enlisted the help of some low-minded accomplices. I will find out just how they acted, but I already know who they are: Hector Gasse and his wife. You are defeated, Logreux. I will give orders for your physical life to be sustained, but your mind will be forever trapped in a paralyzed body! Pépito, go run and tell your father to come with Luisa."

And turning to Nieve, he added:

"Without any more delay, I must see Soca and Vitto. Meanwhile, help me disassemble the essential elements of this machine. We will wrap them into packages, which we shall take away when we leave this house and never return."

The work was done when Soca and Vitto showed up. The former did not wait to be questioned. He said:

"It was very simple. Every day, Anna Gasse went to Beech Grove to bring eggs, milk and cheese. She remained an hour or two in the kitchen, and chatted with all the servants, including her daughter, Jeannette. Without thinking of evil, without suspecting that they were informing the enemy, all spoke in such a way that Anna could then inform Logreux of the smallest permanent or temporary changes in the existence of the residents of Beech Grove."

"Yes," said Saint-Clair. "That is how Logreux knew about the changes in sleeping quarters I made recently."

Then Nieve, with a new audacity and extraordinarily intimate tone, said:

"What about Basilie's role?"

"Logreux was a master of what we sometimes call 'astral projection' in the West. Having met Basilie and placed her under his magnetic influence, he could then, with much concentration and for brief periods of time, literally see though her eyes."

"There remains only one thing to explain: the voluptuous and mortal ecstasy on the pedestal of the statue, and the luminous nimbus."

"I knew that from the first day!" said Saint-Clair. "Remote suggestion for ecstasy of pain; projection of a powerful portable electric torch for the luminous nimbus."

And he concluded, smiling, with that gentle skepticism that he sometimes showed:

"Jacques d'Hermont will never believe me when, to explain and sum up everything, I tell him: magnetic waves and the power of suggestion. But that's just it! Armand Logreux d'Albury was a great physician doubled with a brilliant physicist who found a way to combine occult sciences of the Orient with the immense progress accomplished in the West in modern optics. The mirrors of his projector were a thousand times more active and more precise than the simple crystal lenses the secret priests of Mount Everest."

Four days later, Basilie was no longer the only one to laugh, sing and love life at Beech Grove. Her father, aunt and elder sister were just as eager to enjoy the happiness of their health.

The Nyctalope remained with them for only one more day, but he will never be forgotten in that small corner of Touraine.

Emmanuel Gorlier: *The Tower of Babel*

CHAPTER I
The Mysterious Hindu

On this beautiful evening, September 10, 1931, the travelers who were leaving the Gare de Lyon poured onto the
sidewalks. Some of them headed for the taxis, others stormed
the bus, a few went on foot, loaded with baggage to one extent
or another. Among the latter were two workers dressed in their
overalls, caps glued to their heads. They walked briskly toward Boulevard Diderot, probably meaning to reach the banks
of the Seine. An attentive observer could have noticed that
they were keeping up with an old man twenty yards in front of
them. This man, slightly bent over, was wearing a big turban
and was obviously a Hindu. With a serious expression on his
face, he looked straight in front of him and apparently paid no
attention to what was happening in the street.

The two men were already far from the station. One of
them, a tall blonde with green eyes, said to his companion:

"Say, Jacques, he walks pretty fast for an old guy."

Jacques, a wiry little fellow with brown hair, smiled
back:

"Don't exaggerate! He's got to be younger than he looks.
I wonder where he's leading us."

"Yeah. Ever since we've been on his tail, he's been
keeping up a good pace," the guy named Stéphane, observed.

The two men belonged to the CID—Committee for Information and Defense—an organization created a few years
earlier by the Nyctalope to defend the interests of France and
its European allies. Its mission was mainly to gather information in order to keep the territory safe. Only the highest of

French and European ministers knew of its guarded existence. The CID worked in collaboration with the Prime Minister and was often called in to intervene in the most secretive and sensitive affairs.

One important branch of the Committee was based in Lyon where it had both headquarters and large-scale means at its disposal. The mysterious man in the turban whom the two agents were trailing had been spotted spying on its facilities several times. Therefore, it was decided to put him under surveillance. He had been followed all over Lyon for a few days without anything in particular to be reported. Then the Hindu had left Lyon unexpectedly and taken the train to Paris. The two men had got on the train with him. When he got off, they continued shadowing him, hoping that he would lead them to his accomplices or put them on the trail of some interesting clue.

They quickly crossed the bridge over the Seine and came to the vicinity of the Gare d'Austerlitz. They were less than ten yards behind the Hindu, in a relatively clear space, exposed and highly likely to be noticed. They looked at each other and made a silent agreement to slow down and get a little more distance between them and the turban.

They continued on, more slowly, across Place Valhubert and found themselves in front of the gates of the Jardin des Plantes. The Natural History Museum on the left inside the park was closed for repairs and surrounded by a wooden fence that prevented access to the work site. The man in the turban headed for the gates, took out a key, unlocked the chains and entered the park. The two agents sped up so they could watch whatever the mysterious Hindu was doing on the other side of the gates. He took a side path and went up to the doors of the museum after slipping through the fence. He took out another key and entered the building. When he closed the heavy glass door, he disappeared from their view, especially since he did not turn on the light in the museum lobby.

"That's surprising," Jacques said. "How did he come up with the keys to a public building?"

"We're going to find out," Stéphane answered. "Get ready!" He slipped his hand into his pocket and brought out a pair of small bolt cutters. "I'm going to cut the chains."

"Be careful, there's a policeman coming this way," Jacques warned him.

With his cape flapping on his back and his baton hanging from his belt a bicycle-riding police agent was cruising along the railings of the Jardin des Plantes. The policeman glanced at the two "workers," then went on his way without paying them any particular attention. Maybe he was wondering what they were doing in the neighborhood that was pretty deserted at this hour? But after all, there was nothing wrong with being in the street at night.

When he was gone, the two men went to work. They quickly got the chains off, went down the sandy path and reached the door of the Museum. Jacques went up first and got a surprised look on his face. He had reached out to grab the handle but his arm was stopped by an invisible force that seemed to be emanating from the inside. His hand remained flat in front of him, as if hanging in mid-air.

"Look! That's weird! Look at my hand!"

Stéphane came up next to him and he too reached out his hand, which was also mysteriously blocked by an invisible object. Stéphane pushed harder, spreading apart his fingers. For an instant the air gave way under the pressure but a strong gust threw his arm back once again.

"Well, there's something blocking it, like a kind of force field that we can't get through. I'll try to push harder. This is just impossible to…"

He did not have time to finish his sentence. All of a sudden, he and his partner were hit by a cloud of little, extremely bright explosions that turned them almost instantly into living torches, consuming them and crumbling them. All their cells imploded and in a matter of seconds they were completely pulverized by the mysterious force.

A minute later, all trace of the phenomenon had disappeared and the night returned to its usual calm…

CHAPTER II
The Tower of Babel

The next afternoon, in the big, sunny office of the Blingy mansion near Versailles, Léo Saint Clair was reading *Le Matin*, his favorite newspaper. He was talking to himself, commenting out loud on the news.

"This Pierre Laval seems a little lazy as Prime Minister. Well, at least, we haven't been affected so far by the financial crisis that's hitting our allies… Hold on, that's weird… A severed hand and forearm were found near the Jardin des Plantes! The locals heard explosions…"

His face, looking very concentrated, stiffened a little and his brow furrowed above his remarkable eyes. Nobody had eyes like this man whom the press had given the nickname of the *Nyctalope*. Huge and golden brown, with dilated pupils, his eyes were like those of a nocturnal animal. It was before the Great War that he had become famous by being the first European permitted to visit the most secret places in Tibet and it was then that he had gotten his nickname. It was well deserved because of the strange power allowing him to see in the dark as well as in the light of day. This particularity, which had been very useful over the course of his many adventures, fascinated the public and for almost thirty years, the Nyctalope was the talk of the town.

"This matter has to be cleared up. There's something very odd about this story," he muttered.

Two pages in was a long, popular science article doubting the existence of canals on Mars. Old memories came back to Saint-Clair. Before 1914, he had had the opportunity to go the red planet. He fought, loved, suffered and set up a French colony… Like every time he recalled this period of his life he tried to remember how the expedition had ended, but in vain. Something terrible must have happened because his mind stubbornly refused to remember. After focusing on recalling the events that might have happened there to no avail, he shook his head and went back to reading.

A few minutes later, someone knocked quietly at his door.

"Come in!" the Nyctalope said.

A big man, dressed in a black servant's outfit, entered. It was Bertrand, his butler.

"Monsieur, Monsieur Michel Dorlange is asking to see you," he said respectfully.

"Show him in, please," Saint-Clair answered.

A tall, well built man with blue eyes full of candor and energy, walked up to him, holding out his hand:

"Bonjour, Monsieur Saint-Clair."

Saint-Clair nodded, glanced at his watch and said:

"Bonjour. Four o'clock on the dot. You're exactly on time, as usual, good old Michel. Come, sit down."

After making sure that the door was firmly closed Saint-Clair went to the bookcase and pressed a button hidden under a shelf. One of the wall panels on the left slid open and revealed a big combination safe containing the files of the CID, of which the Nyctalope was now the president. Michel Dorlange, his visitor, was the Secretary General of the organization and Saint-Clair's chief collaborator. They met regularly to go over their cases and make any necessary decisions. The meeting today had been organized weeks ago.

The Nyctalope grabbed a few documents, dropped them on the desk and began:

"OK. The agenda today is a little busy. Let's first deal with the priorities. Where do we stand with the final French members of the Cult of the Blood Worshippers?"

"As agreed in our last meeting, I sent a few agents to check if the pact you made with Princess Alou T'Hô has been honored by her adepts. I can assure you that, since coming back from China, they have done nothing on French territory."

"Great! So, she's kept her word. I'm relieved. I would've hated to start another conflict with her. And the affair ended in a treaty. And how about the other important operation concerning the Radion?"

"The engineer Yves Le Moal has informed us that he found the missing element. He resumed the experiment that was interrupted by Gorillard and he's succeeded in perfecting the Radion. The final tests to make the invention completely operational are being carried out."

"Very well. This vehicle, with its seven different ways of locomotion, will give us a serious advantage if enemies come to attack us. I guess you don't have only good news for me?"

"On the crucial files, yes. But in other matters, some very disturbing events have happened in the last few weeks. Some of our agents, on completely unrelated missions, have disappeared without a trace. At first, we figured they were just coincidences. But six in three weeks is a little much and we might be dealing with a sneaky, organized attack."

"Do you suspect anybody in particular?"

"Nobody. The men disappeared. Like they just vanished in thin air and the missions they were on have nothing in common. Some of them were simply routine."

"This sounds very serious indeed. We have to put the entire CID on maximum alert immediately. Our agents have to be at the ready and tell us right away about any suspicious incident... Contact all the offices and get them to beef up security. Double up the teams so our men won't be isolated. We have to be able to face any possibility. I'll alert my contacts in the Ministry of the Interior and Defense so they can send us reinforcements. Vanished, you say? That reminds me of something... Monsieur Dorlange, you'll have to investigate this story of the severed limbs found at the Jardin des Plantes. There might be a connection with the matter at hand, but in any case it's a curious event that deserves to be cleared up."

"Right away, Monsieur Saint-Clair, I'll open a file and take the necessary measures."

"Great! Let's look at the missions of our agents in the various European capitals. Let's begin with Berlin. The political situation there is getting more and more tense..."

The two men started studying the different files in progress and their meeting ended around 7:30 p.m. When they had gone through the agenda, Dorlange got up to leave.

The Nyctalope smiled at him, "You won't stay for dinner tonight? We had the pleasure of inviting my old friend Hubert de Pibriac."

"Unfortunately, I can't. I have to meet my wife at the Opera."

"That's really too bad. And how are things going with dear Erin? By marrying you, one of the best CID agents was taken away from us," the Nyctalope smiled again.

"You're exaggerating a little, Léo," Dorlange smiled back. "She's only cut back a little on her work. Anyway, I'll warn her, too, about the disappearances so she'll be on the alert."

"Obviously. No matter what, don't forget to do it! Besides, we'll certainly find another time soon to have dinner together."

The Nyctalope stood up and Michel Dorlange to the door. His collaborator was at the bottom of the front steps when Saint-Clair saw three men at the gate, heading toward the mansion. When they passed Dorlange, they gave him a polite greeting.

One of them, a real athlete, a force of nature, was Saint-Clair's friend, Comte Hubert de Pibriac, nicknamed Herkulos, the old sportsman of world-renowned talent. It was with him that the Nyctalope had conquered Mount Everest. The other visitors, two young men in their 20s, with brown hair and blue eyes, looked strangely alike and were clearly twin brothers. Although he had never seen them before, Saint-Clair figured they were Pir and Bob O'Connell, whom he had invited to dinner at Hubert's request.

When they were at the foot of the steps, Saint-Clair greeted them cordially.

Hubert de Pibriac came next to his friend and pointed at the two young men. "Hello, Léo. I hope you're well. Let me introduce Pir and Bob O'Connell. As I've told you before they'll be taking part in my next expedition."

"Welcome all of you! Come in, come in! We'll be more comfortable talking in the salon."

Saint-Clair and his guests crossed the entrance hall and entered a big room, brightly lit by two Art Deco iron lamps.

They were comfortably seated in oversized armchairs around a low table on which Bertrand had set cases of cigarettes, cigars and pipe tobacco. Bottles of various alcohol and fruit juice stood next to tobacco. The Nyctalope invited his guests to serve themselves, taking a cigarette and saying:

"We'll eat in half an hour. My wife Sylvie and my son Pierre will be joining us. We're still waiting for your friend Professor Nicolas Noque who should be here soon. But Hubert, in the meantime, maybe you could tell me something about this famous expedition?"

Comte de Pibriac was just about to begin when Sylvie and Pierre walked into the room.

As always, Sylvie made a strong impression on the people present. She was, without a doubt, exceptionally beautiful. Slender, blonde, with green eyes, she exuded a strong charisma. After years of marriage, Saint-Clair could still not look at her without being deeply moved. He jumped up and offered her a seat. Meanwhile, Pierre, a hearty, eighteen-year old young man, said hello to his father's guests and sat next to Pir and Bob, who were almost the same age.

When everyone was settled in, Hubert started talking again:

"As you know, after the discovery of the strange wall inscriptions in that lost Aztec pyramid in Mexico, I've made several expeditions there. I've carefully recopied the texts, written in an unknown language, completely different from those identified and used by the pre-Columbian civilizations. In vain I followed some clues that always led to dead ends. So, I came back to France to study the documents with respected linguists in order to draw parallels, if need be, that might direct my search. You have to understand that it was fruitless at first. Until one day, by chance, I got in touch with a specialist in Semitic languages who confirmed that the document could have been written in a language that was a very ancient form of Hebrew and that almost nobody today was able to decipher. I admit that I couldn't imagine what kind of text could be written in a language from the Middle East and found in the heart of an Aztec pyramid. But the specialist had said 'almost' and I was intrigued. Therefore, I asked him about who exactly could decipher the writing and he gave me only one name: Professor Nicolas Noque, the leading authority in France and maybe in the world in this matter.

"It was a pleasant surprise when the professor readily granted me a meeting in his office at La Sorbonne. I remember that first meeting like it was yesterday. I was a little taken aback at his age: thirty-five at most and he seemed too young to have such an eminent reputation. Tall and athletic, dark eyes, both warm and penetrating at the same time. He was friendly and after the normal courtesies he spent a long time scrutinizing the papers on which I'd recopied the signs from the bas-relief.

"He looked surprised as well but he stayed calm and professional. He got up without saying a word, went to a bookshelf and took down two fat files full of yellow sheets. He sat back down at his desk, opened a folder and leafed through the pages, stopping at a document covered with small, fine writing in an ancient hand. Then he asked me:

" 'Where did you say you found this text?'

" 'In an Aztec pyramid, hidden down in Baja California,' I answered. 'No one knew of the existence of these important remains in a region that was sparsely inhabited, mountainous and quite unwelcoming. I should also tell you that I have Aztec ancestors. I learned about them a few years ago when I had a falling out with the descendants of an ancient, pre-Columbian tribe that has a small community today. They saw me as the heir of the royal Aztec crown. Obviously it was flattering but far from getting crowned, I was almost sacrificed to their gods because it was the only way for them to bring back the ancient regime. Thanks to a fortunate series of events I managed to escape this gruesome fate but with knowledge of my origins I decided to redirect my research from Africa to the mysteries of the Mesoamerican past.

" 'Thanks to my lineage I was able to make different contacts in the region and through them I discovered this hitherto unknown site. The pyramid was thought to contain the mummy of a high priest of a secret cult dedicated to Quetzalcoatl, the plumed serpent god whose return was awaited by the Aztecs. I made a meticulous search of the monument but I found no trace of the mummy. Some of my companions lost their lives during the expedition because the tomb was booby-trapped and had a number of lethal traps to protect it. The only real discovery we made was this bas-relief surrounded by numbers and some metallic objects that were badly deteriorated by time. We don't really know what the objects were used for, but I'm tempted to think of them as some kind of technological artifact, understood, of course, in a relative historical sense because given their state they must have been very old when the Aztec civilization emerged.'

" 'And how far back would you date these objects?' the professor asked me.

" 'They must go back thousands of years, which is obviously impossible.'

" 'The translation of the bas-relief likewise presents an impossible interpretation...'

" 'What do you mean?' I asked Professor Noque.

" 'I'll need more time to decipher the text in detail,' he said, 'but I can tell you that it is a pre-Semitic language considered by many experts as dating back to before the Flood. Moreover, the word you see here means *Tower* and this one means *Babel*...'

" 'The Tower of Babel on a Mexican bas-relief!'

" 'Indeed!'"

At this moment, in the Nyctalope's salon, the almost religious silence around Hubert de Pibriac's story was interrupted by Professor Noque's arrival. Wearing an old frock coat like university professors often do, he looked around the room with a big smile on his face. Even though Hubert had told them how young he was, which clashed with his old-fashioned clothes, everyone was surprised.

Pibriac stood up to shake his hand and introduce him. Everyone sat back down and the explorer turned to Nicolas Noque, "I think the professor can relate what he discovered in translating the text."

"Gladly, if you'd like, Madame and Messieurs."

They all nodded.

"To sum up the situation," the professor began, "the text that your friend Pibriac brought me was written in a language that is the oldest known form of Hebrew and it tells a very strange story. According to what it says, at a time that is already very remote from when it was written, a powerful civilization had evolved. The author marveled at the tremendous knowledge that it had and the incredible inventions that the men of that time had perfected. This knowledge seemed to have been given to them by men coming from a distant continent who traveled through the air in chariots of fire. The strangers called themselves *Watchers* and indeed seemed to be always on guard, scared of the arrival of far-off enemies who were hunting them. Their supreme chief answered to the name of Shemehaza and his right-hand man was Azazel. They wanted to form a strong alliance, protected by fortresses built in the four corners of the earth, to be ready to fight against the enemies who were coming for them from this distant continent. After a period of prosperity, war broke out between the Watchers and their enemies. The conflict ended in a cataclysm that destroyed both peoples.

"The story in general as well as the names of the protagonists instantly reminded me, being a specialist in the Semitic tradition, of a passage in Genesis that described the fall of the rebel angels before the Flood. The details, moreover, seemed to agree with events recounted in an apocryphal text: the *Book of Enoch*, which has a long narration of the myth. According to its authors, angels were seduced by women on earth and left

213

their celestial home to live on our planet, bringing to men extensive knowledge in all sciences. The children they produced were the legendary giants who lived on this world before the Flood. Having deeply disturbed Creation by mixing the spiritual with the material, they had caused serious damage that could lead to the extinction of the human race. God, therefore, decided to act and drown them in the Flood, with men surviving thanks to Noah. The Watchers, who could not die, were imprisoned in the depths of a desolate plain, in the heart of a hell on fire.

"The bas-relief tells the general story of this legend, in its way, with one exception. The most spectacular invention of this civilization had been a gigantic tower known as the *Tower of Babel*, although all the ancient texts say it was built *after* the Flood. Nevertheless, finding this story in this place is quite astonishing."

Hubert de Pibriac went on from here:

"Even more so since the text gives the location of this tower starting from a reference point that had not yet been defined, unfortunately. At first I thought it might be the pyramid itself but the directions led us to a point that, after checking it over and over, would put us in the middle of the Pacific Ocean. After a lot of trial and error, the professor got the idea of looking at the numbers as an x-axis on a graph with the point on the y-axis determined by starting at the temple. This would put us in the middle of the Atlantic Ocean. On the basis of this hypothesis, using the coordinates of the supposed site of the Tower of Babel, we were finally able to locate it."

"The Tower," Noque broke in, "would be situated in Africa, in an unexplored territory beyond Lake Chad."

"Professor Noque and I went on an expedition to see if there really was something in the spot we identified. After the long, hard trip across the hitherto unknown region, we came to a mountainous zone. I must tell you that we were a little discouraged because the high altitude didn't seem to fit the idea of being submerged in a flood. Still, we marched on and ended up in a very humid valley, on the bottom of which was a lake surrounded by virgin forests and in the center of it, to our great surprise, the top of a tower was sticking out. The sky over this site was constantly covered with clouds but the light seemed to pass through them and brighten the valley. We might very well have been the first men, in thousands of years, to look upon what could be the Tower of Babel!

"The fact remains that there was a building there with the top rising about fifteen feet above the water. Its walls were round, seen from a distance, and looked very smooth, reflecting the light from around. The construction appears to have resisted the ages. At the very top was a terrace with a circular building in the middle of it.

"When we got down to the lake, we built a raft to sail out to the monument. It was easy going but the water was infested with crocodiles whose presence at this altitude could be explained by the unusually humid microclimate for a valley walled in by two huge mountains. The noxious air, maybe from a volcano, was surely coming out of the steep slopes of clayey soil.

"When we got near the tower we noticed that if we climbed over the wall we could enter the building from the top. But the walls were smooth as glass and nothing to sneeze at. It was obvious that if the upper part were sticking out any higher, we would have had a much more difficult time reaching the terrace crowning the building. We had just stepped down on it when we saw that the platform was clearly not meant to be the final summit of the tower. In fact, it looked like the work was interrupted. The tower must have been a spectacular project but it had been abandoned before it was finished. A door opened onto a big, empty room whose walls were decorated in bas-reliefs of the same type we found in Mexico."

"While I was trying to decipher them," the professor picked up, "Hubert explored the back of the room and discovered stairs leading down inside the building. Unfortunately, after a few steps, it appeared that the lower part of the tower was flooded and inaccessible without some extra equipment.

The bas-reliefs were not very well preserved but they still led us to believe that this tower was the main temple-palace of a city called Babel, the capital of the country of Nod..."

The Nyctalope interrupted the professor:

"Nod, east of Eden! That's unbelievable! If the facts are confirmed, it'll be the greatest archaeological find in history!"

"I'm sure of it" responded the professor. "That's why Hubert and I have decided to mount another expedition to go back to explore the tower."

"This extraordinary story is beyond anything I've ever heard," Saint-Clair said. "It makes me think, although I'm no expert in ancient history, of those legends told about the invasion of Earth by Martians in the distant past, or of Plato's description of Atlantis. To him too it was a very advanced civilization that met its end in a flood. During my military service one of my officer friends had told me about the discovery of the remains of Atlantis found in the Sahara desert at the end of the 19th century. But they were far from being as important as this. Your discovery is really exciting."

"I think we can indeed say that," continued Hubert. "But our expedition required a lot of preparation. Even with the underwater equipment we're taking, it won't be easy. The lake is infested with crocodiles and the tower might be booby-trapped. Moreover, the climate is unhealthy. Professor Noque got sick soon after we arrived in the valley and he didn't completely recover until we were far away from it. I carried him on my back for over ten miles through the jungle surrounding the lake before the healthier air of the mountains could restore him. At the same time, the expedition was attacked by a primitive tribe that lives in the heart of the forest. The men were led by a huge chief with light skin and a very different type of body than the others. This time, to avoid running into the natives, we're taking a hydroplane and landing directly on the lake. To explore the depths of the lake and the flooded tower we have diving suits with an independent supply of oxygen. It's to take care of these kinds of problems that Pir and Bob are coming along."

The Nyctalope spoke up again, full of curiosity.

"I know that kind of diving suit. I used one recently in Spain. But how are your young friends going to help you?"

"Well," Hubert answered. "The O'Connell brothers invented a small submarine with mechanical propulsion that will take us down to the bottom of the lake and without having to face the crocodiles. The *veloscaphe* they built is even equipped with an electric generator for lights to scare away the big lizards."

"You've apparently thought of everything," said Saint-Clair, smiling.

Just then Bernard entered the room and announced in a solemn voice: "Dinner is served!"

The Nyctalope and his guests stood up and went into the dining room where the discussion became even livelier. Léo and Sylvie chatted with Hubert and Professor Noque while at the end of the table Pierre and the O'Connell brothers were deep in conversation: Saint-Clair's son was passionate about traveling and listened eagerly to their tales.

Pir and Bob were talking about their expedition to the Sudan. It had almost ended in failure and several of their companions had been killed. Pierre was clearly fascinated and was asking all kinds of questions. He was passionate about these stories and you could feel that he would have willingly participated in one of the adventures. As a result, at the end of the meal, Bob offered to take him with them on the voyage they were preparing. Pierre, of course, accepted right away. Bob turned to Hubert and asked him out loud:

"Monsieur de Pibriac, Pierre Saint-Clair wants to join us in our exploration of the Tower of Babel. Given our precautions, the expedition should not be too risky, so we could bring him with us…"

"Or perhaps riskier than you think," Hubert answered. "Still, if Monsieur Saint-Clair has no objections…"

Hubert de Pibriac, a little surprised nonetheless, looked at Léo questioningly. The Nyctalope, who was talking with the professor, went silent and raised an eyebrow at Pierre. Then his face relaxed and he even cracked a smile. Without a doubt he remembered that at that age he would also have loved to go on such an adventure. In a serious tone he said:

"Pierre has to return to college in mid-October. I would let him go with you but he would have to be back by then. I'm not sure that's possible."

"In fact, he could go with us for the first weeks of the trip and come back to France on the plane that'll bring us supplies, which would be done a little before mid-October."

"Great!" the Nyctalope exclaimed. "In that case, Pierre, now you're about to leave on your first great adventure. Come on, let's drink to your discoveries that will revolutionize modern archaeology!"

The champagne glasses clinked and everyone toasted the success of the expedition. It was decided that they would leave in two days!

CHAPTER III
The Pibriac Expedition

On the morning of September 13, the members of the Pibriac expedition were at Le Bourget airport standing in front of a Latécoère 28-3M 8-seater seaplane, with enough tonnage to transport all the members and their equipment. It was a modified version of the one in which Jean Mermoz had made the first transatlantic commercial crossing the year before. In this version specially designed for the expedition, the plane was equipped with wheels and pontoons that allowed it, as the pilot chose and the landing required, to set down on both land and water. The night before the diving suits and the veloscaphe, or underwater bicycle, as well as a big, dismantled boat to navigate the lake, had been loaded with the rest of the material. Professor Noque had also put on two mysterious crates, one medium-sized, the other much larger, without giving the members any indication of their contents. He obviously wanted to surprise them. Pierre and the O'Connell brothers were consumed with curiosity and had managed to find where the two crates came from: The Academy of Sciences.

Sylvie and Léo lavished all kinds of advice on their son who was leaving on his first big adventure. Hubert de Pibriac, aware of the parents' worries, smiled on them kindly while Pir and Bob paced around, in a hurry to set off.

Around 8 a.m., the plane was gassed up and the final checks were finished by Hubert. The plane was ready to take off.

The Nyctalope spoke to his friend Pibriac and Professor Noque:

"Don't forget to keep us informed. You know, we've got fast planes at the ready and if necessary can fly out there or at least send help if you have problems."

"Don't worry, we'll get you regular updates," Hubert promised.

Sylvie and Léo moved to the side of the runway and all the members of the expedition took their seats on the plane. The motor started, the plane began to taxi and then crawled up into the air. After floating once around the airport, it sped off to the south.

It would have a layover in Tunis, then at Fort-Lamy, the capital of Chad in French Equatorial Africa. After this it would finally reach the end of its journey, the mysterious Tower of Babel.

The first day of the flight passed without incident. The sky was clear and the Latécoère easily reached its cruising speed of 135 mph. Hubert de Pibriac was one of the most renowned amateur pilots in France. To pilot this ultramodern seaplane, therefore, presented no problems. He was more than pleased to be at the commands in such a newly designed cockpit. It only took three hours to cross France and once the Mediterranean was skimmed over, the plane landed on the runway at the airport in El Aouina in Tunis, on time, a little before 5 p.m.

The members of the expedition stepped off the plane and spent a nice, quiet evening dining together in a wonderful restaurant on the seaside. Meanwhile, the mechanics checked the plane and filled it with gas.

After dinner Hubert had tried to get in touch with the Nyctalope to inform him of the smooth first leg of the journey. To his great surprise he could not reach him. *No doubt some technical problem with Léo's phone*, he thought. *It's surprising because his machines are usually in tip-top shape. No problem, I'll just try again tomorrow night when we get into Fort-Lamy.*

The next day, they had to cross the Sahara and fly over Lake Chad to arrive at their second destination in the afternoon. The 1800 miles could have been dangerous if any mechanical failures occurred because the area was deserted or at best inhabited by tribes that often proved hostile. In Tunis Hubert asked the radio service about the weather conditions of the regions they had to cross to reach the heart of Africa. In theory, they would have no disturbances over the desert but heavy rains were forecast around Fort-Lamy. The landing, therefore, might be a little trickier than planned. However, since rain was frequent at this time of the year and they would see plenty of it over the next few days, they decided not to postpone their departure. He would keep in touch with the radio service about the weather as much as possible to be prepared for any eventuality.

Considering the length of the flight, they decided to leave at five in the morning. The sky was clear and the plane was soon flying over the desert. The first part of the trip went well. The only hitch was to the west of the Libyan Desert when the plane had to climb in order to avoid a sudden sandstorm that clouded the horizon.

When they arrived at Lake Chad, the weather turned cloudy all of a sudden and it started to rain. The plane gained altitude to climb above the clouds but being beaten by the rain and battered by the winds it had trouble ascending, even though it performed stunningly under normally turbulent conditions.

This storm, however, forced them slow the plane down and at nightfall it was still in the air, not being able to reach Fort-Lamy. In the pouring rain that hammered the fuselage and in total darkness, it was hard to get their bearings, even more so as the area was sparsely inhabited and the villages they flew over were not lit up at night. Hubert had to rely on the navigation instruments. He was skilled in this but he still started to worry about not being able to see the city lights.

Around 8 p.m., while Pibriac was wondering if it might not be wiser to try landing and start off again the next morning, Bob was peering into dark night. Off to the left he saw lights, not many and not bright, but they must have been Fort-Lamy. Hubert spotted a relatively open field that could serve as an emergency landing strip. Without too much difficulty and with great care he managed to set the plane down on the muddy, soggy soil which did not make it easy for him.

They left the plane in the open space, where it should be safe, and headed for the city. This was their last layover in the civilized world. The next day they would begin the most dangerous part of their trip, the one that would bring them to the Tower of Babel.

They found some rooms in a simple but comfortable hotel and ate a frugal dinner while looking out the windows at the torrents of water pelting Fort-Lamy. When they were done Hubert tried once again to contact the Nyctalope. He got through. The conversation was broken, the connection on and off, but he was a little upset hearing the terrible news about Versailles while they were flying over Africa.

CHAPTER IV
Surprise Attack

On September 13, at 8 a.m., in the garden of the Blingy mansion, Louis, Saint-Clair's gardener, was pruning a rose bush that had just lost its last flowers. He was piling up the dead branches in a wheelbarrow next to him. Despite the early hour it was already warm and Louis work in his shirtsleeves.

His employers had left early to take their son to Le Bourget airport. Julienne, the maid, had finished cleaning the rooms and was walking across the yard on her way to do the shopping for breakfast. She stopped next to Louis and asked him:

"Is it going to take you long to finish up with the roses?"

"No. See, I have to finish this one and cut back this vine that's getting a little out-of-hand. Looky there, it's almost up to the second story," he pointed at the branches of the invasive plant.

Julienne looked up but her eyes were drawn to a dot that showed up in the sky and seemed to grow bigger every second. She said to Louis:

"Do you see that... that thing up there... over the roof?"

Louis looked to where she was pointing and saw the weird thing. It was a metal object, very big now, six-sided, and flying through the air. It was not a blimp because there was no balloon. It was not a plane either because it had no wings. It moved by propellers stuck on top of the cabin. They must have had an extremely powerful engine somewhere because the ship was as tall as a three-story building and it was moving fast. Maybe it was a helicopter but of a revolutionary design because no machine like that had been able to fly for more than a mile.

As the aircraft got closer and closer the sound of the spinning propellers became deafening.

Faced with such an extraordinary spectacle, Louis called out to his father and Mademoiselle Bron, the governess:

"Come over and see what's flying around up there!"

A window opened on the second floor, revealing the dazed face of Mademoiselle Bron, then Bertrand the butler.

The aircraft was hovering over the mansion. The propellers were blowing a strong wind over the yard, stirring up the leaves around Louis and Julienne. A few passers-by on the road outside the gates stopped and watched the spectacle. Everyone made comments about the appearance of the strange machine.

"Monstrous! I didn't think such a thing existed," the governess told Bertrand, who in turn whispered back:

"Me neither. It's incredible. Hey, it looks like a door is opening under the thing!"

Indeed, a panel in the lower part of the helicopter had just slid open, sliding into the side. For a minute nothing happened, then a kind of huge soap bubble appeared in the doorway and despite the blasts from the propellers it started drifting slowly to the ground. A second one showed up, followed by others. It was raining bubbles, slightly iridescent, glistening in the morning sun, falling over the mansion.

At this stupefying sight the onlookers started laughing, maybe to evade the fright that they were no doubt feeling. Louis even started clapping, as if they he were watching a circus show.

At this moment one of the bubbles touched down and exploded with a booming "pop." A clear liquid spread over the ground. At the place where it spilled the grass seemed to stand straight up, as if drawn by a mysterious force. Another bubble popped, then another and another... Every time, some liquid poured out over the plants and bushes, effecting some kind of powerful pull over them, uprooting them and forcing them upward. Louis was hit by the liquid and his feet left the ground. He started floating up. He turned to Julienne and saw that she, too, had been touched. She was already six feet off the ground.

The mansion was not spared. The roof tiles, washed with the weird substance, were flying off as if carried away in a windstorm. The whole atmosphere was supernatural, surreal. Only the walls resisted the magnetic force. Mademoiselle Bron, whose arms had been splashed by the strange liquid, was floating out of the window. Bertrand had grabbed her leg and was trying to hold her back as she clutched desperately to the window frame.

The helicopter had regained altitude. The yard was completely devastated. Julienne was waving her arms 30 feet in the air, just over Louis who had held onto a branch at the top of an oak tree, trying to stop "falling into the sky," so to speak. The mansion was being torn apart. Its roof, attic and even the walls now were crumbling, stone by stone.

Bertrand was trying to keep himself inside the window and had to let go of Mademoiselle Bron, who was swept away. But he struggled in vain. Like his son in the yard, who was soaring up along with the old oak tree, he too was inevitably dragged up.

Five minutes later, the magnificent Saint-Clair residence was nothing but a pile of rubble. All the personnel had been sucked up into the sky by a mysterious, merciless enemy. The Nyctalope and his family owed their lives to the trip to Le Bourget airport whereby they were not home at the time of the terrible attack.

CHAPTER V
Inside the Tower

Hubert de Pibriac and his companions had talked all night long about the attack on the Versailles residence of the Nyctalope. Hubert had learned about it during the conversation he had had with the radio service. Saint-Clair had told him the details in a calm voice, interrupted only by the static and breaks caused by the storm hitting Fort-Lamy and that disrupted radio communication. Pibriac found out that the mansion had been destroyed, his personnel decimated and a few passers-by, who happened to be in the vicinity of the mansion, had stated seeing the poor people literally "fall into the sky" and suffer a ghastly death in the higher atmosphere. Pierre was called in by Hubert and listened painfully to his father.

Hubert then told the facts to his comrades and informed them about what Saint-Clair had found on returning from Le Bourget. The extraordinary and tragic event left them all speechless. Pierre, who had known the servants of the mansion since childhood, was deeply shocked. Everyone tried to comfort him the best they could. After telling Saint-Clair that his thoughts and support were with him, Hubert bid farewell to him and promised to contact him again when they got to the Tower of Babel.

They started forming hypotheses about what might have happened, but they saw right away that Pierre was having a hard time getting over the awful news and they should not be talking about the event. They stopped, therefore, their speculations and did all they could to help the young man deal with his grief.

At the end of the evening, in order to distract him, they brought the conversation around to the last leg of their journey and what was awaiting them the next day. They went to bed pretty late since the departure was scheduled for 8 a.m. sharp, right after breakfast. In spite of his friends' attention, Pierre could not forget the tragedy of Versailles and had slept badly, not dozing off until dawn.

At the appointed hour the plane was ready to take off. The sky was clear, which was a good omen for the crucial day. When they were in their seats the plane took off without a problem, despite the muddy ground, and headed south. Nicolas Noque acted as copilot and the first part of the trip was made over the vast, little explored lands of French Equatorial Africa. After a few hundred miles they got to the point where traditional maps, which lack precision, become useless. Professor Noque, therefore, turned to a map that Hubert and he had drawn up during their last expedition. They had to fly over a real *terra incognita* where they had designated their own landmarks, being the first to venture into this region. They spotted the remarkable plain in the shape of an anvil near a long crevasse open to the sky, to the east a village whose only totem was a vulture and farther west an exceptionally tall tree that broke the monotony of the savanna.

After two hours in the air they saw in the distance a short range of mountains in the middle of which they had discovered the valley hiding the Tower of Babel. The approach was made without any particular difficulties while they saw below them a thick layer of clouds that stretched out between two steep peaks. On the first circling over the valley the fog looked impenetrable.

"Without the directions found in the pyramid," Hubert said, "we would never have found this valley that's constantly hidden by this fog. I'm going to put the plane on its theoretically axis... There we go... Now we'll get through these clouds..."

The others watched Hubert at the controls, trusting his skill as a pilot and explorer.

The plane plunged through the clouds. Everything went dark. It only lasted one or two minutes. Then they saw a tropical valley under the leaden sky, but lit by a weird glow. At the bottom of the valley was a big lake with the summit of the tower sticking out of the middle. They had arrived.

Hubert pulled in the landing gear so he could use the pontoons to land. He set down on the still lake and steered the Latécoère so that it stopped only ten yards from the tower.

Then he said, "We'll set up camp directly on the terrace at the top of the tower. The shore is unsafe because of the natives. Plus, we'll have a good lookout point and can defend ourselves easily in case of attack. The time it takes any would-be attackers to cross the lake, climb the tower and reach us, will leave us free to organize our defense."

Everyone agreed with this wise decision.

But first of all they had to put together the boat to load the material and bring it to the tower platform. It was done quickly and in less than an hour the essential equipment was waiting at their campsite. At the start of the afternoon they were ready to start their investigations.

Hubert led the members of the expedition inside the tower in order to show them what he himself had discovered during the last voyage. Everyone followed him, with the exception of Professor Noque who was in a hurry to set up some of his equipment. Moreover, as he reminded them, he remembered the inside of the tower just fine and did not want to waste precious time. He looked a little feverish and was sweating big drops. Unusually, his movements, which were normally very precise, were becoming hesitant and clumsy. When they saw him struggle to open the smallest of his two mysterious crates, his companions, although a little surprised, did not press him and just exchanged understanding glances.

Half an hour later they came out of the tower, definitely convinced that only an underwater passage was possible to enter the building. They found the professor in front of a complex machine: a metal box with multi-colored lights and a big, parabolic antenna that was spinning slowly.

Nicolas Noque looked like he was back to his old self. He told them:

"It's an experimental machine that one of my colleagues at the Academy of Sciences asked me to test out on our expedition. It detects all the rays emitted within a three-mile radius.

The lights flash different colors depending on the type of radiation. You can also detect radium, X-rays, even heat waves... For us here I saw that the first results are troubling. You see this blinking red light? It tells us that there's radiation, some kind of energy, but it's impossible to determine its nature. The machine was designed to spot all kinds of radiation, so this one is totally unknown and I'm wondering what it could be..."

"That is curious," Hubert said, "but I have to admit that I'm no expert on the matter. Maybe we'll discover it by exploring the lower levels of the tower. Anyway, we'll make good use of it. Pir and Bob, it's your turn now. Set up the veloscaphe so we can explore the lake."

The two young men went over to a big crate in which the pieces of their invention had been packed. Pierre Saint-Clair was interested, so he went to help them out. He grabbed a jimmy and pried open the top. The three of them together quickly had the pieces laid out on the ground.

The veloscaphe, or more precisely the diving velocipede, was basically an underwater bicycle for two people. It was shaped like a cigar, around twenty feet long by five feet wide at the fattest part of its diameter. It was built of steel sheets placed over an inner frame made of duralumin rods. The diver-cyclists sitting on bicycle seats were protected inside a cylindrical compartment and controlled the up and down movement with lateral fins. When they were pointed down the machine started diving and when they were turned up it rose. The front of the vehicle was equipped with an electric spotlight and a steel spur that could send out a strong electrical discharge, which made for a powerful weapon.

It was called the Motor II. The first Motor had been used two years earlier by the O'Connell brothers in the exploration of an underground lake in Switzerland. It had taken them all the way to a network of grottoes that were the home of prehistoric animals which, unfortunately, had destroyed the prototype.

While the two young inventors got to work on their machine, Hubert, Professor Noque and Pierre, who had joined them now, took the boat to the shore in order to cut some wood. They had to build a hoist to get the Motor into the water from the top of the tower and to bring it back up again when needed. They took turns keeping watch while cutting down a tall, tropical tree and slicing up the trunk.

This work took up the rest of the afternoon. They attached the logs to the back of the boat and towed them back to the tower. Using some rope they hauled the logs up the walls and put them on the terrace.

During dinner it was decided that they would build the hoist the next morning and start exploring the lake early in the afternoon. If everything went as planned they could hope to have a picture of the submerged tower by evening.

Bob took the first watch. He would be relieved two hours later. The deep, dark night passed with nothing to report. Jungle sounds echoed under the cloudy vault. All kinds of noises filled the darkness: birds squawking, wild beasts roaring, branches rustling when prey fled predators, grunts and howls and whining and wailing... Sometimes a crocodile splashed into the water and the man on watch had to keep a close eye on the walls of the tower to make sure that there were not natives coming to attack them. But after a few minutes of relative silence, interrupted by the eerie snap of the lizard's jaws as it devoured its prey, the tension relaxed; it was a false alarm.

Early the next morning, as the first days of dawn were crawling over the valley, Pierre, who was on watch, thought he saw a light in the sky. It was like a metal object had passed through the clouds at breakneck speed before disappearing in the tall trees of the jungle. It happened so fast that he could not tell exactly what he had seen. Without waking up his companions he stared at the spot where he thought the thing had vanished. For more than half an hour nothing happened. His watch, the last of the night, was just about over and Pierre was ready to let it go and wake up his companions when he saw the same object, more clearly this time, rise out of the jungle and shoot up into the clouds. The first time he had no idea what it was but now he saw it clearly. It was a machine of un-known design. A huge metal tower, six-sided, with propellers on top. He had never seen anything like it but it looked exactly like his father's description of the helicopter that had attacked the mansion. What was this weird aircraft doing in the middle of an African forest right next to their camp? Why had it come only to leave right away? It was a complete mystery. But Pierre had to tell the others without delay because its presence here was a bad sign.

CHAPTER VI
Under Siege

When they got back from the airport, the Nyctalope and his wife had found what remained of their demolished residence. They were first struck with horror by the incomprehensible sight. Saint-Clair got out of the car and started inspecting the ruins. He could not understand what had happened. Everything was destroyed but it did not look like an explosion.

Saint-Clair was a veteran of the Great War. He had seen battlefields but nothing like what he had before his eyes, even from afar: a huge pit at the bottom of which were the foundations and the remains of the walls of his mansion. And no trace of burns indicating that the disaster was the result of a fire! He was contemplating this when some passers-by who had witnessed the scene arrived. Listening to their statements he got a better idea of what occurred. His mansion was the victim of an extraordinarily violent attack that had targeted it directly; he had only escaped by the slim chance that had called him to Le Bourget to see off his son! An attack by an unreal helicopter with a formidable weapon!

The unknown threat could strike again at any moment. He had to get Sylvie to safety before he could think of his next step.

Therefore, to get his wife under protection he made a complicated journey through country roads to arrive in Paris. Saint-Clair took her to a little house he had bought the year before on Rue Montbrun in the 14th *arrondissement*. Then he called the Paris office of the CID to send ten agents to guard the mansion and keep anyone from entering the ruins.

Nevertheless, the offensive power of this unknown enemy was such that he wondered if these measures, despite a certain level of protection, were enough to counter an attack like the one carried out that morning, which had taken the lives of all his household staff.

He consulted one of his old friends and agreed that Sylvie's security should be strengthened. Immediately he called the Minister of War, André Maginot, to get the protection he deemed necessary for his wife's safety. The two men had known each other for a long time and kept on friendly terms. The Nyctalope wasted no time getting to the point:

"Hello André. This morning at Versailles my mansion was destroyed in an aerial attack by an unknown party. I got my family to safety in my house in Paris and I've already taken some measures, but I'm afraid it won't be enough and I need reinforcements."

"My poor friend, what you're telling me is absolutely incredible! Such an attack, just a few miles from Paris! In any case, you can count on the government's support in this matter. As for a defense, you won't find anything better. You know that I've earned a reputation for this and I'll make sure that your house is as impregnable as France itself will soon be. Tell me, about these measures you've taken: what exactly have you organized and what extra help do you need to step it up?"

"Ten CID agents are protecting the house, but as I said, it was an aerial attack and I don't really have the means to do much against this kind of assault…"

"I'll place a company of soldiers around the house. We'll back them up with a few 75mm field guns that should be able to destroy the machine in case it comes back. Furthermore, I'll ask my colleague Dumesnil, the Air Force Minister, to deploy a squadron of fighter jets to make regular rounds of the area and be ready to strike at the least incident."

"Thank you, André. I think that should do the trick. For my part, now that I feel better about my wife, I'll start an investigation to find out where this attack came from. According to the description of the helicopter by the witnesses I'm thinking of one of my old enemies. But it seems highly unlikely to me because he's dead and I saw him buried. Nevertheless, I'll start there. It's the only lead I have and it just might lead somewhere."

"Very well. My men will be in place in a few hours and I think the squad of fighters will start flying over your neighborhood by the end of the afternoon. At least this aircraft isn't invisible, by God! We should be able to spot it in the air. The air force will be standing by to intercept it whenever and wherever we see it."

"Thanks again, André. Anyway, I'll keep you up-to-date on any new developments."

"Goodbye, Léo, and good luck."

After finishing his conversation with André Maginot, Saint-Clair called the Secretary General of the CID, Michel Dorlange.

"Michel, the Blingy mansion has been destroyed. We're holed up at Rue Montbrun. Can you get over here to protect Sylvie while I start the investigation?"

"No problem, Monsieur Saint-Clair. I'll tell my wife and be right over. Hold on, please…"

The conversation was interrupted for a couple of minutes during which Saint-Clair heard Dorlange talk with his wife. Then Michel was back on the line.

"Erin's worried about Sylvie and is offering to stay with her. She insists since she's also a CID agent and in a position to help us… I'll be over with her. She'll keep your wife company. Moreover, I think we should inform all our services in case of another surprise attack…"

"OK, you can do it from here. The telephone here is, as you know, is completely integrated—special standard plus the radio and wireless, all the latest innovations needed."

"Good. We'll be over around four."

"Great. I'm going to take a little trip to Spain to clear up something that's been nagging me. See you later, Michel."

The Nyctalope made two quick phone calls. The first was to his chauffeur and to his mechanic, Vitto and Soca, who were with him at Le Bourget and had escaped the attack.

"Hello, Vitto? Take the special car with Soca and go to Saint-Jean-du-Gard as soon as possible. I've been in touch with my friend who lives there and he'll give us a hand in this affair. Bring him back quickly."

"Fine, Monsieur. If we drive in shifts through the night, Soca and I should be there tomorrow morning and back in Paris by evening."

"Great! Tonight I'm going to Madrid with the Zig. Stay in touch with me by radio because the situation might change fast and we have to be ready for any eventuality."

"Understood! We'll prepare to leave right away. Until tomorrow, Monsieur."

Then he called to notify the airport at Villacoublay where he had set up an ultramodern hangar. His personal plane, the Zig, was kept there and the pilot and mechanic were ready to take off at any time he needed.

The Zig was a six-seater, high-speed aircraft that could get him to Madrid at 140 mph. Léo would take turns at the commands with the pilot and leaving at 6 p.m. he would arrive by midnight. Then he could get in touch with the Spanish authorities first thing in the morning.

Early in the afternoon he was told by one of the CID agents who was posted on the roof of the house that a convoy of military trucks had turned onto Rue Montbrun. A few minutes later Captain Gougeon, the company leader, introduced himself to organize the plan that he had in mind to defend the building. After a brief meeting the two men went their ways, the officer to give orders to his soldiers. The trucks parked along the sidewalk and a barrier was set up on both ends of the street, one at Rue Dumoncel, the other at Rue Bézout. Within minutes the whole block of Rue Montbrun was literally invaded by soldiers. The orders were clear. All traffic was banned except for residents who had to prove their identity and would be taken home by a soldier. The idea of bringing in field guns had been rejected in the end by the General Staff, given the risk of using such weapons in the middle of Paris. However, a heavy machine gun was set up on the roof to be used, if need be, as an anti-aircraft defense.

Around 4 p.m., a continual roar was heard for the first time. The squadron sent by Dumesnil had arrived. From now on it would make regular flyovers around Rue Montbrun, ready to intercept any non-authorized aircraft.

It was also around four that Dorlange and his wife arrived at Saint-Clair's house, along with two soldiers who were on guard in front. They settled in to start their mission of protection and coordination.

The Nyctalope was satisfied with the organized defense that brought together all the means at his disposal. So, he went to prepare for his departure.

His Torpedo was parked in the courtyard, ready to go. He threw a couple of suitcases in the trunk and left Rue Montbrun for the Villacoublay airport.

So far, I've been a victim. Now I have to find out the truth and do what needs to be done. Otherwise, my merciless enemy is going to kill my whole family and all my friends along with destroying all my work, he thought as the car sped through the barriers and headed out of Paris towards a theoretical revenge.

CHAPTER VII
The Enemy

The train was barreling through the countryside. In the early morning, the passengers heading for the capital were starting to see the wheat fields. In a first class car on board the train coming from Marseille, two men in dark suits were sitting across from each other, looking at the landscape and talking.

"I guess we'll get in on time," one of them glanced at his watch.

"Yes. To get to Rue Montbrun we'd better take a taxi," the other responded.

When Michel Dorlange had contacted them the two agents from the Marseille CID office had jumped on the first train for Paris to join forces with the troops deployed around the house of their boss, the Nyctalope. They were both armed with large caliber Brownings hidden in a holster under their arm. Their trip went smoothly and the tension they had felt on leaving the Saint-Charles station gradually dwindled away. Now they were relaxed and thinking about ironing out the final details of their arrival in Paris.

A strange person came down the corridor, glanced into the compartment and on seeing an empty seat entered. He was a big, fat man wearing a long coat that covered his whole body and a hat pulled down so that only the lower half of his face was visible. The most surprising aspect of this man was his enormous volume. The huge coat hid all his body but it was so big he must have been obese.

He plopped down after nodding to the two travelers. He had to sit in the middle of the bench where there was no armrest because his body was so massive that it took up almost two full seats. The two men, not wanting the stranger to hear their conversation, stopped talking and looked out the window.

After a few minutes of silence broken only by the sound of the rails, the man spoke up:

"Hello, Messieurs. I'm going to Rue Montbrun in Paris. Do you know how I should get there from Gare de Lyon? I'm from the country and don't know the capital very well."

The two men looked at each other, stunned. The newcomer could not have heard the conversation that his arrival had interrupted. Was it a simple coincidence?

"Rue Montbrun, Rue Montbrun... Let's see... Do you know that street, Richard?" one of them asked the other to get a little more time to find a good answer.

His partner hesitated before saying:

"No, I don't it. Sorry, Monsieur."

"Oh well, I thought the Nyctalope lived there and that you were going to see him."

After this response, as unexpected as the previous question, Richard said:

"You know Monsieur Saint-Clair?"

"Yes, very well. We're old friends and I've got an old debt to settle with him. But it doesn't matter, it'll soon be over. Accounts will soon be balanced. Today I'm just going to make a little down payment..."

His menacing tone and the glare in his eyes, barely visible under the big, black hat, made the two men recoil and reach for their holsters. But before they could do anything the fat man was on them, too fast for someone so obese.

His two hands grabbed the agents' necks and lifted them out of their seats with extraordinary ease. Then he banged their heads together with terrible violence. In the hands of this monstrous individual the two men were nothing but puppets and they were knocked senseless, unable to react. The attacker narrowed his eyes and said:

"Yes, today, two members of the CID are going to die."

And he smashed their heads together again and again into a bloody pulp and dropped them on the floor.

The fat man stepped over the two corpses and opened the door leading outside the train. He stood there for a minute, watching the houses in the Parisian suburb roll by. When the train started to cross a short bridge over an empty road the man jumped. He leaped more than 30 feet and landed on his huge legs without hurting himself. Not far from where he landed a limousine was parked with a man at the wheel who looked prematurely aged and had a cruel smile on his face. His dark, mean eyes, deep-set under arching eyebrows, glared at the fat man.

"So, how was the trip?" he asked ironically.

"Very amusing. But the best is yet to come," the fat man snickered.

He climbed into the car and they sped off.

CHAPTER VIII
The Engineer

The Nyctalope arrived in Madrid in good time, a little after midnight. He hurried through customs and spent the rest of the night in a big hotel.

Early in the morning he got in touch with the Spanish authorities to get urgent authorization to exhume a body. After the abdication of King Alfonso XIII, the Nyctalope had lost the main contacts he had used in Spain during the monarchy. The brand new Second Republic was still going through birth pangs. While waiting to elect a president of the Republic, the executive power lay in the hands of a Catholic liberal, the president of the provisional government, Niceto Alcala-Zamora.

The Nyctalope knew practically no one in the new government. Nevertheless, the CID still had privilege in Spain, since the royalty had helped create the organization and it had not denounced the government that succeeded Alfonso XIII.

Through the French embassy Saint-Clair got in touch with the Ministry of the Interior and made an appointment for the afternoon with the Chief of Staff. Thus he could explain his business.

He wanted to get authorization to exhume the body of his old enemy, Maur Korridès, who had been known everywhere as "The Engineer." He was a scientific genius whose inventions had revolutionized entire fields from mechanics to chemistry. Before the Great War, he had managed to isolate a new substance, *heliose*, an incredible fuel that allowed him to overcome gravity. Moreover, he had created extraordinary vehicles that could travel into the most hostile environments, from the depths of the ocean up to the rarest atmosphere, even into the ether that separates the worlds in space. Among his many inventions, he had built a helicopter: the description given by the witnesses of the machine that destroyed the mansion in Versailles had brought back the memory of Korridès.

The Engineer and the Nyctalope had faced off for the last time in Spain, four years earlier. The Engineer and his wife, the Red Princess, were at the head of a revolutionary and terrorist organization, the Hashishin. The Nyctalope had captured its leaders and the organization was shut down. He had given Korridès and his lieutenants over to the Spanish authorities. Unfortunately, when he still had the Red Princess in custody, she was murdered by one of Saint-Clair's allies. The Engineer was heartbroken and killed himself in his cell. Saint-Clair always regretted her death, which he had not wanted but which, despite himself, he was somewhat responsible for. Of course, the Red Princess had been a merciless enemy, ready to wipe out entire families, but still he had not wanted her dead when he captured her even though he knew that the Spanish authorities, to whom he was planning to turn her over, would probably have executed her like the other Hashishin leaders.

Engineer Korridès had been buried in the cemetery of the Madrid prison. But the Nyctalope wanted to verify his death and now he wanted the necessary documents to exhume the body as soon as possible.

He got to the Ministry on time and was surprised to be welcomed by the minister in person. He even had the opportunity to talk directly with the president of the provisional government, Alcala-Zamora. From the start of the meeting the Nyctalope was encouraged by the Spanish authorities. The republicans wanted to continue the good relations that the monarchy had kept up with France and as a result they were ready to help one of its most renowned citizens. The Minister got the authorization for him and scheduled the exhumation for the next day. The head of the provisional government had wanted to speak with him in person as a sign of good faith and to seal the Franco-Spanish friendship.

The Nyctalope left the ministry quite satisfied. The permit for the exhumation would arrive in the evening. It was then that he contacted the members of the expedition in Africa to get news from them and tell them about the tragedy in Versailles.

The night passed without any particular incident.

The next morning, at the break of a beautiful sunny day, they started digging up Korridès' grave in the Madrid prison cemetery.

The most pessimistic fears of the Nyctalope were confirmed. The coffin was empty. Maur Korridès was back!

CHAPTER IX
Battle on the Lake

The sun had risen over the Tower of Babel. The sky above the valley was still covered by heavy clouds but the light was bright. A white mist lay on the dark water of the lake, slowly rising over the tropical forest. After all the noises in the night, the forest was silent now.

The explorers awoke one by one. While some of them cleaned themselves up, the others made coffee. Pierre was still distracted by the weird machine he had seen in the sky just before dawn. He kept hold of his rifle and was watching the lakeshore, waiting for all his companions to get ready so he could tell them about the strange sight.

Hubert finished preparing breakfast while Pir and Bob were making the final checks on their mini-submarine that had to go in the water very soon.

As he put down his weapon to head to the campfire Pierre gave one last look at the beach. And he saw something moving there. He looked more carefully and could make out ten people whose bare skin was striped with red and black, sneaking down the bank and in total silence putting a canoe in the water. Armed with spears, carrying long, oval shields and covered in geometric designs, all the men were short except for one whose height and light skin stood out from the others. From his authoritative air and gestures, he was obviously the chief. When they started paddling on the lake a second group of natives, identically equipped, came out of the forest and put another canoe in the water. The first boat was slicing through the water without a sound and coming quickly toward the tower. If nothing stopped them, they would reach the camp in a few minutes. Pierre cried out:

"Alert! The natives are attacking!"

He hid behind the short wall encircling the tower and prepared to fire. The others grabbed their rifles and joined him immediately.

"It's them and their giant white chief who attacked during our last expedition" shouted Hubert. "Let's try to avoid a massacre. Just fire a little in front of them and they'll understand that they'll die if they come any closer."

Everyone agreed.

"Ready? Fire!"

A hail of bullets struck the water in front of the attackers. The surface of the lake started boiling and in the bow of the first boat the wood burst into a thousand splinters.

The natives stopped rowing and looked hesitant to continue. None of them had been hit and they understood that their enemies had not missed by chance but had spared their lives. They remembered, moreover, that several of their brothers had perished in the last confrontation with these white men and they knew now by experience that the noisy weapons of their enemy had a devastating effect.

The big white chief was thinking that the fact of being discovered before reaching the tower reduced their chance of victory considerably. He cursed the superstitions that dismayed his warriors: because of them they had refused to attack at night although their chances of success were much better. He would have to find another way to chase the whites off the taboo place, the House of the Gods. He had already faced them once and had managed to make them leave.

Now he was especially worried about his men being slaughtered. He stood up straight in the front of the canoe and let loose a savage cry, giving directions with his arms, ordering a halt to the attack. The natives spun their boats around and rowed slowly away from the tower along the riverbank.

Before coming up with a new plan of attack, the chief did not want to lose face and he started insulting the explorers and shaking his fist at them.

"Looks like he's challenging us," said Hubert. "Too bad I can't understand a word he's saying."

In the meantime, Professor Noque was staring at the chief, straining to hear what the enemy was saying. He nodded his head and murmured:

"Yes, it's a little vague but there's a connection coming from an old but common base. Hubert, I understand what he's telling us, at least the gist of it."

"How's that possible?"

"In fact, it's a language that vaguely resembles Hebrew. Of course it branched off long ago. Maybe it goes back to the time when the bas-reliefs in Mexico were written. Anyway, the pronunciation is completely different from modern Hebrew but thanks to my knowledge of ancient Semitic languages I can pick up a lot of what he's saying. He's calling us cowards because, he says, we're hiding behind our deadly weapons and without them we're nothing. He and his men will hunt down cowards like us, relentlessly, and the first chance they get they'll strike us dead."

"Do you think you can talk to him and be understood?" Hubert asked.

"I can try. What do you want me to say?"

"Well, do you think they've got traditions similar to the ancient Hebrews?"

"That's hard to say. The Bible tells us that the peoples who lived before the Flood, the forefathers of this tribe here, had customs like the Hebrews, although very corrupted. And let's not forget that we might be dealing with an anachronism. Personally, I think there might be a cultural relation, but I can't say for sure with so little information."

After thinking about it for a minute Hubert stated firmly:

"In that case, we have to take the risk. Tell him that I challenge him to individual combat. If he wins, we'll leave the tower. If he loses, that means that God or the gods are on our side and they'll let us stay in the valley. Then it'll be him and his men who have to leave."

"And what makes you think he'll accept?"

"David and Goliath!"

"Hmm, OK, we can give it a try."

In a loud and halting voice the professor launched into a speech that sounded a lot like the language used by the great white chief. His companions could obviously not understand what he was saying in this ancient tongue, but at his first words the natives froze and stared at the tower in disbelief. Even more surprised was the chief who could not understand how these strangers knew their language, even if they spoke it with a strong accent and made many mistakes.

The professor's speech was as follows:

"Greeting to you, O Great Chief! I am the spokesman for our own Chief and I am come from the Heavens with him on a great iron bird. Our Chief, the great Hubert de Pibriac, challenges you to hand-to-hand combat. If victorious, we will stay here because that is the will of God. If defeated, we will go back to our celestial abode but that will not be the case because we cannot be defeated."

The great white chief, a real giant at six and a half feet tall, flexed his powerful muscles that had no war paint. His men yelled in triumph, sure of their chief's victory.

"I see that you know us well, Spokesman, since you invoke this old tradition that I cannot refuse! You, Chief of the white men, you have given me a solemn challenge and as is the custom you have told me your name. Therefore, I have to tell you mine: I am Nimrod and I am the champion of Nod. I propose that we meet in the middle of the lake on canoes. We will face each other in one and the last man on board will be declared the victor."

The professor translated this to Hubert.

"Tell him I accept," de Pibriac said.

The professor looked at Hubert. In the strange glimmer in his eyes there was undeniable admiration. Turning to face Nimrod he said:

"It's agreed, O champion of Nod. Our Chief, the champion of Heaven, will face you on a big boat that we'll get from this tower. Both of you can get on board and when you're ready you can fight."

"So be it," Nimrod answered. "I can only admire the bravery of your chief. To engage in a traditional combat whose only outcome can be death, simply to remain in the House of the Gods, is very courageous of him. But he must know that I have never been defeated in combat!"

Professor Noque translated the native Chief, then turned to Hubert and said:

"There might still be time to stop this madness."

While he was speaking Hubert stood straight up and faced Nimrod. Spreading out his legs, he took off his coat and pith helmet and showed off his own muscles, which were as brawny as his enemy's.

"Don't worry, professor. I think the fight is far from a foregone conclusion. Remember that when I was in the Olympics, not so long ago, the sports commentators called me Herkulos!"

With a firm and determined step Hubert went to the boat that was hanging over the water by the hoist and he climbed in. Pir and Bob came over and started to pull the ropes to lower it into the lake.

When it hit the water Hubert untied it and started rowing slowly toward Nimrod's canoe. He drew alongside the natives' canoe, the giant scrambled on board and Hubert pushed the boat a few yards away so the two champions could fight without being disturbed by the other warriors. Neither Nimrod nor his men did anything to hinder the preparations.

The two fighters stood up and faced each other. Nimrod was two heads taller than Hubert and looked down on his adversary with a smile on his lips. Although shorter than him Hubert's muscles were the same size. Moreover, he was a grand champion and had competed internationally. Indeed, he had perfected his fighting techniques with the Nyctalope who had learned his from the greatest of Tibetan and Chinese Masters and he had taught Hubert during their training sessions.

The boat was narrow and the balance unstable: every step, every move could have toppled them over.

Abruptly, Nimrod jumped forward and tried to punch his enemy in the face. With a graceful movement of his chest Hubert easily dodged the attack. The other was now vulnerable, so Hubert threw an uppercut that dazed his adversary for a moment. The giant was still feeling the shock when Pibriac spun around, grabbed his arms and tossed him to the far end of the boat where he crashed on his back.

Nimrod turned on his side and jumped up his feet, scowling. His eyes burned with rage. Until this moment he had never met an enemy who could, even for an instant, get the better of him.

They faced off again. This time Nimrod was more cautious, staying just out of arm's reach. He was also protecting his face. At the last moment he spread his arms to get his enemy in a bear hug.

Pibriac was too close to the gunwale and could not back up. He dodged the attack by squatting down. He wrapped around this waist and spun behind him. This allowed him to try a hold known to wrestlers as the Double Nelson, which would immobilize the adversary by securing his arms over this neck. But Nimrod had almost supernatural strength and under his weighty pressure Hubert was forced to release his hold. Looking triumphant the giant turned around and started charging but his show of force, which made him overly confident, had made him careless. Sure of his victory he forgot to protect himself. For an Olympic level athlete such a mistake was valuable.

Hubert grabbed one arm, bent it back and spun him around. Then he pushed Nimrod backward where he flew into the prow, his spine crashing into the wooden frame. The hull of the boat, already weakened by previous shocks, started to crack and under the 250 pounds of the giant, the solid boat started coming apart.

The two men fell into the water amid the floating debris. Nimrod, handicapped by his wound, could not swim and sunk straight down. When Hubert surfaced he searched for his adversary. Just as he was about to dive down to save him, the water was stirred up by a strong current coming from riverbank. The crocodiles who had been lazing on the lakeshore were rushing into the water and heading for them. Hubert saw them coming, the biggest of them over twenty feet long. He had to get to safety quickly if he wanted to escape these predators.

As fast as he could he started swimming for the shore. The lizards were busy with Nimrod for the moment and forgot about Hubert who was able to cross most of the distance to the shore with ease. But the final few yards could prove dangerous because the feast was over and the huge reptiles were concentrating on him now.

He had only a few yards to go to safety but was about to be caught when his companions opened fire on the crocodiles. At this short distance and with their precision weapons Pir, Bob, Pierre and Professor Noque slaughtered them. The few crocs who were not hit ignored their prey to deal with their wounded brothers. Thus, Hubert was able to get back to the tower without any more trouble.

When "Herkulos" was safe and sound he stared at the rough water being agitated by the wild movements of its ferocious inhabitants. At last everything became calm again and the explorers' attention was turned to the natives. To their great surprise they saw that the warriors had already left the lake and were going back into the jungle.

"I don't think we have anything more to fear from them," Professor Noque said. "This ritual combat was a divine endorsement of our presence in the House of the Gods."

"True, but we've also seen that the crocodiles are very quick to act. I hope we can avoid them in the veloscaphe," Hubert said.

"Now it's our turn," Pir and Bob said in unison. "It's time to launch."

CHAPTER X
Sabotage

On the runway at the Madrid airport the Nyctalope was walking to the hangar where the Zig was parked. It was 4 a.m., the air was fresh and he could see as clear as day thanks to his extraordinary night vision.

The memory of his battle against Engineer Korridès had kept him from sleeping. In the past Korridès had already attacked his family and kidnapped his wife and son. As the Nyctalope had feared, they were once again in danger.

Korridès was without a doubt one of the greatest scientific geniuses of the 20th century. Unfortunately, his unbalanced mind made his behavior unstable and unpredictable. In his youth he had been locked up for a few years and he had left the mental asylum only because a rich American had needed his inventions to go in search of an unreachable treasure. For a time during his second marriage he had been relatively stable. After a few years he had decided to explore the planet Mars with his wife. That was when the Nyctalope had met him for the first time, beaming and friendly in the French colony of Argyre. They had not seen each other for a long time after that trip. But then it had been to fight. Korridès had prematurely aged for reasons unknown and his third marriage was to one of the Nyctalope's old enemies, the Red Princess, always hungry for vengeance. The scientist had founded the Hashishin with her, the diabolical organization that Léo had broken up. Their confrontation had ended in the death of his two enemies. At least that was what Saint-Clair had thought until he had opened the coffin where Korridès was believed to lie.

Worried and troubled the Nyctalope decided to depart earlier than planned and leave Madrid as soon as possible, whenever his plane was ready to go.

From a distance Saint-Clair saw that the door of the hangar was open, which seemed strange to him. No light shined through the windows. He had a bad feeling, so he walked off to the side, staying out of sight of the doorway. Nevertheless, the night was dark and his nyctalopic ability let him see as clear as day, which was not the case with whoever was inside. He snuck a peek through the open door to try to see if anything unusual was happening. The huge hangar was completely dark. He saw a light glowing in front of the plane as if someone was doing some night work on it. He was just about to step in when he saw the upper body lying on the ground, halfway out the doorway leading to the crew quarters. The nocturnal visitors who were working on the plane obviously had hostile intentions.

Saint-Clair snuck silently through the shadows to get as close to the light as he could. Two men were bent over the engine. The Nyctalope could not yet see exactly what they were doing, but he knew that it was some kind of sabotage. He had got within a few feet of them when the man on the left of the cockpit raised his head, probably to say something to his accomplice. He was just opening his mouth when he saw the Nyctalope coming out of the shadows.

Saint-Clair knew he was discovered and figuring that the other man would be taken by surprise and probably not react, he dove forward and smashed his head into the fuselage. The villain was knocked out and dropped to the ground. As the Nyctalope stepped up to the second man, the guy grabbed a crowbar and swung it hard at the Nyctalope. The attempt was so clumsy that Saint-Clair saw exactly where it was going and easily sidestepped it. His adversary, on the other hand, did not manage to dodge the karate chop that the Nyctalope delivered to the right side of his neck. The man stumbled to the left as he dropped his improvised weapon. Before he could get his balance Saint-Clair threw a strong hook into his solar plexus and put an end to the fight.

The hangar fell silent again. Saint-Clair looked all around the place to make sure that the two men had no more partners, then he headed toward the room where the pilot and mechanic stayed.

There was nothing he could do for them: they were lying in a pool of blood. They had obviously been attacked in their sleep and the pilot had the strength to drag himself to the door, which had given, whether he knew it or not, a warning to the Nyctalope about something wrong in the hangar.

Saint-Clair went back to the plane and tried to determine the extent of the damage caused by the two men. The engine was completely destroyed and it would take a long time to find the spare parts to get it working again, especially since it was ultramodern and most of the parts were not available in Spain.

He looked at the two men to make sure they could not escape. There was nothing to fear on this score because they would be unconscious for a quite a while.

He put them in chairs and tied them up. Then he went to search the cockpit for the medical kit that was always kept there. He opened it, took out a vial and a syringe, drew out the contents of the small bottle and gave one of the men an injection. A few seconds went by and saboteur opened his eyes. He looked a little groggy but you could see in his eyes that he knew he was the Nyctalope's prisoner. Saint-Clair started interrogating him without delay:

"Who sent you to sabotage my plane?"

The man clenched his jaw, looked defiantly at Saint-Clair and remained silent. The Nyctalope understood that he would have to change methods if he wanted to get anything out of him. He could, of course, always resort to strong-arm tactics but his adversary looked like a fanatic and it would probably turn out to be futile. Besides, he hated to use violence. Therefore, he decided to use hypnosis. When he was traveling through the secret regions of Tibet many years ago, he had learned to develop his psychic abilities among the lamas who had initiated him into the occult sciences. Since then he had had several opportunities to practice hypnosis with some success. In order to make it easier, he injected his prisoner with a narcotic that would break down his resistance. After locking eyes he made a few hypnotic hand movements, then fixed the guy's attention by swinging a watch before his eyes, all the while whispering calmly to put him into a trance. When the man was staring straight ahead, Saint-Clair smiled with satisfaction. The interrogation could begin. He asked his original question:

"Speak! Who sent you to sabotage my plane?"

There were a few seconds of silence, then the criminal started talking in a flat voice:

"I was sent by our boss... Engineer Korridès."

"Tell me everything you know about it."

"Yesterday we were contacted by the Engineer. We thought he'd died years ago when he had killed himself in that Madrid prison. But he's back and he told us that his old enemy, the Nyctalope, was in Spain and we had to sabotage his plane. The Engineer said we had to do it so he could fulfill his plan. And that's what we did."

"What's this plan?"

"The Engineer didn't say. I have no idea."

"Did he give you any other instructions?"

"Yes, we got orders to kill all the Nyctalope's collaborators to avenge the Hashishin who were killed because of him."

"Do you have any way to communicate with the Engineer?"

"No. He said that if need be he'd contact us by radio."

Seeing that there was nothing more to get from the prisoner, the Nyctalope finished up:

"When I snap my fingers you'll forget this conversation and fall asleep."

The Nyctalope snapped his fingers and the Hashishin—since he was indeed a member of this enemy organization—slumped down in the chair and slept.

Saint-Clair could not get over it. Not only was it confirmed now that the enemy who attacked his mansion was the Engineer, but he just learned that Korridès was back in contact with members of the organization that he had led and he had sent them after him, his family and his men. An organization that the Nyctalope, a few days ago, had sworn was totally annihilated and no longer existed! From now on he had to double his guard because his enemy had obviously been preparing his revenge for a long time and would leave nothing to chance. A few hours earlier he learned that some of his men had simply disappeared. Now he was seeing that the attack was on a much bigger scale. He had never before felt such a serious threat and for the time being he had no real clue or lead to follow! He had to be ready for any eventuality because the battle was certainly going to be pitiless.

He left the hangar and headed for one of the control towers. He had to inform the police and start contacting the different companies to get the spare parts he needed. But this was going to take time. Korridès, once again, had struck first and won the round.

He was thinking, not without a certain pain in his heart, *Korridès 2, Nyctalope 0. Luckily this round is over and he didn't win the match. However, his mysterious plan that the saboteur mentioned is troubling and I have to be ready to retaliate at any moment.*

CHAPTER XI
Exploring the Tower

Pir and Bob had taken their seats in the veloscaphe. They were wearing their diving suits and fastened to it with seat-belts. After giving them some final encouragement the other members of the expedition watched them manipulating their machine. They put the lateral blades in down position and started pedaling. The veloscaphe slowly descended. They were already sunk up to their helmets, which soon disappeared under the dark water.

Going down only three or four feet they were already blind and had to turn on the spotlight on the front of the machine. In the impenetrable darkness only the zones lit by this spot were visible. There were almost no fish. But Pir and Bob were more interested in what they were hoping to find at the bottom of the tower that was buried in the depths of the lake.

Gradually as they descended the two underwater cyclists saw that the only openings visible along the smooth-as-glass walls were long, narrow windows, like arrow slits in a fortress, which must have let in a very meager light when the tower was built. The tower, although strong and built to last, seemed to have been shaken up pretty badly by the Flood. The walls were cracked, some parts in very bad shape and they could easily imagine that the inside of the building must have suffered a great deal of damage. The whole thing looked fragile and entering it might prove difficult and dangerous.

About ten yards down they saw that the tower had a big circular terrace under which the tower grew bigger. Archways opened up at this level but like higher up the passages were completely blocked by rocks and other debris.

The two young men shot each other an understanding glance and were about to continue their descent when a huge crocodile surged out of the shadows right in front of them. It was gigantic, probably twenty feet long, and its crooked fangs were frightening. With a strong whip of its tail it came shooting forward, its jaws wide open.

Pir and Bob turned on the electric feed to their spur and pointed it at the animal. The lizard was quickly on top of it. An electric flash, brighter than the spotlight, blinded them. The crocodile started shaking and then went stiff. The luminous arc was cut off and the two divers saw that the body of their monstrous adversary was not moving. It started sinking slowly and disappeared out of sight.

Confident now in their system of defense, they continued their descent along the tower.

Fifty feet farther down they saw a second balcony under which the tower was fatter again. The building, in fact, was like a round pyramid whose perimeter, going up from the base to the summit, got progressively smaller. Once again, big stone blocks forbid access inside the building.

They kept descending and finally reached the bottom of the lake. The walls were as smooth as higher up but they seemed to be stronger. There were fewer and smaller cracks. They figured that there had to be an entrance at his lower level, so they decided to go all the way around to check.

After going a quarter of the way around the tower they found a monumental double-door built of massive stones. Around ten feet high by ten feet wide, it had no ornate decorations but was sculpted in austere motifs that represented huge hieratic statues in relief with inscriptions identical to those discovered in Mexico.

They looked at the lake bottom in front of the door and saw traces of what must have been a road long, long ago. The same width as the door, a flat surface covered with algae formed a long ribbon that wound away into the darkness. Pir and Bob gave each other knowing looks and decided to follow the road that might lead to other remains. On each side, every fifteen feet, stood time-ruined statues whose exact forms were no longer traceable. They turned the spotlight along the road and saw all kinds of ruins. The tower, apparently, had once been surrounded by a city but the material used to build it was of lesser quality and the constructions did not stand the test of time. Under the thick layer of algae they saw only a few mounds that they imagined were houses. The city architecture was built along a geometric, circular plan. Roads started at the tower like rays and were connected by concentric streets, parallel to the tower that was the heart of a complex, well-designed system.

After exploring around the tower for fifteen minutes, the two brothers, having seen what there was to see, decided to go back up without delay so that their companions would not worry. The ascent was easy until at around fifteen feet from the surface they saw two crocodiles rushing toward them. The reptiles were smaller than the previous one but they were coming from different directions and using the electric spur might prove tricky. However, when preparing for the expedition, Pir and Bob had envisaged such a possibility. They turned the veloscaphe so their backs were to the tower. Then they swung it around fast and skillfully just as they had practiced so often in a Swiss lake to make it turn in every direction.

Thanks to this maneuver the two crocodiles, when they were in range, were right before the spur. Thus, when the first was hit, since they were touching each other, they were both struck by the electric arc and were wiped out in a split second.

After this brief encounter the two young men resurfaced without any other nuisance. The main entrance to the tower had been found but the hardest part lay ahead: nothing less than to actually enter the building whose massive doors would be nearly impossible to get through and they were one hundred thirty feet down!

Their companions, who were waiting above, ran to the hoist when they saw them appear. When the two brothers had slung the ropes around the veloscaphe, they were pulled out of the water and set down on the dry terrace of the tower.

They were barely out of the bicycle when Pierre, Hubert and Professor Noque ran over to know what they had discovered. The twins told them everything and looked especially proud that thanks to their care and attention but also to the exceptional power of their invention they had fended off the crocodiles quite efficiently. Hubert wound up the discussion saying:

"Next time it won't be so easy. We were hoping to find an open underwater access but apparently that's not the case. We're going to have to break down a colossal door one hundred thirty feet underwater. Moreover, the inside might not be filled with water down there. But if we open the door the lake could flood in and cause all kinds of damage to the remains that might have withstood time and be intact. I don't know how we should proceed. To get down there is easy enough and we can attack the door with the excavation tools that we brought with us. But how to do it underwater without too many problems and above all without flooding the tower and destroying everything inside, that I really can't imagine... Can you?"

The O'Connell brothers and Pierre looked at each other, visibly discouraged. They had no solution to overcome the various obstacles that Pibriac was enumerating. But the professor cracked a smile. His companions saw this and stared at him expectantly.

"Well, yes, my friends, I might just have the solution to our dilemma. In fact, I think it's there." He pointed at the big crate that he had loaded in Paris and whose contents were still a mystery. "Come and help me open it."

Hubert and Pierre used the crowbar and quickly had the crate open. Inside were several metal pieces of different sizes, carefully packed. With the help of his companions the professor started to put the thing together. It was fairly simple to assemble and in less than an hour the machine was ready.

It was a metal chamber, a kind of big cube, fifteen feet square, and on one face was a door surrounded by a frame made of flexible material that could fit onto different shaped structures. On the other side were two doors inside each other making a small airlock. The professor explained:

"The principle is as follows: the cube has to be put at the bottom of the lake in front of the door. The flexible frame can fit over the door and make it airtight, the airlock will let us get into the cube and work like in a diving bell. Keep in mind that water can be drained from the cube through a valve system. Therefore, we can stay dry while working on opening a passage inside the tower, hoping, of course, that it's in suitable condition."

Hubert, who was smiling at him, turned suddenly grim:

"But we'll have to be very careful and keep a watch over our camp while we're working under the lake. Let's not forget the weird thing Pierre saw this morning. One of us should always be on guard up here."

"No problem," the professor said. "Anyway, setting up the machine and working on the bottom of the lake to force the stone door open isn't going to be a picnic so we should work in shifts. We'll also have to watch out for crocodiles trying to attack us, even if we have the means to protect ourselves. OK, let's get on it. We'd better start right away. We'll take the cube apart and help Pir and Bob bring it to the bottom of the lake.

CHAPTER XII
Code Joan of Arc

The Nyctalope was satisfied. Three hours earlier he was desperate to leave Spain as soon as possible but early in the morning he got good news.

The Hashishin did not have time to sabotage the radio equipment in the Zig. The Nyctalope sat in the cockpit and tried to contact various people to get some help.

At 7:30 a.m., he was able to reach Rue Montbrun in Paris and talk to Michel Dorlange. The connection was very bad and the conversation kept cutting out but this did not prevent him from explaining the situation and asking for what he needed. Dorlange would contact the different CID offices in Europe to see what was the fastest way to get the spare parts for the plane and especially a new engine.

Around 9:30 a.m., the Nyctalope learned that the same kind of plane as the Zig was available at the Marseille airport. The CID could get it for a price but a pilot still had to be found to fly it to Madrid.

Around the same time he managed to contact Petro d'Arendar, his closest Spanish friend, who was very surprised to learn that he was in Madrid. Petro was even more surprised to hear that their old enemy Maur Korridès, whom everyone believed was dead, had reappeared.

A few years before Saint-Clair had helped the duke in a delicate matter in which the honor of the Arendars was at stake. They had become good friends and the duke had given the Nyctalope a helping hand on several occasions when he was operating on Spanish soil. The last time they had worked together was when they had confronted the famous Korridès who was reappearing today. Of course, the duke assured Léo that he would do whatever he could to help. He would contact some mechanics in Madrid whom he knew and who could probably help the Nyctalope when the spare parts arrived.

After spending long hours in front of the radio, Saint-Clair left the hangar to get a little fresh air. He walked along the runways and headed for the control tower. After a quick talk with the director there, he got authorization to use the wireless and send a coded message to the CID office in Marseille, Lyon, Lille and Bordeaux. With this task done he went back to his plane and waited for responses to the messages he had sent.

Around 10 a.m., Dorlange called Saint-Clair to tell him that he had found a pilot. The plane had just left Marseille and would land in Madrid around 1 p.m. Once again the CID had demonstrated its efficiency. The Nyctalope took the opportunity to ask how things were going on Rue Montbrun. Dorlange reassured him. Everything was fine and given the deployment of force, he did not see how the enemy could touch them. Saint-Clair advised extreme caution and reminded him that the Engineer was one of the most innovative geniuses of the 20th century and, more than once in the past, had proved his ability to surprise his enemies and rise to the wildest challenges. Especially since at this stage they had no idea where he was.

Just then Dorlange remembered that he had forgotten to give the Nyctalope some important information. After their last meeting at Blingy, he had launched an investigation into the "severed hand affair" at the Jardin des Plantes. Only minutes ago he had received disturbing news. The police had also started investigating, got fingerprints from the hand and its "owner" was identified: it was Jacques Dubosque, a CID agent who had disappeared days before along with his partner Stéphane Dampierre. The macabre discovery might be a useful clue that he could still not piece it together.

The Nyctalope made no comment, but it was clear that this news had struck a chord because during the rest of the conversation he sounded distracted and evasive. While Dorlange was talking, Saint-Clair was thinking. His face hardened as if he was starting to glimpse the solution to their problem and was getting ready to go into action.

At noon, the mechanics from the duke arrived and waited together for the plane from Marseille, which landed at 1:15 p.m. They immediately took out the engine. Saint-Clair preferred to transfer the parts from the newly arrived plane into the Zig because his plane had the telecommunication system and was equipped with two machine guns that might come in very handy in the present situation.

Around 5:15 p.m. the plane was operational. Before taking off the Nyctalope still had one more order to give. He contacted Dorlange and said:

"In less than an hour I'll leave Madrid with the Zig. Tell Vitto and Soca to do as planned with the special car and our friend. Code Joan of Arc. I repeat, Code Joan of Arc. I'll be in Villacoublay around 3 a.m. See you soon."

He went to the control tower to inform them of his imminent departure and used the wireless to recontact the CID office that he had called in the morning. He received a series of coded messages that he deciphered immediately. When he looked up, despite the critical situation he was facing, he looked completely satisfied. Things were moving forward.

At 6 p.m. on the dot, after filling up with fuel and checking over the whole plane, he flew off for Paris. At the commands of the plane he was concentrating on what lay ahead. He knew that the final phase of that battle against Korridès was starting, but his enemy seemed so determined and so well organized that Saint-Clair was not sure who would come out on top.

CHAPTER XIII
The Turbaned Man Strikes

At the same time, the afternoon was dying out in the land of Nod. Everything was calm. No wave disturbed the lake. At the top of the tower Bob was taking his first turn on watch. He was pacing around, watching the sandy shore that bordered the jungle. Nothing seemed to be threatening the tranquil evening. From time to time some animals, antelopes, warthogs or groups of little monkeys came to drink from the lake. Their peaceful activities were sometimes interrupted by predators who crept out of the trees. Bob discovered that the jungle was inhabited by cheetahs. He thought he even saw some lions prowling around the edge of the forest.

In fact, the most important activity was taking place one hundred thirty feet below the dark waters of the lake.

The explorers had not stopped working all afternoon. They had assembled the metal cube so it would be dry when they tried to open the monumental door. The system of valves worked perfectly and they now had a waterproof chamber in which the air was chemically recycled with pressurized oxygen.

Hubert and Pir had started attacking the door with the excavation tools. But the stone was hard, the work was slow and tiring and so they set up teams to work in shifts. Now it was the turn of Pierre and Professor Noque to take over. In the meantime, Hubert and Pir were outside the cube in their diving suits, doing their best to memorize the inscriptions engraved in the doorframe so they could write them down inside the airlock. Professor Noque would translate them later. This headwork relied on the physical work they had done earlier. Two bright spots had been set up fifteen feet behind the cube to light up the door.

Hubert went to the airlock to draw a part of the bas-relief from memory. Pir, who was next to him, turned around and saw a strange metal object coming into the zone lit by the spotlights.

It resembled a crate standing on end with a kind of point at the top, which made it look like a big ammunition shell. The base of the object was flat and fitted with wheels so it could move. The upper part had two metallic, jointed arms ending in pincers to grab things. The mechanism that worked its arms must have been very strong and the pincers could also be used for a terribly destructive purpose. In the upper part of this strange submersible, a kind of super diving suit, a thick window showed the head of the man controlling it. He looked Indian both because of his olive tainted skin and the fact that he was wearing a turban. This was a most surprising accessory for an underwater explorer!

Pir signaled to Hubert to alert him since he was busy with the airlock. When Hubert turned around the diver was right next to him. He leaned over trying to get a good look at the pilot. But he quickly realized that the claws of the machine were trying to grab him and he barely had time to step back out of reach. The wheels on the machine shot it forward and Hubert could not get far enough away. He could only avoid it by stepping to the side every time the pincers reached out. The man with the turban seemed surprised by his resistance.

In the meantime Pir got to the veloscaphe and sat in the back. Unfortunately the underwater bicycle was a tandem and needed two people to drive it comfortably. Hubert, who was fully concentrated on dodging the lethal blows of the machine, could obviously not join him. After a great deal of effort Pir managed to point the veloscaphe at the super-diver. He waved desperately to Hubert to move away, hoping that he could launch the bike and hit the enemy with the electric spur.

Hubert, unlike the enemy who kept up his attack, was showing signs of fatigue. The weight of the lead-ballasted diving suit made it hard to move. If it were not for his incredible strength, he would have collapsed, totally exhausted, long ago.

He had just managed to sidestep one more blow when he saw, out of the corner of his eye, Pir waving to him. He understood immediately. With a revival of hope came a surge of energy. By moving directly backwards he was headed straight for the veloscaphe. He had almost got the two machines face-to-face but he was hit hard by one of the arms. Fatigue had slowed down his movements and the super-diver got him.

Even with the water's resistance he was hit terribly hard in the arm and pain shot through his entire body. He was thrown a few yards away and his arm, lying at a weird angle, became completely numb. The bone was broken. With blurry vision and his mind dazed by the pain, Hubert was left powerless. He struggled to his feet thanks to his lead shoes and tired desperately not to pass out, which he felt he was about to do.

The super-diver was coming to finish him off. But Hubert's backpedaling had put the machine in reach of the veloscaphe. Pir gave a hard kick to the pedal to push it forward, knowing that he would have only one chance to hit his target. He fired an electric charge strong enough to down an elephant and it hit the enemy on the left side, just under his arm. A bright flash filled the suit and it stopped moving immediately. Then the lights went out.

Pir, in a panic, saw the super-diving suit start moving again. The designers of the machine had obviously foreseen the possibility of an electric attack and equipped it with an insulation system. It was absolutely unbelievable!

The veloscaphe was brought to a stop when it ran into the super-diver. Even though he was alone inside, Pir did not have enough room to wriggle free in time. The machine had turned and was coming at him, claws forward. Pir was out of reach, protected by the hood, which was much longer than the jointed arms, but this did not stop the turbaned man for long. One of the claws grabbed the spur and snapped it off. Then he pointed both arms at the veloscaphe's frame and started tearing it apart. Fragments of metal went swimming away into the depths and drifting slowly to the floor of the lake. Pir wanted to get out of the veloscaphe to escape the enemy but his diving suit was caught on one of the duralumin rods and he could not get free. The claw was only inches away from his copper helmet now.

He aimed the bright spotlight at the helmet of the superdiving suit to blind the enemy and gain a little time. The inventor of the suit must have been a victim of an electrical attack in the past and compensated for this weakness in his machine, but he had done nothing to protect against a bright light shining straight into the eyes of the pilot. The turbaned man was, therefore, blinded and could only strike haphazardly while waiting for his sight to return to normal.

Pir took advantage of the delay to shake himself free and get out of the veloscaphe without damage. But just as he was about to escape the enemy, he was hit on the side with a wild blow from one of the pincers. He was not hit with a sharp edge but the violence of it sent him sailing off and he hit his head on the tower wall. The copper helmet was strong enough not to break but Pir lost consciousness as a result.

The man with the turban, on the other hand, got his visibility back. He saw that the bottom of the lake was calm now. Before him were the remains of the veloscaphe and a little farther the motionless body of Pir. He turned around to look for Hubert. At first he saw nothing but looking more carefully he made out the lead boots and chest plate of the diving suit lying on the ground. Pibriac must have taken them off to swim back to the surface. The Indian was probably thinking that he could settle accounts with him later because he turned back around and started straight for the cube.

Inside the cube Professor Noque had worked hard on the monumental door. Pierre was surprised by the strength of his partner who, being a scholar, must have lived a relatively sedentary life. Noque had torn out a block of stone and was trying to make a crack in the door.

This was when Hubert should be replacing Pierre in the excavation and the young man was already getting into his diving suit. Hubert was a few minutes late but he was probably absorbed in the bas-reliefs and had lost track of time.

Pierre was stepping into the airlock when a violent shock shook the cube. The professor, who could not understand what caused the phenomenon, looked up suspiciously. The cube was shaken again. The sound of metal echoed through the walls, which were under great pressure. But the cube was designed to be used up to three hundred feet down and so this could not be an effect of water pressure. The thought of an attack from the outside crossed their minds and they wondered what had happened to Pir and Hubert.

Pierre tried to open the airlock to go and see what was going on but it was stuck. He looked at the gauge to the right of the door and saw that the airlock was filling up with water. It had been designed so that the opening mechanism would be blocked in such an emergency in order to prevent total immersion.

"The airlock's flooding!" he turned to the professor. "It's not normal. You'd better put on your suit."

Before the professor had time to answer, a heavy blow struck the inner door of the airlock. Another followed and dented the sheet. Given the thickness of the material, the strength needed to do this must have been extraordinary.

Pierre stepped back and looked around the room. He saw only a big mallet to use as a weapon. He was leaning over to grab it when another blow shook the door. Now it was starting to bend and a crack near the frame was leaking water, spitting it inside the small space.

Professor Noque did not yet have time to put on his suit while Pierre stood at the ready with the mallet, waiting for the door to give way. Another blow literally ripped through the steel door.

Water came pouring into the space and Pierre was thrown backward. The whole cube was flooded within seconds. Pierre saw a weird metallic machine burst in behind two jointed arms with pincers that were aimed at his helmet. With the water now an obstacle, Pierre could not use his mallet and felt totally helpless. The professor next to him had already passed out. Pierre grabbed a small pickaxe that was in reach and swung it at the enemy's helmet in which he could see the strange man wearing a turban. As hard as he could he struck at the window but the pick slipped off the glass without even scratching it. Then the young man felt one of the metal claws hit him on his helmet. The copper bent and the glass shattered under the blow. Water rushed into the suit and Pierre lost consciousness. His last thought was for his father who was also being threatened by a relentless enemy.

CHAPTER XIV
Revenge!

In the back of the car Duke Petro d'Arendar was reading the morning mail. The business at the airport had made him late and at the end of the afternoon the chauffeur was driving him back home, a few miles outside of Madrid.

He had been glad to be of service to his old friend Léo Saint-Clair, but the more he concentrated on the mail and the political situation in Spain, which was a mess, the more his mind turned away from the Korridès affair. He had been one of the strongest supporters of King Alfonso XIII who was living in exile in France today. The future of the Spanish Republic was in jeopardy because the forces that had taken over the country were divided and a good number of extremists were seizing power. The duke could not do much about this. On the other hand, he could work with the different monarchist factions to defuse the situation and to keep the whole country from blowing up in a civil war.

He had just received a letter from a general who was writing to offer him nothing less than the restoration of the monarchy by force. This Francisco Franco, whom the head of the government said in private was the most dangerous Spanish officer, was asking him to appeal to the King so that he could enlist the help of Victor Emmanuel III of Italy and Benito Mussolini to bring back the House of Bourbon to Spain. An intervention of the Italian army in Spain—now that was a really hare-brained idea!

The duke took a sheet of paper from his briefcase to write a kind but firm response. Spain would have to deal with its own problems and do so through negotiation and dialogue, not with arms. He wondered sometimes is this were really possible, but it was too soon to say for sure.

While the duke was thinking of this letter, his car had left the suburbs of Madrid and was on the country highway. A sidecar that had been following for a few minutes sped up. It was starting to pass. When it pulled alongside the back door, the passenger in the sidecar threw a tarp off his knees and raised a machine gun. Before Pedro d'Arendar was even aware of what was happening the man emptied his clip into him. He was killed on the spot. The chauffeur lost control of the car, bounced off the highway and went rolling into the fields.

The sidecar sped off and was lost to sight.

The old enemies of Engineer Korridès could be hit anywhere and at any time.

CHAPTER XV
The Return of the Master

Night fell over the house on Rue Montbrun in Paris.

The soldiers had set up roadblocks on either end of the street. In front of the door of Léo Saint-Clair's residence two guards kept watch, with bayonets fixed. Inside, twenty CID agents were ready to act at any moment. They had organized shifts to keep watch during the night to face any possible attack. On the roof an anti-aircraft gun had been set up. In the sky there were squadrons of fighter jets making rounds every five minutes around the house. The defense organized by the Nyctalope with the help of the government seemed flawless.

In the salon on the second floor Michel Dorlange, his wife Erin and Sylvie Saint-Clair, were coordinating the defense of the house and the actions of the CID agents. In the four corners of Europe, the members of the organization run by Saint-Clair had suffered numerous surprise attacks by Korridès without being able to react effectively.

In the afternoon the Nyctalope himself had launched an operation that he called "Joan of Arc." He was hoping that maybe the next morning it could offer serious opposition to the Engineer's attacks. Meanwhile, Dorlange, Erin and Sylvie were preparing for a night of siege in the house transformed into a trench camp.

In the street, there were fewer cars driving up to the barricade. In fact, more often than not they were not let through and this discouraged journalists and rubberneckers. Delivery drivers and cabbies called to Rue Montbrun for professional reasons had to park at a distance and go on foot to get authorization to enter the street in their car and park briefly.

A coalman was doing just that, chatting with the soldiers to get his truck up to his clients so he would not have to haul the heavy sacks by hand in separate loads. Behind him was a potato deliveryman ready to ask the same thing and looking worriedly at the huge canvas bags that he had to take all way up to the fifth floor sometimes.

A little farther away, behind these horse carts, a covered truck was parked. A fat man in a big coat and a wide-brimmed hat that hid part of his face scrambled out and went around the back of the truck. Despite his weight he jumped into the back rather agilely.

The soldiers who were busy talking to the coal man paid no attention to him.

The man turned on a flashlight and carefully closed the cover behind him. Inside what looked like a delivery truck was a weird, bulky, mechanical assembly whose use would no doubt baffle the cleverest engineers at the Ecole Polytechnique. To the right of this machine was a kind of control panel covered with lights, different colored buttons and a series of sliding controls and rheostats that must have regulated the energy or whatever unknown force powered the device.

The control panel ran the machine whose function, it must be said, was hard to determine at first sight. It looked like a huge "storage battery" with all kinds of different movable parts. Over it, fit into the right side of the machine was a tube whose end flared out like a huge phonograph horn. On the side of the control panel, connected to it by a thick cable, was a helmet riddled with electrical wires ending in rubber caps. The thing was obviously meant to be worn so it could connect to different parts of the brain.

The man sat in front of the control panel and pulled off his gloves. He started playing with the controls and quickly had it adjusted. The machine started to purr.

He took off his hat and his face appeared pale and sinister in the light. His eyes were a strange blue with gold sparkles. His hair was cut very short, making his skull look almost bald. His face was deeply lined, like someone who had lived a hard life.

What was most surprising about this giant was his head, held up by a collar of metal cables and by a kind of steel neck brace that kept it vertical with the rest of his body. Above his neck was an electric cable that entered directly into his skull.

His hands, now bare, were also reinforced with a strong steel frame all the way to the tips of his fingers. Moving them seemed to be controlled by the metal joints hidden under his coat.

The man looked like a quadriplegic who could only move thanks to a steel exoskeleton that he managed to control with his mind. His overdeveloped brain had realized the impossible.

He put the helmet of the weird machine on his head and adjusted the rubber tips very carefully so they would line up with the correct areas of his brain. His haircut was obviously to make the operation easier. While he was fitting the various tips to his head, the lights of the control panel lit up one by one. When the last one was on, the man turned a small crank that worked the flared tube to point it at the Nyctalope's house, along with all the security around it.

His hands being controlled by the metal cables ran over the control panel like a concert pianist grazing his keyboard. The purring became shriller. One of the barricades heard this weird sound coming from the truck and started looking more closely at it. His gaze was attracted by the tube sticking out of the back. Intrigued, the soldier walked around the checkpoint and the sandbags and approached the vehicle. Armed with his bayonet he strolled up casually, not really worried about anything.

The sound coming out of the truck suddenly turned into a screech. The soldier stopped, seemed to hesitate. His face was frozen and he started sweating bullets. He was clearly trying to fight against some outside force but all he could do was turn around slowly and head back to the barricade where his colleague was still talking with the coalman wanting authorization to do his deliveries on Rue Montbrun.

The coalman finally went back to his cart and the guard stepped aside to let them pass. When the soldier came back holding his rifle, he stood in front of his colleague and stuck the bayonet into his belly. With a violent thrust he ripped open his belly all the way up to his chest. The guard's face twisted in pain and surprise, watching his attacker with unbelieving eyes. Then he dropped to the ground in a pool of his own blood.

The soldiers posted a little farther down the street watched the scene in horror, not understanding what was going on. Frozen in terror, they all went silent. Soon they heard the buzzing of the fighter jets making their pass over the street.

Two things happened at the same time. The soldier who had just killed his comrade started running across the street, his bayonet dripping with blood and guts held out like a spear. He stabbed two pedestrians who went down screaming in pain. Simultaneously the jet over the house made a wide turn and got in line with the anti-aircraft gun, which was set up to protect the house. The fighter was also equipped with machine guns in front. He started firing, aiming deliberately at the roof. The first bullets ricocheted off the gutter but the next round hit the gunner in the head. He collapsed as his partner was hit in the legs, barely having time to jump to the side and hit the deck, groaning in pain. It took only a few seconds to put out of commission the gun meant to protect Saint-Clair's house.

In the street and around the house the soldiers did not know which way to turn. Four of them tried to bring down the murderous guard while others pointed their rifles at the sky in some mad hope of taking the fighter jet out of play.

Inside the house the CID agents heard the shouting and shooting. They pulled out their Brownings and took position at the windows to defend the house. Although they did not understand what was happening, they were ready for anything.

The raving mad soldier was stabbed twice in the belly with a bayonet and dropped to the ground.

The fighter jet disappeared from sight; soon it was back and coming down the street. It started gunning for the soldiers trying to shoot it down and it targeted the trucks parked along the sidewalk as well. Several men were mowed down; others were hit by bullets ricocheting off the pavement. A truck whose gas tank had been hit exploded and the fire spread to two other vehicles.

This brutal attack left nothing untouched except for one truck whose driver was trying to back up to avoid the flames that were jumping off the other vehicles. In the meantime, the unharmed soldiers sought shelter under porches and fired wildly with their rifles. In fact, it was possible that one of them might hit the maniacal plane as it was flying low, apparently beyond danger.

The jet was getting ready for a third run. Its machine guns started firing on the few soldiers still alive. A few shots answered from the windows of the house. Most of the agents had Brownings but two of them had brought machine guns and were aiming at the plane. Finally hit in the arm by someone, the pilot lost control of the plane, which swerved to the left and crashed into the house directly across the street from the Nyctalope's residence. The tide seemed to have turned, until shots were heard coming from inside the house itself.

In a few seconds, as they were still stationed at the windows for defense, some of the agents were shot in the back by their own colleagues who stared blankly ahead and acted like sleepwalkers trying to kill everything in their path.

On the second floor, in the salon where all the doors had been locked, Dorlange and his wife were shielding Sylvie Saint-Clair and trying to understand what was happening. All three of them were armed with Brownings and ready to fire. They watched the doors of the room anxiously.

"It's coming from everywhere," Dorlange said. "The enemy's apparently got into the house. I wonder how they did it."

"A fighter jet was shot down just before we locked ourselves in here. But I have the feeling that it was being flown by an enemy," his wife answered. "I don't get it."

Sylvie spoke up, "In fact, it's like the men who are supposed to be protecting us have gone mad and are trying to kill one another... That doesn't seem possible! Unless we're the victims of a very powerful psychic attack. Léo told me about one of his enemies who was capable of such madness. It was not Engineer Korridès but…"

She was cut off because the door leading to the stairs just flew open. A dazed and haunted looking agent stepped into the room, waving his Browning at all of them until it finally settled on Dorlange. But before he had time to pull the trigger, Sylvie, much to her chagrin, stuck a bullet between his eyes. She saw her hypothesis confirmed: just as she had said their enemy was using some extraordinary psychic power to turn the agents against one another until everyone was killed.

"Michel, lock the door! We have to cut off all contact with the others if we don't want to shoot them all!"

Dorlange locked the door while shots continued ringing out throughout the house, often broken up by machine gun fire. The three of them looked at each other in bewilderment.

"It could be an old enemy of my husband, Lucifer," said Sylvie, "but I think Léo killed him with his own hands. That's why I was leaning more toward Armand Logreux d'Albury, who was called 'The Master of the Seven Lights.' He, too, had psychic powers and could kill his enemies at a distance."

Then she saw that Dorlange was starting to sweat and seemed to be fighting against forces rising up inside of him. His eyes turned glassy. He slowly raised his weapon and pointed it at his wife Erin. He fired and killed her with one bullet in the heart. She was so astonished that she did not make a move to protect herself. The enemy's power was really limitless if it could push a loving, caring husband like Dorlange to murder his young wife in cold blood.

Then he aimed his Browning at Sylvie. But she had understood the danger and had ducked behind a table to defend herself. He shot but the bullet lodged in the wood. He started walking around the table to get to his target. Sylvie snuck around the other side, keeping the table between them, but crouching down as she was, she moved more slowly than Michel and in no time he would be in position to shoot her.

As a last resort and since no other solution seemed possible, she raised her weapon and shot. He was hit in the arm and dropped his gun, wobbling on his feet. The wound, however, was not serious enough to neutralize him completely. He looked around like a robot. He saw another gun lying on the table and with his good hand reached out for it. He kept staring, glassy-eyed, at Sylvie and brought the gun up slowly. The young lady saw no other solution: she put a bullet in his head to stop him for good.

Erin and Dorlange, one of her best friends and the partner of her husband, were now lying at her feet, swimming in their own blood, which was pooling over the carpet.

She stood there panting in the middle of the room, drained of all energy. Gradually the gunshots died down in the house. After a few minutes there was nothing but a mysterious, agonizing silence.

Sylvie listened hard. She heard nothing. She went to the door, gripping her gun. She put her ear up to the wood and listened. Not a sound. She turned the key in the lock and opened the door. In the next room a few corpses of CID agents were lying on the floor. Bullet holes pocked the walls. The furniture was riddled with lead and almost all the decorations were broken. She crossed the room and looked out the window.

In the street the trucks continued to burn. The soldiers' corpses, lying in their own blood, were scattered over the sidewalk, sometimes in bizarre positions. A few civilians had also died during the battle.

Then she saw a fat man waving to her from behind the control panel in the truck. She started raising her weapon but froze in mid-air. Her arm fell to her side and she dropped the Browning. Like a robot she walked down the stairs, crossed the hallway, left the house and headed for the man. During this time he had climbed back into truck behind the wheel.

She reached the truck and sat next to him, in an almost cataleptic state, as if mesmerized.

"Bonjour, Madame Saint-Clair," he said. "Let me introduce myself. I am Armand Logreux d'Albury, an old friend of your husband. We haven't had the pleasure of meeting each other before but I believe we have one friend in common, Engineer Maur Korridès. He wishes to speak with you and your husband and he has given me the most pleasant part of the mission—coming to fetch you. I'm glad you accepted his invitation on such short notice."

He seemed very satisfied with his bit of humor and snickered. Then he continued.

"This little experiment allowed me to test the improved version of my psychic amplifier, which gives me total control over people's behavior when they're hit by the ray. Impressive, isn't it?"

During this speech, Sylvie sat like a statue. She was still under the influence of the mysterious machine and her will was completely submissive. Her husband, thanks to his great spiritual strength, might be able to resist this infernal machine, but Sylvie could not fight back.

Logreux went on with his monologue. He knew that Sylvie could not answer but he was having fun bragging about his crushing victory over the forces of the Nyctalope.

"Yes, Korridès thinks he's boss but it's me who organized everything. When I met him, he'd been beaten, made a prisoner in Spain. In fact, he was even thinking of ways to put an end to all his suffering. That was the moment I was waiting for. I got in touch with him through telepathy and said: *Korridès, you're not giving up now when you have the means to overcome your enemy once and for all?*

"After hesitating a moment, he answered me, concentrating hard: *Who are you?*

"And I sent out: *I'm Armand Logreux d'Albury, whom some call the Master of the Seven Lights. I'm offering to join forces to crush the Nyctalope, our common enemy. I'll take care of breaking you out and you will use your mechanical knowledge to build an exoskeleton for me so I can once again move freely. In fact, when I met the Nyctalope, he tricked me and made me a quadriplegic by injecting a toxic chemical into my blood that killed my nervous system below the neck.*

"The pact was made on the spot. Later, Korridès said he thought it would be easy to do what I wanted and it was like a scientific challenge that interested him. Especially if the exoskeleton had to be controlled by my mind. A psychomechanical machine in a way, a first of its kind! He loved being the first in anything. I knew this and thereby could lead him where I wanted him to go. The pact was concluded. Using one of the guards that I controlled mentally, I snuck into the prison a Tibetan drug that makes one appear dead. I only had to wait for them to bury him. Then I would go and get him. I put my Indian servant in charge of that. So, he made the contraption I had asked for and turned an invalid into a superman. Because, go figure, he used the opportunity to give me extraordinary strength! Then all we had to do was plan our revenge to destroy all the work and the family of your husband before he destroyed us."

The Master of Seven Lights stopped talking, apparently lost in thought.

Sylvie was in no condition to do anything about all this new information. And despite her knowledge of Paris, she was not even able to memorize the route taken by the truck. The vehicle was still driving around the capital but the buildings were sailing by her eyes without her recognizing a single one or figuring out where they were headed.

After a while it seemed that they had crossed the Seine. The truck stopped alongside a fence. She watched herself climb out of the truck and cross a construction site. Then she entered a big building whose door shut behind her.

CHAPTER XVI
The Destruction of the Nyctalope

At 1 a.m., the Nyctalope's airplane was soaring through darkness. He was still far from Paris and could only make out a few lights down below.

Saint-Clair was piloting automatically. His mind was totally absorbed by the conversation that he was having with Captain Gougeon on the radio. He had just learned that his house had been attacked, his friends killed and his wife kidnapped.

"Yes, Monsieur Saint-Clair, it's a real disaster. More than thirty soldiers are dead along with ten CID agents. The others are all pretty gravely injured. I myself managed to pull through. I only got a bayonet in the leg and got knocked out. When I came to the battle was over and I was being rescued by the army medical services that was just arriving on the scene."

"And my wife has disappeared?"

The Nyctalope could barely contain himself. His voice trembled. He had not imagined that his enemy would retaliate so quickly and he felt completely overwhelmed by the events. But already, without even being fully conscious of it, his remarkable mental faculties, perfectly honed over the years, were at work on getting the upper hand. He had had the greatest Tibetan lamas as masters and controlling his emotions had become second nature to him. But he knew, and it always frightened him, that in extreme cases he could fall apart, like when his mother died a few years earlier. He asked for more information in order to reduce his stress by thinking about and analyzing the situation:

"Are you sure?" he asked.

"Highly likely. We didn't find her body in the salon where she was holed up. Plus, a few wounded soldiers say they saw a beautiful blonde woman leave the house walking like a puppet and get into a truck. Given the nature of the attack, kidnapping looks like the most reasonable assumption."

"And... the Dorlanges?"

"Unfortunately, they're both dead and we found their bodies. We're interrogating possible witnesses to..."

Static had been cutting off Captain Goujon's words until he finally became inaudible. Saint-Clair tried adjusting the radio and changing frequencies to reestablish contact but to no avail. All of a sudden the crackling stopped and a voice boomed through the speaker:

"Léo Saint-Clair... The Nyctalope?"

"I hear you loud and clear. Who is this?"

The voice sounded triumphant:

"Hello, Monsieur Saint-Clair. This is Maur Korridès. I think the time for explanations has finally come..."

"Maur Korridès! You dare... after killing my friends and kidnapping my wife..."

Saint-Clair, who did not want to lose control before his enemy, had difficulties keeping a lid on his anger. He managed, however, to calm down a little and let Korridès talk:

"Well, yes, I dare! And with your limited means, you're right to be surprised at hearing my voice over your radio."

"It's your gall that surprises me! I have no doubt that you're the one who's been intercepting my radio communications. So much interference and static isn't normal. But you still don't know all my plans. I thought, of course, about a double agent infiltrating the CID... but there are so few people who are in the know that an outside spy using technology is the most probable explanation. So, I figured it was you with your scientific knowledge who was pirating my conversations and messages. No, I'm not surprised but you could have done it with less interference, less static while you were listening in. A genius like you, it should have been right up your alley. When your men attacked me in Madrid I had no more doubt about it. There was no other explanation."

In a less triumphant tone Korridès answered:

"Perhaps… Perhaps… But as faulty as it was, my invention did the job. I knew that I might be discovered. So, I compensated for the technological shortfall with the speed of my actions. And as you will see, it won't matter a bit to my final victory. I've already hit you hard and I will hit you again, you and yours, until you're all completely exterminated."

"I just learned that you attacked my house on Rue Montbrun and you kidnapped my wife…"

By saying this Léo was trying to get more information about the fate of his wife.

"Of course I did!" Korridès roared. "I succeeded in destroying the CID and now I'm going to finish off the rest of your people: your son, your first wife, your friends… In the next few hours you yourself will be executed. Then it'll be your wife's turn. You can't do anything for her! I've prepared an unprecedented, scientific end worthy of her beauty. But if you'd like, I can explain the different stages of my crusade against the Nyctalope and how I'm going to destroy you."

The Nyctalope thought he could outwit his opponent, but he needed more time. The plan he had in mind would be easier to put in play for two reasons, on the technical side, if he were closer to Paris. As things stood he was not sure that his counter-attack would succeed. Therefore, he had to stretch out the conversation so he could make the best use of his teams. He kept talking:

"In fact, the key is to know why you even started this crusade. Of course, we confronted each other in the past but I don't really understand how such a vendetta could have come out of that…"

"You don't understand! You ruined my life and I was supposed to just lie down and accept it?"

"Ruined your life? Oh, right, your wife, Diana Krosnoview, the Red Princess, was killed when she was my prisoner. But I wasn't behind it and she was in prison because you and she had kidnapped my wife and son to avenge the death of Leonid Zattan, her old boss, whom I had managed to destroy."

Saint-Clair did not feel very convincing. Korridès was in a rage:

"But you were responsible for the death of my third wife! Like a coward you let her get murdered! For this I have to take revenge personally and you can't wriggle your way out of it and pretend you had nothing to do with what happened!"

The Nyctalope was very surprised by this unexpected answer. He said:

"How could I have hurt you before we fought in Spain? We had only met each other once before and it was very brief. On Mars, in the French colony of Argyre, just before it was destroyed…"

The Engineer went off on a long speech during which his voice softened, as if it got lost, gradually, in a maze of memories:

"Yes, it was the day all the colonists went crazy. That cursed day when they killed one another, when husband murdered wife, father slayed son, friend slaughtered friend. As you know you were not the only one there. I was there, too, with my wife Marguerite. I remember: the day she and I left, we were walking in one of those gorgeous forests on Mars. The leaves of the majestic trees were all different shades of red and rustling gently in the Martian breeze. The fantastic animals running around the forest were a pleasure to our eyes. We were trying to imagine how these weird animals lived.

"That morning we had watched from a distance the movements of a kind of giant, yellow millipede that was forging its way through the thick bushes. After our walk, when we had strolled back to the colony, we were still talking about the impressive sight. It was then that we heard the screams and explosions. We didn't yet know it but the colonists had started their day of destruction. At first we tried to get closer but when we saw how the peaceful people had suddenly, for no apparent reason, turned into wild, rabid beasts, killing one another, we knew we had to stay away. Hiding behind a nearby hill we saw an old man being chased down by young colonist armed with an iron bar. It looked like Oxus, who had founded the Argyre colony long before the French expedition got there, at a time when it was still a secret base of the organization known as the XV. The young man caught up to Oxus and hit him over the head. The old scientist fell down and never got back up.

"Horrified, we decided to skirt around the living quarters and head for our ship, which we'd left near the place they parked the radio-planes. As opposed to those interplanetary ships imagined by the XV that moved on a force field emitted between the organization's Congo base and the one near the Mars colony, my ship ran on heliose, an energy source of my own invention that left me independent. It was a synthetic metal with a strong attraction to the sun. By using butterfly valves I could regulate this magnetic pull, thereby traveling in space. After a bunch of detours my wife and I were almost at our rocket ship when you showed up, wild-eyed and covered in blood. You looked like you had lost your mind. You were heading straight for my ship, no doubt to steal it so you could get off the red planet. But unfortunately for you, we stood in your way, apparently insignificant objects in your eyes...

"I was protecting Marguerite. I stepped forward and asked you to leave us alone and go your way. You karate chopped me on the neck with your bloody hand. I felt a sharp pain run through my body and I passed out almost immediately. When I came to, next to Marguerite who was rubbing my face gently, we had been abandoned on Mars. In the sky our ship was speeding off until it finally disappeared. You left the planet in our ship and we were marooned among the lunatic colonists.

"We decided to hide while waiting for things to calm down. But before we could find shelter, some of them spotted us and gave chase. We ran as fast as we could. With the light gravity on Mars we were taking giant leaps and this chase through the air had something unreal about it. Maybe we would've lost them if Marguerite hadn't twisted her ankle after jumping a little too high. I helped her up and we kept going, but we were slowed down and the mad hunters were getting closer every second. We were almost at the edge of the forest when I was hit on the back of the neck. I dropped to my knees. Before I could get up I was hit again and this time I passed out.

"When I came to I had a bunch of cuts and bruises all over my body. I still bear the marks of this attack today. But this was nothing because a few feet away I saw the body of Marguerite, hacked and slashed with a knife. She had obviously defended herself bravely before falling under the blows of her enemies. Her hand still grasped a bloody stone, one of those stones that were already naturally red that you find all over Mars. Near her, only a few feet away, our attackers were lying lifeless on the ground. They had fought and killed one another. I was the sole survivor but I was physically and emotionally shattered.

"Why did I not die that day with my wife? I don't know. Why did I escape the strange effect that drove the other colonists insane? This, too, remains a mystery. But with time I came to believe that Léo Saint-Clair, whom all of France considered a hero, a paragon of virtue, had left us to die, me and my dear Marguerite, out of cowardice, only to save his own hide. If it wasn't for him, we would've been able to escape. He was the one who dug our graves. I had to punish him. I survived all this time to avenge Marguerite by punishing the one who was responsible for her death. At first I failed and I almost died myself. But today the time has finally come to settle accounts."

Saint-Clair let the Engineer talk, primarily for strategic reasons, but also because the story both interested and troubled him. He could not believe what his enemy was telling him. He remembered the Martian colony, of course, where he had lived with Xavière, his first wife, and their three children. Xavière had died giving birth to their son Pierre. She was closed up in a transparent sarcophagus and thanks to a treatment discovered by a scientist in Argyre, her body would remain eternally young and vital, as if ready to be reborn.

But the events that had caused the destruction of the colony had remained, until now, buried in the depths of his memory, as if hidden behind a veil of ignorance. The shock he felt was no doubt caused by a long amnesia. The Engineer's speech was, therefore, a real revelation for him. But now he was starting to remember and all the tragic events were slowly coming back to the surface of his memory. The protective veil was finally being lifted and memories were flooding in.

The colonists had been contaminated by an intelligent virus that tried to control their bodies and that drove them mad. He, too, had been affected. He did indeed return to Earth in Korridès' rocket and was found completely dazed. Because before this, he had suffered the most terrible tragedy. He had not just shoved aside the Engineer to take his ship but like the other colonists driven insane by the Martian parasite, he had participated in the massacre. He had killed. He thinks he had even killed his own children. For Saint-Clair the shock was unbearable. While he was trying to get over this, Maur Korridès spoke again, as if lost in his own memories:

"Yes, I wandered over the Martian plains not knowing where I was going, completely hopeless. Without Marguerite my life was meaningless. A long and happy marriage had just come to an end. I had no reason to live. My life was over. But your savage face kept haunting my nights. After I don't know how long, I saw there remained only one thing for me: vengeance. Yes, before leaving for the farther shores I had to avenge Marguerite and punish the man who ruined my existence. I went back, therefore, to the remains of Argyre. Nothing but silence and death. Lifeless bodies all over the city. Death had done its work but the equipment was not too damaged. Going through the laboratories I noticed that the radio-wave propulsion system could be repaired easily. My wife had died for nothing because you could have taken a radio-plane to leave the planet.

"After a few hours of work the propulsion system was up and running. I got into one of the radio-planes and flew to Earth. After a week I was back in France. Then I needed to prepare my revenge. I found out that you were busy with the war against the Germans. You were hopping from one trench to the next, which made it hard for me to reach you. I had to be patient and wait for the right moment. It was just before the end of the war when I met Princess Diana Ivanovna Krosnoview. She was setting up a network of Bolshevik agents whose mission was to spread the revolution in the west when the fighting had stopped for good. Me teaming up with Bolsheviks! Everything about them disgusted me! The rule of mediocrity! Only exceptional beings like myself should lead the human race. But in the final count, as Lenin used to say, the end justifies the means. And my revenge trumped everything. I helped Diana as much as I could to set up her network.

"Very quickly it became one of the best organized on the planet and its renown reached the ears of Leonid Zattan, who also had a secret international organization. His genius was to federate different occult networks and they were about to take over the whole world when you caught him and broke up his organization. He died soon afterward, in exile, abandoned on an island in the Pacific. At his side was my future wife, who had also been captured. She was tortured but managed to escape her enemies by the sole power of her genius. It was you who had delivered her to them!

"We decided to unite our forces once and for all to fight you. She became my third wife and we created the Hashishin who were becoming as powerful as the organization founded by Zattan. And the moment I'd been waiting for finally came: our confrontation! Everything was ready to make you suffer the worst torments. Unfortunately, I have to admit I underestimated you. Thanks to a ploy you managed to beat us. My wife lost her life because of you and I was on the verge of suicide…"

"I thought you did kill yourself. I was at your funeral in Madrid," the Nyctalope broke in, deeply disturbed by the discussion and trying to change the tone just the same.

A hint of amusement flavored the voice of Korridès when he answered:

"Yes, that's what I wanted you to believe. A strong ally helped me. But you will never know exactly how I managed it. It's time to get the friendly conversation back on track and tell you exactly how I figure on exacting my revenge on you. Of course, you know that we've attacked and killed a bunch of your agents..."

"Yes, yes, I know," the Nyctalope answered dryly.

"And that we destroyed your mansion in Versailles and your house in Paris where we captured your wife Sylvie, who will have to die soon. But we also murdered your friend, Duke Petro d'Arandar, who was helping you fight against me and Diana in Spain."

Saint-Clair was stunned and babbled:

"Duke d'Arandar... murdered..."

"And that's not all. We also wiped out the expedition of your friend Hubert de Pibriac, including your son Pierre. When I learned that he was going off to Africa I sent one of my old inventions against them. They should all be dead as we speak but their bodies will never be found."

"Pierre... Dead..." The Nyctalope felt the world collapsing around him and he could not utter another sound.

"Yes, dead, just like you and your wife will be soon. But before reaching my final step, I still have a little surprise in store for you. Listen..."

With his heart crushed and broken, Saint-Clair listened. At first he heard nothing. Then all of a sudden the noise of an explosion was clearly heard over the speaker. Then another and another. There were six in all. Although distressed and anxious, Saint-Clair kept silent, waiting for his enemy to explain, which Korridès was postponing out of sick pleasure.

"Nice explosions, weren't they?"

"What was that?"

"The sound of the six main CID offices in France and Europe disappearing." He paused dramatically before adding, "Now there's nothing left of the Nyctalope and I'll be able to kill Léo Saint-Clair."

Shocked by the revelations of Maur Korridès, Saint-Clair was shaken to the very core of his being. He had suddenly remembered the awful events that had caused the destruction of the French colony on Mars along with the death of his two older children, killed by his own hands while he was oblivious, under the spell of the Martian virus that made him crazy. He had just learned of the death of his son Pierre and the destruction of the CID. His wife was being held prisoner by his enemies and her life was on the line. He sat there in a daze, totally devastated...

A light started flashing on the instrument panel. Saint-Clair shook himself and looked at the screen to see what was coming at the Zig. He saw a huge metal machine. There was no doubt about it: it was the helicopter powered by solar energy designed by Korridès. Once, in Spain, during one of their first encounters, he had the chance to see a prototype. He prepared his machine guns and got ready to give a big welcome to his enemy. They were a hundred yards from each other and the helicopter was coming on fast. The Nyctalope opened fire. The machine guns rattled. Saint-Clair had aimed well and the bullets hit the fuselage, but it must have been thick and reinforced because in spite of the heavy fire Korridès' aircraft seemed unaffected by the attack.

The Nyctalope's plane flew as close as possible to the helicopter in order to give it another flurry of bullets. Just then the copter spun around and shot a yellow ray that barely missed. The Zip, skillfully piloted by Saint-Clair, made a long spiral to escape the powerful weapon. In the past the Engineer had developed a disintegrating ray. If he were dealing with that weapon here, he had every reason to be afraid.

After flying around he was facing the helicopter again, searching desperately for a way to fight his enemy effectively. His machine guns could not pierce the armored fuselage, so he had to try to hit a more vulnerable spot. He saw two possibilities: he could target the windows, but they were small and the outcome was uncertain; or he could fire at the rotor blades whose armor, if there were any, would be much thinner. This last idea seemed a lot easier to accomplish.

He got closer and started firing continually at the rotor, hoping to break them and bring down the copter. At first the bullets were lost in the whirling blades. Then there was a slight disturbance in the rapid whirling that made them almost invisible. One of them must have been hit and a piece thrown off had hit the other. The rhythm of the rotation slowed down and the blades, which could clearly be seen now, were coming to a stop. The helicopter stalled and dropped down, but the blades started spinning again and aircraft stabilized.

Saint-Clair made a wide loop to get next to the helicopter. He was hoping to do the same thing again but this time finish off his enemy. He was only 20 yards from his target when he was caught off guard by an unexpected maneuver: the helicopter spun around 90 degrees. The ray hit the Nyctalope's plane on the right wing, which tore apart like paper. Another ray shot out and ripped off the end of the other wing. The plane, which the Nyctalope was having a hard time controlling, swerved away, turned back and headed straight for the blades of the helicopter. Saint-Clair was trying one final attack: to ram into it. But at the moment when he was about to smash into the helicopter, it shot up into the sky and avoided the collision.

A third ray hit his plane right in the engine and the fuel caught fire immediately. The Zip exploded; shards of metal flew through the sky for hundreds of yards around before falling to the ground. Nothing remained of the Nyctalope's plane.

The helicopter made several turns around the site of the explosion, no doubt to verify that nobody had time to eject and possibly survive. The combat had taken place at over 1600 feet altitude, so if the pilot had managed to jump out with a parachute like the Germans used during the Great War, he would easily be spotted.

The rotor blades of the helicopter, damaged in the battle, were completely twisted and were starting to make a weird noise. With the deformed metal it was getting harder for them to spin around and the helicopter could obviously not stay long in the air. Korridès had conquered the Nyctalope but the victory had cost him. He decided to leave the battlefield and get as far away as possible.

Of course, the Engineer could be satisfied. The death of the Nyctalope had cost him his helicopter but this did not really matter: he had had his revenge. Now he just had to execute his enemy's wife. And he was ready to do so in a very original manner, as befit his genius.

CHAPTER XVII
The Artificial Man

Pierre Saint-Clair felt a sharp pain in his head and he could not think straight. He felt like he was floating in a vacuum. A painful vacuum. He had never thought that he would suffer so much after death. Maybe, just maybe, he was still alive, as surprising as it might seem. The window in his diving suit had been broken by the claw and the glass had splintered into his face. It hurt like mad. At more than 130 feet down the frighteningly destructive power of the underwater enemy had probably killed him. But blood was still beating in his veins; an awful pain was hammering his head; and all these sensations meant that he was still alive. He was out of the water, in a dry place, apparently lying on the ground, abandoned in a strange land. He made a great effort to open his eyes but he could not. What could have happened after he passed out on the bottom of the lake?

Someone was shaking him gently and putting a wet cloth on his forehead. A voice called out, sounding very far away. It was Bob's voice.

"Pierre, wake up! How do you feel?"

Pierre concentrated all his energy on answering the call and he finally managed to open his eyes. Bob, dressed in a diving suit without his helmet, was leaning over him. Behind him was Pir, smiling down on him. He, too, must have been hit in the face because his left cheek was swollen.

Pierre gradually came around. He tried to figure out where he was. Pir and Bob were standing there but he did not see Professor Noque or Hubert de Pibriac.

The big, high room was decorated with monumental statues of Semitic-looking men wearing long robes and beards. Their clothes, however, looked practical and they were holding in their hands objects that seemed modern, although they could have been designed by advanced technology: boxes covered with buttons, switches and a control panel, rods that could have been firearms, a kind of earpiece that was probably for communicating at a distance.

On one side of the room was a double door opposite the monumental gate that was open.

Pierre struggled to his feet, looked at the entrance and managed to ask:

"How did you get inside the tower? When I passed out I was still in the cube and the door was still shut tight."

"It's a mystery," answered Bob. "I was on the tower, keeping watch, when I saw Hubert come up to the surface. His arm was broken and he was having trouble staying afloat. I used the hoist to help him up and he crawled onto the tower before the crocodiles could get to him. I asked him what happened and where the others were. He was out of breath but told me that you'd been attacked by some diabolical machine, a kind of underwater capsule equipped with huge, metal pincers. It had broken his arm like a matchstick. Hubert escaped by taking off his lead boots and everything else that was heavy on his suit. He said to me: 'We have to do something, Bob. The others are in grave danger. But I don't see how we can fight this monstrous underwater machine.'

"I thought about it for a moment and offered to put on my diving suit to go and see what could be done. Hubert winced in pain and suggested that I take two harpoons from the plane. He said: 'I don't know if it'll make any difference but you can always try.' He leaned back against the railing, closed his eyes and tried to fight against the pain. I went to get the harpoons, put on my diving suit and then I dove all the way to the entrance of the tower. I was lucky not to run into any crocodiles and got to the bottom quickly. In the spotlights I saw my brother unconscious near the veloscaphe. Given the condition of our prototype I knew that there'd been a bad fight. Pir was passed out but his suit wasn't damaged and he was still alive.

"I left him there and went to the cube. The exterior door had been torn clean off. Stuck in the airlock in front of the inner door, which was also in bad shape, was the machine Hubert had described. Or what remained of it. The back of it was ripped out and the window was smashed. A dead man wearing a turban was sitting inside it at the commands. His head had been literally torn off. Pools of blood floated in the water and I was afraid the scent would attract the crocodiles around the lake. I managed to free the door and I saw that there was an opening in the tower. But nobody was inside. You and Professor Noque seemed to have disappeared. I went to get my brother and we entered this room where I found you, unconscious. My brother had been knocked out but not injured and I woke him up. Then I got to work on you. Now the three of us are up and around but Professor Noque is still missing. I wonder where he could be? And what are we going to do? Keep exploring this part of the tower or go back to the surface to get Hubert?"

Pierre thought for a minute before saying:

"That depends on Hubert's condition. Do you think he's able to dive with his injuries?"

"He was hit pretty hard. He would certainly have trouble getting through the rubble and may not be of much use to us. On the other hand, he's the most experienced explorer among us and his advice would be valuable."

"Let's not forget that the lake is infested with crocodiles," Pir added, "and we don't have the veloscaphe to protect us anymore. So, we have to be careful where and how we move and not try to do too much."

"Maybe we should start checking out the tower," Bob conclude. "Maybe we'll be able to find the Professor. I'm starting to worry about him. Maybe this 'mysterious benefactor' who helped Pierre has taken him inside the tower. But if we want to go exploring the monument, maybe it'd be better to fetch Hubert. He can help us if we have to make any tricky decisions about dangerous situations."

They made some quick arrangements. As much out of curiosity as out of desire to find Professor Noque they decided to go back up to the surface later to get Hubert.

The hall was lit by a dim light whose source was hidden. They headed for the second door from which a brighter light was coming. It opened onto a huge room. The floor was littered with rubble. The ceiling was cracked and looked unstable. On the right was a monumental staircase going up to the upper floors. On the left was a similar staircase that descended into the underground. In the opposite wall were numerous openings into darkened rooms.

Huge frescoes decorated the walls around the room. The patterns told of an epoch that obviously stretched far into the past.

The first fresco represented a fertile valley flooded with sunlight and watered by a wide river. A strange machine, vaguely resembling an insect, was sitting on the riverbank. Four men dressed in long robes like the ones on the statues in the hall appeared to have got out of the machine and were standing around it. The weird vehicle had no wheels and probably flew through the air, which the explorers refused to believe at first because of the antiquity of the tower.

The next fresco showed a city being built in the same location as the first. The city spread out from a tower, itself under construction. On observing the second painting, it was no longer possible to deny the existence of technological machines in ancient times. Even in this contemporary age, they looked like something straight out of the fertile imagination of Jules Verne or Albert Robida. Huge digging machines along with flying vehicles bigger than existing airplanes. The traces that these men were seeing at the bottom of the lake were unquestionably the remains of this tower in the fresco and the city around it.

The three young men could not believe their eyes. The frescoes proved undeniably the existence of the advanced civilization that Professor Noque had talked about. They must have been painted very long ago because the weather in the valley had changed and the geography of the place seemed to have evolved as well: in the background was a mountaintop much higher than the others and that no longer existed in the 20th century. As for the lake, it had still not appeared.

The three of them discussed their discovery while hustling to the third fresco, eager to see the sequel to this extraordinary history. It was a very surprising picture. There was no more valley but a futuristic city that extended as far as the eye could see. In the foreground a group of men dressed in the same clothes as those in the other frescoes were in deep discussion. The way their faces were drawn and their gestures made, it was clear that there was an argument. To the side, one of them was walking away and pointing to other characters whose faces seemed frozen in a cold expression and who were dressed in metallic gray outfits.

Three other frescoes were painted on the wall across from them. Very excited now, the young men crossed the room in a hurry.

A battle scene, totally unexpected, was painted. Numerous metal tanks faced off on the ground among cannons that were shooting multicolored rays. In the sky were swarms of flying machines fighting one another and bombing the machines on the ground. It was a battle comparable to Verdun but with weapons that looked even more destructive.

The faces of the young explorers turned pale. They had not yet seen what the last two scenes had to show but they had the feeling that they already knew the end of the story.

The next painting was, unfortunately, very damaged. They could, however, make out a big aircraft but it was hard to understand its use and the whole subject of the fresco was not at all clear. On the side with the weird ship was some kind of transmitting machine of unknown purpose.

The last picture showed the population of the city, obviously celebrating a great victory. Men were being covered in glory and decorations. In the background the futuristic city had sunk beneath the ocean, destroyed by weapons of frightening power that had put an end to the ancient civilization.

The three young men, a little shocked by this last picture, looked at each other in silence.

Bob finally spoke up:

"A civil war tore apart a great nation in the far past. A big city was swallowed up by the ocean because of some powerful weapon that we can't even imagine... it's dreadful!"

"Yes, Bob, it sounds like the destruction of Atlantis that Pierre's father talked about at the Blingy mansion a few days before we left for Africa. What do you think, Pierre?"

"It's completely unbelievable. Such technology at a time when Europe was still prehistoric! If anyone told me this, I'd never believe him. Anyway, we still don't know what's happened to Professor Noque. This room is covered with debris from when the building was destroyed. Stones and pieces of the ceiling and layers of dust. If anyone else walked in here, we'd have seen traces of their footsteps."

They started examining the floor, searching for some clue or indication. At first they saw only their own but Pierre suddenly called our when he noticed prints that did not belong to their shoes. The O'Connell brothers came over to him.

"Pir, Bob, I've found some footprints. Look, they go from the stone door we came through and head to the left, toward the staircase that goes down. And they clearly belong to only one person. Either the professor or our mysterious savoir... But there's no way to know right now."

"It could be this person in question who took the professor if he was wounded."

"That's possible because the professor would have waited for us. The best thing would be to follow the prints. What do you think?"

"Well, since we intend to explore the tower, we might as well start with this. What do you say, Pierre?"

Pierre looked at the stone stairs and nodded.

"Let's go," he said.

The young men got to the top of the stairs. The footprints continued down and they followed. 30 feet down they came out in a vast room full of damaged furniture and a multitude of corridors leading off from it. Apparently it was some kind of entrance hall. The footprints crossed the room, avoiding the remains of what might have been a control room or guardroom or even an information booth.

A sliding metal door had once closed off the corridor that now opened before them. The door was broken, the metal twisted as if under enormous pressure. The three of them were about to step through when Pierre noticed something.

"Look! Here... and there! The metal is bare and the coating's been entirely removed. But there's no sign of corrosion. That's weird. I wonder what kind of metal could do this. It has to be completely rustproof. Let's see if we can find the other doors lying around the room and see if they're made of the same stuff. If their coating's been damaged they should all be rusted."

"But this door must have been broken down a long time ago. I don't get it. Look, there's no dust at all on the floor of the corridor after the door. It's like that zone was totally cut off from this part. Which would fit with the idea that the door was destroyed recently and the traces we found are not the professor's but the mysterious savior. He would have to be incredibly strong. And that explains how he could destroy the underwater attacker and kill the turbaned man inside it."

The young men decided to go down the corridor, which passed by a series of futuristic laboratories. In this part of the tower there was less damage caused by the tower's submersion. The laboratories were intact, as if they had been abandoned only a few hours before. The visitors, in awe and wonder, wandered through the rooms without saying a word, each of them trying to find logical explanations for these strange phenomena. It took them thirty minutes to explore the place, without discovering anything to help them understand what had happened in this lower part of the tower. At the end of the corridor they stood before another massive door, built to resist time and battering.

Like the other door, this one was open and seemed to have been broken recently and easily. The few inches of unknown alloy, no doubt the strongest material at the time, was not enough to protect it from being torn off its hinges.

Pierre, Pir and Bob climbed carefully over the obstacle. The door opened onto a big room full of gigantic machines.

Before them lay the body of a tall man dressed in armor. He must have been hit very violently because his helmet was bent out of shape, clearly the cause of death. The three men leaned over the corpse to get a closer look.

"But it's not a man!" exclaimed Pierre. "It's a machine. A machine in the shape of a man!"

Under the armor there were no signs of flesh and blood but they saw the damaged metal components, bathed in a viscous fluid, a thick, dark brown oil. Near him lay a weapon, a kind of pistol attached to the humanoid by a cable. It looked badly damaged and the power cable had been yanked out.

Pierre stood up straight.

"It's a mechanical, artificial guardian. Whatever science created it is far beyond us. I can't even understand the basic principles of how it works. In any case, the metal it's made of is strong and it must have taken a colossal force to smash it like that and put it out of commission."

Bob pointed to some residue of synthetic matter dripped on the floor near the door and said:

"Look. It might be that the attacker who broke in here was injured by the guard before getting the better of it."

"You're probably right. I propose we explore this room. I hope that we can find the professor and that the creature endowed with amazing strength who came in here before us doesn't get a bad impression of us. I'll bet we're getting close to winding up this mystery…"

They went to the back of the room where they saw various control panels to unknown machines whose use was incomprehensible. The devices were in working order, to tell by the constantly blinking lights. They got closer and saw a dozen glass sarcophagi inside of which lay a dozen sleeping men.

One man was sitting in the middle of the control panels. They saw only the top of his head over the back of his chair. When they were within a few feet of him, he spoke:

"Welcome, my friends. I've been waiting for you."

They recognized the voice of Professor Noque, who turned around to face them. The professor was smiling. The three young men stepped back. The professor's left cheek had been badly burned and the skin torn off. His left eye had disappeared. But instead of the living flesh and bone that should have been in the hole, they saw the synthetic structure of a plastic skull. The smooth, light blue material must have been able to resist intense heat because the burn had completely melted Noque's flesh.

A hint of irony was in that gaze as he watched the three of them with his artificial eye that looked exactly like a human pupil. Professor Etienne Noque, distinguished linguist of the Sorbonne, was an artificial man.

CHAPTER XVIII
The Invisible Man

Two lights darted through the night sky. All of a sudden a bright ray shot out of one and struck the other, which caught fire right away. It was obviously an airplane that was flying at a high altitude and had just been hit by a mysterious weapon. The plane exploded and a ball of flames and sparks lit up the night. Burning pieces fell to the ground as the attacker, after making a few extra rounds, shot off into the distance. Nothing remained of the battle between these two flying objects. Nothing but silence.

A few miles from the spot where the confrontation had taken place, four men sitting in a car were watching the scene attentively. Three of them looked indifferent but the fourth was much more intense. He was surrounded by instruments that took up almost all the space in the back of the car. He sat in front of a screen, now completely black, but on which he had watched the scene as if he were in the cockpit of the plane that had been destroyed. Under this screen were a bunch of dials, levers and even a wheel. All this equipment was an exact reproduction of an airplane's commands. The man was wearing a helmet with headphones and a microphone so that he could communicate by radio as if he were inside the plane itself.

In order to be totally incognito, the car was parked with all its lights off. But this did not bother the man controlling the screens because it was none other than Léo Saint-Clair, the Nyctalope, whose enemy, Maur Korridès, believed he was killed in the plane crash. The plane that the Engineer had had a little trouble destroying was, in fact, a decoy, a remote-controlled machine.

In the front of the car that contained the remote-controlled commands were two of Saint-Clair's aides, Vitto and Soca, and sitting next to him was his old friend Jacques

Roll. The four men looked at each in silence for a moment. Saint-Clair was the first to speak.

"He's gone. Everything went as planned and I almost beat him. I gained some time while talking to him so I could connect the plane to my manual controls, which allowed me to maneuver with the necessary precision. It's like I was on board the Zig. The battle went off normally thanks to this exact replica of the commands. He thinks I've been killed and he's going to let his guard down. We'll be able to strike back!"

"But even like this it won't be easy," Jacques Roll said. "His helicopter has unsurpassable firepower."

"I'm sure it does. But I managed to damage it and I doubt he can use its full capacity any time soon. Besides, we've also got our strike force and he'll find out about that soon enough. Vitto, take us to Villacoublay."

"OK."

After a moment of silence the Nyctalope turned to Jacques Roll and said:

"In everything Korridès told me, what surprises me the most is what I did on Mars when the French colony was destroyed. Some psychological mechanisms must have gone haywire because I don't remember a thing..."

Saint-Clair was very upset by this breakdown that he did not understand. Never before had he had such memory gaps. He anxiously wondered whether he had forgotten other events in his life. For the first time his powerful brain was floundering. Jacques Roll, who was seeing the telltale signs of serious doubt on his friend's face, tried to reassure him:

"Considering the painful nature of those events, it's possible that your brain set up some defense mechanisms to spare you constant remorse for the actions that you were in no way responsible for. In fact, if I believe what the Engineer said, the colonists including yourself were driven mad by an unknown Martian force, which would relieve you of any responsibility for the actions you committed in that fit of madness."

Saint-Clair frowned and responded:

"And yet, it seems that I killed a bunch of people, maybe even my children... The worst thing is that now these memories are slowly coming back to me. I think Korridès was telling the truth. Yes, I have a gnawing dread, like a criminal must feel while seeing his murderous acts committed over and over again in his mind... Yes, I'm catching glimpses of men, completely changed, and a woman, my wife, whom I thought was dead for so long... Yes, as if the virus took over the bodies of some of the colonists... I'll have to investigate this after I've beaten Korridès..."

The Nyctalope shook his head to chase away these terrible, nagging questions. He turned to his friend again and spoke in a firm voice:

"But in the meantime, we have to concentrate on our present enemy."

"That sounds like the only thing to do right now. He wiped out the CID and he's holding your wife with every intention of killing her. So, we have to act quickly. Tell me, Léo, how did you know that Korridès was going to attack your plane? You said that you had some suspicions about the security of your communications system..."

"Indeed. He was not very effective in hiding the fact that he was spying on me through the radio. First of all I noticed that all my radio communications were being broken up by interference. At the start it didn't seem too suspicious to me, but after I got to Madrid it looked really fishy. I wondered how the two men sent by Korridès could have known about me being there. In other words, how did my enemy locate me? Of course, he could have guessed that I would go there, knowing that I would automatically think of him after the very particular kind of attack on the Blingy mansion. But the destruction of my plane and the precise instructions he had given to his men got me thinking that he was too well informed about my movements, which allowed me to react more favorably. And when he finally told me just now that he was spying on me with a special radio, it only confirmed what I already suspected.

"I had worked in this kind of thing in the past, with my father who was an expert. We studied the possibility of creating an ultra-powerful two-way radio that could spy on whatever conversations we chose of all those crossing the air. If we could do it, there's no reason why one of the greatest scientists of our time couldn't also build such a device. For some mysterious reason his pirating, which should have gone completely undetected, scrambled the signals he intercepted and caused static. Korridès was probably in such a hurry to get his revenge that he used it before it was perfected. Anyway, that's what put the bug in my ear."

"So, you thought he was going to attack you on your way home?"

"Yes, that was the most likely. And I thought right away of using the remote-controlled plane to foil his plan. But I had to change planes without him noticing. Otherwise there was a good chance that he wouldn't try to fight to the death! Therefore, I used a code name for the CID to make the exchange: 'Protocol' meant the remote-controlled plane and 'Joan of Arc' meant Orléans, the place where the exchange would be made. I did indeed figure that he would attack my plane on the way home, close to Paris..."

"Why's that?"

"In fact, thanks to his monitoring system, he knew that I'd be going back to Paris to join my wife. For him, in theory, any place on my route between Madrid and Paris would do. But it was easier for him to spot the plane closer to the point of departure or arrival. Of these two, Paris seemed to me the most plausible since Korridès was hiding out near Paris."

"Great! You've found his lair!"

"In fact, from the start of this affair I gathered the clues that led me, one by one, to know where he's hiding."

"How's that?"

"First of all, one fine morning while reading the newspaper my attention was drawn to an article that reported a severed hand found in Paris near the Jardin des Plantes. I asked Michel Dorlange to investigate it in the guise of national defense. Before being killed in the attack on my house he had time to inform me that the macabre relic belonged to one of the CID agents who was tailing a spy who was spotted in one of our Lyon buildings. This must have been to place the mines that Korridès set off not long ago. But in the end, our agent and his colleague followed him to the Jardin des Plantes, more precisely to the Museum of Natural History, which was having work done on it. At first the agent's disappearance went unnoticed because of all of Korridès' attacks. There were fingerprints lifted by the police that identified him."

"But none of this was enough to locate his lair."

"That's right. In fact, it only confirmed the information that I'd already gathered."

"But what did you do then?"

"When I was sure that Korridès was spying on my conversations, I snuck into the control tower at the Madrid airport and used the radio there. I contacted the main French offices of the CID and changed the transmitter to throw off the enemy. Moreover, I sent my messages using a secret code known only to CID agents. Obviously, as the outcome has shown, Korridès couldn't pirate these communications. I asked our offices to use new equipment and call this counter-espionage mission 'Gorillard.' Now they could detect the origin of a radio message as well as its destination. The different offices located pretty much everywhere in France got to work and thus we had a good chance of finding exactly where Korridès' equipment was located. If he had only used his technology to spy on our conversations, he would have been safe. But in our case he also used his equipment to get in contact with his organization in Spain. He gave them instructions, notably and unfortunately to organize the attack in which our friend Pedro d'Arendar lost his life. These transmissions were coded and therefore not deciphered in time to save him. But his transmitter was so powerful that it could be identified and located easily. That same evening I found out where his hideout was. He was broadcasting from Paris and he was hiding in the Natural

History Museum in the Jardin des Plantes where my two agents were murdered a few days ago."

"Impressive discovery! So, we'll be able to organize an attack and arrest the Engineer and his accomplice..."

"Sadly no and for several reasons. First of all, Sylvie, my wife, is their prisoner and we have to act discreetly to keep her from being killed during the attack. Then, Korridès must have a spectacular defense system. There was nothing found of two CID agents who approached his headquarters except a hand. When Korridès attacked my plane he used a terribly formidable disintegrating ray. He probably has one set up inside his lair as well. Furthermore, he told me that he had a powerful ally. So, he might have other means that we can't imagine and he would certainly be able to fend off a frontal attack. No, no, we have to have a surprise attack, breach the defenses using a method that he can't suspect. For this I have a plan and you're part of it."

"What are you waiting for, my friend? Tell me what Jacques Roll can do for you."

"In fact, it's not Jacques Roll I need but the Invisible Man!"

Jacques Roll answered with a smile. Saint-Clair and him had met a few years ago when Roll had become Prime Minister. Before the War, since the Ciserat Affair and the conquest of Argyre on Mars, the Nyctalope had had special relations with the Prime Minister. He even had a special telephone line that connected directly with him to coordinate actions with the government. When Jacques Roll had become Prime Minister in 1924 the two men got along great and had since remained good friends. During a confidential affair that involved certain parties well-known to the public, Saint-Clair had found out that the Prime Minister also had a superpower. Thanks to a mysterious chemical he could become invisible, both his body and his clothes. Several times, in the interest of the state, he had used this power and shared some of Saint-Clair's adventures. After his marriage in 1925, the Invisible Man had retired and Jacques Roll had become a doctor again in the south of

France. Since then the Nyctalope had not called on him, leaving him to enjoy his family life in peace. Only the extreme gravity of this present situation had forced him to ask for his old friend's help.

When the Nyctalope had contacted him, Jacques Roll accepted without hesitation. Vitto and Soca went to pick him up in the car and all three of them prepared the Orléans Protocol, which had saved the Nyctalope's life.

However, he still did not know the reason why the Nyctalope had called him or why he needed his special power. The information he was just given was starting to give him some idea. He answered his friend:

"After what you just told me, I think I'm starting to understand."

"Yes, I'm sure. But my plan is more complicated than it seems and now I'll enlighten you as we approach Villacoublay."

CHAPTER XIX
Professor Noque's Secret

Professor Noque smiled at his friends. His face, ravaged by the flames, was hideous to see and the three explorers were shocked. How could they have imagined that their partner in adventure, the learned professor of the Sorbonne, was nothing but a machine? But what a machine! An incredible artificial man! A creation far beyond the wildest imaginations of Mary Shelley and Victor Frankenstein. The professor spoke to them, trying to sound reassuring:

"Yes, my friends, I'm not human. I'm what my designers called an android, a mechanical creature that looks like a man."

"But who designed you? And where do you come from?" Pierre blurted out.

"I was created a long time ago, more than 10,000 years ago. My creators lived on a continent that has now disappeared: Atlantis."

"Atlantis! But we should go get Hubert de Pibriac right away. He'd want to hear this and get some answers to the questions he's had since he found the symbols in the Mexican pyramid," Pir interrupted.

"That's true. But he's already with us. Follow me," Noque said.

The three men looked around in astonishment. The professor went to a big machine in the middle of which was a glass sarcophagus.

"Yes, look. He's inside. While you were exploring the labs in the underground tower, I went to get him and put him in this machine. In a few more minutes his broken bones will be mended, he'll be completely healed and he can take part in our discussion."

The three men and the android made small talk about the state their own health in order to pass the time before their friend could be with them. Concerning this, Professor Noque explained:

"I was shot with a laser right in the face…"

"A laser gun?"

"Yes. It was a powerful weapon that shoots a concentrated light ray of extreme heat. My face mask was damaged but underneath is made of an alloy of orichalchum and is very resistant. I'd say it's indestructible and only the worst disaster could do it any serious harm. I'll have to fix up the protective mask, however, because I can't go back to civilization looking like this. Look there! The green light just lit up. Hubert is healed. I'll get him out of the regenerating machine and we can continue our discussion."

Professor Noque went to a control panel. His fingers tapped a keyboard and the glass door of the sarcophagus slid open.

Hubert de Pibriac climbed out. He was smiling while examining his arm. Then he turned to his companions and said:

"Unbelievable! This machine is a technological marvel that will revolutionize the modern world!"

"Not necessarily," Noque objected. "I think the moment has come to tell you everything, to answer your questions and explain what I expect of you."

"Well, thank you," Hubert said. "For the last half hour I've understood nothing at all about this world I'm in."

Professor Noque paused a few seconds before speaking:

"It's a long story that dates back to ancient times. Everything started around 10,000 years ago on a continent that is gone today, which used to be in the Atlantic between Africa and Central America. In that distant epoch this continent, Atlantis, had a civilization that had an advanced technology, unknown to the rest of the world. The Atlantis Empire flourished. The people reached a level of technology that's never been equaled. They conquered the skies, the depths of the seas, space… One of their expeditions got them to Mars, that dangerous planet. The Atlanteans devoted their lives to research, art and philosophy. They lived in perfect harmony and their civilization made constant progress in all domains. It seemed like it would never stop.

"However, the beautiful harmony was bound to break one day because of a disagreement over an important matter: should the Atlanteans subdue the primitive men who lived on the other continents or should they continue to live in isolation, which had been so beneficial so far? At first the problem was confined to peaceful discussions among philosophers. The isolationism had been so advantageous that most of them wanted to maintain the status quo. But a minority, which kept growing in numbers, were arguing for political expansion so the Empire could have access to the natural resources on the other continents and also the possibility of making the savages work in their place in exchange for the benefits of Atlantean civilization. Ultimately they intended to implement a colonialism like the British and French Empire practice today.

"But simple philosophical discussions can sometimes cause the fall of nations. A group of determined men decided to ignore the general opinion and go out and conquer Africa and Central America. Some very well equipped individuals set up a few colonies like in the land of Nod where we are right now. Their main city was farther east in a valley that's in Palestine now.

"The Atlanteans decided not to impose sanctions against these dissidents but they kept a close watch over them so they wouldn't have any nasty surprises in the future. A battalion of machines shaped like humans was created and these androids were in charge of the supervision. I was one of them. 10,000 years after being built I'm the last survivor.

"For decades our coexistence was relatively peaceful. The Watchers, as the rebels would call themselves later, concentrated all their efforts on the conquest of savage continents. They came in contact with the natives to whom they appeared on board their flying ships in a great display of colors and sounds. Their goal was to be taken as gods and they succeeded brilliantly. Thousands of years later they're still talking about the arrival of Quetzalcoatl, the plumed serpent, and the celestial Watchers who seduced the women before the Flood...

"And they truly lived as gods. They got luxurious cities built, extraordinary monuments and the tower we are in right now is a good example. They devoted themselves to pleasure, to research and to philosophy. They took their wives from among the barbarous women and lived a life of leisure. But in a few decades they had lost their creative power. Idleness and a life focused solely on satisfying the senses quickly led them into decadence.

"During this whole period, the army of androids kept an eye on them. Living in the colonies, these creatures assured the maintenance of peace merely by their presence. The situation would have lasted for centuries if the Earth had not entered the ice age that the modern men call Würm. The climatic disturbances that caused glaciers to spread over Europe, Asia and North America weakened the Atlantis Empire as much as the Watchers. Their hedonistic civilization, however, was much harder hit than the industrious world of the Empire. The Atlanteans made extraordinary efforts to adapt to the situation whereas the Watchers let themselves go and couldn't keep up their level of civilization. More and more often they looked out to sea with envy, out to the shores of Atlantis.

"The situation became tense. Envy turned into jealousy. At the same time the presence of the androids, even thought they were more necessary than ever, became totally unbearable to the colonists. They felt like they were breast-feeding an enemy who only wanted to beat them down.

"Over time the androids saw that the Watchers were starting on what you'd call today a war effort. Building military equipment took on serious proportions and the leaders hardened their tone. The worst was to be feared. However, as long as my fellow androids had the power to intervene, there could be no real risk of war. The situation became more and more tense but the battalion of androids kept everything in check.

"That was when Azazel invented the neutralizer. Azazel was one of the Watcher leaders. Like the others he had devoted his life to pleasure, but his favorite hobby was research. All his spare time was spent finding ways to beat the androids. After a few years of dogged work he managed to create a revolutionary machine that emitted a ray whose nature was unknown but that paralyzed and then destroyed the artificial brain in the androids without harming humans.

"The Watchers decided to get rid of us before attacking Atlantis with the aim of snatching its economic potential. Neutralizers were built and set up secretly in all their cities. They were all turned on at the same time and most of the androids were destroyed. I was working in Atlantis at the time to get some equipment that would make it easier for me to investigate an arsenal I'd found that the Watchers had built in secret. I was lucky to escape destruction.

"The next day the Watchers attacked Atlantis. They didn't use any weapons that were too destructive because they wanted to profit from their future conquest. They caused a lot of damage but the continent's defense was strong and their wisdom had led them to keep their military in good shape.

"When the attack failed, they retaliated. That was how the terrible war started and all the horrible devastation that followed.

"Little by little the Empire got the upper hand but the losses were huge on both sides. The war seemed like it would never end. It was during this period that the Atlantean colonists took the name Watchers as they are called in the books that were written about these legendary times much later. Both camps were awaiting more and more destructive attacks from their enemy.

"It was the colonists' fault that the fatal escalation began. Azazel and the scientists in Nod created the ultimate weapon, a machine so frightening, generating a wave so powerful that pointed into space it could pull an asteroid off course and send it plummeting toward the Earth. The colonists, after losing so many battles, knew that they would never get hold of the Empire's riches. For one, the wealth had been spent or destroyed in battle; then again, without some last ditch effort, they would lose the war within months. So, they used their infernal machine to destroy Atlantis. An asteroid was captured by the ray and hurled at their enemy. They barely missed the continent itself and the big rock plunged into the sea but the force of the impact caused a huge tidal wave, over three hundred feet high, that swept over the continent and killed almost the entire population.

"In the days that followed the very foundations of Atlantis, which had been weakened by the shock wave, cracked: the continent and the ancient civilization it contained disappeared forever under the waves. The colonists' ships flew over the sea where the capital of the Empire used to be but they saw nothing but the raging sea. They had won the war and could now celebrate their victory.

"In fact, contrary to what they believed, they were far from a total victory. A few hours before the total annihilation of Atlantis, the Emperor had summoned the few surviving androids into an underground shelter that was protected from the tidal wave. He was desperate and vanquished. He gave us one last order before sinking into a morbid depression that would lead to his death.

"*I, Antinoüs, Emperor of Atlantis, am giving you an order that will be valid for eternity. Destroy our enemies and their descendants unto the last generation. Thus will your creators and their glorious Empire be avenged. Go now and may nothing stop your strong arm of justice.*"

"Determined to obey, we left the refuge and went to the secret arsenal where we organized our action. There were seven of us, seven avenging angels who were going to retaliate against the enemies of Atlantis. I didn't know it then but for me that was the start of a mission that after more than 10,000 years has still not been fulfilled. You should know this: once an android has been programmed for an action, it will complete its mission no matter what. Since I was built to last and

I'm practically indestructible, my goal might not be reached for a long time to come.

"After agreeing on our plans, the other androids and I went about our tasks. To destroy the Tower of Babel was my first mission. Our enemies were not the only ones to control nature for their own good. We had machines that could affect the weather. Our science in this field allowed us to create the best meteorological conditions possible for a pleasant human existence, all the while preserving nature, crops and livestock. Most of the weather stations had, of course, been destroyed when Atlantis sank. There was one left, in the North Pole, and it was still working. It was therefore possible to use the power of the ice age in the climate.

"When I went there, I reprogrammed the station to turn it into a weapon of war. I used all its power to radically change the climate of this valley here. Rains and storms raged for forty days and forty nights. A tempest so violent and for so long left little chance of survival for the people. A few of them were able to leave the city in the first days, but all the others were drowned in the flood. You've noticed that 10,000 years later the weather in this valley has still not returned to normal. A lake has flooded it, a layer of clouds covers it constantly and it's humid everywhere, always.

"While I was taking care of Nod, the other androids were destroying all the cities that belonged to our enemy. However, the battles carried heavy losses. The Watchers still had their neutralizers and one by one my companions were 'neutralized.'

"A few years later the main installations had been destroyed but I was the only one left to continue the fight. All the other androids had been wiped out. Then began the long epoch in which you are sharing the latest adventure.

"In accordance with the permanent orders I received, I hunted relentlessly those who had destroyed Atlantis and their descendants to the four corners of the world. A tireless wanderer I flushed them out wherever they were hiding. Over the years they became a holy terror to me. I knew they had a base near Palestine that my comrades had found but they didn't know exactly where it was. I looked long but in vain and live for generations in the region. Seeing how I conducted my investigations and the effects of certain techniques that I used, and also because of my longevity, the inhabitants started to think I had semi-divine powers. That's where the legend of Enoch was born, the patriarch who was taken into heaven by God. According to the legend there had been a revelation about the fallen angels, the Watchers that God had destroyed in the Flood.

"After many centuries I discovered by pure luck the hideout of my enemy thanks to a herdsman named Lot whom they had captured. They were hiding near Sodom and Gomorrah in a maze of underground grottoes. I destroyed the entire region with a very powerful bomb…"

"All those innocent victims," Pierre broke in. "Why massacre them as well?"

"I'm just a machine who carries out orders no matter what. Besides, the Watchers were among the local people and were starting to take an aggressive stance against the neighboring towns. Their expansionist, conquering ideology was back in play. But the leading group of Watchers had apparently escaped me. I thought I found them much later on the island of Santorini. I destroyed the site using a volcanic eruption and wiped out the entire colony but still did not get the head Watchers. And to think that some scholars have published the idea that this colony was Atlantis!

"I kept looking and once again thought I'd found them in Rome at the time of Nero. But this time they escaped me by setting fire to the city. Still, I didn't give up. The fall of the Roman Empire and the troubles that followed protected my enemies from me. Every time I thought I'd found them, they got a new lair before I had time to exterminate them. Sometimes I killed one or two but never enough.

"Over the years and with their constant flight I ended up seeing that they had lost a lot of their power. Their last neutralizer had been destroyed, no doubt in Santorini. They couldn't really hurt me except by some miraculous stroke of luck. The little power they had left made them look like sorcerers and in the Middle Ages it was easy for me to rely on the Church to help me in the fight. A great many descendants of the Watchers were burned alive during this terrible time.

"Much later the last of them left Europe for the New World where they hoped to escape me for good. This time they did indeed manage to lose me. For two hundred years they were completely out of circulation without a clue to their whereabouts. It was at the start of the 20th century, on reading an article on pre-Socratic symbolism in an esoteric journal, that I found some hints as to where I might find my old enemies. After a discreet investigation I found that they were hiding around San Francisco. I went there but couldn't find them and the author of the article had died in the meantime. But with an underground explosion I caused a very strong earthquake that I hoped would destroy their lair..."

"The 1906 earthquake!" Hubert de Pibriac exclaimed. "You destroyed a city of 250,000 people just to get to a hideout with a few old descendants of the Atlantean renegades! That's insane!"

"Sorry, Hubert," the professor responded, "I'm not programmed to reason like that. But let's continue. After spending some time in the USA to see if any more Watchers were there, I went back to Europe where my research had been interrupted by the Great War. At the end of the conflict I took the identity of Nicolas Noque to get the position at the university, which would aide me."

"Nicolas Noque," Pir cut in. "N. Noque. Enoch."

"Well, yes. A little joke," Professor Noque said. "Now I've told you almost everything. When Hubert came to see me, it was easy to see that the text from the pyramid had been in Atlantean. I thought it could be interesting to come back to Nod to look for any possible clues that might have stood the test of time. I'm pretty much eternal and I'm always attracted to interesting leads, even if I know there's a good chance I'm wasting my time. During our first expedition, when we 'discovered' the site, I was really surprised when I got near the tower. A neutralizer was still working somewhere in the ruins. If it weren't for Hubert I'd have been destroyed.

"I pretended to get a fever when in fact my artificial organism was being ravaged by the only weapon able to kill me. Hubert was chased by the natives but managed to get me away quickly so I could recover before suffering irreversible damage. I had to go with him because the existence of the neutralizer was certainly protecting a Watchers setup. But before going back I had to protect myself from the neutralizer. To do this I procured some chemical pills that would allow me to resist its effects for a little while. Moreover, I got hold of a scrambler to cancel the effects of the neutralizer by emitting a disruptive wave.

"When we got there, the pills didn't really protect me and I almost couldn't set up the scrambler. But I did get it turned on the first day and it was supposed to detect and protect against all kinds of waves. Then I helped you get in the tower. When the super-diver attacked it was easy for me to defeat him. My body is built of an alloy so strong that I could tear off that mechanical arm with no problem, smash the helmet and kill the pilot. Then I dragged the wounded to safety and started looking around the underwater tower.

"And I made a fantastic discovery. Of course all these machines built with technology not equaled since the fall of Atlantis could qualify as such. But these are not what I'm talking about. Look at what really counts for me: these twelve glass sarcophagi! They contain the hibernating bodies of the twelve historical chiefs of the Watchers. Azazel and Shemêhaza are even here!

"After all these centuries, the destroyers of Atlantis are finally going to get what they deserve and it'll be by my hand. I never thought I'd see the day when I could proudly kill the very enemies of last Emperor of Atlantis. I thought they died a long time ago, killed by one of the androids who still existed at the start of my quest.

"I'm going to disconnect the hibernators and they should all die in a few minutes. Then I'll destroy the tower because I can't leave a copy of the neutralizer and I can't seem to locate it. It has to be somewhere inaccessible for the moment, maybe in one of the upper floors.

"We have explored and fought together. Hubert even helped me escape certain destruction and today I reach the end of my age-old mission. Therefore, you should leave the valley and return to France. I'll remodel my face and take on a new identity to continue my mission of vengeance. When I'm back in civilization, I'll get back in touch with you and you can help me find the last of the surviving Watchers. Thanks to you I can spot them more precisely and I'll be able to avoid all that massive destruction that seems to bother you so much. Of course, you won't be able to brag about finding the Tower of Babel because I'm going to destroy it. But I've kept something for you, inside the crate, some beautiful archeological pieces that will at least help compensate for your lost discovery. What do you say?"

Hubert de Pibriac looked deeply affected by the story Enoch had just told. He answered haltingly:

"Why not... It's hard to say anything about such extraordinary events..."

"I understand. Don't worry. You can give me your final answer when I get back in touch with you in Paris in a few months. In fact, whatever your decision, I have no fear. Who would believe such a story anyway? Go on now because I have to finish my mission here. I've already put down some explosives that will blow up the tower in one hour."

The four men looked at each other in silence. They felt like there was nothing more to say and they should leave the place. They headed for the entrance of the tower and put on their suits. They had to make two trips because some of their equipment had been damaged during the attack.

When they got to the top of the tower they were still lost in thought and said nothing. The story told to them by the machine-man was incredible. From what they had seen here, however, they could not doubt the truth of it. They had heard the story of an extraordinary epoch in history that they could never retell without being taken for madmen. They had learned about a war that was still being waged 10,000 years later. They had adventured with a living weapon capable of destroying everything in its way at the mere hint of suspicion.

Even if they wanted to stop him—and how could they not want to?—they had no way to do it.

Unless... Hubert de Pibriac was thinking. He glanced around and spotted the scrambler. *In fact, there is one way.*

He went over to a pile of excavation tools and grabbed a pickaxe. He approached the scrambler and looked at his companions. They all nodded silently. Then he lifted the pickaxe and brought it smashing down on the machine, which flew into pieces.

With this simple gesture, a conflict that had lasted since the ice age came to an end.

CHAPTER XX
Face to Face

Through the window Léo Saint-Clair and Jacques Roll were watching the runway. Half an hour earlier it had started to drizzle. At the end of the night the two men were looking unto the sky. The Nyctalope could not see a thing.

Tense and pensive Saint-Clair stayed silent. He feared what was happening to Sylvie. Now and again Roll, who was also pondering the situation, spied on him out of the corner of his eye. He was thinking about everything the Nyctalope had told him in the car about the plan of attack that he was putting into operation so they could get into Korridès' secret base in the Natural History Museum in the Jardin des Plantes.

Saint-Clair had said that a frontal attack was too dangerous, completely out of the question. For one, if he were cornered, the Engineer could kill Sylvie to keep the Nyctalope from ever being able to save her. Moreover, his lair was protected by a powerful defense system that the severed hand had borne witness to when the CID agent tried to get close. Therefore, they needed a surprise attack, without the risk of being exposed to the disintegrating rays.

That was where the Radion came in. It was perfected now and the two men were waiting for it at the Villacoublay runway. It was a revolutionary machine that could move using seven different kinds of locomotion. It could move on land, in the air, on and under water, under the ground, on ice and even in space. This was going to get the Nyctalope and his allies into the museum. Once inside Saint-Clair was counting on Roll, the Invisible Man, to help defeat the Engineer and his stooge.

Saint-Clair waved to his friend. In the sky, to the west, some lights appeared that were now getting closer. It was an airplane but was it really the Radion?

The plane landed father down the runway, turning towards them and slowly rolling forward. Vitto handed them umbrellas before Saint-Clair and Roll left the car to approach the plane. The Nyctalope started smiling. It was indeed the Radion they saw before them.

The Radion did not look like a normal plane. It was a monoplane. Its streamlined body and triangular wings made a very curious flying machine. Strangely, the propeller was situated in the rear. The Radion looked hermetically sealed, which would allow it to fly at very high altitudes.

Closer to the machine they could see that it was equipped with landing gear and floats that were retractable and allowed it to set down on both land and water...

A door opened in its side and a tall man stepped out. Saint-Clair walked up to greet him.

"Hello, Monsieur Le Moal. I hope you had a nice trip and that the Radion will meet our needs."

"It's working fine and I can make it fly a lot faster than during the trials. As a plane it's a match for the best of them."

"I don't doubt it. But we don't need it to fly today."

"The three CID agents you sent to me are inside with their equipment."

"Very well. Vitto and Soca are going to take care of getting our equipment on board, then we'll get on ourselves. Every member of this expedition will be carrying a machine gun, a Browning, a hunting knife and a grenade. And be careful! The grenade should be used only in an emergency and with great caution because in a closed space it'll cause a lot of damage. Everyone will also have a flashlight so they can work in total darkness. Ah, there they are."

Vitto and Soca came to load all the material that Saint-Clair was talking about. They got it on board the Radion, then Saint-Clair, Roll and Le Moal climbed on board and greeted their Breton colleagues. Le Moal shut the door.

The five men took their seats. The mission to free Sylvie Saint-Clair could now begin.

Le Moal took off gently. The engine was almost totally silent, which surprised the passengers. Saint-Clair, who was an expert pilot, whistled in admiration.

"Well, well, Yves, you've built a real marvel here."

"Thanks, Léo. And to think that if it wasn't for Gorillard, France would have been using the Radion years ago. But let's concentrate on our mission. I'm heading for Paris, right?"

"Yes," Saint-Clair said. "Get to the Seine near Bercy. You have nothing to worry about there, the airspace in the capital is clear and I sent a discreet message to the Air Force so we won't be harassed by any military craft."

A few minutes later they were over Paris, heading to Bercy. At this early hour the barges docked along the quays were delivering casks and barrels to the wine warehouses—there were many of them in this area. Saint-Clair glanced out and said:

"Set down on the Seine to the right of the barges."

Le Moal circled the Radion around at 90 degrees to come straight down on the river in front of an empty lot on the shore. The pilot brought out the floats under the wings and the vehicle settled gently on the river. Its propeller pushed it effortlessly through the water.

"Prepare to dive and head for the center of Paris," said Saint-Clair. "Underwater we'll go all the way to the Austerlitz Bridge."

Le Moal filled the ballasts and the Radion dove. The water in the Seine was dark and dirty and they had to turn on the headlights to see. The plane turned submarine disturbed a few fish and had to veer off to avoid hitting the bottom of a barge.

During this voyage under the Seine, Roll opened a case that he had taken out of the trunk of Saint-Clair's car. It was empty. At least, it looked empty because he took out a box of pills and swallowed one.

A few seconds later he started becoming transparent until he had completely disappeared in a short time. Jacques Roll had become invisible. The mysterious chemical that brought about this transformation had been discovered years before by an English scientist who had tested his invention on himself. But the substance was very toxic and ended up making him crazy. Roll had managed to get hold of the formula and improve it. The result was a product that could be used without any risk to mental health. He also succeeded in making objects invisible. Thus his case looked empty but it contained the clothes that were already treated with the chemical.

Roll took off his suit and put on the invisible clothes and the shoes that made no sound when he walked. The Invisible Man was now ready to go. Saint-Clair hoped that he would be the critical asset in the fight to come.

While Roll was transforming, the Radion arrived at the Austerlitz Bridge. Saint-Clair said to Le Moal:

"This is the last leg of the journey. We have to get out of the river and proceed underground to the Natural History Museum."

"No problem. Let's go."

Le Moal turned his vehicle to the left and adjusted the thrust to compensate for the light current that ran through the Seine at this point. Then he leaned the machine forward forty-five degrees. Out of the end of the tapered nose came a drill that started turning at high speed.

He readjusted the forward thrust as the vehicle reached the bottom of the river, which it was starting to drill into. Slowly but precisely the Radion dug into the ground and started its underground voyage. The museum was not far from the Seine, so this would actually be the shortest leg of their journey. The engine had to drill thirty or forty feet underground to pass under the street and the sewers, then move forward another 100 feet to come up under the museum.

The Radion's progress became faster as the rock became softer. Everything was going as planned and when the vehicle reached a good depth it straightened out to horizontal. Le Moal warned his passengers:

"Get ready because, even going slowly to avoid too many tremors that might be detected by the enemy, we're going to be there in just a few minutes."

The members of the commando team put on their black military outfits. Their equipment was exactly as Saint-Clair had said: a shoulder holster with a Browning, a sheathed hunting knife in the belt and a flashlight; the grenade was hooked to the holster. They quickly checked their machine guns and they were ready to go.

Le Moal pulled a lever to bring the Radion back to the surface. The passengers were huddled around the two exits to jump out when the vehicle entered the museum.

The Radion had no trouble swallowing up the layers of earth under the museum and the basement was drilled through easily. Through the window the Nyctalope scrutinized the dark room where they surfaced. It had clearly not been used in a long time. It looked like an old laboratory whose outdated furniture and obsolete equipment was covered in dust and cobwebs. Saint-Clair signed to Le Moal to continue moving up. The Radion attacked the ceiling. Above them should be the big exhibition hall on the ground floor.

A few seconds later, a bright light shined into the vehicle. The Radion had broken into a part of the museum that was usually open to the public. Through the windows the Nyctalope and his companions could see what was happening. The Radion had come in lengthwise and was turned to the back of the room. The space usually contained the skeletons of various species of living animals while the remains of prehistoric wildlife were on the second floor. But all the bones had been pushed to the back of the room and an ultra-modern laboratory took up the rest of the space.

On either side of the rows of skeletons, two aisles led to doors that gave access to different parts of the museum, normally off limits to the public. In the laboratory part several tables were set up and around them stood a dozen technicians in white coats, frozen and paralyzed by surprise. To their left an iron staircase decorated with metal flowers led up to the second floor.

Behind them, next to the main door, were more work tables and on the left, all around an armchair, a huge machine with lights that was hooked up to a helmet lying on the control panel. It was a "large size" version of the machine Armand Logreux d'Albury had used at Rue Montbrun.

But what was most stunning was the sight of Logreux without the big coat he usually wore. Saint-Clair was amazed by the how different his enemy looked, though he still recognized him immediately. Now he knew who Korridès' "powerful ally" was.

Logreux's face had not changed and it was still brightened by the unusual radiance of his gold-flecked blue eyes. But his head was shaved. Cables in insulated sheathing connected him to a crazy, metal frame that covered his whole body. The Nyctalope and his friends were seeing the exoskeleton that Engineer Korridès had created for the villain. His body was covered in a metal lattice soldered to a jointed, steel structure that ran up his spine and down his limbs all the way to the tips of his fingers and toes. Saint-Clair could see how Logreux, hooked up this machine by conducting wires, could use his mental energy and move the structure and himself within it despite being a quadriplegic.

The great strength he must possess thanks to this equipment, along with the mental powers he had acquired among the Tibetans, made the former Master of the Cross of Blood a formidable adversary.

The lab technicians' surprise did not last long. They were soon busy trying to respond to the intrusion. They ran to a gun rack on the wall while the count grabbed a table and flipped it over with one hand.

But the Nyctalope and his team were not just standing there. The two doors of the Radion opened on the command of Le Moal and they jumped out in two groups. The first, on the left, consisted of the Nyctalope and the two CID agents with the goal of reaching Logreux, now hiding behind the overturned table. The second group with Vitto and Soca and the third agent, was responsible for attacking the right wing and covering their backs in case their enemies got back up. The

Invisible Man was still inside the vehicle. He was supposed to leave when he was certain not to be caught in any crossfire.

The two groups started firing before the technicians had time to organize any real defense. The machine gun fire swept over the big room and in a few seconds most of their enemies were out of commission. Only two of them were firing back but their shots were off the mark and hit no one.

Saint-Clair tried to hit Logreux but he was too well covered, hiding behind the table that doubled as a metal shield. This was protection against the small caliber bullets from both the Brownings and the machine guns. The Nyctalope started to wonder if he should use the grenade to flush him out.

When the last technicians were knocked out and the Invisible Man could leave the Radion without getting shot, two events, one right after the other, jeopardized the chances of success of what seemed to have started well.

First of all, the two doors in the back of the room near the skeletons flew open. Two pairs of men stood in the doorways. One of the two was holding a short-barreled rifle with a cable attached, held by the second one and unrolled in the corridor behind them. The two "rifles" opened fire on the Nyctalope's men. A weird sound resonated and a table behind Saint-Clair completely disappeared while the CID agent with Vitto and Soca, standing near the door on the right, had his upper body pulverized. The Nyctalope recognized the horrible effects of the disintegrator ray that Korridès had perfected and he slipped behind the Radion to protect himself.

For their part, Vitto and Soca, responsible for guarding the doors where these armed men showed up, were plenty busy. When the doors flew open, they had aimed their machine guns in that direction to hit the invaders. For a few seconds they were blocked by the CID agent who was in their line of fire. But when he was struck down by the lethal ray, they could open fire on the door to the right. Two bursts sent a hail of bullets through the air before the enemies had time to move their disintegrator rifles. The weapon was phenomenally destructive but it was also heavy and unwieldy, making it a lot less easy than a machine gun to maneuver. The two men were dropped on the spot.

The rows of skeletons kept Vitto and Soca from hitting the two men standing in the left doorway. While reloading, therefore, they slipped around to get a better shot. All this happened in a matter of seconds. But a second event followed that almost turned the victory into defeat.

A very powerful mental wave swept across the room and hit Saint-Clair's men. An order written in letters on fire in their brains:

YOU ARE SURROUNDED BY ENEMIES. FIRE ON EVERYTHING THAT MOVES, INDISCRIMINATELY! DON'T EVEN THINK ABOUT WHAT YOU'RE FIRING AT!

The Nyctalope's allies hesitated. As happened to the soldiers guarding Sylvie Saint-Clair at her home, they immediately lost their free will and the control of their movements. A superior will took the place of their own. The mind amplifier that the Master of the Seven Lights was using gave them no chance. Armand Logreux d'Albury, endowed with psychic powers, could have taken control of their minds even without the machine. With that device, much stronger even than the one he had used on Rue Montbrun, he would have total control over all the members of the commando team. Even the Nyctalope, whose metal strength had been developed during his stay in Tibet, trained and honed as it was during his confrontations with enemies as fearsome as Lucifer, could only put up a weak resistance to such an assault.

The two men armed with the disintegrator had not entered the room and therefore were not influenced by Logreux's psychic power. They kept their reason and could continue their attack. They had seen the Nyctalope hide behind the Radion to escape the disintegrator ray. They exchanged a sly look and decided to get rid of the object, to vaporize the Radion.

They aimed their rifle at the vehicle and fired. The ray hit the front of it, which disappeared in a cloud of dust. They kept destroying it progressively, piece by piece, in order to reach Saint-Clair who was hiding in the back near the propeller. Le Moal, who had stayed inside the Radion, vanished at the same time as his invention, without realizing what was happening, completely preoccupied with finding a weapon to obey the Logreux's mental order and kill his companions.

On the Nyctalope's side, the destruction of the Radion unleashed true madness. The two close allies, childhood friends, Vitto and Soca, started trying to kill each other. On the left the two agents who were with the Nyctalope stopped heading toward the table where Logreux was hiding with his death machine and turned their weapons against each other in answer to the pitiless order that was hammering away at their brains. Jaws clenched, they opened fire and fell to the ground simultaneously.

A few feet away, the Nyctalope was mustering all the force of his hardened mind to resist the Master of Seven Lights. But his efforts were in vain. Gradually, his will weakened and he slowly raised the Browning to fire at his friends. He could not resist the inevitable. His will to fight the psychic influence was bolstered by the obsessive thought that he was about to kill his friends just like he had killed his children on Mars. He was suffering, struggling. Sweat started pouring down his face, twisted into a horrible grimace, tormented by terror. Little by little his sweat turned red, infused with blood. Nevertheless, he raised his weapon, inch by inch.

On the other side, Vitto and Soca, who were sneaking around a pile of bones, stopped abruptly and started circling around each other. They pulled the trigger at almost the same time. But also at the same time, the two machine guns jammed. In fact, at the moment the mental order was given, they were both reloading and interrupted their action. In a way, this saved their lives because the clips were not fully loaded and the guns would not fire. But it was only a pause because their desire to kill each other was still there. They threw down their machine guns and unsheathed their hunting knives.

The Invisible Man had also been hit by the Master's mental order. He raised his Browning and shot... the man carrying the disintegrator rifle, whom he hit right between the eyes. In fact, when the two had showed up, he had used his invisibility to get close to them so he could take them out. When the psychic attack hit, he was only a few feet away and the two men closest to him were his designated targets.

The one holding the cable looked around in total surprise. He was clearly wondering where the shot had come from. He was about to draw the pistol out the holster on his belt but a second bullet stopped him clean when it pierced his heart.

The Nyctalope was still fighting against the awful feeling inside of him. When he saw his two companions collapse after killing each other right in front of him, the situation took a sudden turn. His nearest enemy was now Logreux d'Albury! He could stop struggling against the psychic order that could now be of some use. But he had to act fast, very fast because the enemy must already be getting ready to change the mental instructions.

Saint-Clair raised his Browning again. His adversary, still protected by the steel-reinforced table, was out of reach. Nevertheless, the Nyctalope pointed his weapon in that direction. He simply raised it a little higher than if he were trying to hit the count, which would do no good since the bullet would only crash uselessly into the metal table. He fired. The bullet flew over the table and hit the mind amplifier that was a lot taller than the improvised shield.

The little 9 mm caused damage that was inversely proportional to its size: shot in a critical spot, the machine started crackling, smoking and then turned off.

The Nyctalope and his three companions immediately felt the control of their thoughts and movements come back them. Vitto and Soca, knives in hand, stood and looked at each other, each feeling the awful fear of having almost killed his best friend with his own hands. The Invisible Man had been a lot luckier. He had only killed enemies whom he had planned to get rid of anyway. He turned and ran to the other side of the room to attack Logreux who was now vulnerable without his psychic amplifier.

At the same time the Nyctalope also snuck up to the Master of the Seven Lights, who was still hiding behind the table. When he was almost there, the heavy table rose up as light as a feather and came flying in his direction. Saint-Clair was expecting to be targeted by a firearm and was ready to shoot his enemy when he popped up—this took him by surprise. He barely managed to dodge the table and push it out of his way. But in the meantime he had dropped his weapon and stumbled back, falling hard onto the ground.

Armand Logreux d'Albury, his enemy, the Master of Seven Lights, was now standing over him, leaning over him, his eyes burning with hate, shouting triumphantly:

"You are going to die, Saint-Clair! I'm going to break your limbs one by one and you will feel the agony that you inflicted on me when you turned me into the living-dead that I am. Only the hope of this moment has kept me alive. And now, it's payback time!"

Vitto and Soca had taken these few moments of the Master's bitter speech to sneak up with their Brownings. They fired at the same time. The two bullets flattened out and dropped to the ground a few inches from the metal frame covering the villain's exoskeleton. They were amazed to see that their enemy was protected by an electromagnetic force field produced by his suit. He was truly invincible.

Logreux raised his steel boot to crush the Nyctalope's head. As the foot came down, Saint-Clair rolled to the right and the boot shattered the floor where his head had been a second before.

The Nyctalope was stuck against the wall now. Vitto and Soca drew their knives and rushed over to stop Logreux from attacking their boss. The Master swung around, grabbed Vitto under his huge arm and threw him violently into Soca. The two men crashed to the floor together ten feet away, completely dazed.

The Nyctalope had taken the opportunity to kick his enemy hard in the back, but Logreux did not react. He turned around with an evil smile on his face and every intention of finishing Saint-Clair off for good.

He leaned forward and grabbed him by the neck, lifting him up easily and holding the Nyctalope a foot over his face. Logreux slapped him hard enough to stun him. The fight was coming to an end and it did not look good for the Nyctalope.

Logreux d'Albury was about to deal the final blow to Saint-Clair with a hook in his left hand. A glimmer of satisfaction sparkled in his eyes and he paused a second to contemplate his vanquished enemy. At the moment he decided to finally administer the coup de grâce, he suddenly froze. He tried to move but could not. His balance looked off and the weight of Saint-Clair in his hand seemed to be dragging him down. His body stiffened and he fell forward, unable to make the slightest move.

The Nyctalope wriggled free and stood up, amazed by this sudden change of events, just like Vitto and Soca a few feet away. Both of them were slowly getting to their feet, still holding their knives, without understanding what happened. Suddenly, a voice rang out next to them, saying:

"Are you OK, Léo?"

Saint-Clair knew then that he owed his life and his victory to the Invisible Man.

"Is that you, Jacques, who stepped in to save me?"

"Yes. I came up behind him and pulled out the cables connecting his exoskeleton to his brain. As soon as they were unplugged, that madman lost control of his armor and fell. The Master of Seven Lights is beaten and I hope this time it'll be his final defeat."

"The hardest part is still to come. Now we have to beat Korridès who's holding my wife hostage. He must be hiding upstairs somewhere. We'll split up into two groups. You, Vitto and Soca, take the main stairs on the right of the entrance hall right by the front door. I'll take the other stairs straight out of the exhibition hall. I should end up in the other room on the second floor, then down the corridor on the mez-zanine that overlooks it, which is on the third floor. Be careful, he still has some henchmen running around."

Without a second to lose the Nyctalope ran to the stairs in the exhibition room. The upper floor was not lit. Saint-Clair thought, *I hope he's not thinking that he'll slow me down by cutting the electricity!*

He walked cautiously up to the second floor. Thanks to his night vision he did not run into any of the obstacles that were in his way. He was as silent as possible so he would not be detected. The ground, indeed, strewn with debris from the renovation work on the building that had barely started when Korridès and his men had discreetly taken possession of the place. The windows were all covered with tarps, which made his nyctalopic powers indispensable.

He reached the second floor and looked around. He thought he saw something moving in the mezzanine corridor on the upper floor. Then he saw the two men at the top of the stairs armed with disintegrator rifles. If he had not been so careful he would have been spotted on the landing where the tarp on the window let in a little light.

All of a sudden he heard two gunshots coming from the main staircase on the right. Vitto and Soca were obviously meeting up with some of the Engineer's men.

Saint-Clair aimed his Browning at one of the men with the disintegrators. He fired. The man was hit in the head and fell back. His partner jumped up and was shot down in the same place. He stumbled over to the railing, lean on it for a second, then his weight carried him over and he plunged to the second floor.

Saint-Clair reloaded and continued his climb. He reached the third floor without a problem and headed to the right to go into the room right over the lobby. Two more shots rang out somewhere in front of him. His friends were still fighting. He got to the doorway of the room that suddenly lit up. The Nyctalope stepped back.

Before him, in a converted alcove in the middle of a bunch of machines, was his old enemy, Engineer Korridès. Saint-Clair thought he looked even more decrepit than the last time he had seen him. Next to him, sitting in a metal armchair, Sylvie was gagged, tied to the chair and wearing a helmet connected by wires to one of the machines.

The Engineer saw the Nyctalope and said:

"Hello, Monsieur Saint-Clair! Come over here, please. I was just beginning a revolutionary experiment with your wife as subject. I wouldn't want you to miss it."

Saint-Clair was about to step forward but something in the Engineer's voice sounded suspicious. He looked more carefully and saw that the space where Sylvie and the Engineer were was a lot brighter than where he himself was. He took his hunting knife and threw it into the bright zone. The blade started sizzling and then burst into flames as it flew across the room. A few charred fragments landed inches from the Engineer's feet. His intuition had been right. The whole area was a trap. If he had stepped in he would have been fried just like the knife.

The Engineer spoke up:

"I suppose you don't really need to come over here. From where you are, you'll have a fine view of this historic first in science. You've witnessed the wonder of my disintegrator rifles on several occasions. This time I'm going to move it up a level. I'm not going to just pulverize your wife, I'm also going to destroy the very fabric of the space she occupies. Nothing at all will be left! Not even ashes! What do you think of that, Monsieur Saint-Clair?"

The Nyctalope looked around anxiously, searching for some solution. But he found nothing! The barrier was impassable and he had no way to keep the Engineer from completing his sinister project and killing his wife. He tried to gain a little time:

"You know, Korridès, this vengeance is unworthy of you. The deeds you blame me for were not done of my own free will. My mind was possessed, contaminated by extraterrestrial parasites. You can't hold me responsible for what happened on Mars, and what you're doing is not getting justice."

"I alone decide what is just or not! I'll punish whomever I consider guilty and I'll let go whoever is innocent in my eyes. As for you, you're guilty and your punishment is coming... right now!"

With a quick flick of his wrist, the Engineer flipped down a lever. The machine started humming and the space around Sylvie started vibrating, trembling like a mirage in the desert heat. All of a sudden there was something like a rip. A deep, dark fracture appeared in the space where his wife was bound. In an instant she was swallowed up, sucked into the void. The crack stayed open for a few more seconds and a strong suction could be felt. All the objects not bolted down were sucked in, vanishing in a flash. Korridès was hanging onto the lever to fight against the suction. His feet lifted off the ground, then his whole body, like it was being levitated, became horizontal. He could certainly not last long in this position.

It was then that one of the machines on the right was torn up and sucked into the crack. The destruction of this machine caused a short-circuit that fried the electricity, not only in the building but in almost the whole *arrondissement*. The museum was plunged into darkness. The force field keeping the Nyctalope from moving was gone.

The Engineer dropped back down and stumbled over to a small table searching for the drawer with his disintegrator pistol, a smaller version of his famous rifle.

Saint-Clair, whose face had nothing human about it, watched him with hatred in his eyes. Whoever could have seen him at this moment would have backed away in terror at his transformation. In his eyes was carved the death of the man who had killed his wife in cold blood.

The Engineer was still feeling around for the drawer. Frustrated, he finally realized that the drawer and all its contents had been sucked into the open fissure of space. Then a hand of steel suddenly grabbed his wrist and pulled him back in total, terrifying silence.

The gunshots on the stairs had stopped; the battle must have been over.

Still in deadly silence Saint-Clair's other hand clutched Korridès' throat and started squeezing with uncommon strength, in an unyielding desire to kill him. The Engineer mumbled something incomprehensible. And in the Nyctalope's fist something gave way. The body of his enemy suddenly went limp: the greatest genius of the 20th century had just died.

Flashlights appeared behind the Nyctalope. His three comrades were just coming in. They, too, had taken down their adversaries. The CID had triumphed, but at an enormous cost. The organization had been almost completely destroyed and nobody could say if it would ever be rebuilt.

Saint-Clair was devastated. He left the museum without saying a word. Engineer Korridès and Armand Logreux d'Albury had almost succeeded in killing him and something in him had snapped. His family and friends had been exterminated and he had practically nothing left. There was nothing more for him to do in Paris, no more reason for him to live.

He looked around at the city that held nothing for him. Like in his youth he had to leave. Go to the other end of the world—Africa? Asia? Mars perhaps?

He looked up. There were clouds in the sky. Behind this veil the red planet was hiding. Yes, the Martians. He remembered now. They, too, had hit him hard. They were dangerous. Yes, he would deal with them. That would give him a new meaning in life and also a little revenge.[12]

First of all he, would pick up the Zig in Orléans, then leave for the Congo. There was an abandoned base there with radio-planes and not a chance in hell that he could not get to

---

[12] See "The Ides of Mars" in *Night of the Nyctalope* and *The Return of the Nyctalope*.

the red planet to do some investigating. He turned to his companions and gave them a final farewell.

A few minutes later an ambulance carried Armand Logreux d'Albury to the hospital while the Nyctalope took a taxi to the Villacoublay airport to get his Torpedo and set out for Orléans, the first leg of his journey back to Mars.

Epilog

Dumuzi, a shepherd, was guarding his sheep in the green hills. Down below in the plain, lying along the banks of the Great River was the prosperous city of Uruk in the middle of which was a grand, terraced pyramid, a ziggurat.

Long days would pass before he went back to his house near the city dedicated to the great goddess. Dumuzi looked over his flock to make sure that no animal was wandering off. Everything was in order and he could resume his contemplation. Would the gods be favorable to him? Would he get a good price for his wool? He would only know when he went back.

All of a sudden he felt a cold wind on his back, unusual at this time of the year. He turned around and what he saw made the hair on the back of his neck stand on end.

In the blue sky, around three feet off the ground, a black shape had just appeared. Like a shroud with torn edges. It got bigger, slowly, and a breeze of icy air came out of it. It was a black spot that reflected no light.

Tiny objects, which he could not identify, were thrown out of the dark shape. Then all of a sudden *she* appeared.

Majestic, royal, eyes the color of the sea, golden hair, sitting on a throne of iron, the Great Goddess just surged out of the center of the black shape. The throne dropped into the green grass. The black spot disappeared. The body of the Goddess was bound to her throne.

Dumuzi fell to his knees, bent forward and placed his hands on the ground. He straightened up and bowed down again several times as a sign of adoration.

In an unknown language that he did not understand, the Goddess pronounced one word, something like, "Eramaï?"

Yes, what he was thinking was just confirmed. "Innana!" He had just heard the name of the Great Goddess! He knew what the dark shape was. Innana was coming back from hell

337

and she was carrying her chains with her. If she allowed him, he would unbind her and lead her gloriously into Uruk where her return would be celebrated as befit her.

On the laboratory's metal armchair Sylvie was slowly regaining consciousness. She saw a man prostrate at her feet and in the distance a city that looked like it was straight out the ancient past. Where had the Engineer sent her with his infernal machine? She did not know but she would do whatever it took to find out and act accordingly.

The man stood up, approached her and untied her from the chair. A few feet away, lying in the grass, she saw a strange-shaped pistol that she knew was the terrible weapon created by her torturer. She grabbed it, figuring that the disintegrator pistol might come in handy. The man who was before her obviously believed she was a supernatural creature. Maybe she could use this to her advantage to guarantee her safety. He was pointing to the city and offering to take her down there. She followed him, wondering what she would do once she was in the city.

That was how Innana came back from the underworld. Many centuries later the people still invoked this Great Goddess, whom they called Ishtar, Astarte, Aphrodite or Venus the fair-haired. Nostradamus himself had a vision of the Goddess when he predicted in his Prophecies the coming of the Golden Virgin whose fate would be determined by the return of the Antichrist. It was this "Golden Virgin" whom Léo Saint-Clair, the Nyctalope, had married after his battle against Leonid Zattan—Sylvie Saint-Clair, *née* Mac Dhul, who was bound to be annihilated by Engineer Korridès on the day that almost saw the destruction of the Nyctalope.